THE LIFE OF FIRE

For the Dreamers, the Philosophers, the Mystics...

THE LIFE OF FIRE

BY

PANAGIOTIS DIMITRIOU

PART 1

DAWN

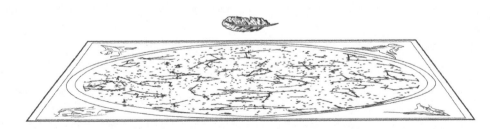

CORRUPTION

He stared back at me. His eyes were blank, empty. His gaze slithered around me, constricting me in a cocoon of dense yet invisible force. With every gasp my lungs achieved, his ghostly reach tightened with the sound of flesh ripping apart. My heart beat deafening. A rotten smell hindered my ability to concentrate.

He was a haze of black cloud engulfing the vibrant glory of the temple. The colourful walls and pillars had disappeared into dark space whose boundaries were nowhere. The priests had not yet arrived. I was alone, and I was captured hanging above his abyss, unmoving, lest I slipped into his darkness.

"Surrender, boy."

He spoke, yet his voice came from inside my head, loud and unyielding. I, still, staring, kept breathing; all I could do to keep his darkness from invading me. And in my breathing, I found a thread of safety, a sense that kept his grip from crushing me.

He stared back at me. In his left hand shone a golden rod, a sceptre or spear with a jackal's head carved at its upper end. As soon as it took shape in my mind, it penetrated my skin just below the chest, blasting shivers around my body. He had not moved. He held the spear upright, its tip now dripping with blood. And yet, it still burned inside me.

I moved my awareness away from pain and onto my breath, again and again. An enormous weight pushed my head downwards while my eyes were still locked in his. Through the haze, a beak appeared below his eyes. He had the shape of a man, but his skin gleamed black. He had no wings on his back, yet iridescent black feathers floated a few fingers around his body, more so around his arms and shoulders, all pointed upwards, moving at the rhythm of his breath.

My chest was being pulled from the inside as if this darkness wanted to suck what was left in my lungs. I kept breathing, keeping alive that place of safety within my chest. How easy it seemed to stop resisting and inhale his darkness. But letting go, fading away into him, felt even more horrific than him.

My chest warmed. A small flame appeared in my heart, growing stronger with every breath until it burned bright inside me. A golden-white fire headed upwards in a pillar of serenity. The safety it bore expanded in my body as it swiftly passed through it. It reached my throat. The force pulling my head down lightened, and I raised my head to the beast. The light now touched my nose. I breathed unafraid again as it reached my brain, gathering into a small sphere that filled my eyes with certainty. A spark of will and power came out of that core of light.

My voice sounded from the centre. "I see you."

His dark cloud erupted like a fire fed by winds. His invisible grip on me became itself dark fire. Like a hurricane, all the darkness blew in a sinistral rush around a sphere of force in front of him. His feathers stretched upwards. He burst, becoming one with the storm that roared unhinged. All vitality was sucked dry. I could breathe no more. His ferocity was crushing my body and pulling my chest towards the centre of the storm.

From that centre, he spoke to me again, with a deep voice that made space tremble. "Yes, child, but I see you too."

The darkness gathered into the sphere. From behind it, a creaking sound brought blinding sunlight into the room. The priests had arrived. They opened the gates and marched inside in two rows. They walked through the sphere and whatever remnants of darkness had yet to dissolve, and separated a few steps before me to proceed in opposite directions. They did not acknowledge the disappearing darkness nor the black smoke latching on to them as they bore it in the inner temple. *They do not see.*

For me, the room was only now taking its place in space again. My ears buzzed with an eerie echo, and my eyes struggled to adapt to whatever sunlight reached me through the open gates. A crack in the stones of the ceiling allowed the sun to shine through and warm my face.

A blurry shadow hid the light. As my eyes focused, the shadow turned into my father, looking down at me. With his usual smile and calm voice, he extended his arm.

"Aletheos, come, my son," he said and brought me to my feet. He led the way as I withdrew into my scattered mind.

A windowless corridor led us to the inner chamber with the priests already in a circle. I halted, letting go of my father's hand, who continued to the other side of the room to take his position in the circle. Behind him, the image of the father of gods was engraved on the wall; a man with a white bird's head and wings looking down at us.

The doors banged shut behind me. The room was sealed. My stomach burned. With my mind still occupied, I placed my palm on the fiery spot. My eyes stuck on my father. I observed his ceremonial movements as if they could somehow give an explanation or maybe comfort me. He looked down for a few moments and silently moved his lips with the words only he was allowed to know. He then took the hands of those next to him, and the rest followed his example. To his left stood his wife, Muttiya, stern as always. To his right was my older brother Favar, whom I didn't know had returned to the palace, followed by my old teacher Meleethos, the high priest and advisor to my father, the king.

"Let us come together," Father exclaimed. His smile now eluded his face. His kindness was swept away. "Come," he commanded me.

With heavy feet, I took a few steps while the burning pain in my stomach grew pulsating. I stopped and shook my head from side to side as if to break free from the pain. It did go away, and I separated the hands of the priests closest to me to join them. From across the circle, Father's furrowed brow alerted me to the present. My brother, to whom I should be standing next to, stared with a smirk twisted on his lips. I just wanted to go home.

Before I even thought of approaching him, my brother grabbed Meleethos's hand and closed the circle. The two priests to my sides shared some discreet glances, and after a few moments of silence, Father took a deep breath and said the words.

"To this, I stand witness. I am you, and you are I. Let me be as you in your light. Here I stand, a beacon for all, from the fiery wheel to the slithering serpent. For all to see and come to me. Until all are one in the presence of You alone."

The ceremony had begun.

I was saying the words and making the movements, but my mind raced back to the beast and his eyes; until the flashing pain in my stomach brought my awareness back to my body. With every move, with every word, the pain grew stronger. I could feel the spear of darkness again, as if it had never left me, now burning its way deeper inside. My lungs found it harder to bring vitality into my body, and the voices, the light from the candles, and the smell of burning incense were excruciating to my senses. The spear now imposed on my consciousness, with its edge breaching my last defence. My body stretched in shock when I felt the spear removed.

All my warmth was pouring out. With a fogged mind, I looked down to cover the wound and save myself. But there was nothing, not a wound nor blood. Overtaken by the sensations, my throat stiffened and eyes swirled up inside my skull as I took my last breath.

My muscles let go, and my body fell to the stone floor. The mumbling voices of the priests brought the precious ceremony to its end. My senses were now released from their hammering, and my consciousness fell into oblivion.

E verything was light, pure light. My body was no more. I was the entirety of that light and, simultaneously, this mist of light enfolded whatever piece of self I could experience, like a warm blanket keeping a baby safe in the arms of his mother. The sweetest female voice rang from each particle of light. Its sound, calm, steady, deep, shaped my core.

"Wake up, my child. It is time. Wake up."

The light curdled, forming calm waves in all directions. The waves moved around me and, like reaching the shore, gradually became lines that shaped the world around me, the sun, the land, everything in between, and the room I found myself in. The cool, soothing light was replaced by the gross material I had known all my life.

Next to me stood a woman in a pearl gown shining yellow and orange-white light from within. I could not move as she leaned down, close to my face. I struggled to move, to awaken my body and free my throat from any hindrances in breathing.

"I will find you. I promise," she said.

She kissed my forehead and looked into my eyes. I employed all my strength to move. Instead, I only managed to cough. I blinked, and she disappeared. All my effort to move now burst out, and I jumped off the bed. I looked around the infirmary; empty. I sighed.

No one was around. Nothing out of the ordinary. The sun shone from the window. I pressed on my stomach; the burning sensations were gone. I let my shoulders drop and laid back on the bed. In my mind, I could still see her eyes, and in them, I saw the whole universe; the stars, the galaxies, the waves of cosmic matter.

A Flower in the Desert

I paced through the dusty corridors, heading towards a room I held dear. The sense of hanging over the beast's abyss had been haunting me for almost a moon cycle now, and I yearned to alleviate myself from it, even for a while.

I took a turn, careful, looking out for any unexpected guards or priests that could give away my whereabouts. I even listened for any voices, even though this part of the palace was long deserted.

The room had always been a mystery to me. It was called 'The Great Bosom,' and it was one of the few places where only a handful of women could enter, only the king's wives and their maidens. The gods permitted neither myself nor my father, the king, to enter.

My mother used to bring me here in secrecy. She would release all her maidens from their duties so she could tell me stories about the stars and wanderers and how they were born. I would often ask about her homeland, but she never talked about it. Her answer was always the same, she came to Erevos, our kingdom, to marry the magnificent king and give birth to me.

I entered the almost empty room and exhaled with relief as I closed the door behind me. It took a few moments for my eyes to adjust to the light coming from the other side of the room, left completely open to oversee nature outside. A big pot carved in white stone stood alone at the centre. My mother had explained it was made in her homeland and kept in one of the temples until it was brought here on the same ship she arrived on. Behind it, a pond, maybe one step wide, full of the only violet lotus flowers in the kingdom, stretched in a straight line to join the river outside.

Around the room, I could feel, and sometimes even see, a milky white mist. My mother had once told me that the pond represented the great waters in which we all live and that the mist was the love of the Great Mother that gives life to all things.

There was always a fresh flower in the small space between the pot and the pond. I would think my mother had put it there, but I never saw her do so. She must have been visiting that room more often than I thought, without me.

My mother's words, her presence, used to make the world brighter, infuse all with life, a higher meaning. After her disappearance, I would slip into this room to bring flowers to the Great Mother as mine used to do. The room changed, though. No one attended it anymore. The mist of vitality was gone. The water of the pond was muddy, and the white stone of the pot was barely apparent below the dust. The only thing that gave a sense of life in this room was my flowers. In that space, if I tried hard enough, I could almost sense my mother. Sometimes, when I fell asleep trying, I would dream that she was there with me, still telling me stories about the stars and wanderers.

Today, I was awakened by some clattering against the stone floor. My head was heavy, and I struggled to open my eyes. The first thing I saw through my blurry mind was one of the lotus flowers in the muddy pond, graceful and bright against the dark sky behind it. Three orbs, a yellow, a blue and pink one, faded into the river as my eyes focused.

The stars shining through the open side of the room indicated that I was in there for longer than intended. My stomach clenched at the prospect of being found in the sacred room for women. With a heavy outbreath, I placed both my hands on the coarse stone floor and pushed with all my strength to awaken the rest of my body that strongly refused to leave this place.

I stood up and walked to the door. No sound reached my ears from the other side, only the sense of cool air between my head and the door. *Maybe it was the wind or the trees from outside.* That seemed more plausible than people walking through the forgotten halls that led to this deserted room. Careful, I opened the door and exposed myself.

I was wrong. People must have passed through here. Their torches still cast shadows from a left turn down the hall. I followed from a distance, my feet scraping the floor, until I reached a door engraved with an open-winged beetle; a sign that the door led to the throne chamber.

Through the side door, the throne chamber was busy with people. *At this hour?* I looked around to see who had led me there, but no one held a torch anymore. I pushed through the small crowd and got to the front. Everyone was either too sleepy or too curious to notice me.

My father Aletheos, for whom I was named, sat on the throne, calm and bright as always as if he could somehow reflect more light off his fair skin than others. The sun had made his face and hands a little browner than the rest of his body, which was barely showing below his white robe adorned with symbols of golden thread. On his head shone his delicate crown made of three golden snakes intermingling with his short hair, raising their heads above his forehead with open mouths and sharp teeth. Each snake had a stone infused into its forehead; one with a sapphire, the other with a ruby, and the middle one gleamed with a diamond.

To his left sat his first royal wife, queen Muttiya. A turquoise beadnet dress held tight her white see-through gown, accentuating her dark skin, which testified of her ancestor's distant origins that she carried oh so proudly. My mother never wore anything like that; even as the second royal wife, she used to carry herself in a simpler manner, never had the taste for imposing appearances.

To his right, as usual, stood his trusted advisor, Meleethos, my old teacher whose wrinkled face had spots of various pigmentations.

The three of them were raised above us by twelve steps. The only people below them were the Starani men, my father's guards, standing in a row. Most Starani men had much darker skin than my father and I, though not as dark as the queen's; undoubtedly descendants of a special tribe of warriors.

From there onwards, the middle section of the room extending from the throne stage to the main gates was empty. The flames of thirty-three torches kept the middle section lit while the two side sections were darker; the lower ceilings and the wide columns did not allow the light of the flames to reach me and the small crowd occupying each of them. Next to me, I recognised the faces of two maidens, a guard or two, and a couple of priests. The rest, I didn't know.

"It's the fleet from Khantara," whispered someone to my left.

I turned. He wasn't talking to me.

"They were returning from an expedition," he continued. "The sea swallowed them, all but one ship."

"It's the middle of the night," his companion yawned.

It was indeed unusual for such a gathering to occur after the sun had set.

"Stand straight!" he answered. "It's a courtesy. The Khantara nation has been a historic ally to Erevos."

He did stand straight, still rubbing his eyes. On the opposite side section, beyond the lit middle part, the queen's brother Valsaris wore his official cape of leopard skin, a sign of his role as religious advisor. I hadn't seen him since he escorted my half-brother, the queen's son, to another city to train in the ways of the gods. Oh, and there he was, my half-brother Favar, standing tall and proud next to him, with Valsaris whispering in his ear.

Swirling around Favar's feet was his beloved cat, always with him since he almost went blind due to an injury he suffered while playing with me. Father got him the cat during his recovery, and while he got his sight back, he still had a bald spot around his temple with two very visible black spots. *But when did he acquire this smug smile? What is Valsaris teaching him down there?*

The gates opened, and all chatter faded into silence. Three men appeared, each holding one small chest, and walked towards the throne. The one in the middle was a few steps to the front. He had long, black hair and a beard mixed with grey patches, but his big trunk and heavy movements showed he was still strong. His clothes, as well as those of his companions, were dark red and blue, colours not often worn in our sunlit kingdom. The other two seemed younger, with short and curly black hair and beards. All three kneeled in front of my father just a few steps before his guards, placing the chests on the floor. *They lost their ships but still bore gifts. How graceful of them.*

The king stood up as his guards in front of him gathered to the sides of the stairway. He gently extended his right arm, giving permission to the guests to rise, and nodded to a lesser official who dealt with writing down my father's instructions and taking notes of the state's affairs and accounts.

The official, wearing his very formal, clean, and light-coloured clothes, hurried to the front and bowed proudly. He said a word in another language, and the oldest guest, their leader, spoke with a loud voice, his slow hand gestures making his appearance all the more dramatic.

"My king, we are blessed with your presence," translated the lesser official, a somewhat strange arrangement since I knew my father to be fluent in the tongues of our affiliated states. He continued, trying to make his voice loud enough to match the guest's.

"Please allow us to present what is left of the ships that were once full of our king's respect and admiration for your magnificence. Please accept his gratefulness on the matters of our states' affiliation. We wish not to insult you with these three chests alone. We hope we can leave all unpleasantness behind."

The translator was still exclaiming his words, but my father seemed to ignore him. His half smile disappeared as he observed the oldest of the three men. He was examining him, weighing and evaluating the truthfulness of each word. His eyes penetrated him, making the words he spoke irrelevant, as his true intentions were veiled no more. The elder visitor seemed uneasy for the first time since his entrance.

They opened the chests. I stretched to make myself taller but I still couldn't see their content. The man in the middle was about to continue, but my father took a few steps forward and talked without ever glancing at the chests.

"How many men have you lost?" he asked.

Father's empathy could never be misconstrued as foolishness or weakness. His voice would somehow find a way inside your head that made his kindness, whose source was true power, very clear.

The translator spoke back and forth. "Too many, my king. Only my ship made it to your shores but not without damages."

"Do you have wounded men?"

After some whispering and some noise, the translator, trying to use a sympathetic tone disproportionate to the strict and almost angry tone of the visitor, continued. "Yes, your Magnificence."

"They will be looked after by our wise men until they are found fit to travel. Your ship will be repaired and escorted beyond our port. Your men should let your ruler, Balluashir, be sure that I am very well aware of his intentions. Give him my sympathy for the unnecessary loss of his men and let them tell him I had the greatest of respect for his brother."

Hearing the words from the translator, the visitor gathered his shoulders to his chest and threw quick glances around the room. I wondered whether the translator was doing a proper job giving my father's good words as they were meant. My father didn't seem to consider that and kept observing the visitors with immovable eyes.

With a deep breath, the visitor stepped forward, speaking our language in a broken accent. "Your kindness and wisdom are known, King. Our devotion is seen by gods who saved the most valuable gift for you."

He took a few steps back, still looking at the king, before nodding at his men to bring the valuable gift. The young men moved not and only exchanged silent looks with him. The main gates opened and several guards came through, forming a line in front of the doors. The older guest clenched his fist before bringing it to his belt, where his sword would be tied. But no weapons were allowed in an audience with the king.

From behind the guards, two priests appeared with a girl. She kept her eyes steady on the floor. She must have been around the same age as me, probably witnessed twelve or thirteen sun cycles. She wore a white robe and had dark curly hair gathered behind her, tied inexpertly, probably by the priests who prepared her. Her shoulders kept sliding forward as if to withdraw. But she kept walking, pushing her spine back up straight as the priests led her forward.

I moved to get closer from behind the shadows of the columns separating us from the middle section. Her big, dark eyes glimmered in the light of the torches as she passed by me and the three guests to stop and offer a clumsy bow to my father.

"Our king sends the most beautiful girl to you," the translator explained.

My father looked deeply at her.

"What is your name?" he asked.

She opened her mouth to speak but coughed instead.

"Idhatora," she finally said in an accent that sounded familiar.

She was beautiful, but I knew her beauty was not what my father looked at. After a few moments of silence, without moving his eyes off her, he replied in a deep voice.

"The gods be good to us." He paused. "The girl's line is pure." He sounded concerned. He had not finished his evaluation; he was still searching. His uncertainty, however subtle, did nothing but feed the worries of the three foreigners.

As the translator gave them that last sentence, my father looked away from the girl and into our visitor's eyes, waiting a few moments to let what was said be truly understood by him.

"You shall tell me all about your misfortune and the new affairs of your state in the morning when you will have your capacities rested."

The guards from all sides of the room proceeded around the three guests, separating them from the rest of the crowd, allowing only a small passage towards the exit. The foreigners were invited to surrender. But they had no weapons. And they came bearing gifts. The people around me started talking again while I tried to make sense of the guards' aggressive stance.

The foreigners protested in their language as a ring of black smoke appeared around them and burst outwards, throwing the guards on the ground and the room into pandemonium. The torches were blown away. The people next to me screamed, blindly rushing backwards. I held my hands up, pushing them from trampling on me as I struggled to get past and towards the foreign girl; my racing breath together with the memory of two blank eyes imposing on my consciousness. Valsaris, the queen's brother, was already shielding the girl, holding the leopard skin he wore up against the attackers.

"Not in my palace!" yelled the king.

He raised his hand, and the dark smoke disappeared. All shouts faded. The torches lit up again.

"There will be no dark forces in my presence," said the king before turning to the guards. "Take them!"

The captives were dragged outside. My brother pushed himself up from the ground and patted his clothes, narrowing his eyes at Valsaris, who must have pushed him aside. The king addressed the small crowd.

"Is everyone well?" He scanned the room.

People around me were fine, other than the many pale faces. I turned to my father, wondering whether he would address the display of magic. He was always very strict about the use of forces in front of laypeople.

"Please, return to your chambers. If anyone needs help, please go to the infirmary," he finally said.

Some kept whispering, probably waiting for more of an explanation as did I. But, after a few moments of my father's silence, they hesitantly exited the throne chamber. My rushing heart was regaining its pace as my father sat on his throne, looking down at the girl comforted by Valsaris.

His wife touched his arm, interrupting his mental processes. "Are you alright?" she whispered in his ear.

The king stayed quiet, looking at Idhatora.

"I will take care of the girl," the queen told him and walked down the steps of the throne stage.

"Are you alright, girl?" she asked her without waiting for an answer.

She turned to her brother and smiled as she straightened the leopard skin on his shoulders with a nod, and looked around the room. At her glance, two maidens shook their shock away and rushed from behind me. Their movement though, brought the queen's attention to me. Her eyes widened. As if repulsed or angry at me. Like that time her son acquired his scar, and she blamed me for it. 'You should just go away,' she had said between her teeth, 'you mother as well.' Her words would come back to me every time she laid her eyes on me. As if I had wronged her by being the son of her husband's second wife; as if the very existence of my mother diminished her standing as queen to the king. But I had never witnessed a confrontation between them; even her late parents were good to me and kind to my mother.

"My queen," said one of the maidens, holding the girl's hand.

The queen withdrew her gaze from me and walked to the exit; her maidens followed, escorting the girl. The chamber was now mostly empty. My father stood with his back to the room, confiding with his advisor, Meleethos, as my brother climbed the steps to join them on the throne stage with his cat always a step behind him.

The king's low voice carried around the silent room. "They are mere soldiers. They have no command over dark forces."

My jaw clenched hearing him. Only friends and advisors now remained in the room.

"Then who did this?" asked my brother.

My father turned to his advisor. "Can you find out?"

Meleethos replied with only a nod, and the three proceeded down the steps behind the throne stage, leading to the king's private apartments. I took a step towards them, but they banged the door shut. *No matter.*

I turned and walked back through the side door and into the hall I came from. Only now did I realise that my legs shook with every step. I leaned on the wall for a few moments. *Father is taking care of it.* "We are safe," I assured myself.

The girl's face came back into my mind. I searched my brain for her name. *Idhatora.*

Through the corridors, an open door caught my eye. It led to the room of The Great Bosom. I was almost certain I had shut it. I peeked inside for any invaders in my mother's great altar. Glimpses of light, probably reflections from the moon outside, shimmered around the violet lotus flowers in the pond. The room was safe. No one was inside.

WINDS RISING

I sighed and leaned back in my chair. Only now did I hear the loud song of the cicadas, reaching me, together with the light of the midday sun, through the library's window. The dry scroll on my lap quivered with the breeze; its depictions of the father of gods, head of a bird, white wings, and all, mocked me in silence, as did the half-empty shelves across from me.

The beast remained hidden, eluding the most informed library in the kingdom. I tossed the scroll to the side, onto the pile of all the useless scrolls I read, and got up.

The halls outside were quiet. At this time, Father should be at the temple for the midday ceremony to the father of gods, alongside his officials and priests. At least he didn't insist I joined them, not since my encounter with the beast.

Having nowhere to be, a joyful prospect brought a smile to my face. I could spend more time with Idhatora; see her before our usual evening rendezvous at the garden, an engagement that had become part of my night routine almost ever since she arrived a couple of moon cycles ago.

With a lighter chest, I paced through the palace corridors and sneaked into the queen's chambers, where my father's first wife, together with her daughter and other high-degree women, were attended to by their maidens. It was a wide room with various levels, each connected with the next by two or three steps. I had not been in there for a long time, not since my mother was here.

The queen's chambers were very different from what I remembered. Before my mother's disappearance, it used to be a place full of natural light, with big ceramic pots adorned with colourful sceneries and green plants and flowers emerging from within them to create a beautifully vibrant space. Now, the room felt darker. Heavy golden statues reflected the reddish light of torches and whatever sunlight made it through the bold coloured curtains.

I remained behind one of the statues next to the entrance, hoping to go unnoticed while searching for my friend. I did not crouch; I did not want to seem guilty of hiding. Queen Muttiya was on the other side of the room talking to our old nan; a woman who took care of me as a child but moved on to look after Hetta, the queen's daughter, when she was born.

Little Hetta galloped in front of me. With a gasp, I pressed my finger on my lips, hoping she would silently carry on. She rolled her eyes and, indeed, ran up to some maiden. Behind her, old nan was still in discussion with the queen.

I finally spotted Idhatora on the level just below mine. She stared at the floor, lost in her thoughts, maybe reminiscing about her homeland again. She was having her hair combed by Cereena, the daughter of Valsaris and niece to the queen.

With one hand, I pressed against the leg of the high statue in front of me, withholding my excitement. The statue was cold and dry on my hand, even when the rest of the room was warm with incense and perfumes.

It was Cereena who saw me first. She greeted me with a small bow of her head and leaned down to Idhatora's ear, alerting her to my presence. I nodded thankful to her as her attendee pushed her hands and comb away to hop up.

My heart beat joyful to share this walk with Idhatora and introduce her to my favourite place. She didn't seem to join me in my sentiment. She was distracted, her eyes wandering away from me.

"Are they treating you well?" I asked.

She put her hand through her neat hair, combed in place according to our nation's fashion. She pulled off the lapis beads that kept it in place and tousled it free.

"They are fine," she answered.

She still looked away, staying all the while one or two steps behind me. I kept checking for her behind my shoulder as we left the palace to walk through the city and the busy affairs of the housekeepers trading with merchants. As I looked back one more time, a man rushing through the street bumped into my shoulder, knocking me to the ground.

"What are you doing, you idiot?" he shouted as he got up. "Look where you..." He stopped when he saw my face. His eyes widened, his tone changed. "I am very sorry, my prince," he said and gave me his hand.

From behind him, a man in a dark cloak pushed him to the side, throwing him away to the ground. The tall man extended his arm down to me. The sun behind him covered his face in shadows. He stood unmoved, waiting for my hand. Unable to find a reason not to, other than a sense of contraction in my chest, I gave it to him.

He pulled me up and drew me close to his face. "Are you okay, Prince Aletheos?"

His voice was calm but almost sarcastic; his concern certainly ungenuine. In his blank eyes, pupils appeared as if out of thick smoke, with irises that seemed to expand and contract with his breath. Cumin reeked through his narrow lips, and his thin face matched his narrow nose below his bald, sunburnt head.

"I am fine," I said with half a breath, turning my nose away from his mouth.

He let go, almost pushing my hand away, and walked past me and Idhatora with a pat on my shoulder.

"Are you okay?" asked Idhatora.

My eyes followed the strange man. He reached the gates of the palace and halted for a moment before walking inside. The guards at the doors never moved.

"Who is he?" I mumbled.

"I don't know. He just fell down when he saw your face, and ran away." She laughed. "As if it's okay to be rude, as long as it's not to the prince."

"No, not him. The guy who pushed him."

"Nobody pushed him." She furrowed her brow.

"I am talking about the..." I pointed towards the palace.

She subtly shook her head.

Did you not see him?

"Shall we move on?" she said after a few moments of silence.

She smiled, seemingly excited about our journey. I sighed and threw a last glance at the guards, still unmoved at the gates.

"There was... Yeah, let's go," I agreed.

She kept walking behind me. I was becoming very conscious of the heat from the sun above us and the uneven pathway that would follow. It usually didn't matter to me, but I was not alone this time. We stopped a few steps before the base of the hill.

"What is that?" she cheered and ran towards some rocks.

She turned to me, enfolding something in her palms. She brought it close to her face, blew away the excess sand, and presented it to me. It was a ball of stone that looked like a flower. She kept turning it around in her hands, inspecting it from all directions, reflecting the sunlight in its almost transparent petals. I had seen them before, but it was unusual to find a sandflower in the shape of a perfect sphere. I looked up into her eyes.

"It's beautiful," I said.

On our way up the rocky side of the hill, I kept a step ahead to help her up if she needed me to. Sweat slicked my skin, and the sand dancing with the wind stuck on my face. Some even crunched in my dry mouth. She slowed her pace after tripping a couple of times. But she did not complain. My stomach clenched, wondering whether I was right in bringing her here.

The ground at the end of our climb was even all across the top of the hill. It seemed as if a piece of the valley had decided by some mysterious force to rise above the rest of the area or as if the kingdom around us had lowered a level. I had pondered on the factors that gave rise to this hill many times. The different levels in the queen's chamber were built according to the wise architect's design. But who were the builders of this hill? And whose design were they acting upon?

We took a few moments to catch our breath before I softly took her hand. I led her to the other side, towards an edge that extended beyond the rest of this small mountain. With a sharp inbreath, she let go of me and stopped a few steps behind me, hesitant to step on the edge.

"It's okay," I said and extended my arm to her.

She looked down at every slow step she took until she reached for my hand and brought herself to me.

"Look," I said, turning to face the world below us.

The city and the whole great kingdom were laid before us, cut in two by the life-carrying river whose path was green and blue. On the right side of the river stood the grandiose temples and the palace, lavished with white, yellow, red, and blue illustrations, surrounded by blocks of clay houses and the lively streets. On the left side stretched the boundless desert.

Her shoulders relaxed. She said not a word.

"The great river reaches the sea," I said in a low voice. "The waters connect this place with your homeland."

She turned to me with wet eyes.

"I am glad you are here," I continued. "And I hope I can make this place feel like a new home for you."

"Thank you," she said and touched my cheek.

We sat on the edge of the cliff. She didn't seem to mind the height now.

"It's true this place reminds me of home," she said. "The temple I grew up in was built on a hill like this one, overlooking the agora and the sea beyond it."

She looked in the distance and smiled at her memory. I let my eyes wander, follow the river until it all turned into a haze. With blurry eyes, only the air on my face woke the sensations on the cage of my consciousness. My head emptied. Whatever currents of consciousness rose in it banged back and forth before exiting altogether.

The howling wind was the only thing I recalled when my contemplation was disrupted. The dry sensations of the sandy ground brought me back to this stone reality. Across from me, high in the blue sky, two white eye-shaped patches watched down on me. They vanished as I blinked. Maybe the sunlight messed with my eyes. Slowly, almost unwillingly, I adjusted my sight.

"Shall we go?" she asked from behind me.

I didn't hear her leaving my side. Finding my legs took a few more moments than usual.

"Why did they bring you here?" I asked.

"I..." She looked away and her shoulders rose with a deep breath. She turned back to me and let the air out of her chest. "I wanted to see the red flowers popping from in between the rocks. They only bloomed for a couple of days each year. The priestess was adamant, 'no aimless wandering instead of studying.' But the humidity carried their fragrance around the temple and in my bedroom; a soft and sharp scent at the same time!" She lifted her head and drew the air in, as if she could smell the flowers.

"So, I sneaked out during resting time. And it was marvellous! The entire hill was alive with red flowers and white butterflies and bees. I laid down among them. And..." Her face changed, darkened. "... I heard screams. I looked up, and they were everywhere; horses and swords. One of the priestesses was coming up towards the temple with a basket of fruits. She was hit from behind by a rider. Her blood splattered on the rocks. It dried almost immediately, as if the earth was thirsty for her blood. The apples and oranges she carried rolled around her on the ground. She saw me as she fell and screamed I should run back to the temple. I turned. The temple seemed so bright, I just wanted to pull myself through and into its walls. But I was grabbed from my waist and carried on the horse."

You were brought here by force? The three men were lying!

She put her hands around her waist. I went closer, serious, concerned. She took a breath that seemed to ground her to the present. "I was then taken to a ship. We were hit by a storm. Things were falling around me, and water had come inside. I remember kneeling on the floor and covering my head, wishing for it to pass. It got quiet, and when I looked up, the water had withdrawn and all the things flying around had fallen away from me, heavy on the floor. After that, I ... I remember being escorted into the throne chamber to meet your father." Her shoulders dropped.

Do you want to go back? My stomach tightened at the thought of uttering my question. I hugged her instead.

"I am very sorry you had to go through any of that," I said.

With her arms still around me, she pulled her head back to see into my eyes. All was silenced. Stillness ensued. With a spark of a heartbeat, I blinked.

"I want to show you one more thing," I said.

I headed towards the centre of this plane. Nothing showed yet, but I knew what was there. Glimpses of fractured light glimmered as we got closer. My walk became slower, almost ceremonial, appropriate for the great wonder that laid before us.

It was now distinguishable, a thin pillar made of clear crystallised liquid. It stretched into the sky twice my height. From its central tube, a few branches extended to the sides, them too, made of the same material.

"It's like a lightning made of glass," she exclaimed.

I allowed a few moments of silence to pay our respect and stepped closer. She followed. I put my hands around it, feeling the centre of my palms vibrating. Seeing it from this close, the material was neither totally clear nor smooth. It had rough edges all over it and what seemed like dirt from the ground trapped inside its coarse material. It didn't matter, though. This was a magnificent demonstration of natural forces, maybe even magical, and I was certain that this crystallised lightning was guarding many mysteries yet. Like the grains of sand trapped in it, they, too, needed a way out, achievable only with proper tools and knowledge of the necessary craft of purification.

My thoughts became too loud in my head. And the wind threw sand on my face again. Next to me, Idhatora's face looked drained. We were ready to go.

We entered the palace gates, almost dragging our feet, dry and warm. I held her hand and looked into her eyes.

"You will always be safe here! I will make sure of it!"

She leaned in my embrace once again. *We are safe, now and always.*

We each went on our way.

A DAY IN THE SUN

The shed did little to cover the heat of the morning, but my teacher Meleethos insisted we come outside again to one of the inner gardens of the palace. He was explaining something about the ways mathematical values manifest in the visible universe over a wooden, table-like board with pebbles arranged in geometrical patterns.

I only heard his every other word. It was too hot beyond the cooling shadows of the palace halls. And I kept thinking of the dark forces in the throne chamber. And the beast. Darkness was creeping closer. I sensed it. Yet everyone kept quiet about it, as if they hadn't witnessed it themselves. Meleethos still talked over the table. *You are not telling me anything, are you?*

"You are not ready," he said without looking up, silencing my thoughts.

I held my breath, said nothing, and, after a few moments, Meleethos continued his lecture. *Did he truly respond to my thought?* Against the bright reflections, I focused on his face, following the deep lines in his skin. He was very old, the oldest man I had ever seen. He must have witnessed dozens of sun cycles already by the time my father's mother called for him and placed him at the side of my father some two decades ago. My father had inherited the throne during his early teenhood and needed an advisor to guide him in wisdom and prudence. Now, Meleethos was slow in everything he did; his movements, his speech, even his listening seemed to be slow.

I wondered how well he knew my mother. He must have been there when she arrived at the kingdom, when she married my father, when she gave birth to me. *Where is she with her magic stories of the great wanderers in the sky?* I let out a deep sigh.

I did not want to insult my teacher, but that sigh just came out. As soon as I realised, the wanderers wandered away from my mind. He looked up from the pebbles on his board and smiled. I sat across from him, but his eyes seemed to miss me. Maybe he had gotten blind too, although that was improbable as he was moving around by himself and seemed to know where all things were.

I thought he would make a remark about me not paying attention, but he remained silent and stood up instead. He took a step back and bowed. *What for?* The doors behind him opened, and two guards came out. *How did he know?* I didn't care for an answer as my chest expanded with joy. It was my father who emerged from behind the guards.

The king greeted his old friend and advisor. They talked for a few moments. I wanted to join them, go to my father and escape the dullness that had been this morning. I remained seated, wondering whether Father would leave again, busy as usual with his important affairs. I tried to overhear, hoping that Meleethos wouldn't mention my absent-mindedness. They only exchanged a few sentences before Father came to me.

"Walk with me," Father said with a smile.

I took his hand and followed him into the garden. The heat didn't matter anymore. Any little time I could have with my father was valued dearly. Being close to him was comfortable and comforting; in a different way than it was with my mother, but equally heart-warming. We walked very slowly, from one bush of flowers to the other. I looked up at my father's face as his hand led my way. His face seemed to shine in the blue background of the sky.

"How are you and your friend, my son?"

Her story rushed back to mind.

"Father, she was brought here by force!"

"I know, Aletheos. The men who brought her here were dishonest from the beginning."

"Is that why you asked them to surrender?"

"Their fleet raided our affiliated states. Their ruler, Balluashir, thought he was powerful enough to pull it through. They thought they would be back before we knew. But we knew by the time they laid foot on your friend's island. We intercepted them on their way back, but a storm had already destroyed most of their ships. They didn't come here bearing gifts."

"What if Idhatora wants to go back?"

"I will prepare a ship and take her. She is free to do whatever she wants," Father said.

"Does she know?"

"I told her myself."

She stays by choice! I nodded.

"Father, did you find out who performed magic in the throne chamber that night? I heard you saying it was not any of the three soldiers. Is it related to that vision I had with the beast? I have been searching through scrolls..."

"Don't worry," he said and looked away. "Forget all that unpleasantness. Look around at this beautiful day."

I sighed, having no choice but to trust him, and let my eyes wander. We had reached the pond on the other side of the garden.

"Do you know what those are?" he asked.

The only thing I could see were the blue flowers in the pond. But he couldn't have meant the flowers; naturally, I knew what they were.

"They are lotus flowers," he continued. "They are very special flowers."

I didn't know they were special, but I knew they were special to me. The pond in my mother's sanctuary was always full of them. Although, these were blue instead of violet.

"Why?" I asked.

"The lotus flower reminds us of the journey of life. Their seed falls in the mud, and through the waters, they develop until they reach the sunlight to blossom."

"Is that the same journey for everyone?" I asked inquisitively.

"Not just everyone, for everything, all that is alive," he answered. "Everything is alive. Everything you will ever see or touch is alive."

"Flowers and stones too?"

"Yes, like us, flowers and stones are made of the earth, from the same grains of sand." He pointed at the lotuses again. "They then close and sink during the nights when life sleeps, to re-emerge with the new day."

"Does everything sleep, Father?"

"All that is alive needs to come to rest at the end of a great day, my son."

"But everything is alive."

We began walking again.

"Yes, they are," he added.

Passing by the different bushes of flowers, my father stopped before a pomegranate tree. "There are many kinds of sleep. Do you see this flower? One day it will have to sleep as a flower in order to awaken as a fruit."

"How about the stars? Do they also sleep?"

"Everything has to sleep, like everything has to awaken. How do you know some of them are not asleep right now?"

"Because they are moving."

"And what if tonight, I come in your chambers during your sleep and take you into my embrace? Will you not be moving then?"

"Yes, but I won't know it."

My answer seemed gratifying. He looked at me and smiled, gently touching my cheek. "So young. So wise," he whispered. "No, my son, you will not."

He gave me a kiss on the forehead and headed towards his guards and some officers who waited to escort him back into the palace. We had already walked around the garden and reached the place we had begun, the place where my teacher awaited in front of the wooden board. Before leading the way inside, Father turned to me one more time.

"Every teaching, as everything in the world, has many levels of understanding," he said as he did so many times before.

I responded in the words he himself had said again and again. "Once you cultivate the innermost meaning, the universe will unfold before you."

"You are doing very well," he said. "Keep thinking. I will see you tonight."

That same night, he did come into my chambers. He moved me, took me into his embrace. I never woke up. But I felt him.

BENEATH THE SKY

With a light chest, I walked past the entrance and out into the night, delighted in the prospect of meeting Idhatora. The garden was the usual starting point for our nightly rendezvous for many moon cycles now.

After the habitual tasks were carried out in the proper ceremonial order, I would be released from my duties, religious, scholar or otherwise, and after the sun had set, the evening was mine to navigate, free from others' expectations and constructs of tradition. I was by myself, especially since old nan moved on to care for young Hetta, the queen's daughter.

The evening was free for Idhatora as well. She was under the care of the queen, who only cared for her role in political affairs and kept herself distant from everyone save her children, Favar and Hetta. Idhatora, the stranger girl from another land, was therefore not one of the cares she attended more than she had to. My friend, then, was usually by herself after her education sessions were over.

Walking a few steps further into the night, Idhatora indeed waited for me, away from the light of torches. She welcomed me with a smile, and we embraced to truly bring ourselves in each other's presence. We then began our casual walk around the garden.

"How was your day?" she asked in a sweet and calm voice.

"I am well, tired into relaxation," I exhaled.

She took a few moments in silence.

"Did you find anything about the man in the dark cloak?" she asked.

My shoulders tensed and chest contracted.

"No. No one seems to be able or willing to tell me anything."

"You have been asking for quite some time now. Are you sure you saw him? I really think no one was around other than the guy who bumped into you."

I halted.

"Idhatora stop. I know what I saw."

She did stop. We resumed walking around the garden in silence.

"Today the teacher told us about the wanderers in the sky!" she finally said with sparkling eyes.

My shoulders relaxed, and the image of that man faded away.

"There," she pointed, "the evening star next to the moon, them two are my favourite."

Indeed, the evening star was right next to the crescent moon.

"Did your teacher tell you about the stars and wanderers?" she asked.

"Yes," I smiled before lowering my voice, "she did."

Meleethos had taught me about the stars in the sky, but it was my mother's words on the matter that I held dear.

"Is it not amazing how all of them dance around us?" she remarked.

No! The stars don't dance around us! It's we that...

I took a moment to think about what she said, hoping that her teacher did not establish a false teaching in her mind. Meleethos had told me that the profane schools may believe that the wanderers circle around us; nonsensical teachings that did not accord with the heliocentric understanding of the initiates.

"What do you mean?" I asked. "What else were you told about?"

She went on to tell me of their official names, how each circles our earth, and for how many sun cycles, while pointing at different directions in the sky; technical aspects I could not recite myself.

By the end of our discussion, all the while walking, we had reached the roof of the palace, overlooking the walled garden, the usual destination before separating for the night. We laid down, looking at the starry firmament.

The seven stars of the plough constellation shone brightly. Those were my mother's favourites, and they became mine as well. I wanted to share what I was taught, but I could not retract from my mind the technical knowledge Idhatora had demonstrated to defend my mother's teaching. And I would not expose it to judgement, nor my mother.

"Back in your temple," I finally said, "did they speak to you of the stars?"

"Yes. But they said it is our earth that wanders around the sun, together with the other wanderers."

"You know, Idhi, maybe they are the ones who got it right," I said.

She turned to me with raised brows. "You think?"

I sat up. "I will speak with my teacher, Meleethos. Maybe you can be schooled with me. He knows best."

She nodded and looked back at the sky.

Meleethos could teach her what I knew. It would be safer then, maybe, to stay open with her. We got up and entered the palace. We hugged goodnight before turning to opposite sides of the hall.

A Point in the Middle

I dismounted my horse before the outer walls of the Black Temple complex. It was early in the morning, and the sunlight made the black stone of the complex look even darker, as if the walls swallowed the light. Two gigantic black towers, fully engraved with rows upon rows of symbols, signified the entrance in between them. In front of each tower, several priests were polishing the white stone of two statues of a man, each standing at least ten times taller than me. The ceremony for the winter solstice would not begin until midday.

A servant rushed to my side. I gave him the reins of my horse and walked through the two towers. Beyond the gate, no ceiling hid the light from the sun. The garden in this first section was attended to by a priest. A second gate with white statues similar to those outside, but half in size, separated this garden from another one. And then a third gate with even smaller statues led to the 'great pathway,' a wide path of black stone plaques splitting the sandy terrain in two and leading to the temple.

No priests were around in this section. There was nothing to take care of here before the ceremony. Only a handful of black stone spheres stood out in the golden sea of sand. Each one was engraved with the name of the family members we lost during the plague a few sun cycles ago; a sad reminder of a troubled time and a great honour for those whose names would forever lay here and be blessed with the waters of the river flooding the entire complex every summer.

The temple was busy with the priests finishing up the preparations, burning incense, and lighting candles. The mud from the last flooding was already cleaned out, and the interior brought to a pristine state to celebrate the end of long nights and the subsequent birth of light, the new era of creation. On the back of the temple, seven steps brought me to a raised stage that would never be submerged. I closed my eyes and took a few deep breaths, setting my mind right, as an act of reverence before I proceeded. I took a lit torch, one of the many around, and descended into a hole, down a narrow stairway, and into the spherical cave.

My torch cast sharp shadows on the coarse surface of the cave's walls. No other light could penetrate this small, underground chamber below the Black Temple. Other than the walls, everything in here was finely sculpted, smoothed out of the same stone.

I went down a few more steps and gently placed the torch on the floor. Amidst the ground of sand that disrupted the spherical shape of the cave stood a square stage in the middle of the chamber. Twelve steps were carved at each of its sides, creating a cross around it, elevating it so that when I climbed up the stage, I stood in the centre of the sphere. Across from me, on the sides of the entrance, stood two pillars, each with a stone orb on its top.

My father had told me this place was created by our forefathers, those who, upon their arrival on this our land, wanted to make sure their origins would not be forgotten by their progeny. They were called the sons of the sun. How strange I thought it was that the sons of sun found it appropriate to create an altar for their origin in this utterly dark cave.

The first time I came here was disappointing. Nothing in this place was telling any story. There were no depictions painted on the walls, and no language scribed on the columns or the stage. Only sand and rock.

During my visits to the temple, I would spend some time in this cave while the priests prepared the rituals above. I hoped to find something I had missed. Nothing ever emerged under the light of my torch, but I kept coming back, maybe as a tribute to our forefathers. This place was created to remind us of our origin, but no one ever came down here. How sad our ancestors would feel that we lost sight of our origin. The thought fired anger in me, at our people who neglected this place and even at them, our forefathers who left nothing more for us to witness their story, our story, other than sand and rock.

I laid down on the central stage, looking at the cave above. My thoughts were long gone. Only the cold sense at the tip of my nose made me aware of every inhalation. Not even the hot sun could reach me. Maybe it was this impenetrable, sacred safety that I sought coming back.

Each breath was dry and short. I remembered I should not be staying down here with a lit torch burning the air. The light around me was fading out. I wondered how long I had been in the cave. As I raised my head, a glimpse of white-blue light sparkled in the shadows between the edges of the stone surroundings. By the time I sat up, it disappeared. My eyes were probably adjusting to the darkening room. I looked at my torch right before the entrance. I tried to stand up, but my breath was cut short as the room blackened around my torch's diminishing flame.

The flame went out. The darkness echoed one single heartbeat before a warm breeze stroked the back of my neck and ears, electrifying the hairs on my skin. The breeze passed to my front and waved back to slowly gain a breathing rhythm. But there was no one there to breathe.

"Where are your thoughts?" I heard exhaled.

I tried to utter words, but my lungs had no air to carry them out.

"Where are you?" the voice said. The sound of breathing became heavier and heavier. I could not decipher whether it was a female or male voice. "You are nowhere. You are home."

There were two voices, both a male and a female speaking the words as one. A spark of light burst above me and around the cave like lightning, filling the darkness with white-blue light. Glyphs blazing with this light now covered all the surfaces in the cave. I was still not breathing. Translating what I saw into something with meaning was getting harder. One of the glyphs looked like a man.

In a moment, everything changed. A flow of warm air rushed through my nose and filled my lungs. I blinked, and the white-blue light disappeared. The cave lit up with innumerable floating flames originating from no source, no torch or candle. In front of me, on the square stage, a being stood breathing. Its warm exhalation became my inhalation. My lungs emptied as this being sucked its air back into its body, only to exhale a moment later, giving me back my breath. With each exchange, the whole cave trembled around us.

The entity radiated with light, and I could not focus my eyes on it. It slowly and gradually took form as the light receded into its body. It had the body of a lion, an ox's tail, enormous wings on its back, and a human head. It stared back at me. My legs shook, with blood rushing through my body. I wanted to run, but I did not move. And I would not take my eyes off this magnificent being.

It did not move its mouth, and yet it talked. "All that exists must come to awareness through life..."

Its voice became deafening. My chest bumped as if it could not contain my beating heart for much longer. I covered my ears, trying to make words of the voice.

"You must forsake us as you have. You must get corrupted and you will. Find us again at the middle point. Search for us when the time is right. Open your eye, and you shall see us and Life."

With my next inhalation, all that radiance from around the room faded in through my nose and into my lungs. All was back to normal. The being disappeared. The flames disappeared. My torch was lit again, casting flickering shadows around the cave. An eerie silence filled the space around me.

My eyes were open wide, searching around the room; for the being, for the symbols on the wall. Nothing. Only sand and rock. I let my knees bend to the ground until my heart paced down. A wave of warmth embraced me into calmness.

Everything in this cave felt more real, more vibrant. I stood up and walked down the stage and towards the steps to the exit. My body was heavy, magnetised to the place I was sitting just moments ago, as if I had grown roots into the heart of this room. Every step up needed extra force. I pulled up my now flaming torch and passed through the two pillars towards the main temple. The temple was empty; the gates closed.

Beyond them, the priests already recited prayers. But in here, all was quiet. I sat down, waiting for the arrival of my father and his priests. I looked around the building and everything in it. They seemed less real. As if the truth that was the vibrancy of the cave was somehow distorted out here. Or rather, corrupted. I tried to go over what took place. But I only recalled glimpses of it, as if from a dream. I remembered the being. And the tremble in my chest as it spoke. *What did it say?*

THE GRAND MOTHER

T he river stretched from our city, Eos, out to the sea. 'Like a silver thread
that leads the way back from the great waters to the golden kingdom,' as my
mother had told me, 'always connecting the two and giving life to all it touched on
its way.'

I lay chest down on the wooden raft flowing through the river. The sun above,
together with the monotonous sound of water, was hypnotising. The water reflected dancing sparks of light, occasionally tricking my eyes with flashes of blue, pink
and yellow from deep below, and we kept floating. My chin rested on my hands on
the edge of the raft so that I would be as close to the water as possible. At times, I
let my palm move with the flow just above the water so that I could almost sense it,
yet never touch it.

I liked floating on the river, and we used to do it often, travelling between the
palaces in different cities. Every day or so, we would make a stop and visit a temple
or stay at another palace while my father attended official business. But when
disease ravaged the kingdom, our trips became scarce. And when the plague took his
mother and the parents of his queen, around the same time my mother disappeared,
our trips stopped altogether, and Father would travel alone.

Even back then, it was not often that my father would leave Eos, the capital, just to
welcome a ship. I tried to recall when he had done this before. After a few moments
of trying to mentally spot such instances, I hurriedly stopped, for what came to
mind was my mother. She had said that when she arrived in this our land, my father
had been waiting for her at the port of Dessha, and welcomed her with honours and
gifts, which, as she revealed to me, mattered not when their eyes met. She had said
that in that moment, all around was silenced, all disappeared from sight, and they
could truly see each other.

This should be a very special guest we were travelling to receive. It would take us
seven days and six nights to reach the sea and the city of Dessha. My small raft was

attached to my father's barge. The vessels were filled with people, my father's priests and guards and servants. The banks on both sides were alive with guards, mostly on horses, moving along with the boats. And yet, when I came down on this raft, I could hardly feel anyone around. There was a beautiful silence that came with the sound of water and the flickering sunlight. Everything else, the voices and the galloping, quietened.

Around midday on the fourth day, I was down on my raft when a cube of black stone, double my height, showed amidst the reeds on the west side. *Another one.* It was the seventh I saw travelling down the river; monuments for all the people taken by the plague. These grim reminders kept stirring the fears in my stomach, never letting them settle down, however much I insisted that Father and Meleethos would keep the darkness at bay. But my ignorance on the matter only swelled the wave of emotions. And my suffering under its pressure was, in any case, inconsequential. With a sigh, I whispered to myself. "Just let me be."

A warm sense on my shoulder made me, as of instinct, look up to the boat. Father's clear gaze enfolded me with his attention. He didn't talk, only nodded, inviting me to join him, always with a smile.

He led me to the front of the boat and pointed to the left bank. This was the side of the river that, for its most part, was empty of houses. Only tombs and altars to the god of death were built there. Thus, it was more common, especially during the day, to see animals resting on that side of the river. He pointed to a group of crocodiles basking in the sun.

"Do you see that animal, my son?"

"The crocodiles."

"They are beautiful, but you need to be careful around them, for they are also deadly." He paused, keeping his eyes on the shore. "They journey through the waters. They dwell in the mud but can emerge and stand on land dried by the sun. They are the symbol of that life that connects the two worlds; of water and of fire, and can traverse through each one at will."

His voice softened. He looked at me for a moment and turned back to the reptiles in admiration.

"Do you know, Aletheos, that the day you were born, the great spiritual Sun sent its rays to wake up the spirit of the great serpent to watch over you? It is your guide and guardian, and the crocodiles are its symbol. They work in silence, and thus you must be very attentive not to miss them. But they are persistent teachers, and they will give you their gift of wisdom. But be aware where your feet stand when they contact you, in which of the two worlds you place yourself."

"How do I know where I stand?"

"Be aware of what you allow to infiltrate your consciousness. You know the world of water is the plane of illusion, the waves of which arise by emotions; it is the world of separation, the mother of illusions. The world of fire is mindful objectivity; it is where our forefathers stand as beacons, shining the light of the central spiritual Sun until we can all swim beyond the waters and stand with them as brothers."

I almost felt another sentence exhaled by him, but never uttered in words. He let his hand fall from my shoulder down behind my heart.

"What difference does it make for them where I stand?" I asked.

"The teacher and the principle are the same. The lesson is the same. And you will receive it! But the way you learn it and the form it takes depends on the world you place yourself in."

"How can I make sure I am in the correct place?"

"Love, my love."

His face was in cool shadows, having the sun high behind, casting golden light around his figure. I hoped to hear more. But his lips were now sealed into a gentle smile, and I accepted that would be enough for now.

I took a step forward, at the stern of the boat, in an attempt to get closer to the reptiles and the mysteries they carried. A faint movement got my attention right below in the water. I only saw a few of its scales before the crocodile submerged itself.

T he morning came soon enough, and we reached the port of Dessha around midday. We descended to shore in a ceremonial order, with horns playing aloud and people mumbling a prayer or a cheer or both. Amongst the curious laymen and serious officials stood my brother Favar, oh so proud, who resided here with his uncle Valsaris. He had shaved his head, maybe to get rid of his bald spot and de-emphasise the dark spots on his temple injury.

He embraced Father while I kept onwards, away from all the noise and towards the port palace. Favar's cat jumped from in between his feet and followed me. *You, kind animal, I can't ignore.* I kneeled and touched the thin fur on her forehead, and after a quick rub around my hand, she returned to her master.

Eager to escape the sun, I dragged myself up the steps to the palace. Right before the entrance, a hand reached out, a few fingers from my neck. I gasped and threw myself back a step as I followed the hand to its owner. Instead, another hand and another and another piled next to it and as high as I could see, carved in the stone of the high wall. There were dozens of severed limbs of stone, hundreds even, and each one seemed to gruesomely punch an invisible grip into my guts.

"None dares oppose us," my brother said from behind me, trying to mimic the image of the man engraved victorious on top of the macabre scene. Favar probably expected of me an equally proud response, for the monument I assumed was his construction. I kept my glance away from him.

"This is an atrocity," Father said as he passed by us.

Favar held his breath.

"You commissioned a war practice, Favar!" Father said. "You should be pleased with your blessing, not having to witness such practice!"

I hid my smile from my brother while he rushed to defend his monument.

"We do not take pride in having to go to war!" Father stopped him. "And the ambassadors who visit this palace should not be met with a threat!"

Favar stayed still, abandoning any attempt to negotiate, while I followed Father inside. All noise was finally shut behind closed gates. For a few moments, all was quiet until the officials brought their reports to the king. I turned away, towards a window on the other side of the room, charmed by the intermingling blues of the sea two or three floors below. From within the stone room, I could almost feel the freedom of the wind and the unbound waters.

"Are you all right?" Father asked from behind, interrupting the officials' serious jobs.

"I just need to rest." My answer was blunt, almost rude, and for the first time, I talked to my father without feeling the vastness of his wisdom separating us.

He turned to some attendants who led me to my room. I didn't even wait for them to leave before I threw myself on the bed, and drifted into a deep sleep. By the time I woke up, the sun was shining red through the window. I sat up, still dry from my sleep, feeling like the decay of ten thousand sun cycles had fallen on my body. As if a veil of lightness had slipped away, and I was left emptier, sad, and maybe a bit corrupted. I became aware of a pain in my stomach just as it faded away. After a few slow heartbeats, I took in a deep breath and got up.

With every step I took towards the main chamber, I felt my body reassuming its age. I could still distinguish that sense of maturity coming from somewhere within. It felt familiar. Maybe it had been covered in child's ignorance all along. By the time I reached the room, ready for the welcoming of whomever it was that we came all the way down here for, a warmth filled my head and torso.

The horns sounded. The guest was almost at our open gates. She stopped at the threshold, and three bangs filled the room as the priests knocked from the outside. My father stood up, came down the steps from his throne, and halted. Never had I seen him stepping down for a guest.

He spoke. "Who is it that wishes to pass the threshold?"

With a full voice, the guest answered. "It is I, the pilgrim on the path, the child of the One who has travelled in the seas and reached the shore. Who is it that receives me?"

My father went on with a very sweet tone in his voice, as if he was truly welcoming in his home, one he had almost truly lost hope of ever seeing again.

"It is I, the dweller on the threshold, the child of the One, who awaits your return, oh pilgrim, and that of all the brethren pilgrims on the path, from the first day to this day 'be with us'."

The silent room echoed thunderous with every word they uttered and every movement they breathed.

"I shall pass the threshold and rejoice with you."

"I shall receive you and rejoice with you as One."

They looked into each other's eyes and slightly bowed their head from across the room. The honourable guest pulled her dress up a little and extended her right leg to make but one small step past the threshold. The light of the torches revealed the enigmatic lady. Her black hair, shaded with silvers was braided around her head, woven with golden threads and pearls. The soft lines on her forehead and around her mouth showed her a little older than my father. Her thin body was browned by the sun, and white gowns floated down to her ankles.

After a moment of stillness, both stepped towards each other. They met in the middle of the room and held hands, looking into each other's eyes. Nothing was said. Then, breaking the invisible grasp they had on the room, Father spoke.

"Chaa," he called her.

"Aletheos," she answered before embracing him. She backed half a step and asked in a serious tone. "The children?"

Father turned to me. The woman followed his eyes and looked behind her shoulder to find mine. My spine shivered at the connection, and instinct straightened my body; I stood tall. Her eyes glowed with tenderness; the firmness on her face had never been replaced. She knew.

She came to me. "Do you know who I am, child?"

My forehead wrinkled as I tried to retrieve a memory I did not have. While I searched my mind for an answer, a sense of love warmed my chest and relaxed my shoulders. I gave up.

"No," I exhaled, cheeks flaming.

"That's all right," she said with eyes immersed in light. I was magnetised. I even lost my balance for half a step when she pulled back to meet my father.

On the third day of our journey back, when the sun headed towards the side of the dead, turning the white sand into fields of yellow, I lay, stomach down, on my raft. The humidity and the wind made the air I breathed so heavy that I was almost falling asleep with my eyes open.

With an idle mind, I lay there, subject to the movement of the water as we floated, and waiting for this day to end. But time, as everything else, stood still during this hour. No sight of the guards moving on the shores, no sound of chatters or songs, just the silence of the watery air that weighed on my mind.

The blurry shores and plants and waters were slowly populated with little creatures that flashed in and out of existence. Some looked like tiny humans, others like obscure animals, all luminous and semi-transparent.

A sweet and refreshing sound rang out of the dreamy beauty in my mother's voice. "Wake up, sweet prince. Wake up and see. Turn your eyes from the waters and breathe with the light of the sun."

Still sleepy, I groaned as I turned around my body and laid on my back. My nose, now exposed above, could receive oh so easier the air. The light, although directly hitting my closed eyes, was almost cool on my face. The plants from the banks rustled through their leaves. Everything was waking up. I opened my eyes. The honoured guest stood watching me from the ship. The sun was almost down. This day was almost over. The fourth almost begun.

We had been on the ship for five days, now almost back at Eos. I sat outside, hiding from the sunlight under the shadows of the white cloth with a scroll thrown on my lap; teachings given by my tutor to keep my mind from falling into slumber. But it was not his scroll that occupied my mind. *How can the very nature of the father of gods be in such a direct contrast, yet his image be so similar to the beast's?*

I sighed in an effort to cool off my body and brain. My exhalation was deep and loud, so much so that I had to regather myself. I tried to recall and resume my thoughts, but they would take me back into the gloomy depths of my mind. Instead, I stretched my arms and gazed over the waters and the shore at a small distance. Freshness, greens, blues, and whites coloured the almost cool breeze that touched my chest and neck under the morning sun.

From the floor, a spark of light caught my attention; a beetle, crawling across the ship, reflecting the sunlight hitting its body. I pushed aside my scroll, and without making a sound, I kneeled to observe it closely. *Magnificent.*

Within the green colours of its iridescent shell, a thin line of orange followed my gaze. How must it feel enclosed in that shell, I wondered. How unimportant its inner body and head seemed, so black that they almost blended with the surface of the wood below them. I stretched my neck to get closer to this creature, staying as far from it as my curiosity would allow. Its fine legs moved and intermingled without ever missing a step.

My throat tightened with despise. How could all those people, those who were supposed to act as intermediates to the Gods, ever mistake this little insect for a god? However beautiful and shiny, it should not have fooled those fools.

"They are as ignorant as this beetle is insignificant," I declared and abruptly pushed myself up.

A figure caught the corner of my eye. It was our honoured guest, Chaa, looking at me. Her body faced outwards, as if she was on her way to shore. She must have been there for at least a few moments. Embarrassed by my thoughts on the beetle's fools, I hurriedly push them away from my head and down into my stomach.

Chaa stood still. The boat stopped. "Walk with me," she said.

What an exceptional mixture of strictness and kindness her command had! One tightened my stomach as of instinct to withdraw; the other opened my chest in joy to be around this woman. Only my father had a similar aura in his presence, but I never wanted to withdraw from him.

I decided to proceed while the priests brought the raft. As we floated across to the east side, she stood tall to my right, with her arm over my shoulder, expanding her presence all around me, almost but not touching. Not a word did she utter. And yet all the people around us seemed to move in accordance with what would have been her directions.

On the shore, two guards received us, stepping down from their horses. They offered a subtle bow, and Chaa gave them a smile and a movement of her hand. They stepped backwards, and we passed between them to walk in the fields of reeds that spread around us.

"We make our prayers, Prince Aletheos," she answered the thought I hadn't even formed yet. "The sun is right above us."

She faced away from me, having taken a few steps forward after I had stopped. Still, I could see her face was turned upwards, towards the sun. "It is the time when the light of the sun reaches us the most." Her explanation wasn't enough.

"The light of the sun gives us life. It gives life to those bodies that are appropriately prepared by the waters of the universe. You see, Life needs a vessel to become itself. Blessed by the gods and gods they become, those who surpass appearances and see the essence the vessels hold.

The whole of nature is alive at this hour. And at this time, we give our gratitude for our life, and pray that we come in harmony with Life, that our wills become one with It, and that we may walk the sacred path aspired by many but dared by very few."

That is why our daily gratitude ceremony at the temple takes place at midday. Her words elucidated a habitual task of mine, one that I had accepted as tradition without asking for explanations.

"You see, my child, all is alive," she said, echoing my father. "The sand we walk on, the reeds all around us, the birds in the sky."

As she finished her sentence, a flock of birds flew above us, shrieking out loud before landing in the distance.

"And all are vessels of the same Life, embodying and carrying out as much of their divine nature as their physical nature allows at each specific moment. Even the beetle we so easily dismiss is blessed and burdened by the same duty," she said with a half-smile.

"Is that the reason the beetle is worshipped?" I asked, eager to understand.

"The priests of this, your land, do worship the beetle. But beware, for only fools worship the vessel. The wise men see and pay tribute to the aspect of the Life it embodies. You see, the beetle is held in high esteem for its habits. Have you ever observed its habits? You should study the habits of all of nature, for they tell you the ways of the universe. The beetle leaves its nest to go out in the world. There, it finds pieces of elements nourishing to it, excrements of other beasts or what remains of them, and it collects them to form a sphere which it pushes into motion until it reaches its nest.

Thus, in its mundane routine, this insignificant creature shows us the routine of our sun and all the stars. Once the time of dawn is reached, life shines forth, vessels are created, and stars are shaped as they move around in the sky, attracting to themselves grains of sand they find in their way, remnants of other stars, previously full of life, merging them with themselves until they are ready in the middle of their day to fully take form. That is why we call the stars wanderers. For they wander around in space, never ceasing until their night comes and the time for them to rest commands them to do so.

Do you know that only the male beetle is worshipped?"

I did know that. I had heard it from a priest, but I would not remember had she not told me again.

"That is because the male is that divine principle that shapes and moves the bodies of the world, constituted by the divine female sea of matter. Life permeates and is the essence of both, and life is the result of their union. Thus, the beetle became a symbol of the divine will that lies beneath the world and moves it."

"Is it in the same way that other animals are praised?"

"Yes. Each animal, each being that is described as sacred, has attributes, habits that represent the ways of the universe, both the seen and unseen. And each one is important. The same applies to all beings, each and every one. It is like these reeds around us. Can you hear the sound they make as the air passes through them?

If you silence your mind, you will hear that each of them makes a different sound according to their shape, the composition of their body formed by the elements of the soil and water, the holes and cracks they acquired as they grew. But it is the same air that goes through them all. It is the breath of God that passes through every being and gives it Life."

"But there are many gods."

"As many as there are reeds. But whose breath gave them life? The same exhalation that rushes through you, me, the beetle, and the world. Each carries out a function of the One; each sounds the sound they must. They are neither the One nor the function they carry out. They are mere vessels for That and Its processes to manifest in this and in many other worlds. There is only One God, the Absolute, and its breath is Life."

Our honoured guest, who had taken a seat on a rock, with a gentle move of her head, nodded me into silence. She closed her eyes and, resting the back of her hands on her knees, opened her palms to the sky. She was giving her prayers. Silently. Internally. I took a few steps back and kneeled on the ground. I moved my gaze from her as if to withdraw my loud thoughts and avoid disturbing her sacred practice. I stayed still as the sand in my mind, moved by her words, settled down. The light of the sun almost passed through my closed eyes, and, for a moment, I decided to just be with that, the clear, warm sense of light.

With a gentle touch on my open palm, she brought me back into wakefulness. The sun was almost gone, and the sky's blues had changed into purples. Not a word was exchanged as we headed back to the boats, only the sound of water passing below the raft. We reached the boat, and each went on our way. Me, straight to my bed, ready to fall into the cold beddings in my now dark room. With no thoughts, no disturbances, I floated into sleep.

BENEATH THE SKY

I n contradiction to the warm walls of the palace, a cooling sensation helped my body into comfort as I went out to the garden. I took a few steps into the breeze of the night before realising that I had walked right by Idhatora, who had been waiting for me. I greeted her with a smile before she joined me for our evening walk, the first since I returned to Eos.

We embraced and slowly made our way, passing by the trees and flowers that adorned the periphery of the yard.

"You never told me about your trip to the shores," she said as we reached one of the ponds that brought the water of the great river into the garden.

When we had arrived back at the palace, Idhi was there, together with queen Muttiya, amongst the many officials and servants that gathered to receive us. As the others headed inside with my father and honoured guest, I went to her, but only for a few moments, as I was too tired to really talk.

"It was... long," I said.

She nodded, and we carried on walking. Whatever might have been happening within me, I needed time to say out loud; I needed time to relax into whatever emotion I had been feeling and gradually experience what was kept safely inside. And my trip was strange; I needed time to feel safe to open up to my companion.

But she knew that. She would always open up first, speak to me about herself, her day, and any issue she might have faced. She then would endure some long silences between her asking me about myself and me actually answering. I needed to first think before crafting into words whatever shade, shape or image of an issue or feeling I was experiencing.

Thus, she gave me my time, and as we kept walking around the garden, I did tell her about my journey; the days on the water, the monuments to those taken by the plague, the ceremonial reception of our guest, my encounter with her in the field of reeds. And she listened with the same openness and grounded presence she always had for me.

"She seemed magnificent!" she said.

"Chaa?" I asked.

She nodded.

"We will have to see," I said and looked away. *Depending on her reasons for coming.*

By the time we reached the roof overlooking the garden, nothing else needed to be said by either one of us. We merely lay beneath the cool dark sky. My sleep promised to be light and content.

Sun Obstructed by Stones

I galloped through the corridors of our palace. With no particular destination, I was projecting my mind onto the empty halls as they unfolded before me.

I reached yet another turn before my pumping chest demanded I catch my breath. The sunlight in the otherwise dark corridor was almost tangible, shining from the narrow windows high on top of the right wall. I walked down three steps to where the sunlight mass began and glanced at the spectacle from the shadows.

Small spheres moved in the light. "Sand," I sighed at the earthly explanation of my mirage. I looked up to the windows beyond the floating particles of sand. All the usual sounds, be it the birds singing through the leaves, the flowing of water or voices in the distance, were all suppressed and dispersed away with the moving sand in the wind. *The voice of silence.*

The hall in front of me was equally silent, other than the almost imperceivable rustling of the grains of sand as they touched each other, dancing in space; each of them accepting the vitality of the sunlight and giving it back as best as they could, reflecting it according to their shape, size, and movement.

I closed my eyes and pushed through the light, sensing the warm sensation on my forehead and right cheek. I then pulled back and opened my eyes in time to see the small spheres spiralling around the space my head just occupied to fill the void it left. *Such a spectacle. Such beauty and order!*

I raised my arm through the light, and the small earthly spheres began to embrace it, keeping their distance of at least two fingers around it. Against the serene sensations, a thump from behind sent my heart racing. Before I turned, a masked figure passed by me. More thumping sounds broke the moment. Six or seven men jumped down the steps with their long dark cloaks fluttering as they hastened onwards.

They passed by me from both sides, imposing on my breath. I could no longer see the windows. Their figures, darkened by the light behind them, disrupted the flow of light and created chaos in the dancing spheres of sand. The dark reds and browns of their clothes filled the room with reflections of the same colours soaring on the walls as the light hit them.

Before they vanished to the left of the long hall, the man second to last, turned back to face me. His eyes behind a golden mask which had the shades of green and brown of age on it, the same worn by the entire group, slowed time down for me. The dust erratically swirling all around, now froze in its place. Only his eyes showed, deep beneath the mask. His face was about to reveal itself in my mind, when the one behind him grabbed his elbow and ended his hesitation in moving on. And thus, they vanished.

A few moments passed in quietness before all went back to how it was. Time resumed. The noises disappeared. The particles of sand reclaimed their position in the light, and I was left rooted in fear, a minor step away from the sunrays. Themselves strongly refused to give way, irrespective of what took place.

My hands were cold; my palms vibrated electric. I brought them close to my face. There was nothing out of the ordinary. Nothing that I could see. But I felt it, and I kept feeling it. I held power but felt powerless. I turned at the end of the hall. No one.

My feet were heavy, as if tied to the ground, with an erratic chaos swirling in my chest. *Masked men. In my home!* I shook my head, took an inbreath, and stood straight. With my outbreath, I pushed myself onwards, and followed their route. After some turns and steps, trusting I was going the right way, I took a left and pushed open a door carved with the winged beetle, entering the side of the throne chamber.

The room was empty, dark, and cold, devoid of its usual liveliness. Only the outline of some columns reflected whatever fracture of light passed through the shut windows high on the middle section. I moved to the central area of the room and looked at my father's throne, raised a little over my height by twelve steps.

Behind it, a vertical line of light escaped the slightly open door of my father's apartments. I leaned on all fours to keep hidden as I ascended the steps, focusing on my breath to keep the fear from rising at the bottom of my spine. Deep in. Warm out. I reached the top and threw myself towards the throne, keeping my body low and leaning against the cold base of this glorified seat.

With one more breath, I crawled towards the door. After the few moments it took my eyes to readjust to the blinding light, the room slowly took form, showing the table where my father and his close advisors would come together. Only this time, my father was nowhere to be seen.

A golden mask rested on the table. Thick lines of dark smoke, coming from what I assumed were burning incense, engulfed the men standing around the room. The chairs were still astray. The business of this meeting had already finished. Three of them stood next to the table on the side closest to me. The man in the middle was talked down to by the other two. He kept quiet, turning away from them. He was not confident on what was decided upon.

The one on the left was taller than the rest, speaking with indifference. It was his mask on the table. He was bald with a thin, long face. My eyes widened. It was he who had helped me up out in the streets and moved unencumbered into the palace some moon cycles ago.

I tried to focus on his lips; only deciphered his last words, "... he must perish." His whispering tone echoed in my head, causing such a tremble in my chest as if the entire palace was collapsing on me. I took half a step before hearing a deep voice in my head.

"I see you, child."

I squinted my eyes to refocus on the man's lips. They were sealed still. The voice was heard again, making my head vibrate in pain.

"I see you, child."

I was burning from within. My stomach was pierced by an invisible blade. Like before, there was no wound, no blood; nothing but the pain on my inside and the heat that wetted my face and palms. *You! No!*

Two enormous, blank eyes opened in front of my face, staring into mine. They disappeared with my blink. From within the room, the man's lips were turning into a smile. A subtle movement of his chin towards me warned of an impending confrontation.

Through my burning stomach, I threw myself backwards away from the door, landing my weight on my tailbone. Against the sharp crash, I pushed with my feet on whatever ground they found below them.

The door opened wide, and the conspirators emerged from inside. I moved my head around in a desperate attempt to see anything while the dark figures passed by me and rushed down the steps from the throne, almost crushing my fingers.

Their feet slammed the hard ground, and robes flapped towards the exit. The last one looked back at me from beneath his golden mask before the door closed with a bang. By the time the echo dissipated, they had all but left, and I was alone in the darkness.

With shaking hands and legs, I grabbed the throne's arm and pulled myself behind it. I brought my knees close to my chest and rested my head on the throne's back. Only then did I allow myself to make a sound; gasping out my fear.

When my heart and breathing gained a bearable pace, I exposed myself to the room. Nothing showed from below. Numb and clumsy, I headed on, pushing the door to the empty meeting room. Dark stripes of smoke were being absorbed in the walls. I pushed my eyes shut for a heartbeat, and the room was clear of them when I opened them. The chairs were in position, set straight around the table. Nothing held witness to what took place mere moments ago. His intentions remained veiled.

My eyes fell on a floating black feather. It dropped softly on the floor. I reached for it, but a spark pushed my hand away. There was not a second when I grabbed it.

After a moment of collecting courage, I faced back the empty throne chamber. I crossed the room and paced out into the gardens, letting my back fall heavy on the engraved door that shut behind me.

With eyes half-closed against the bright day, I brought the feather close to my face. It shone dark greens and purples wherever the sun hit it. I sighed, and stretched my neck towards the blue sky, letting the fresh air and sunlight give my chest a small but warm sense of safety.

The wind had ceased. The grains of sand had fallen into their new positions. It was another day.

A VIEW FROM ABOVE

I walked in the yard behind one of my tutors who insisted on talking about history and the marvels of previous kings, the kinds depicted on the palace walls. I was absentminded, having been prematurely woken up from a nightmare, the same one I had since I saw the conspirators in the throne chamber.

My father was about to ride beyond the gates when I became aware of him. He halted, already smiling, looking down from his horse at me.

"My son," he exclaimed, releasing the horse's reins.

"Father!" I approached.

"How are you doing today?"

Before I answered the question, Father looked up to my tutor with his scriptures in hands, having failed to establish a route to my brain. With no response from him, my father looked back at me.

"Would you like to join me? Come, ride with me." He had already extended his arm and helped me up on his horse.

He asked the two men that rode with him to proceed alone, and we left the city, galloping through sandy terrain. I let my head rest on his back while my arms embraced his waist. A few fingers away from my closed eyes, his garments fluttered with the wind, accompanied by the sound of the horse's steady rhythm.

The pace slowed down until it stopped altogether. He had brought us to a very familiar place. I got off the horse and turned around, only to become sure of it. With a smile on my face, I moved to the edge of my favourite hill to see our kingdom below. My father stood behind me, touching my shoulder. He pointed at our house, the palace's gardens, where he would take me for a walk and speak in riddles about the sacred sciences and matters of consciousness. I had observed all these places from this exact point oh so many times, but sharing it with my father added one more reason to hold this place dear.

"So much beauty," he exhaled, pleased at the view. "From up here, you can see, truthfully. I come here often...."

I wondered how we had never met up here.

"Seeing things from above allows you to remember what and who you truly are. When you leave the terrain behind you, travel above all waters to see them from above, allowing only the fire of the sun to touch your face and eyes and mouth, then you can more easily discover your true self, cleaned from any impermanence."

It was this space I needed coming up here, the detachment from the waves of daily life.

"You need that warmth in your chest," he continued, "and clarity in your mind to align your will with the good of humanity and take the appropriate decisions and actions. Especially us, whose actions and decisions determine the lives of so many people, our brothers, and sisters."

Not my decisions. You are the king. And Favar will succeed you someday... Not mine.

"You should sustain such a viewpoint," he said. "For it is easy to forget what clarity even feels like as soon as you are enclosed in those earthly walls we call house. You should know that, in truth, our house is our bodies and the body of the land, with the sandy terrain and stony hills, all permeated by the waters of life. All of this is our house, all coming to be within and under the light of the sun. The earth is our house, but the sun is our home."

I remembered our ancestors, whose shrine was the dark cave below the Black Temple.

"Father, how is the sun our home?"

I turned my eyes towards the sun, only to be blinded by white light before I turned back to my father.

"Our ancestors are the people of the Sun, you know that. After relieving ourselves from all these earthly garments and remain clean under the sun, we connect to them and to our home. My son, whom I know and love, is not this body made of sand. The houses made of sand shall inevitably dissolve back into sand. But my son, my true son, shall know not such decay, for he shall always exist in the light.

And for us, the sun represents and embodies the Fire born from no source, the cause of Life. It is the same fire that shall melt away your darkest impulses, through which shall emerge steady effort according to your divine will.

And, so must we be, suns for our people. Give them the flame we receive, for it is not ours to keep. Help them feed their torches and strengthen their flame in the darkness of their nights. I know you will do a great job, my son."

I wondered whether he had such faith in my brother as well. I pushed such thoughts away and returned to his words that made my chest expand, as if more air came through, smoother and more refined than before. My head was now cleared. I almost felt that I was not just a child with his parent but a pilgrim finding himself in the long-awaited presence of another who had taken a few more steps in the sacred path and turned back to guide the rest.

"Come, sit," he said as he kneeled on the cliff's edge.

I sat down next to him, feet hanging from the edge.

"Who are you, my son?"

I took a moment in silence, looking at the distance, searching for the right answer. I turned to him, hesitant.

He asked again, "Who are you?"

I glanced at the horizon. I spoke with my next heartbeat.

"I am me, he who holds the chief of the gods satisfied, son of my father the magnificent, named after my father Aletheos who holds the chief of the gods satisfied, the king of Erevos, this land of the sacred sciences and the servants of divinity, and son of my mother the graceful who can hold the light and make it beauty, the water in the flowers, now departed from this land."

The sun was warm on my face. And as I allowed the sun to shine over me, the source of my gaze repositioned itself higher than my eyes, a small distance behind the centre of my forehead. And as I kept looking at the distance, I could see all the houses and temples and the palace below us. But now they were houses and temples and palace no more. They were all sand. I could see and understand how all that grandeur was but sand, carefully positioned with intention to serve a purpose, maybe painted or adorned, but nothing could now hide that all they truly were, was sand. How could I have missed that reality? How could the purpose assigned to them by men appear more prominent in my perception than their true nature?

All thoughts were silenced. I looked beyond the desert. The validity of my answer was now fading. Determined, I stood up and exclaimed to my father, "I am me. I am the son of the Fire. I am who I am."

He came to me with a smile, placed his palms just below my ears, leaned and kissed my forehead. My eyes shut at the warmth of his lips. My shoulders dropped, and as he embraced me, I became his son again, and I raised my arms around him.

We sat, quiet. The sun kept his journey towards the horizon, changing with it the colours of the sky.

"How are you, my son?"

"Right now, I am at peace."

My own words stirred the waters within, or rather, by bringing myself to peace, I had the space to see what lay inside.

"Do you miss grandmother?" I asked.

He sighed. "Sometimes I do. She had been with me since my father died a long time ago. When I was called to the throne, she always guided my way and protected me. And she made sure that I had all the assistance I could need.

She held my sense of direction. And when she was taken from us, I had to find it within me. And I know that my mother, her consciousness, is always alive; only her body of sand was dispersed."

"She was very weak towards the end," I said.

"Yes. She had been such a strong woman. But the plague did that to her, together with Muttiya's parents and countless others."

I looked away. The busy streets were now emptying, the city was preparing for rest under the orange horizon and purple sky.

"Did you find out who released the dark force in the throne chamber?"

"Don't worry about that."

"You keep saying that, but... I am not a child anymore, almost fourteen now."

He laughed, gently. "That's not many," he said before turning serious. "You have always been extraordinary... But even you need time to develop."

Even me? I never knew he held me in any high regard. How would I? He was never around. Hadn't felt it either.

"I am taking care of it, my son."

No, you are not! "They were in your private apartments!" I blurted out.

He locked his eyes on me but kept a calm facade. "What did you see?" he asked in a low voice.

"Six or seven men. With masks."

His eyes widened. His tone changed. "You shouldn't have been there! I am taking care of it!"

"Are you?" I asked.

He took a moment to exhale his tension and let his shoulders drop. "Son, I know you worry. But I don't want you involved in any of this. We have people to protect us."

My emotions swirled up from my stomach up to my throat. "Father, and where have you been? Your mother held your sense of direction. How about mine?"

He said nothing. My throat tightened, and my eyes filled up. I shook the tears away and swallowed the knot so that my words wouldn't be drowned.

"I miss you. And I miss Mother," I finally said.

My father looked down. He took my hand and slowly walked me towards the centre of this hill, to the precious lightning made of glass.

"Do you see this wonder, my son?"

I locked my eyes on his.

"This pillar made of lightning holds many mysteries. And it can hold one more. Do you see how it encapsulates the light before releasing fractures of it through its walls?"

It was true. The inside of this glass tube seemed empty. And it always seemed that in that emptiness, a thread of light showed in pieces through its coarse texture.

My father brought my hands gently around the pillar, which remained rooted in the ground. He then placed both his hands on the tube as well. He closed his eyes, and a breath later, his whole body radiated with light. His hands shone bright, with light passing into the tube and spiralling in all the colours of the rainbow.

My brain rumbled with questions but my chest warmed. Before I could ask anything, I was overtaken by the sensations; I vibrated from within. Light burst through each cell of my body, overflowing to fill the space of about two fingers around me. I shut my eyes as my spine straightened and my head was pulled upwards. My light flowed through the tube and connected with my father's in a circular movement. Their fusion shaped an effulgent white sphere, sending a thrust of powerful force outwards.

In a deep voice that caused silence in my head, Father said: "Our streams are now connected. It is done."

The force dissipated as we slowly returned to everyday consciousness, and my body calmed down.

"Whenever you miss me," he said, "whenever you feel alone or far from me, come here. See the world below, and let the sun bathe you. Touch the crystal, and I shall be here with you."

My chest filled with lightness. The sun had disappeared, and the sky was dark blue with only a few strokes of pink, violet, and yellow just above the horizon. He extended his arm, waiting for my own.

"Come, my son, let us go home."

BENEATH THE SKY

I was very eager to find Idhatora. I wanted to share my experience with her. As soon as all my duties were done with, I rushed to our usual meeting place in the garden. The sun had set but probably only moments ago. *I am too early.* The red and purple hues were still quite high and visible in the sky.

I didn't mind, though. I could practise re-enacting what we did with Father on the hill. I had been feeling my palms pulsating electric since then, and once, I even manifested that force to shine through my hands.

Father always said that no practitioner of the sacred sciences should ever create phenomena in front of laymen, so I walked further into the garden and sat on a bench of stone hidden between trees. I adjusted my posture and took a couple of breaths to be sure all else faded away. I recalled the sense of vibration in my hands when the light from the pillar went through them. With it, another memory flashed to mind. It was of my brother, trying to show me how he could direct energy. It was the same day he had gained the two black spots on his temple. His energy hadn't come through, and it was probably the last time he showed any interest in my company before moving on to play adult.

I let the thought dissolve and focused on my body, my feet firmly touching the ground, my knees bent, the base of my spine straight on the bench. I allowed my abdomen to relax, my chest to open, and my shoulders to fall to the sides, with my palms resting on my thighs facing upwards. When each part of my face dropped, I encompassed into awareness my whole body, relaxed and rooted on the ground, with my breath lighting its course through it.

My concentration was now in my hands. They pulsated more electric with every heartbeat my attention remained with them. I visualised my body electric as well, filling it with light in an attempt to emulate what I had experienced up on the hill with my father.

I failed. My body didn't respond to the fantasy. I sighed and opened my eyes to my hands. At least they seemed to spark with force, however fading. Before I could get up, a sharp pain in my stomach stretched my body with a shock of heat. My vision was overtaken. All I could see were my hands, now burning with a golden mask that melted into red liquid, dripping through my fingers. I could not move them; I could not shake the dense liquid away. With all my might, I pushed the air out into a scream.

A sudden weight on my shoulder dissolved the image into oblivion, replacing it with a blurry face in front of mine. To my salvation, it was Idhatora. As soon as my body responded, I jumped off my seat and, in frantic moves, looked all around, not knowing what for.

The palace was there; the trees and flowers and the ponds were there. The sun had disappeared. My friend was there. She grabbed and pulled me into her embrace. "It's okay," she repeated.

Some many sharp breaths later, I managed to regain control of myself. All had passed. I raised my hands to hug her back and stayed with her warmth on my body.

We didn't talk that night. I merely sat down at the bench, and she... she was right there with me, in silence, giving me my time. We did not talk that night. I walked her to her room and only gave her a look before leaving her goodnight; a thank you and maybe a confirmation that I was, or would be, okay.

Dark Pathways

I was back in the hallways that had been occupying my dreams for some time now. I touched the walls, their dryness scraping my palm. I even took my sandals off, brushing the dusty stones below with every step.

With steady movements, I tried to glimpse what had happened that day. As if the stones could whisper what they had witnessed that morning in exchange for me being quiet. Nothing. Nothing more than what myself could recall; the fluttering of the robes, the heavy steps, and the golden masks with the shades of green and brown of age on them. That and the accompanying terror that ached in my chest.

That same night, I was back in my bedroom, trying to maintain the coolness from the open window amongst the warm walls and sheets that covered only my hip. Unlike other nights, the nightmare would not be unexpected. Unlike other nights, I would not force out of my mind the same fluttering of the robes, the heavy steps, and the golden masks. Thus, I knew; I expected the terror that my dream would surely bring.

A few moments of blankness led me from wakefulness into sleep. I opened my eyes. I was quiet, cold. The room, the air around me, felt different. I stood up with the thought of looking out the window, but a sense of urgency in my stomach led the way.

The corridors were empty, sparkling with a constant howling from the distance. Everything was more fluid. The stones of the walls seemed to wobble, glowing a warm light from at least six fingers within them, but as soon as my eyes were upon them, they reassumed their solidity. The pillars cast flickering shadows, and the source of light seemed to change with the direction of my focus.

My breath was warm in an otherwise cold body. I knew I was not awake in the physical world, but I somehow remained conscious of this one. And this world was dense, almost solid, but swayed by emotion.

Before my thought was complete, my chest contracted. The stones around me were melting. As I turned my gaze on them, they assumed their prior position on the wall. As if the stones mocked me. On guard, I let my underlying desire lead me on. I passed through the corridor that had become the object and the cause of my disturbed sleep. I thought of touching the walls again, but my emotions led me astray and placed me in another hall in a moment's time; the private chambers wing. In front of me, a cat was frenzied, scratching a door. I wanted to open it, but instead, I passed through it as if both the door and myself were made of liquid.

In the unlit room, a man kneeled before the bed with his back to me. Shadows floated above his head, clusters of black smoke or black flame. I remained still. The smoke constituting each one was moving, albeit slightly. I wanted to go near, give my hand to the tormented man. But I took only a single step. A mask lay on the bed, right in front of him.

I tried to move onwards, this time not to offer my support but to uncover a conspiracy. Before raising my foot off the floor, an invisible veil grasped me tight. I could only move my eyes, desperately searching for an escape. My heart beat deafening. With each beat, the invisible grasp tightened.

I turned my eyes to the floor, now covered by dark smoke. Behind my shoulders, I could feel, even if not see, small dark flames. I fixated on the window across the room. Beyond the shadows, the moonlight blazed through thin fabrics. I focused on the light, trying to breathe it in against the darkness swallowing the walls and the bed and whomever the man was. A glimpse of the shiny mask captured my eyes before it disappeared too. A path to the window was still free in front of me, at the height of my chest. I struggled to move, to break through. Nothing changed. I was powerless here.

The smoke rose, spiralling in two columns around the window before they twisted around each other and flooded down on me. Only a ray of moonlight remained as the clouds of darkness raged in the room. I closed my eyes right before they collapsed on me. With a sharp burst, I opened them, and the small ray had become an enormous shield before me. In the oval barrier of light, glowed a luminous human figure. She turned to me. It was she that had become the shield itself.

"You should not be here," she exclaimed as the clouds hit her strong.

She raised her arm and pressed the middle of my forehead with two fingers, sending through me a wave of force that pulled me backwards. All things around me dissolved into each other, and I jumped up from my bed. I looked around the room to make sure I was back, and paced around as its physicality was substantiated.

"Was this a dream?" I asked out loud.

I went to the window as I recalled what had happened. The moonlight pressed tight on my head. Images flashed in front of me. The mask on the bed. The fluttering robes. The men in Father's chamber. The whispering. '... he must perish,' one had said. One of them was hesitant. He now took prominence in my thoughts. And in my mind, his mask fell. I saw him.

My eyes shut and opened wide into soberness. All fell into place. I knew. They are going to kill him! "Father!" I yelled.

I ran out of my bedroom. I ran with all my strength. I ran and ran. "I am not too late!" I repeated. I reached the private chambers wing, found the door from my vision. The cat was there, hissing at a big black feather in front of it. I knew those feathers. Without a second thought, I ran over it and pushed through the door.

The man from my vision was still kneeling in front of the bed. The room around him showed nothing of the affair that I had previously experienced. The cat came through and ran to him as he jumped up at my intrusion. Above his hollow cheeks, dark circles weighed his wet eyes. His face relaxed when he recognised me. I turned to the mask on the bed. Next to it, an adorned double-edged dagger was already pulled from its sheath.

His gaze followed mine towards the mask. And his smile vanished. A burning pain flashed in my stomach. With widened, unblinking eyes, he grabbed the dagger and opened his mouth but exhaled no words. My arms were already around his neck, pushing him back until his body hit the wall. The cat was jumping, grabbing on my arms, falling, and jumping again. All my weight pushed on my hands. My face burned. My fingers tightened more and more. Tears ran down his cheeks.

The cold blade of his dagger shivered on my throat. I wanted to let him go. I was desperately searching his eyes for a sign, for an explanation. I could find nothing, not even the willingness for me to let go. I kept pushing with all my strength, refusing to accept the reality of what I was doing. With my arms tightly grasped, I pushed my face as far as possible from his, wanting nothing more than for this to be not. His dagger fell, banging on the floor. He raised his hands to touch mine before the muscles on his neck twitched, and his ghostly exhalation went through my fingers.

I slowly released him as his weight came down, his legs gave way, and his whole body fell to the floor. My arms shivered as I stepped back, shaking my face to clear the hot tears. I uttered not a word; only leaned down, all shaking, and kissed the centre of his forehead before stepping back. I could not think anything. I could not do anything.

With my next breath, I sat down on my legs, facing him. I don't know for how long. All senses were numb, my consciousness idle. The sun was shining through the window before the first steps sounded behind me; probably one of the servants. I remained there. Nothing moved me. I was strongly disassociated from the world around me.

The room was suddenly full of people. A woman passed by me, bashing on my shoulder as she collapsed in front of her son, screaming. Everything was blurry and quiet for me. Her cries only echoed in the distance. My father's hands on my shoulders woke me up in the reality of death. The crying became deafening. I stood up shivering, still facing the breathless vessel that used to be a son, below the heartbroken mother embracing him.

Dried up inside, I turned around. My father's hands slipped away. He did not raise them again, himself remained looking at the horror. I heard him kneeling down with the woman, taking her into his embrace as I left the room. Freezing from within, I dragged myself to my mother's chamber and closed the door behind me.

The sunlight coming in from the open side of the room filled space with warm yellow light. I hid from it behind the big pot, facing the door. Deep cat scratches on my arms dripped red as I brought my palms up and buried my face in them. I leaned back and, with a last deep but cold exhalation, all my capacities ceased to be.

PROCESSION

I sat in the long hallway outside the chamber where my brother Favar was. The sun hit the floor through the open arches across from me. It was early in the morning, and there was still coolness in the shadows. I was alone, and, in my mind, I heard children's laughter. The sharp footsteps of queen Muttiya almost brought me back to this coarse reality, but as she walked past me and into the chamber, I escaped once more into my childhood.

I hadn't seen my cousins in a while. We hadn't spent any substantial time together, but I did have fond memories of them. They must have visited the kingdom only a handful of times. But I still felt close, maybe because of the desire I had to befriend them, the same desire I had about my brother. My cousins, however, were kind. I remember running with them on the sandhills outside the city. I had fallen trying to catch up to them, and they rushed to my need. The older one, Cyrus, even tore his robe and folded the cloth around his hand to push away a scorpion that I had bothered with my fall. My brother, still mocking me, wanted to move on.

And he did move on. The last time I remembered spending time with him was when he wanted to demonstrate how he could direct energy through his hands. He had brought me to Father's chambers and held his hands up.

"Will you teach me how to do it too?" I had asked.

"You are too young! Besides, Meleethos taught me because I will be king someday. I don't think you are allowed to learn the sacred sciences."

He kept squinting his eyes. Nothing happened.

"It's because of you! Stay back!" he said and shook his hands.

He paced around the room, mumbling through his teeth.

"It doesn't matter," I said, "you will get better."

He stopped in front of the altar. On a transparent crystal with sharp edges laid Father's delicate crown with the three intermingling golden snakes.

"It will be yours one day," I consoled him.

He took it in his arms and looked at me. He placed it on his head, with eyes gleaming with joy, or was it pride? The golden snakes sparkled; the gems on their heads shimmering lively.

Favar frowned. He shook his head, moaning. The golden snakes seemed to move, tightening through his hair. He tried to take off the crown but scratched his hand on the snake's needle-thin teeth. With a hiss, one of the snakes bent and pierced his temple.

My heart beat as loud as his screams, trying to pull it out. I ran to him. The crown was pressing hard. His mother, the queen, stormed in, pushing me out of her way. She managed to remove the crown as guards came in and took my brother away. The queen turned to me. She raised her arm and slapped my cheek. Beyond my pulsating face, it was her eyes that made my jaw clench.

"What did you do?" She stared me down. "You should just go away. Your mother too!" she said before going after her son.

The crown was on the floor. The snakes reassumed their position. The gold was cold in my hands, solid. I placed it back on the crystal altar and left to find Favar. It had taken a few moon cycles for him to recover. He had almost lost his sight. After that, he completely withdrew from me.

The chamber door opened wide in a screeching sound that made my hair stand on the back of my neck, bringing me back to the present moment. I sighed and got on my feet. The priests emerged first, carrying all the dead weight of the coffin. Behind them followed the queen, with my father only a step behind. They came to a stop right outside the door. Father looked at me in sympathy as I crossed my arms to hide the cat's scratches from that night. His wife kept straight ahead. No one had talked to me since that night. No one confronted me. But they must have known.

I proceeded right behind them, moving at their pace. The engraved doors of the temple slammed open. I breathed in all the silence of the hallway before the sun hit me in a wave of blinding heat with the first step down the temple. Crowds had gathered on both sides, leaving a long path in the middle for us. On the left, priests stood in a row, and a little further, old nan held Hetta's little hand, with Idhatora by her side. My uncle and two cousins were surely there. Both had gotten taller. They even had short beards on their faces, wearing some very official outfits. How must it have felt to merely be there, detached from grief; how comforting it must have felt for them to know they would leave this place thereafter.

I turned to the front; it would be a long way before this day was over. I had already retreated within. I was in a chamber inside my body, cold and dark, my breath echoing in the emptiness around it while without, the sun was making me sweat. Every now and again, we would stop for the priests to exclaim out loud the correct words in the right manner to ensure favours with the gods.

I started walking again, trying to keep up until we reached the great river. How insignificant it seemed, dirty, muddy, slow. The priests alleviated their shoulders, placing all the weight down before the water. They turned away from the vessel, again shouting their prayers. *Meaningless.* They placed the vessel on a ceremonial boat that awaited to transfer them to the land of the dead. My father and his wife followed on another boat, myself with the third or fourth. Only priests and the family continued beyond the river. There was no crowd across, no clear path to follow, just the procession going through the wind that howled over the sandhills, blasting sand on our faces, making sure we knew how unwelcome we were.

The wind had gotten so strong that I faced down for a moment, just to find an angle where the striking sand hurt the least. I stayed hidden in my arms, with the roar of wind drowning my thoughts. The sun must have gotten closer to the horizon, for what little light reached my eyes shined red. Taking one last breath from my hiding state, I looked up. No one was there. I was alone in a sandstorm that had turned into a brown-red beast of a whirlwind around me. Blank eyes looked down at me from what little sky showed above.

"What do you want?" I yelled through the winds. "What is this darkness you are corrupting the kingdom with? Corrupting me..."

No answer, only the deafening rustling of the sandstorm encircling me.

"What are you," I asked in a low voice, "other than a shadow of a blank gaze looking down at me?"

I exhaled, tired. At least I could stay alone, hidden for a little while longer. The pressure hit me strong, and my royal attire fluttered around me, hanging on to this insignificant vessel. I kneeled and stayed there, head down, twisting whatever part of me touched the sand to sink a little, gaining some sense of stability.

Through the walls of sand raised around me, someone approached. *It's her!* The figure of light, the one that had shielded me from darkness that night. She reached me, and the whirlwind backed off, growing away and relieving the pressure. She was not a figure of light anymore; she was our honoured lady guest, Chaa, whom we had travelled down the river to receive.

Firm as always, she stood unmoved. "Come, child."

She held her hand out, waiting to receive mine. My shoulders dropped; my burden fell in the sand. I looked up into her strong eyes and reached out. I shook my head to bring my mind to where I wanted it to be, and started walking. She followed half a step behind, touching my upper back with the tips of her fingers, gently showing the way. Only a few steps later did I realise there was no wind. The hills were idle, quiet. The others were a few steps ahead, moving on, indifferent to my ordeal.

Lighter, having the storm within me silenced, we reached the others at an entrance to a temple. This one was smaller, with far less grandiosity. It was the tomb.

The priests that led the sleigh carrying the deceased turned to face the procession and my father with his queen at the front, while two priestesses waited at the entrance behind them.

The priests raised from the coffin the empty vessel of my brother. At the sight of him, the first one after that dark night, my heart seemed to have stopped, and my chest was heavy, pulling me down. This thin vessel, now facing us, wrapped in a ceremonial way, used to laugh and run around. It used to stand strong and speak in arrogance, and perhaps kindness and sweetness at times. Now, it was just an empty vessel that would do nothing but lay still for eternity.

The priests kept on. They touched several points of the body already prepared according to the godly instructions. At each point, a prayer was said, this time in low voices. Several amulets were passed from those points and positioned where the body was destined to lay.

One of the priests, having completed the remaining ritual, touched with a ceremonial blade the mouth of what used to contain my brother and placed on it another amulet, accompanied by a prayer yet again; safely to speak the correct words in front of the judges beyond. The priests then took him up the steps while the gates to his resting place creaked open by the priestesses. The latter welcomed him, murmuring in their turn the words before he was passed inside and placed in two additional layers of chests, all shaped like a human form and adorned in a way that was supposed to represent and glorify him.

How estranged they seemed from his true temperament. I was told that the gods judge in absolute just, in truth, and in the light. But these chests would only serve to hide his truthfulness. They were meant to falsely represent and glorify a son preparing to murder his own father, conspiring with faceless men to bring down the sun and replace it with a muddy stone. How could a son end up going down these dark pathways? How could he have given himself to the dark clouds to swallow whole? The only thing he should have been covered with was his golden mask with the shades of green and brown of age.

As I was going over what had taken place, I walked up the steps, raised my head, and pulled from an inner pocket of my robe his golden mask. I kneeled and placed the mask on the higher step, leaving it to stare back at the people behind me, leaving it so that his true face would be clear to see.

"Farewell, brother."

THE IGNORANTS' PLAYGROUND

S everal days had passed since my brother's funeral. Early that morning, as customs demanded, we revisited the site to pay our respects and witness the sealing of the tomb. It was now time for the separation of the worlds. I was taught that only with the separation of the sea from the land can the departed walk the path created in the middle therein, and go freely through the trials, healings, and teachings of the Guardians. Going through this process, his fate would be determined based on the merit of his achievements, and the world he belonged to would become the next step on his path, be it the world of sand, the world of the waters, or the world of fire.

Meleethos, who insisted on resuming our lessons the day after the funeral, had explained that this world of ours, our kingdom, and the bodies of our families and friends, all that we could see throughout this world, was made of sand. This path is chosen for the departed by the celestial judges according to his deeds. The path of the water is the intermediate path where one goes after departing the world of sand if he is not yet as light as a feather to be taken by the wind of Life beyond the waves and into the fire. Most people remained there fighting the storms until they sank to touch the sand below their feet or until they learned to master the waves and earned a second trial. The path of fire is only for the gods, our brothers and fathers, and we shall rejoice with them when we master all the other paths.

The worlds and how they might feel to the recently departed were heavy on my mind, tightening my stomach. I was trying to place my brother on the most appropriate path, incapable of deciding which one was such and, in all instances, having no authority on the matter.

The priest turned to the small crowd. "Each where he belongs!"

My father repeated the words, and the others followed. *Each where he belongs.*

My shoulders dropped. I could but trust that through the wisdom and love of the Judges and the Guardians, my brother would indeed proceed on the path most appropriate for him, the one he paved himself.

T he sunlight, enchanted with jasmine essence, flooded my room. I was calmer than I had been for a while. "We are all where we belong," I said, contented, wondering what that meant about my deeds, those that led me to walk on this path of sand.

The day itself felt calm. The exhaustion from carrying around the burden of the imminent threat that came to be my brother had finally forced me to alleviate myself from it. Out of reflex, the habit of fear rushed through my body. *What about the beast? His companions?*

But I wanted to remain light, even for a while. I stood up and escaped into the beautiful cool morning, out in the tranquil but lively gardens of the palace.

I was about to be touched by the sunlight when I heard some friendly voices. Beyond the arched doorway, my two cousins, Cyrus and Mythus, talked with Idhatora. My chest warmed up. I held back a step and continued to join them. They lowered their voices, seeing me. *Do they know?*

"Hello, Aletheos. Come. Join us! How are you?" said my older cousin Cyrus, extending sympathetic touches on my arm and back.

I nodded, saying nothing.

My cousins had witnessed a couple of sun cycles more than I had, now well in their late teenhood. Cyrus was taller than me and his brother both.

"Idhatora here was telling us she is from the Five-Pointed Star island as well!" said Cyrus with cheeks reddened by the sun below his short brown hair.

It was the small nation their father was presiding over.

"The place she was raised is a beautiful sanctuary next to the sea," said Mythus in a sharp voice that contrasted the sweet tone of his brother, as did his straight, short dark hair. "The temples reside over the agora and overlook far into the horizon facing towards this great kingdom," he said and turned to Idhi, who confirmed his words with sparkling eyes.

"We have been there a few times," said Cyrus, "but never had the honour to meet beautiful Idhatora; although we met the high priestess, and she is a force to be reckoned with!"

He was trying to demonstrate a certain grandeur in his mannerisms that did not really fit his gentle character and age. Idhatora looked down at his reference to the high priestess before she half-heartedly agreed. Conveniently, my cousin continued to cheerfully address other matters.

We all walked amongst the trees and even sat down for some time. I was gradually falling out of my presence, disregarding their pleasant stories and anecdotes. *Would they still welcome me if they knew I had done away with my brother?* No one really asked me or said anything after they found me sitting before his breathless body. *Why?*

Their voices now sounded like mumbling in the background, and my face was getting more and more irritated under the hot sun. I jumped off my seat and gave them a half-smile with the promise to see them later.

I kept my breath and paced towards the inside, urgently searching for the safety of the walls to breathe out my dense sadness. I leaned on the first wall I found and managed to cool down a little. With Father's image flashing to mind, I continued through the palace. I needed to open up. *If they know it was me, Father needs to learn why!* And I needed to know why they kept silent. I headed for the throne chamber, as unlikely as it was to find him there.

The throne room was almost dark in the absence of torches or metal mirrors to reflect the light from the small windows above the columns. *Maybe he has businesses beyond the palace, as usual.* I sighed, before a voice broke the silence.

The columns were in between me and the throne stage, at the feet of which I could place the voices of two individuals. I took a few moments to listen before deciding to leave or join them. The voices sounded relaxed and friendly, and I assumed the meeting was not of an official degree. I took a few more steps before the voices were assigned to their possessors, my father and his dear friend Galias, whom I came to call uncle, although he wasn't one by blood.

I could still not see them behind the columns. Their relaxed tone was crashed by a loud voice of a person whose presence I had just noticed. She was the honoured lady guest, Chaa. Her composed nature and comforting manners I had come to witness were in sharp contrast to her outburst as she emerged from behind the columns, pacing around the room. Her thunderous tone made me abandon all notions of taking another step. I should leave. But I remained still in my position. She addressed Galias.

"You should have never used your powers in such an irresponsible manner! You only have them to prevent a war, not avenge one!"

Galias replied in a somewhat apologetic manner. "They ravaged our shores, sister! They killed and stole!"

"Regardless!" she dismissed him.

"And where were you to prevent this?" he answered.

"My responsibility is a spiritual one! My temples and priestesses were safe! Wars amongst nations do not concern me! That is the responsibility your position bears; it is for you to carry out!"

"They attacked us suddenly. We couldn't have known."

"You would have known had you been standing guard in the realms your powers emerge from instead of indulging yourself in the material pleasures circumstantial to your position."

My father intervened. "Sister, you know that this is not the case. Our brother is not entangled in such materialistic webs."

Sister?

Galias, encouraged by my father's words, continued. "It is your priestess they took! You did not manage to offer the safety you claim you did!"

"The young girl was safe all the while," she exhaled before raising her voice again. "Even when you so thoughtlessly rampaged their ships with your storms!"

"Nothing happened to her," said Galias in a wavering voice.

"Because of my protection, not your meticulous execution! You, beloved brother, have behaved irresponsibly using means you evidently do not fully understand! She could have been lost by nothing else than your intervention alone. Irrespective of the girl, your vengeance is an action to be pitied and feared! For, surely, you knew that your actions were inconsequential to the safety of anyone! No one would benefit from the loss of those lives. Your heart and mind were gravely misplaced, dear brother."

My father intervened again. "Chaa, please."

She glanced at my father and stopped moving. She brought her hands to her chest, took a breath, and continued in a more sympathetic tone. "Using waves to sink their ships will not go unrecorded. The lords of the sea have not granted you such power. The entities you worked with to carry out such atrocity are beings you should have never come in contact with!"

Listening to her words made it very clear that she did not mean to strike down my uncle but was merely explaining the consequences his actions bore, knowing very well that the records of the Lords cannot be undone.

My blood rushed around my body, thinking of what the records would reflect about me. I quickly justified my ill actions on the willingness and urgency to do good and pushed the thought away, hoping that my intention would be sufficient in the balancing of the heart.

Galias hunched. He seemed to realise the burden he had placed on himself.

"Can you even visit the realms of fire now?" Chaa asked.

Galias looked down, shaking his head.

"Did you see her?" Chaa continued. She did not wait for his reply. "The girl is here. She is safe."

"She is here?" He turned to my father, eager to hear him confirm it.

"Yes. They brought her here along with what remained of their ships. She shall remain here as is her path," Father explained.

"And Balluashir's men?"

"The three surviving commanders are held here for crimes against the kingdom. Their subordinates were sent home."

"Why?" Galias asked.

It was Chaa that answered. "How could you still ask that?"

My father abandoned his calm tone. "Enough!" His outburst echoed around us all.

He took a few steps and sat down on the steps below the throne. He remained silent. Only now did I see the vast sadness on his face. He brought his hands to his face, hiding for a moment his vacant look. I had seen him being contemplative during the funeral; I had seen him strong and firm and supportive towards my brother's mother, but only now did I see him sad.

"Enough!" he pleaded again in a lower voice. "I have lost my eldest son to the hands of my youngest because the former conspired to kill me... Enough."

Galias froze at the revelation. My face heated, and eyes blurred with tears, as if having it said somehow solidified my ordeal. Galias looked at Chaa, probably waiting for an explanation. For a few heartbeats, he received none.

She then responded in a low voice. "The night he died, the boy was overtaken by his co-conspirators' darkness. Aletheos somehow witnessed it in the land of mud, and I was alerted just before he was struck."

Galias took a few steps back before turning to Chaa. "In the land of mud? Did you show him how to go there? Should he be able to go there?"

"No. But his line is pure; his mind already well developed. I don't think he is conscious of his capacities yet, but we don't really know what aspects in him are awakened. And not only did he find himself in the land of mud, but his mind was able to accurately translate the impressions of that world. And in the knowingness of the grave danger his father was in, the boy resorted to taking his brother's life."

My father kept looking down, unmoved.

"Could you not have intervened otherwise?" Galias asked.

"It was too late," Chaa said, protecting my father from having to explain. "When I sent the boy back to his body, the conspirators' attack truly began in both worlds. They stormed the palace with the support of dark forces. By the time we subdued their clouds, it was done."

"Is it over?" Uncle Galias asked.

"Far from it," my father said. "Our interference has stirred many gears. Tradition maintains too strong a hold on the nation. Their dogmas are too persistent, and so are the devotees. And the fallen ones have gained a strong grip."

"Brother," Galias answered, extending his arm to my father as a sign of his willingness to assist, only to let it fall midway, recognising his inability to change anything. "I am deeply sorry, Aletheos," he finally exhaled.

Father said nothing. She spoke. "The boy had witnessed one of their meetings in this very palace." She turned to my father. "You need to tell Muttiya about her brother."

"Hasn't she suffered enough?" Father asked.

Galias opened his mouth, but before he spoke, my father, as if alerted by something, raised his eyes and met mine. He knew everything. He had been fighting a war he kept secret from me. And he left me to do the unspeakable. I took a step backwards, still looking at him. The waves of emotion swelled within; it was all that I could do not to be swept away by them.

He pushed himself up and only took a step while I put all my strength into confining the bursts of thought currents. And I turned my back to my father, the king.

Instead of the main gate, an enormous blackness stood only fingers away from my face. Itself, never moving, sent a thrusting gust of force that swept me off my feet and sent me flying on the ground.

My head pulsated from hitting the floor. My eyes struggled through the dizziness. I saw the beak below the eyes, the black skin, and the floating black feathers pointing upwards around his wingless body, the sceptre in his left hand. It was the dark beast. Only this time, he stood as tall as the building would accommodate, blocking the main gate, facing down on me. He was more physical, more real than the last time.

I pushed myself up as he conjured a dark sphere that burst into a ring of black smoke towards us. As of instinct, I stretched my hands, and from them emerged white light that met his rolling darkness with an explosion that nailed me back to the ground.

I pushed my hands below my back to move as far as I could. But my wrist gave way, and I fell hard on the stone floor. Below me, a thunderous sensation passed through the ground, making it vibrate electric. Unbalanced on my elbow, I resorted to the people behind me.

Father stood tall with Chaa to his left and Galias a step behind. They all radiated light from within them. They didn't move, just stood there facing the creature. A bright wall of light emitted from the ground upwards now separated us from the dark entity. The whole chamber, save the place occupied by the creature, shimmered bright.

The beast did not move. I took a sharp breath with a sense of hope and rushed to the three beacons of light. With a swift move, Father grabbed my arm and pulled me to his side. I, too, faced the creature, shifting my focus between him and my father.

No one uttered a word. No one moved. Each expected to see how the other's intentions would unfold. The enormous dark entity at the other end of the room stared back at us, his only movement distinguishable only by the feathers around him, floating at the rhythm of his breath.

The creature's head moved at a painfully slow pace. Each moment passing served so to impose his gigantic size on us. As his head tilted downwards, the air in the room, as if a solid composite, was being misplaced to accommodate him, creating a deafening sound that made the whole room and everything in it tremble. The creature now faced down on me. His eyes focused on mine. Father raised his arm, hiding my face behind it, interrupting the creature's invisible grip on me.

A heartbeat later, everything was back to how it used to be. The air I breathed had cooled down, vibrating no more. The room had assumed its original place, almost dark in the absence of torches or metal mirrors to reflect the light from the small windows high above. The whole throne chamber was as dull as it would be on any day. My father, our honoured guest, and my uncle held their stance, unmovable, looking across the room.

"He is gone," Chaa said in a whispering voice.

Father turned back to me and bent his knees just in time to catch me as my senses were released from my body.

I floated in boundless darkness. I could discern nothing other than darkness all around. And I drifted, or rather sank, in deep waters, all the while content with my fate and calm in my chest.

Suddenly, I sank no more. I turned down. Nothingness still. I looked up. The creature was there. He was not as enormous as before, now about the height of a man. He stared back at me from a small distance with his sceptre in hand. His eyes were blank, empty. But now, he clearly had no intention of remaining still. He opened his palm as he came closer. A small eruption of light came out of nowhere and disappeared as suddenly into the darkness, forcing him backwards. He frowned and looked around from amidst the black feathers that flashed in and out of existence on all sides of him. Nothing. He tried again, and again, and again, but every time, a small explosion of golden-white light forced him to abandon his offence.

Each hit made him more furious, more ferocious in his next attack. This last time, he paused, gathering strength, and forcedly pushed himself towards me. I remained watching his attacks, unable to move or float intentionally, hoping for another burst of light. And surely it came. Proportionate to his force, the light was now brighter and more powerful, keeping his aggression at bay. As he pushed, so did the light grow bigger and brighter until it filled the darkness around me, and all I could see was this golden-white light.

Everything was quiet. Only the calm light pulsated throughout space. And I breathed in the light. Through it, I thought I glimpsed the entity I encountered in the cave of our ancestors; the being with the body of a lion, the tail of an ox, and great wings on its back; only now, it had the head of a reptile instead of a human. Before I had time to be sure, a new process had begun. Having no authority, I gravitated back into my physical body as the light dissipated into the dense material that constituted the room around me.

I was in one of the chambers of the royal infirmary. As I was coming back to my senses, flames floated around me, originating from no source. I tried to focus my gaze on them, but they, together with the still fading light, disappeared altogether.

"Father," I said, my voice breaking.

"I am here. You are safe," he replied. With a sigh of relief, he touched the temples of my face and kissed my forehead. "I am here. You are safe," he repeated, keeping his eyes on mine.

In his assurance, I let my head fall back on the bed and into a sleep of warmth and hope. *He is here.* The last spark of awareness faded away with my consciousness.

Oh, how I wished to believe him...

CLOUDS OVER THE CITY

T he avenue before the palace was empty. Only clouds raged close with thunder.
It had rained before, a few years back. But then, it was celebrated as life-giving.
Now, the guards moved around the city with warnings, and people ran to gather
their stock, pulled their children inside, and sealed the windows.

Such was life within the palace as well, silent but ruled by an underlying tension.
I had seen priests detained by guards as they passed through the halls. Another
day, officials were taken away at blade's threat. The entire palace seemed emptier
or quieter of people. Many of those close to my father, be it advisors, guards, or
officials, were released from their duties and prohibited from entering the palace.
Even housekeepers seemed to be absent.

It had been a few moon cycles now, and we hadn't really talked. I had barely even
seen Father. He was at unrest since that day in the throne chamber, pursuing an
enemy that was lurking in the shadows. He couldn't find the beast, but he searched
for those amongst us who made its attack possible, bringing the darkness inside.
And all was taking place in silence, again kept from me, even though, I was certain
now, that this was my war.

The air filled with an earthly scent. A single drop fell on my forehead. Then it
began, soft. The cold water awakened my skin as a man rode by me through the
gates, splashing mud under his horse. It was the queen's brother, Valsaris.

By the time he disappeared into narrow streets, the rain had already stopped. The
heavy clouds must have missed the city. Beyond the houses, the hills were scorched
by the thunderstorm.

T he expectation of another intrusion had been waking me up very early in the morning, sometimes long before the sun showed in the sky. My throat filled with a drowning sensation that demanded I check for any threats.

Thus, I was awake again. The smell of humidity stuffed my nose. Through the window, the sunlight barely appeared over the horizon, sky still dark blue with some purples and oranges. Looking across my bed was our nan, who had, after a very long time, returned to watch over me. She was asleep on the chair with her neck bent in what looked like a very uncomfortable position.

I tried to convince myself to stay in bed, unsuccessfully. I pushed my sheet away, trying not to alert her. What a dry woman. Strict as she may have been, though, she honestly cared for our wellbeing. But I was too young, and she was too set in her ways to be able to establish a tender connection. And before I was able to consciously try, she moved to concentrate her duties on my sister Hetta. Until now.

I gently shook my head and got up. With carefully planned steps, I left the room. The palace was quiet, and the hall was alleviated from the dampness by a minor cool draft above the warm stones of the floor.

My eyes were dry and my face warm, my senses not yet fully awake. I took a careful look at each corridor before exposing my body. But after a few turns, I admitted to myself that I was not really expecting to find someone. It was only fear that drove me out of bed.

At the next turn, below a window in the hall, laid scattered pieces of a broken vase. *Was this the wind? Maybe another official who protested before thrown out...* I kneeled and gathered all the pieces into a small tidy pile, an act of reconciliation with my ominous anxiety. *Where are the maidens?*

Before reaching the end of the hall, somebody emerged from behind the left corner. I remained still. He did the same. He bore the black uniform of the Starani guards, but his skin was as light as mine; definitely not a descendant of the Starani warriors. He held a spear and had a dagger wrapped around his waist. Aware of his weapons, I focused on his face. He was a young man with soft features, probably having such guard duties assigned to him only very recently. My eyes met his. He wouldn't blink.

I let the tension on my chest and shoulders drop. He abandoned his offensive stance and stood up straight, followed by a nod that I perceived to be paying of respects. I customarily returned his salutation while he adjusted his clothing and stood straight as I passed by him.

It wasn't unheard of for the Starani to accept outsiders in their ranks. He was probably such an instance. It would otherwise be foolish of him to dress as one. If the proud Starani caught him impersonating them... I sighed.

When I entered my bedroom once more, nan was already expecting me, eyes wide open with the usual frown that made her eyebrows come together. "Where have you been?"

I didn't give an answer. I mumbled some low noises and let my weight fall on the warm bed, pulling the sheet up to my hip and looking towards the window, away from her. The sun was now showing whole, just above the horizon.

When I woke up again, late in the morning, nan was not there. The parts of my body that touched the bed were damp with sweat. I stood up and rearranged my clothes from sticking to my skin before looking out the door of my bedroom. Nan was not there. To my left, at some distance, the young guard stood still, looking straight ahead at the opposite wall. I passed by him, keeping the corner of my eye on him until I took a turn and moved on with my day.

I headed to the library. The space of scholars and scribes who spent their whole days studying and recording, was diminishing into a room devoid of light throughout big cases of scrolls. My old teacher, Meleethos, was busy counselling my father and had left my education to another. He was absent as well. Before leaving this lifeless room, I tripped on some scrolls. I picked them up and tidied them on a table. Behind it, further into the library, some big and complex instruments that dealt with the movement of the wanderers were tumbled on their side, with pieces of them lying around. My jaw clenched at whatever conflict might have taken place here.

My scrolls! With only a breath's hesitation, I paced through to the inner isles and towards the case containing all the written knowledge on the gods' genealogy. It looked untouched, only as messed up as I had left it. Not that there was something of value in them. I had gone through almost all of them with nothing in return.

With a sigh of relief and disappointment, I returned to the corridor and headed outside. Maybe my tutor would be in one of the inner gardens, where we occasionally met. Beyond the palace, the heat was overwhelming. I walked towards a shed made of wooden pillars and white cloths hanging between them. No one was around, another anomaly, another sign of disorder.

Nevertheless, I stayed for a while, under the somewhat protective shadow of the garments, with eyes almost closed, away from the light-reflecting ground. Across from me stood the palace; its intricate masonry stretching up to the blue sky. My eyes opened wide as an urge pressed me to see things from up high.

I hurried up to the roof, and looked down at the garden I came from and further beyond it, beyond the palace walls. Next to me, would usually lie Idhatora observing the stars at the end of our walks. My heart ached at her absence. I had not enjoyed the refuge of her company for some time now.

I went for her at the queen's chambers. I stopped at the entrance as a mere courtesy in entering a women's chamber and searched to find my friend. Only Idhatora and two other girls were inside. She was whispering with Cereena.

They both looked so formal and courteous. Idhatora was taller and more feminine than I knew. *Am I changing as well?* I had noticed changes in the measurements of my clothes and sandals but thought nothing of it. For a moment, I wondered what kind of development, beyond the physical, we might have gone through during this time away from each other. *How short was it really?*

When our eyes met, Idhi embraced her friend goodbye and rose from her seat in a manner of elegance. We headed to a dusty room we sometimes visited when it was too hot or cold to go in the garden. It was a room reserved for when the queen's parents stayed at the palace. No one used it after they died, in superstitious fear it might still hold the illness that killed them. Even the servants kept away.

We embraced and sat in front of the big window facing each other. Her black hair was straightened, carefully combed to position. Her big dark eyes seemed even bigger by the dark lines drawn around them. And her face was a little thinner, making her cheekbones more apparent.

"How have you been?" I asked her.

"Did you find what you have been looking for?" she asked back.

Her gaze was gathered, as if she was more grounded in her body.

"No," I answered. "No scrolls mention the beast."

"And the man?"

I only shook my head.

"I worry, Aletheos," she said with a deep outbreath. "What do you expect to do when you do find them?"

"Fight!"

"Fight?" she burst out. "How? With what means?"

My stomach stiffened with a loud heartbeat and the thought of Father, tormented by responsibility.

"I will find a way! I am not letting the beast plague the kingdom."

I threw a glance at my palms, already warm with invisible force. *If I could only understand... If Father could only guide me instead of hiding in silence...*

She shook her head and pressed her lips together. "Do you know why people are thrown out of the palace?" she finally asked.

I sighed before speaking. "The same night I..." My stomach burned at the thought of confessing. "The night Favar died, conspirators tried to kill my father. And people in the palace were amongst them."

Her eyes widened. "Do you know who they are?"

"No. All these people gone; I think my father is trying to find those we can trust."

"But Cereena's..." She mumbled something and turned away. "Are we safe now?"

"I... I don't know."

We both sat in silence. She was looking out the window, and I at her. I kept thinking about what Chaa had said about the young priestess taken away from her temple.

"Tell me about the temple you were raised in," I said.

"Back on the island?"

I nodded.

"I think I already told you what I remember. It was the temple of the Great Goddess. Although it was not as big as the temples we have here, it was simple and beautiful, built on a hill. One thing I remember for sure is the beauty of the blue sea viewed from up there."

I smiled, delighted by the picture painted in my mind. "What else do you remember?"

She sat straight and continued in a more cheerful tone.

"I have an image of a very kind priestess with long black hair. I remember meeting her on the beach long before she came to the temple. But she must have been very knowledgeable on the ways of the Goddess, because she began tutoring us as soon as she joined. We had a strict schedule, teaching, chores, not a lot of playtime. Although, I would cheat some of the resting time to wander around. But the priestesses had a set routine, overseen by the high priestess."

"And how was she?"

"The high priestess? I didn't really know her; she didn't attend the lives of us little girls. But I know she was a woman that commanded respect and order. Everyone would do their best for her. Once, I remember, we had spent days preparing for a ritual orchestrated by her. We gathered in the garden late at night, around a ceremonial pot, as she overlooked the ritual. She stood higher than us, on the entrance of the temple, chanting. Us girls were behind several rows of priestesses, and I didn't really see her. But I remember her voice though, deep, commanding, safe."

Safe?

"Why do you ask?"

I smiled and shook my head. She came next to me, leaning her head on my shoulder. "It was beautiful back then. But this is my home now."

I fondled my cheek on her hair. "I am very glad you are here, Idhi."

She looked up at me. "Are we safe, Aletheos?"

"You will always be safe! I will make sure of it," I said, hugging her tight.

UNCERTAIN GROUND

I made my way up my favourite hill. It had changed since my last visit. My path had collapsed into a steep cliff that I had to climb with care and effort. Sharp stones had emerged from it, guarding the crystallised lightning at its top. I wondered what kind of force could have changed this place so much and whether the path my father had used to get us there had changed as well. His path was all the way around the hill; I had never used it myself. *The storm!* I remembered the thunderstorm, seeing how the side of the hill had subsided into vertical dried rivers.

The sharp stones cut my wrist. As of instinct, I brought the burning wound close to my lips, with the taste of blood catching me by surprise. With lips pressed together, I shook my hand for the remaining drops to fall off. Sweat flew away as well.

Willingly, I brought my mind back to the task. I pulled my weight up to the level plane and reached the end of my ascent. All the miniscule stones of the ground pushed hard into my hand, never breaching the skin but sticking to it. I stood up and rubbed my palms together, seeing the different shapes pressed on my hands. With squinted eyes, I swiped the sweat from my forehead and looked around. There was nothing to cover me from the heat directly above.

Looking back at the city below, I acknowledged my success in reaching this place. I sat down, legs crossed, looking down at Eos and beyond, far into the horizon, following the course of the great river. I wasn't feeling as I had hoped when I decided to come up here, away from everything. The heat was almost unbearable, and my eyes were hazy from the sweat and the light reflected all around me.

"Now what?" I said out loud with a deep exhalation and a dry mouth. I stood up indecisive; which direction should I head in, what steps should I take? I thought of going back, but not before I saw the lightning of glass, more out of ceremonial habit than anything else.

By some pull I did not resist, I approached and grabbed the transparent pillar with both hands. A great wave of energy came outwards, swiftly filling my whole body and pushing my head upwards. The light had touched my innermost need and carried it out with it.

"Father!" I yelled, commanding his presence.

The rush of force dissipated. My father appeared on the other side of the pillar. He just stood there, calm, smiling, radiating cooling light. I hesitantly removed my hands from the pillar, not knowing whether it would affect his presence. It didn't.

"My son!" he said in the kind tone I used to know he had.

"Father!" It took a lot of restraint to hold back my tears. I wanted to run to him. *Where have you been?* I stood still and silent.

"Oh, my son," he said in a sad tone, "my sweet son, I am very, deeply sorry I have not been present for you."

"Why?" I finally cried out.

He took a hard swallow before speaking. "I have been striving to restore order. What took place in the throne chamber was obscene. It is dark magic of high degree. Such atrocities should not have been able to infiltrate the palace!"

His words violently unburied a memory in my mind's eye, that of dark smoke being absorbed in the walls of the room behind the throne.

"Have you found anything?" I asked, hoping. "The beast?"

He shook his head. "But I have been crafting our safety," Father continued, "all of ours and especially yours; yours and that of your future."

Mine? No! Your absence does not benefit me! It's your guidance I need!

"Oh, my son, I wish I could tell you everything. I cannot. Not yet. But I can promise you this, we shall head into your future together. You will learn the truth, this and many others; It is your future. It is your future and sacred duty."

He walked around the pillar, coming closer to me. He brought his arm to my back, leading the way and myself to the edge of the hill, and pointed at the city below. "This is your duty. You will be king one day. This city, the entire kingdom, and its people will all be yours to guide, to rule, to serve!"

The extent of what he now bestowed upon me seemed unimaginable. The capacities I considered one should have for such position seemed so distant, impossible to cultivate. And I had already corrupted myself by taking a life. I could never succeed him; maybe my sister.

"But..." I hesitated for a moment, yet, incapable of holding back, I continued, "but my brother..."

"Your brother is gone now."

"But... I..."

"You did what you thought was right, my beloved. That is the best you can do; that is the best anybody can do."

His words fuelled the anger that had been burning in me for a while. I was angry at him for whom I had committed fratricide. And I was angry at my brother, whose stupidity consumed him and took him from me. And I was angry at myself! I could still feel his last exhalation engraved in my hands.

"I killed him, Father," I shouted, ready, or rather desperate, to face the consequences. "I killed him."

"I know my son," he said in a soft voice.

I tried to catch my breath in an attempt to hold it all back, but I was rendered powerless. I had been alone, lost, and thirsty for absolution in a desert of guilt and anger. His words were like rain in this vast dry land. With a gasp of air, my tears drowned me, and through my blurry sight, Father continued.

"I am so very sorry you had to go through that. Your brother was my responsibility. I should have dealt with him when I could. But I loved him so, and I hid from my responsibility and burden. It was my inadequacy that killed him. And his actions. So, shed the burden off your shoulders, my son. Let me carry it. All of it."

The guilt had been pressing on my chest, obstructing my breathing; now cleared by the rivers I was crying.

"Come home, my son. Come home to me," he said, extending his right arm and inviting mine.

Through the tears, I gave him a half smile that truly came from within. I nodded. He gave me a last smile before he vanished into a mist of light that dispersed around the level ground of the hill.

I turned to see the kingdom one last time before heading back. I pulled the black feather from my robe. I had kept it close since my first encounter with the masked men. It shined with reflections of dark greens and purples as it flew away with the wind. This time, I took the path of my father. A path that was smooth and wide, turning mildly until it reached the base of the hill.

At the gate of the palace, he waited. He was calm; his arm ready to receive mine.

"Welcome back, my son. Welcome home."

PART 2
SUNRISE

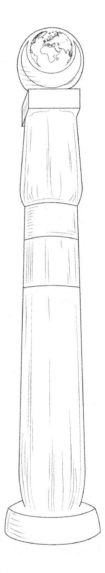

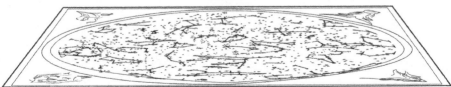

STREETS OF SAND

The sun shone down through the cobbled passages of the city. I observed the people, their lives. I would grow to be responsible for this place, my father had said, for these people, the kingdom. And I was determined to be a good ruler after him, a good server and protector.

Having marched through the main avenue, adorned with statues and altars to the gods, I walked down the narrow streets of clay houses. People were so very busy. None looked away from their chores. The continuous murmur of daily life carried my mind smoothly until a naked babe ran out of a house laughing. Her mischievous nature was followed by the angry worries of the mother, and her laughter was cut short when the woman caught up and slapped the babe's buttocks.

Her cry disappeared back into the house before I moved on. A few steps later, a man rushed out from a corner, clumsily screaming towards me. I tried to figure out what he was saying. He pointed at a chick that sprinted between my legs, chased by a cat. *Surely screaming won't help.* I smiled as he ran by me, following the chick and cat in their affliction.

Further down the street, a smith of copper banged his metal with a small hammer in a compact space built around a furnace. Most of his stock was almost green now, but each piece had some veins that still caught the light. In no way did it remind of our smith areas at the palace, full of shining stock and refined artefacts.

From among the busy people, a group of five or six men in dark hooded cloaks walked towards me. The first one bumped on my shoulder as they passed by me. He didn't act to care, but as he spared me a look with the corner of his eye, his long face and narrow nose showed below his hood.

They moved on as whispers filled my ears. I stretched my neck, staying still and quiet to make sure. No one was close to me; the people went about their daily lives, all at some distance. But the whispers continued from no apparent source. I could but follow them, and the hooded men, into the main avenue.

To the left stood the palace over the simple lives of people. Amidst the crowd, a hooded man turned into a passageway. The whispers were guiding me to him, becoming louder in my head.

With an eye out for his companions, I marched behind him. I could not make words out of the hissing sounds that chiselled my brain. So, I only focused on the man. I peeked down the street with sweaty palms and a racing heart as his cloak fluttered, disappearing behind a house.

By the time I reached the corner, he disappeared into another one, and again, and again. I paced after him, faster and faster, only to see his cloak as he took yet another turn. Each street was quieter than the last one, while the whispers and the hissing got louder. They then ceased altogether as I turned into an empty alley.

I halted with my heart pounding. I looked around, breathing fast through my mouth. The street was a dead end, enclosed by buildings on all sides. All windows were shut. Only a door remained half-open on the other end of the street. Nothing showed from inside, as if there was a veil swallowing whatever light reached through.

The whispers came back, louder with every heartbeat. They invited me inside. With a deep inhalation, I stood up straight, ready to march in. Before my foot left the ground, a figure emerged as if from nowhere, firmly rooted in front of me. The whispers stopped.

"Chaa!"

"Turn away," she said, pressing on my shoulder.

All courage flew out of me as we ran back through the narrow streets. My legs shook, trying to keep up. I didn't talk, and neither did she. We merely paced through until I stumbled on the coarse pathway. We didn't stop. She grabbed my hand and led the way, never letting go until we were out on the main road with the sun shining down all around us. She then brought her hands to my head.

"Are you all right?" she asked with inspecting eyes.

A guard ran to us, gasping for air. It was that young man I met in the hallway.

"I am sorry, I lost you," he said.

She only gave him a quick glance before taking my hand and rushing to the palace. The gates closed with a bang behind us. Still panting, I waited for her explanation. Instead, she turned and grabbed my arms below the shoulders.

"Your ignorance will kill us all!" she said.

I gulped at the change of heart. All tension rumbled within me. "Then teach me!"

She backed off. She did not expect my outburst either. With a sigh, she composed her posture and looked deep into my eyes before finally exhaling.

"Find me tomorrow at midday."

AT THE FEET OF THE MOUNT

T he sun finally showed above the horizon and I jumped up from the bed. Nan
had laid out my clothes, like old times when I was too young. Still unaware of
the terms of our meeting with Chaa, I prepared myself and rushed to find Father.
He should know. I kept looking around for the high priestess as I made my way to
the throne room.

Father stood next to the throne, speaking to his elder advisor, Meleethos, with a
few others around in the room. I kept my distance, waiting for his acknowledge-
ment. He did see me and came down the steps. Before I could ask for his approval,
he leaned down and whispered in my ear before moving on to greet another.

I hurried out into the halls and towards my mother's room, according to his
instruction. The room looked attended to; the stone of the floors was clean of sand,
the water in the pond more vibrant. *Beautiful.*

"You are early," I heard from across the room, the open side of it. It was Chaa. She
was facing outside.

"Come with me, observe," she said.

I joined her.

"What do you see, child?"

I looked for anything in particular. I found nothing out of the ordinary.

"I see the trees."

"Yes?"

"I see the blue sky. Three, no, four clouds, small, almost transparent."

"What else?"

"I see the water from our pond here connecting with the great river, flowing."

The sun was high, its light casting but small shadows on the ground.

She spoke. "Allow your perception to expand. Let that which is beyond this gross
world show itself and let your brain open to those impressions."

I did not know how to follow that.

"Just relax with your intention. Obtain a passive stance," she said.

I let my shoulders fall and tried to retrieve my mind.

"That's it," she said. She positioned her open palm behind my head. "Now observe again, truly see with your eye."

I led my concentration to a tree. With eyes relaxed, I saw hazy movement where there was none before. I tried to ground my mind in my body, tighten its reins, and looked again. My heartbeat was slowing, and, in my calmness, every branch and every leaf danced in an almost indiscernible rhythm, gracefully through the air. I enfolded with my awareness more trees, them too dancing through all their parts, flowing together in perfect harmony.

The river flowed with vitality, and the heavy boundaries of my body slipped into a deep connection with it, feeling what the body of water met on its way, embracing within it the ground and the stones and the peduncles of the lotus flowers. A breeze scraped the water, carrying miniscule drops up through the air and onto my face, centring my awareness back in my head.

I looked around. Everything was vitality. All was actually, physically interconnected; each movement of the leaf would direct the breeze that altered, even at the most minor degree, the currents of the water that touched the bottom of the lotuses.

"How do you feel, my dear?" she asked in a low voice.

I did not wish to speak; I did not want to break the charm. I was content with maintaining a passive stance.

Glimpses of light emerged through and above all that I focused on. The trees vibrated, lively. Their substance seemed to extend beyond their physical bodies into immateriality and then into an invisible but very perceivable vibration that permeated everything; all that I could bring to mind and beyond. All was esoterically interwoven as well.

And from each spark of light came out dispersed waves of colours; layers upon layers of colours. I shook my head and shut my eyes to return to reality. Before a moment had passed, the colours were back, insisting on existing in and all around me, now flashing with visions of creatures; human-like, animal-like, they all appeared and disappeared with every heartbeat.

"There are many worlds, my child. They are all interconnected and equally real. Each entity, as do we, needs an appropriate vessel to exist in each world, and all of them precede this physical existence. What you see now is a mixture of the bodies and the worlds. This chaos you witness is chaos only to your inability to distinguish them from one another. But you shall learn to differentiate them for what they are. Their existence, though, is real, irrespective of your ability to perceive them. They are even more real than this, our physical reality."

Over the beauty of it all, an urgency rushed to mind. "How is this going to help us?" I asked. "Help me against the darkness?"

She smiled. "You don't look for darkness in the abyss. Darkness there, merely is. Only from the light you may discern what lies in its depths. But to find the light is to find yourself. And to do so, you must first learn how to look for him."

She stood in front of me. With one hand, she touched my forehead. With the other, my heart. I was pushed within.

Dark space now surrounded me. In the distance glimmered a single source of light. With a calm chest, I made my way to it, as each step echoed with dripping water over the slightly submerged floor. The light came from a small barred window on a door. I stretched my feet to peek inside, but the light was blinding.

Without a second thought, I push the door open. The light in the chamber was no longer fierce; it was soothing, inviting, embracing. I stepped inside a hemispherical room. The smooth stone floor was dry, engraved with symbols. The walls were coarse, like a cave.

From the centre, shined the light. A flame. No. Three flames, intertwined. A golden, a pink, and a blue flame spiralling around each other. I smiled through a warm heart.

"This is the essence of you that inhabits your body, in the sacred chamber of the heart," Chaa said.

I was deep in concentration. Her words didn't move me from my experience. I opened my arms to the threefold flame. The golden one came first. It went through my hands and expanded in my entire body, energising each cell. My thoughts subsided. I had trust, certainty. The pink followed. It calmed me like a warm embrace that healed and united. The blue followed. I would walk the path. I was strong.

"Your divine nature is hereby expressed as wisdom, love, and power," Chaa said.

I opened my eyes.

"Never forget, each and all worlds are vessels themselves," she said. "One by one shall dissolve for the eye of the seer, and one by one give way to that which is even more real. Until the innermost, the highest truth is uncovered."

A highest truth... The reassurance of its very existence over chaos shaped a longed smile within.

"This is what this room represents." She looked around the chamber before settling her gaze on the white pot. "The one vessel of Life."

She paused.

"Now, the time is upon us. The sun is almost directly above; it is the middle of the day."

The rays of the sun now touched us. I had never realised before that the floor extended one step beyond the covered area of the room. And now, at this hour, we stood between the open lands under the sun and the room still in the shadows. She held her arms up towards the sun. The light reached her body, which seemed to absorb it until it overflowed, bouncing off her like a thick liquid, shining all around.

She radiated from within. I took a step away, my eyes never turning. She turned to the pot in the middle of the room, extending her arms and projecting onto it all the light she exuded. Its white stone absorbed it like the dry earth does the water, before emitting it back in the room in a thick white mist.

The water of the pond cast refracted light, creating a mirage of multicoloured shades floating around through the glowing mist. I opened my arms wide and closed my eyes, letting all the vibrancy go through me and settle deep within.

T he mist had faded, now visible only a few fingers above the floor.

"My mother was performing this ritual," I said, half asking, half knowing. She smiled.

"Who are you?" I asked. "Truly?"

She sighed and turned to me. "My name is Chaa. I am the high priestess of the temple of the Great Mother. And I am your mother's mother."

ASHES OF DOUBT

I walked along the river, moving against its stream. This was one of many small islands that stood between the kingdom's two sides. Across from me, beyond the river, stood the city, busy, full, lively. Behind me stretched boundless deserts, quiet, solitary, ghostly. And I was in neither of them but at a point in the middle.

My forehead dripped with sweat. The teachings Chaa had shared in our handful of meetings, finally giving meaning as they did to my existence, were still settling in my brain, and her voice kept banging around in my head, 'I am your mother's mother.'

I wasn't paying any attention to my path. I just walked, my feet almost dragging in the sand until I stepped into muddy ground. A wall of reeds stood in front of me. I pushed through, mingling my feet with the reeds in the mud, some grabbing my clothes, others scratching my skin.

A crackling sound followed me. Something else was coming through, bending or breaking the plants on its way. I hurried onwards. Before I stepped out on the sandy bank, my foot got caught in the mud or a branch, and I fell, knee first, beyond the wall of reeds and onto a stone.

With a groan, I swung my arm at the sand, and caught my breath, listening for whatever might have been following me. Nothing out of the ordinary. Only the water burbling on its way to the sea.

My knee bled muddy. I crouched next to the river, observing my wound. It was all that now occupied my mind as I washed it clean. The smell of blood grounded me, solid into physicality.

The sweat now weighed on my eyelids. Across the river stretched the city, busy, full, lively. Men took their nets out of the water. A small child gripped the clothes of a woman whose hands were full with a clay pot. A priest came down the steps of the temple, another going up, both carrying out their duty in some way.

The gates of the temple opened. From within emerged a man with dark robes and a leopard skin around his shoulders. He stopped at the top of the stairs, inspecting the others below, showing himself arrogantly. His bald, thin, and long face looked distorted by a small grim smile. His image alone was unpleasant to hold.

Before I dismissed him, I realised it was him again. I jumped up. The river was in between us. I looked around for the fastest way to him. *Should I just swim? The river is strong. He could see me.* I turned around.

"Is it me you are looking for, child?" He stood there in front of me.

I gasped, falling back a few steps. The pale semblance I thought I saw was now a man of dark complexion.

"Valsaris, it's you!" The queen's brother. "No, I was trying to..."

"What did you tell them?" he asked.

What? "What are you talking about? I need to go."

He grabbed me below the elbow as I walked by him. "No, Aletheos."

I turned to him, searching in his eyes. He stood unmoved. And my arm was now in pain. I remembered my brother, hesitant behind his mask. *No!* I pushed away his hand.

"You are with him?" I pointed at the grim man at the temple. He was not there anymore. "It was you! You are with them! That day in the palace! You were the masked man grabbing my brother's arm, pushing him!"

He said nothing.

"Who is he?" I asked.

"Stop asking about us, child. Stop meddling in affairs you don't remotely understand!"

I am not a child. "Is that why you left after the beast's attack? Was it you that brought it into the palace?"

"I didn't leave!"

"Father exiled you," I realised.

I pointed back at where that man stood a few moments ago. "I saw him in the city. Were you with him? He wanted me to follow him! Why?"

"We wanted you to know the truth, child. But your grandmother interfered."

My eyes now focused on his. *My grandmother?*

He smiled. "We know everything about you. But she doesn't want you to know."

"How did you... What truth?"

"I am not the foe here, child. It is your father that has gone mad! Interfering with the high traditions because of what that stranger of a witch tells him; dismissing the gods into fury!"

"That beast? That's your god?"

"You are as ignorant as your father!"

"My father is a good man!"

"And you think that's enough to rule the kingdom? He wants to bring to ruins all that our ancestors worked for! All that we have learned! He wants to take the sacred sciences from us, let the people use them!" He burst out a short laughter. "As if they could! Beware, child, for he would have us stripped of all the gifts from the gods and feed them to the pigs."

"Is that why you convinced my brother to kill him?"

"Your brother knew of our true power. He could help protect it. But you murdered him! And now you think you saved your father. But who will save us? And the people?"

His nostrils flared up below his swollen eyes. I backed up as he approached.

"Let me show you, child."

His arm was already flashing with sparks. He raised his hand towards my forehead. But he stopped midway. A blade on his throat held him still.

"Enough! No closer!" a man said, emerging from behind Valsaris. It was the young guard from the palace, placing himself in between me and the priest, always keeping the blade at his throat. "You will not have him! Get away."

I tried to push through, but the guard was firmly grounded, one hand holding me back, the other holding his blade high. I wanted to hear more. Valsaris grinned.

"Watch out, child. He shall be our downfall!" Valsaris said and vanished into myriads of locusts, flying like a wave around the blade.

I raised my hands, willing them away. For a moment, they remained still, hitting on an invisible wall my intention had created. But as the guard threw himself onto me, stretching his body to protect me, what might have held them back collapsed, and all came flying down on us. The insects covered us, mostly the guard on top of me. He stood up, pushing them off me, and jumped around to get them away from his back. I shook one from my hand and slapped another from my shoulder. Most flew away. On the ground, some were already dismembered, prey to beetles.

The guard gave me his hand, but I pushed myself up.

"What are you doing here?" I asked him.

He gave a clumsy bow. "My duty, my prince!"

"Did my father send you?"

"He did!"

I pushed the door to the king's private apartments. My father was discussing with some officials, his calm face filling with concern as he glanced at me. He sent everyone away.

The young guard passed me a black cloth we had torn from his uniform. I unfolded it to show my father the locust we managed to capture. In its place, ashes had already greyed the fabric.

Disgusted, I threw it on the ground.

We were now only the three of us in my mother's sacred room. It was the first time I saw another man in this room. Maybe the urgency had done away with the courtesies. The sun was almost setting, making everything turn orange-red.

"Somebody just talk! Tell me!" I exclaimed. "Why aren't you saying something?"

The king and the priestess were on opposite sides of the room, looking away from me and from each other.

"Father! Did you order the guard to follow me?"

"I did," he answered.

"It's for your own good, Aletheos," Chaa added.

"Why? What kind of danger am I in?"

"You have already witnessed their power!" she said.

"It was Valsaris. He wanted to talk!"

"You do not know that," she said.

"But I do. That's what he did!"

"What did he say?" my father asked.

"He said..." I held back. "Your guard interrupted us."

My father walked to me. "He is a dangerous man, Aletheos."

"He said the same of you!"

The grandmother walked closer as well. "What did he say?"

"He said... that you are changing things, the sacred ways."

"Ha!" my father exclaimed. "The sacred ways! Son, we are the sacred ways! They only carry out imitations of parts of them!"

"Who is they? You..." I turned to Chaa, "you said you would tell me!"

"I said I would teach you. And that is what I have been doing."

"Teach me what?"

"The sacred ways. The true ways, the one way."

"If it is us, you, that know the sacred ways, why don't you show them? Why are they against us?"

"My son, this city, the entire kingdom of Erevos, is overseen by the priests, the self-proclaimed hands of the gods on earth. Many of the kingdom's resources go to them. But most importantly, the people go to them. Having control over all that effort, do you think they would like to change anything?"

"If they are in the wrong, why do we keep acting out the ceremonies of old?"

"It's not the ceremonies at fault here, but the people performing them. The ceremonies, the mysteries, and initiations of this tradition, as of many others, were designed correctly and in harmony with the truth. It is the personal merit of the people carrying them out that has rotten through the ages. Sadly, it is the orders that identified the need for secrecy and hold the initiations that fell prey to the same inadequacy themselves! Now, only a handful of initiates remain in their ranks, diminishing against those led completely astray. And here we are, trying to bring the order to its former standing, finding against us those who swore to protect the truth."

"Why?" I asked.

"Because they do not wish to see the truth, child," Chaa said. "They wish to cling to the compartments of the truth they already claim to possess. Their way offers them power and money and the effort of the people."

"They prefer power over finding the truth?" I asked.

They both exhaled in disappointment. None spoke for a while. I was in contemplation. Calmly, honestly, acceptingly, I finally talked. "How do you know the way?"

"We, child, work in the ranks of the Brotherhood of Fire. Our order originates back to those who embodied the truth on earth, the same truth that transcends traditions and cultures, respects them all but oversees them both."

"Was my mother part of your order?"

"She was," Father said.

"Do you know what happened to her?"

My father took a pause. His eyes fell on the ground before taking a deep inhalation. He opened his mouth.

Chaa sounded from the other side of the room. "I told you before, sweet prince. We don't know."

I turned back to my father. His mouth was now sealed.

"Will I be a member of the order?"

"What do you think your training is for?" she answered.

I turned to my father yet again.

"Yes, my son," he said proudly.

"The queen?" I asked. "Is she with them, with her brother?"

"Muttiya is a woman of honour," Father proclaimed.

"Okay," I said. "I shall accept the guard as I did with nan. But only him, none other."

"That is fine, my son. Thank you."

Before leaving, I turned to them one last time. "Will you teach me to protect myself?"

They both nodded.

The young guard awaited outside the room. He expected my welcoming. I looked at him for only a moment; that was approval enough. He escorted me to my room, already prepared by the nan.

BENEATH THE SKY

I had missed some of our rendezvous with Idhatora. I had been staying late with Chaa, absorbing everything she would tell me, preparing myself. But tonight, my heart beat with a smile, waiting for Idhi.

The young guard was in the garden with me, standing by the arched gateway to the palace. I wondered how he must have been experiencing his daily life, following me around and having to be by me throughout the day. He seemed tired. He looked down, leaning on the wall, and his nose and cheeks were red under whatever light reached us from inside.

"Is she a romantic relationship?" he asked.

By the time he looked up to me, he must have realised how inappropriate his enquiry was and regained a straight posture.

"Idhatora? She..." I decided to answer. "... we are close friends."

It was probably a fair assumption on his behalf. I was now well into my teenhood. Others were already married at my age.

"I didn't mean to speak out of place," he apologised.

I exhaled in the warmth of the night.

"What is your name?" I asked.

"Innok."

"It is okay, Innok," I said, led by the circumstances. "We can talk."

He didn't say anything, just nodded, squeezing his lips together.

I looked at the door again and the hall that stretched beyond it. *She must be otherwise engaged.* I sighed.

"I am going for a short walk," I told Innok, "and then we go back inside. It is okay for you to stay here."

He agreed to wait, probably because of his previous indiscretion. I walked away from him and in between the trees. No light from the palace halls could reach me now, only moonlight. I left my thoughts to say what they may until they faded into quietness. And I walked further into the garden, further into thought dissolution.

In between the trees, stood a woman. I squinted my eyes. It wasn't Idhatora. Her pearl gown shone yellow and orange-white light from within. Although different, she did remind me of Idhi; and, albeit young, she was beyond the age of my friend. Her hands were gathered to her chest, with eyes fixated on the ground.

"I am glad you made it," she said, raising her gaze.

I gasped as a man approached from behind me.

"Did you make it?" he asked.

She shook her head. They did not acknowledge my presence.

My eyes stayed on the man. He was... familiar. A man some sun cycles older than me, strong, wearing a bright blue-white robe with radiating violet symbols. They walked towards each other; slowly, gently, tenderly, sad. They raised their hands but never touched, as if they could not. The space between their palms sparkled with light; I was certain. They looked into each other's eyes and said with one voice, "Until we meet again." They backed up. The growing distance between them ripped my heart with every step they took. I choked at the pain in my chest.

The man dissolved into a rising windstorm and the woman into a pillar of sand that was scattered in his wind. I tried to catch it, frantically moving my hands to withhold whatever grains passed through my fingers.

Two hands grabbed mine. Everything around me changed. Idhatora stood in front of me amidst the trees.

"It is okay," she said. "You are okay. You made it."

"What..." I managed to speak.

"You are back. You are okay."

I looked around. The young guard had run to me as well. "Are you okay?" he asked, looking around with his sword at hand. "You screamed! What happened?"

T he guard, Innok, would not leave me now but kept some distance.

"Are you feeling better?" She sounded relaxed.

"What happened?" I asked.

"I came to find you. Your friend told me you were up ahead, and before I reached you, I heard your voice."

"He is not my friend. My father assigned my safety to him."

"What happened back there? One of your visions?"

"I don't know. I just... saw something."

"Have you talked to her about it?"

"Chaa?"

"Or your father. Maybe they can help you."

"Maybe," I said.

W e sat next to the quiet water of the pond. Me with crossed legs, she with her legs down, back straight, and hands on her thighs.

"What do they teach you about?" she inquired with a cheerful voice.

"She talks to me about nature and the different worlds... and spirit." I smiled.

"What about it?" She leaned towards me.

I sat straight and took a breath. "We all live within the light of a hyperconsciousness. From that light, all worlds spring forth into existence. And there are many worlds, all connected by that light. While we are used to experiencing life through our physical form, this world of ours," I pointed at our surroundings, "this physical world, is only one of many that extend beyond of what we can see with our eyes and feel with our hands."

"What kind of worlds? Could anyone visit them?"

"It is not only a matter of visiting them but rather of perceiving them. You see, Chaa says, many of these worlds are intermingled. How many we can see and touch and feel depends on the development of our faculties."

"What is it that you perceive?"

I searched my brain for the words to describe my experiences with Chaa. "You may see them as colours interacting with this world. Or you can feel them on your skin as you pass by them. You can hear or smell them as well. All the senses we use in our world have their counterparts to perceive the higher ones. And you can also transfer your consciousness to them alone. As you said, in a way, visit them and experience life not only through our physical body but the bodies that correspond to each of those worlds."

I wanted to include her as much as I could in this life I was now emerging into. Maybe we could proceed together.

"Now, come on." I jumped up. "Let me show you this."

I took her palms and turned them upwards. I touched their centre with my middle fingers and placed my hands above hers at a small distance. I closed my eyes and followed my breath into my chest. With my exhalation, I led light out through my hands and onto hers. She could not see it.

"Can you feel this?" I asked.

"Umm... I am not sure. What am I supposed to be feeling?"

"Anything, a tingle, warmth or a breeze, any sensation localised at the centre of your palms."

"A kind of tingle maybe... oh." Her eyes sparkled, and, never losing her charming mannerisms, she sat on the edge of the bench. "I feel pinching."

I exhaled, relieved.

"Now stand up," I said. "Relax and follow your breath into your heart. Don't worry about it. Just set your intention in energy coming from your chest out through your palms."

"My hands are getting warmer." She brought them towards her face, inspecting what was happening.

"Turn them towards mine," I said.

She was fast to follow my instruction. I took my hands to hers, kept them close until I established a connection, an almost tangible, magnetising sensation between us. She examined her hands; she must have felt it as well.

In an instance, her eyes locked into mine and all faded away; all around was silenced, all disappeared from sight, and we could truly see each other. A sudden heartbeat seemed to awaken my heart from a slumber I never knew was there. It was only the two of us, our eyes alone. Time was yet not. I closed my eyes for only a moment.

Time resumed. I pushed the warm sensation in my chest away from my mind, hid it, for now. I moved my hands back a little and waited for her to notice the difference. She nodded she did. I moved further away, then close again, and then afar. Our connection was bold and dense. We stood many steps apart. Chaa had helped me practise seeing the colours of the forces, pink and yellow at this instance. But I didn't mention them, not to dishearten Idhi, who couldn't see them.

I walked to her and touched her palms, looking into her eyes. "Now touch your chest and will your energy back to you."

She said nothing. Her smile was everything.

"It is force. It exists everywhere and in everything. And we can direct it," I said, breaking the silence.

"What else can you do?"

That wasn't enough?

"With your hands, I mean, with the energy," she laughed.

"Oh." I rubbed the back of my head. "I can direct it and attach an intention to it."

"Meaning?"

"You can attach a feeling or a thought to the energy before letting it out. And circumstances allowing, it can take effect," I answered, expanding my chest.

She tilted her head, waiting for more. I raised my hands, gathered force, and created an orb of energy. I found within me a sense of calmness and poured it into the sphere. She couldn't see it. I made it pink.

"Watch Innok," I said.

He stood on alert, turning from one side to the other.

I sent the sphere close to the guard and waited a few moments. Around him, the layers of his own force, fiery reds and browns, connected to the orb's pinks. His neck relaxed. He placed his sword back into its sheath. His movements became slower as Idhi observed him carefully.

"That's amazing!" she said.

At the sound of her voice, the guard regained his aggressive stance. His reds reawakened around him, swallowing the pinks. He drew his sword, always on the lookout. I sighed. Idhatora came closer and gave me a kiss on the cheek.

"You... are extraordinary," she said.

The sense of her lips on my cheek followed me back to my room and all the way into the comfort of sleep.

At the Feet of the Mount

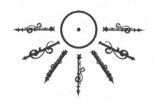

C haa sat on the floor across from me. In between us floated the violet lotus flowers on the narrow strip of water, extending outside my mother's room and into the night.

"Find me in the land of men's fire," she said and closed her eyes.

I was becoming accustomed to the process, needing less guidance each time. I nodded and closed my eyes, slowly bringing my awareness to the sacred chamber of the heart and the threefold flame. From it, I moved up my spine until I reached the crown of my head and upwards into the golden column of light that stretched above my head and through all worlds.

"Higher," she said in the flesh.

Each world had many levels; the higher I went, the purer they became.

"Higher," she repeated.

I kept going up.

"Hello, sweet prince," she said when I found her at the level intended. "Now, this is the highest part of the land of the mind, of men's fire. Below us lay the fields of experience. Above us is the land of the true Fire, the cosmic spiritual realms. Here we stand in the middle. From this point, we can oversee the subjective nature without it subjecting us to the waves of emotion and currents of thought that howl in the lower mind."

Above us, winds of white fire roared for as far as I could see.

"Take my hand," Chaa said.

She led me into the land of Fire, with another layer of me left behind. My consciousness was freer by one heavy clothe.

"Coming here, you can see things from above. You can understand the inner meaning of affairs and allow your consciousness to receive the ideal of the cosmic fire and take it down to the body. But for it to manifest, it must go through all the levels underneath us, take shape into the mind of he who perceives it, and get infused with the necessary desire to exist.

This is true for all human affairs and is the process that leads to the realisation of all. But not many have developed their capacities to perceive ideals from the realms of light and, unavoidably unaware, they shape into their minds their unconscious darkness and feed it with fear into reality.

We who walk this path take upon us a sacred duty, the responsibility to carry out the light, until all our brothers have the capacity to embody it themselves. Therefore, we must always keep an eye on the state of our emotions and thoughts, for the ideal to go through them as unaltered as possible. Now, allow this white light to enter your consciousness and when you are ready, meet me in the flesh."

I took a few moments with the Fire. As it burned deep inside me, it illuminated certain dark spots, releasing me from their burden. When I was as light as the wind, I slipped down through the golden column into the mother's room and back into my body, slowly opening my eyes to the flickering flames of torches.

I remained looking at the night while Chaa worked her way through the room, now a place of sacred items or maybe of ordinary items used in a sacred way.

"Chaa, how do I translate the light into something I understand?"

"Practice, my dear. The more you use your mind, the more it will train your brain. But know that on those pure levels, you can meet our brethren that have walked a few more steps on their pilgrimage and have chosen to face back and assist their brothers and sisters. They act as intermediates between us and the higher levels, and they can help you understand until you can contact and perceive that aspect of you that dwells in the realms of Fire."

"Thank you," I exhaled with a warm chest.

She came closer and touched my cheek.

"You have earned this, dear brother. It is your efforts and their merit that have allowed you to relearn."

She turned away and continued with her tasks.

"Bear in mind," she said with her back to me, "whatever reality is embodied by men is coloured by their individuality. And remember the process, for there are dangers involved. Men can and have been slain by the forms they create. Feeding the ideal too much mental material without the analogous material of desire, or vice versa, will render it unable to pass into this physical reality. And remaining there, it will poison the mind and lead its creator into a labyrinth of obsession.

Unable to connect to the light of the higher worlds or the love of those around him, that darkness of isolation shall brew in him feelings that will inevitably lead to self-destruction."

I allowed her words to settle deep in me, determined I would only stand for truth; the true ideal. The flickering flames were almost gone. It was time to rest.

Birds of the Morning

"**D**id you choose this life?" I asked Innok.

The cool morning out in the gardens was refreshing for us both.

"What do you mean?" he replied.

"This; being a soldier, a guard in the palace. Spending your days with me."

"Yes, I did. It's good to know I can serve."

"Serve whom? The king?"

"No, not the king. The kingdom!" he replied. "I serve your father's commands to do what is best for the people."

I did not expect him to express such noble intentions, not by a man of his young age.

"Do you have a spouse you returned to before being assigned to me?"

"No. Maybe someday."

"Family?"

"All gone."

"I am sorry," I said.

"Illness," he continued.

"Did the priests not help them?"

"They tried. But in the end, it didn't matter."

I did not respond.

"You see," he said, "the help of the gods seems to be reserved for people of higher ranks. Those whose lives are inconsequential usually face the demons alone." He took a pause before changing his sentiment into a more innocently vibrant one. "Being a soldier though means to protect all people, keep order. Your father is a good man. He wants peace for the people. Under his rule, the kingdom has been thriving. And the people love him; all people, not just the rich, especially not the rich. Before him, the servants were lifetime slaves. Now they work for wage, and when they want to retire, the masters must provide property in exchange for their servitude."

I never knew that this was not always the way.

"You should never believe Valsaris's accusations nor any others of men lesser than your father."

"Your father? Was he a good man?" I asked.

"No. He was not."

His lips remained closed. His eyes kept falling. Around us, the birds chirped. I hopped up with a smile.

"Is there someone you like?" I asked, lifting his eyes.

"Not really." He turned his face at me as I walked around him.

"No one of your fellow guards? Or a girl?"

He laughed. "Is there someone you like?"

"Have you ever liked someone?" I asked back.

"Yes, of course," he said.

I hoped he'd speak of his experience. Instead, he asked about me. "That friend of yours?"

I stopped moving and faced the blue sky.

"She is exquisite," he said. "What changed? Last time you said she was just a friend."

"I don't know. But every time I meet her... I get warm with a smile; my mind loses its grip on myself, and I just want to get closer. Thinking of her makes my heart spark open. She raises my spirit."

"That's not your spirit rising. That's falling in love," he said.

"Have you ever been?"

"I have... Sometimes it goes away; sometimes it's worth more than letting it so."

"What do you think?" I asked.

"You can wait awhile, see if it passes or even if you want it to pass. You don't always have to act on it. Just be with it, enjoy your... raised spirit."

His casual response grounded my emotions, and I settled down in what my feelings urged me to act upon. I nodded.

"Is it time for your lesson? Should we head inside?" he asked.

It was.

BENEATH THE SKY

I dhi and I sat next to the pond. We played with energy, sending it back and forth to each other. Innok was always around but kept his distance.

"Is it green now?" she asked.

She was beginning to see the colours as well. First, according to my descriptions. Then, I changed the colour, waiting for her to notice.

"Pink?" she asked, focusing on the space between our hands.

I nodded and, with an exhalation, I touched her open palms. White sparks flew around as our skin came together.

"Do you think the beast is gone?" she asked out of nowhere, amidst the sanctity of our practice. "It's been a while now," she continued, hopeful against reality, as if my days had not been coloured by his threat.

The force around my hands turned to brown, as my stomach clenched and smile vanished. I said nothing of it and touched my chest as usual; an end to our practice. She did the same and remained in silence.

I shook my hands to cool them down while she sank hers in the pond. Seeing she didn't insist on the matter, I dipped mine as well, letting them flow around in the water, maybe even touch hers.

She, very calm, took my hand below the water before she stood up and hugged me; a ceremonial embrace that followed each session. The cold drops from her hands ran down my spine, making me jump. The sound of her laugh at my reaction pulled me out a swelling feeling of sinking, and, with a lighter chest, we made our way inside.

Innok waited to escort us back. I glanced at him as we passed by, and he must have understood; he didn't follow.

I walked her to her chambers, letting my hand brush against hers. When we reached her door, she turned to me. My heart pounded as I wasted precious moments in stillness. She placed her hand on my chest and leaned to kiss my cheek. I kissed hers, but did not withdraw. Neither did she. I let my lips slip on her soft cheek until they found hers in a moment that was everything. My hand went through her dark hair and grazed her neck. We remained close. Her eyes sparkled; her breath still on the tip of my lip. I gave her a smile, finally falling into the reality of our connection. She gently touched my cheek before we parted.

I turned away only after she closed her door. Innok waited at the next corner with a smile and a gentle pat on the back. We didn't say anything as I almost hopped through the halls, my chest full of liveliness. In my room, nan sat at the foot of the bed. I gave her a big kiss on the cheek, turning her usual frown into a big smile, so alien to her face.

I then dropped on the bed with a warm heart and sweet Idhi in my mind.

AT THE FEET OF THE MOUNT

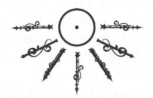

T he midday ceremony of the sun had long ended, and Chaa had already shared the words of wisdom she intended to. She sat amidst the dissipating mist on the floor next to me, facing the sunset outside.

"Chaa," I said, "why do people die?"

She turned to me, calm. "What's on your mind, my dear?"

I hesitated. "A friend of mine, his family died."

She waited for more.

"He told me the priests performed some healing rituals, but after a while they died anyway."

"What is your question?"

"Why did it not work?"

"My dear grandson... First of all, remember the process of manifesting an ideal. You must know that our physical incarnation is the realisation of our consciousness through the same process. Part of our spirit, extending downwards, passes through the worlds below it, attracting to itself matter from all planes to shape all its bodies until it can exist in this dense world of ours. The matter's condition will be such as recorded in the Records during his previous ascend when the bodies died and disintegrated, for it to reconnect with the Fire."

I nodded.

"The health of the body while on earth depends fundamentally on the conditions of those elements within men, and the changes we produce upon them during our lifetime. But all men must die, for there is a significance in the cycles of descent on earth and ascent to spirit. With each incarnation, we rebuilt our bodies, refined to the degree reached in our previous embodiment. And thereby, our consciousness has the opportunity to express itself through more developed vessels."

"What is healing, then?"

"The rituals you spoke of, if performed by priests who only hold the technical aspects of the sacred sciences but lack proper understanding of the inner functions of the cosmos and man, will necessarily fail to bring true healing. For true healing to occur, it must shine through all levels, not the physical alone. But the truth, the higher science, cannot unfold to those whose personal efforts don't reflect that which is good and merciful and wise. They heal the body but not the essence. That is why the ailments they treat will come back to those afflicted. Afflictions are of an inner nature, not bodily. The body only responds thereafter to bring man's awareness to his wrongdoings, his behaviour, his dense emotions, and troubled thoughts, even if from another lifetime."

"Is this the inadequacy you and Father spoke of concerning the priests of the old tradition?

"Not all of them, for there are still some initiated to the highest of degrees. But for many of them, yes. The merits of their personal efforts will be the downfall of what they pretend to hold sacred. Unfortunately, what they destroy is what, for the laymen, resembles the truth. Truth can never be destroyed but will remain hidden for as long as men trample their divine nature."

My eyelids were heavy. I had remained seated under the flickering torches of this sacred room while the grandmother attended the flowers in the pond. I thought of transferring my consciousness to one of the higher worlds, contact the light one more time before ending our meeting.

I sat straight and let the stars dim out as I closed my eyes. Different thoughts burst in my mind, leading me astray. I insisted. I followed the proper route and ascended through the crown of my head and into the column of light above it. The thought of Innok losing his family flashed in my mind, stuffing my chest.

"Uh..." I shook my head, reorienting my awareness back in the column and brought my consciousness flying through it. My mind slipped again, this time into the desire for Idhatora. In an act of will, I brought myself back and went on until I was at the mental level, that of men's fire. Above me, flowed marvellous the white flames, their purity shining over me.

Some alteration in the light invited my glance back down in front of me. My brother stood there, looking at me.

"Hello, little brother," he said with cheer.

A flash of heat contracted my chest.

"Brother!" I said in a broken voice. "You... You are here!"

"An aspect of me, yes." He smiled from a glowing face.

My heartbeat from all the way down in my body weighed on my consciousness. The plane I was in began to dissolve around me, and I sank in dense substance. The now muddy ground covered me whole until I dropped below it, floating in colours of dark blues and browns and reds. There was no ground, yet I stood as if on an invisible plane.

Someone crouched in the distance. It was Favar again. Only this time, he was hammered in torture. He was alone, gasping. He kept hitting himself in the stomach.

"Brother!" I cried to him.

He faced up to me. He tilted his head and got up. His was disfigured with big lumps throughout his body; some bigger than his head with skin as if scorched away. Black liquid floated around him, pouring out of his temple where Father's crown had injured him. He screamed and ran to me. His eyes were shut under bloody masses. With the scream of a wounded beast, he raised his arms just before he reached me. I managed a few steps back before he forced them down, slamming his own guts. His face was only fingers away from mine, groaning, with thick liquids splattering out his mouth.

I stood still, breathing fast. He kept facing me, unmoved. He wasn't going to hurt me. His pain was self-inflicted. With a shaking hand, I gently touched his bleeding shoulder. My touch shocked him, forcing his eyes to open and lock on mine, observing me as if trying to realise who I was. Beyond the gross material around his eyes, I could still see a faint glimpse of him.

"Brother," I said in a wavering voice.

He squinted. Tears kept running on his deformed face.

"Help me," he moaned.

I took a breath and gathered myself. And I hugged him with all the love I could find within me. He shivered. His struggle was slowly dissipating in my embrace. He breathed wearied.

"Brother," I repeated as if to remind him of himself. "It's me. I am here."

"What is happening?" he asked in a broken voice.

Orbs of light, three, maybe four, floated around him. From them, light burst all around us. The aspect of my brother I had met in the higher plane, the calm, smiling one, appeared as well.

"Thank you," he said.

"What is happening?" I asked.

"My dear brother... I have been trying to reach this part of me for a long time. How long has it been, really?"

"I... about a sun cycle," I said confused.

He shook his head. "Aspects of my consciousness remain trapped in this muddy land."

"Why?" I asked in tears, already assuming the answer but unwilling to accept it.

"For the same reason you burden yourself for protecting our father. I was lost, Aletheos. I got lost. And a part of me could never forgive myself for what I did, for letting myself go down those dark pathways. And I have been punishing myself for the same reason."

I looked at his wretched part, breathing like an animal ordered to stay in its place. "Now what?" I asked.

"Through the clouds of self-torturing, your love sparked a glimpse of light in this creature I have become. Now, I can move on. The messengers from the Guardians and Rulers have been trying to reach me."

He pointed at the orbs of light around him and continued. "But self-infliction is strong. It becomes impenetrable until the one who built the walls learns to bring them down. With that spark you ignited, the messengers will help me free myself. Once I do, they will help me heal. At least as much as possible. Afterwards, well, I don't really know."

He smiled in contentment.

"And you?" I asked.

"All my aspects need healing. Now I can attempt to recollect myself. The messengers explained that I will be guarded against any communication and focus on getting better."

"Can you forgive me?" I hurried to ask.

"Brother, I have already forgiven you. Please forgive me too. And please, please forgive yourself. Allow your guilt to be absolved. And know they will come for you again and for all we hold dear. Guard yourself within the light. Become the light. I never could."

He came closer and embraced me tight, speaking in a low voice close to my ear.

"Thank you for releasing me, dear brother. I am forever grateful. May we meet again."

He stepped back towards his counterpart. The orbs of light moved around them, hiding them in clouds of reds, browns, and yellows. All was now quiet, and the colours around me were as ugly as before.

A child's voice broke the silence. I looked down to my left. A child, running.

"I told you to stand guard of your thoughts and emotions." Chaa appeared behind me. "Lest they lead you astray."

Her calm presence made my shoulders drop and breath safe.

"Now, since you are here, focus," she said. "Gather your mind. Become aware in distinguishing what is real and what is projected by you." She pointed at the running child. "Let's go. Let's see what images your emotional body creates."

By intention alone, we floated down, closer to the child wearing royal attire. His course was created before his feet as he ran into a wide arena of black and white squares.

The kid ran and hopped around, sometimes landing on the white tiles, others falling on the black. An enormous crocodile, tens of times bigger than the boy, flew below and around the arena. At the end of it, three squares were raised, and three black, man-like creatures appeared on top of them. The child stood before them, and the creatures melted, dripping down from their black tiles. The crocodile now headed for the boy. I raised my arm, and before he was eaten whole, the crocodile vanished in his movement.

The stage disappeared as well. The boy was now confronted with the appearance of a pyramid, guarded by two monsters as tall as the pyramid itself. They had the bodies of men but the heads of animals. One was a brown bull holding a big hammer, the other a black and white bird holding an axe. Their weapons crossed in front of the pyramid until they raised them high and let them fall on the child. I gasped, trying to reach him, but Chaa held me still. Himself calm, raised his arms high, and the monsters withdrew their attacks and stepped aside. Unencumbered, he passed through the gate. Upon his entrance, the pyramid lit up, blinding me.

When I opened my eyes, I was already back in my body. Chaa stood above me. She leaned and kissed my forehead.

"You are tired, young prince." She smiled through her kind eyes. "Go to sleep. Your big day is coming up."

BLADES

Darkness surrounded me. Confined as I was in this burial container, itself within another within another, I laid on my back, unable to move. The chants of my father and priests had long disappeared.

At first, my fingertips intermingled with the coarse fibres of the wood below them. I did not know what to expect. Unaware, I tried to just be. After a short while, my back began to hurt. My shoulders and neck needed to stretch and my legs to move. I was enclosed, unmovable. With my breath, I tried to calm all sensations, all the discomfort of the body, and with them, all of its needs and desires.

I stayed with the cold sensation at the tip of my nose that soon became warm. The smell of sandalwood and frankincense oil used to draw symbols on my naked body, combined with the dampness of decay in the container, forced a point of pressure between my eyebrows.

The pressure grew stronger. I wanted to burst open the containers towards the fresh sunlight. I couldn't. Unable to take my awareness away from the tension, I included my breathing with it. The pressure eased for an instant before it spread throughout my head and body until the same sensation encapsulated my whole being.

The container disappeared from around me. The darkness expanded and dissolved everything in its way. Darkness was now space, stretching in all directions with no end. And I floated, drifting into nothingness. My mind had begun to dissolve, becoming one with the all. The all had become nothingness. I vanished in a limitless void, a dreamless sleep.

Aeons could have passed. Time was not. With a heartbeat, a voice set the particles of space into trembling motion, causing light to be born out of this dark sea of nothingness. My eye opened, the centre of my forehead erupted in a ray of light that met the trembling space and united with it. An abstract sense of self was born again. The Word was about to be uttered.

Sharp pains within my whole body invaded the process of genesis, like blades burning their way out of my veins. The Word began to form the Sound as the pain became excruciating, and my breathing was hindered, my lungs unable to expand and draw in life. I was about to hear the Word! But a blinding light pulled me away from the centre, out of which the Word would emerge. I opened my physical eyes as the third and final seal of my confinement was pulled open. Through my blurry vision, Father threw the seal to the side. Only with his touch were my lungs shocked into an inhalation.

"Son!" he kept saying, patting my face to draw my eyes to him.

Father pulled me out of the coffin. I could barely assist him. With body still numb, all I could do was just breathe in his embrace. Something slipped off me, scraping my skin on its way. Below me, the container was no longer empty. Big black feathers overflowed it, shimmering with blood. And whatever parts of me I could see were covered in dripping cuts.

"Father?" I managed to exhale.

"You are fine, you are fine now," he kept saying, moving his hands around me to manage the bleeding.

Exhausted and injured, I leaned on my father's back as we rode away from the sacred white pyramid. My white robe was stained brown through the wrapped wounds and oily ointments. My initiation was incomplete. I had not received the Word. The Word remained unheard.

REFUGE

T wo days had passed since my return from the pyramid, wounded in more ways than one. All I wanted to do was be in Idhatora's presence. But, upon waking, nan told me to go outside and wait for my father at the gates. I had not seen him since our return, and Chaa had left the palace shortly after.

I went to the gates in the company of my guard, Innok.

"Is everything okay?" he asked, seeing me lost in my thoughts. "Did something happen with your friend?"

"No," I said, unable to pretend a smile. "It's something else."

My father joined us, alone.

"Hello, my son." He greeted Innok as well. "Come." A servant brought a horse for me. Father turned to Innok again. "Go to the room of the mother."

Innok bowed and waited until we marched beyond the gates to leave his post. And we reined our horses up on our hill and sat on the edge, overlooking the city. Above us, clouds hid the sky, although unlikely to bring rain so soon after the last time.

In the silence, I hesitated to enquire about the initiation. But it was not the only thing on my mind.

"Father," I said after a while. "You knew about Favar."

"I did."

"Why did you let me... do what I did?"

"No, no! My dear son, I did not know it would end up the way it did. I would never willingly let you... I knew your brother was losing his way, and I knew the intentions of those who found a way to corrupt him. But, you see, to know what time shall bring, you must stand watch of the currents of force in all realms. And still, you can never truly know. It is like feeling the wind. You can sense its power and learn its direction. But you cannot always predict the places it will reach and the damage it will cause on its way."

"I saw him."

"I know." He smiled.

"You know?"

"He told me. After his death... His personal afflictions would not let him proceed through to the second trial."

"Did you meet him?"

"Yes. I helped him clear his mind. But I could not force his emotions to release their grip on his consciousness. And then he found you."

"Did he truly move on?"

"Yes. He is out of our reach now. This means he is undergoing healing in the infirmaries of the higher planes. You did him a great service, my son."

His reassurance of my brother's fate released my mind from many hammering thoughts. I could now keep Favar with me, as that light aspect of him I encountered in the higher levels. I kept quiet.

"Aletheos..." He sighed. "What happened in the pyramid..."

I turned to him.

"My son, we cannot protect you here. The mysteries and rituals of this land are now overseen by them, whose power depends on the truth remaining hidden."

"Can I not proceed on my path? Can I not help our people?"

"The rituals have been a way to pass through the initiations, to find the light within against all this darkness. But they are not the only way. The one way, the true way, the way whose merit mostly counts, will accord you with more aspects of the truth and even more powers than the rituals ever could. But we can no longer guide you here, if your safety is to remain intact."

I waited to hear his next words.

"My son..." His eyes were now sparkling with tears. "You have a choice to make."

I jumped off the horse before it even stopped. It was too late to find Idhi in the gardens; night had followed me back to the palace. I rushed through the halls and knocked on her door. Idhatora opened. She smiled upon seeing me. I stood still until she met me in my state of mind. With eyes open wide, she did, and I took a step, and kissed her lips. She leaned into kissing me back. I pulled her into my embrace and closed the door behind us.

T he sun, still below the horizon, lightened the blue of the sky. The sheets were loose on our naked bodies. With her hand resting on my chest, I stared at the ceiling and the colours cast by the sun's awakening. I knew what this dawn was about to bring. I turned to her and kissed her lips. She smiled before half opening her eyes.

"I need to go," I whispered.

She nodded.

"I will come back to you. I promise."

I left the bed to dress up. She stopped me before the door, kissed me. We remained in each other's eyes before taking refuge in each other's arms.

"This is for you," she said. "You should keep this until your return."

She gave me the sandflower we had found on the hill. I forced a smile, looking at her with all my love.

A t the next corner of the halls, my hand was grabbed by one who took me a moment to recognise.

"We are late," Innok said.

"I am here."

He led the way through the palace. As we passed by my mother's room, my feet became heavy. I couldn't but stop. I opened the door and looked inside, touching with my mind all in the cool chamber that remained indifferent to my emotions. Innok allowed me a moment before gently touching my arm.

We went through an underground passing carved through rocky ground and reached a wider cave whose opening was covered by reeds from the outside. Two horses were tied on a pole. We mounted and turned to the exit.

"Son."

Father emerged from the shadows. I dismounted. He touched my cheeks and held my arms.

"You will be back. This is the right choice." His eyes were already wet.

"I believe you," I said.

He hugged me tight. "Now, go."

I got up on the horse and looked back one last time.

"Until we meet again," he said.

I bowed my head to him and rode beyond the reeds, out in the sun.

WANDERERS

"Are we lost?" I asked Innok.

The wind threw sand on my sweaty skin.

"No," Innok shouted.

He was on the ground looking at some notes, then at the distance, and back at his notes. The vastness of the desert almost drowned the shrieking of a bird of prey circling above us. He took out his bow and reached for arrows.

"What are you doing?" I protested.

"She said they might be following us."

"No. Wait." I jumped off my horse to stop him.

He kept the arrow pointed downwards while I followed my breath within, trying to ignore the discomfort in my body. I took my awareness through my heart, into my head, and projected my consciousness out of my forehead and onto the bird.

"The bird is not a spy," I said with a smile and opened my eyes. "It's a guide."

He abandoned his stance. I wasn't sure he believed me until he got on his horse and urged me to do the same. The bird now led the way through the desert.

My thighs pulsated, burning. But finally, something showed in the distance. He saw it as well. He turned back to me in joy and marched on. *We are close.*

When I got off my horse, my legs almost gave way. The bird had landed on a wooden hawk atop a roof. It let out a sharp shriek and flew away.

"Is this... what is this?" I asked.

Seeing it from afar, I assumed it was a village. But there were only four houses separated by a crossing in between them. And the bad shape of their walls of mud could accommodate no one. He didn't answer. He looked around. Four carriages were already tied to horses, one in front of each house.

"Welcome." A man considerably older than us emerged from the house below the wooden hawk, inviting us in.

Innok went first, keeping me close. Six or seven men sat inside; some drinking from their cups, others leaning quiet on the table.

"Here." He gave us a small pile of clothes.

Innok took off his black uniform and wore the beige clothes before turning to me. I looked at the men around, who never even glanced at us, and changed into the stiff clothes. Our host took my ornate garments from the floor and threw them into a furnace that flared up.

"We need to go now," said our host before offering us water and bread with nuts.

The others got up. All wore the same clothes as us. I quickly swallowed a bite of bread before we followed them, and saved the rest in Innok's bag.

The older man led us into one of the carriages. The others, without a word, moved on to the carriages across the street. These were bigger chariots than we had in the city. They had a shed standing on four narrow wooden pillars with fabrics hanging from them, which our host untied loose. He mounted the horse and signalled the others. All four teams rode at once, each in a different direction.

We were mostly quiet on our way. At least the pulse on my thighs had eased now, and we were protected from the intense sunlight.

"Did you say your goodbye to her?" Innok asked.

I faced away from him, out to the dunes of sand. "I did."

We kept a constant pace. The sun was close to the horizon behind us. The white, rocky mountains that stretched to my right now seemed purple. Innok, sitting across from me, was asleep. His boy face was stripped of worries, and his age was clearer to see in his innocence. The chariot bumped over a stone, forcing stiffness back onto his forehead as he pushed his eyes open.

The sky darkened with every blink of the eye. And finally, we stopped. The shadows between the trees almost hid the houses of stone below the cliff. The light of the torches through the windows, though, gave a sense of structure. We descended.

Our guide proceeded, and we followed some steps behind. Another received us into a house. It was almost empty; only some pots and furniture to make it habitable. The calm faces of its inhabitants, however welcoming, could not make the unknown feel safer.

"You would like to wash up?" A young maiden grounded me to the present. We weren't that far from the kingdom, but her appearance, brown skin with thick black hair, gave away her foreign origins, as that of the others staying here.

She led me to a room built around a rock that was carved into a tub. I undressed and left my clothes on the rock, then immersed myself in the water that was already extruding essences of sandalwood. All the scratches and pain I had gained through the day burned their way to awareness, but soon enough, the warmth and the oils enfolded my body. I let my shoulders drop into the water, and my head rest on the stone.

The same maiden came in, pulling me out of my transparent state. I gathered my legs to my chest. She never looked, only left new clothes on the stone and, in a low voice, said that I was expected.

"Thank you," I said as she exited.

I stood up with the water dripping away from my body. The girl, waiting in the next room, escorted me to the back, in a garden closed on all sides by other houses.

"Hello, my grandson."

Chaa sat in the middle of the garden. She poured some boiling water in a cup full of leaves while she sipped some from hers. Innok, together with our hosts, sat by her side. Their faces all flickered cheerful with the light of the torches.

"Food will be ready in a while," the maiden said and went inside.

Now that grandmother was with us, my stomach unclenched. I could eat.

"Come join us," she said.

I walked through the pots sprung with flowers and sat across from her. She passed me the cup of tea.

"We should talk," I said in a low voice.

"Not tonight, my dear. Rest, eat, enjoy. We shall talk in the morning."

It didn't take long before the garden echoed with laughter, and I... I rested, I ate, I enjoyed.

I woke up early to a quiet house. Out in the garden, Chaa alone drank her morning tea. The liveliness of the people from last night was now exchanged with the silent but vibrant colours of the flowers under the morning sun. I sat with her.

"When do we leave?" I asked.

"In a short while. Your friend is preparing our carriage."

I had hoped I was wrong in believing we would leave the garden. And indeed, a little while later, we stepped onto another carriage. This was a bigger one, made of dark brown wood, finely carved all over.

"Where are we heading?" I asked when the three of us were inside, and the horses marched on.

"But of course," she said, "to the feet of the mount."

SAND AND FLIES

I stretched my arms, looking around at the desert, devoid of any signs of human exploitation. Only the hills of rock stood like islands in the sea of sand. Our camp was prepared by Innok and another man who led our way. I went close to assist, but no one told me how. After I failed to grab their attention, I backed off and untied the horses to share some affection with them.

By the time the sun had set, our fire was already boiling tea water.

"What is your name, boy?" Chaa asked my guard.

"Innok."

"Do you remember your duty, Innok?"

The young guard frowned and stood up. "Of course!" he declared, pushing his hand on his blade around his waist.

"Sit down, Innok. I need you to remember that your sole responsibility is your prince. None of the rest of us. Do you understand?"

He looked at me and nodded hesitantly before re-joining us around the small fire.

"Chaa..." I tried to protest.

"Listen carefully, both of you." She turned to him. "If there ever comes a time you need to choose whom to keep safe, it must always be Aletheos."

He agreed. My objection was inconsequential.

"Tomorrow, we enter territories beyond the kingdom," Chaa continued.

"All neighbouring states are affiliated with my father," I said.

"They are. But you will not expose yourself as the prince of Erevos. None of us will make our origins known."

Our escort remained silent and unfaced.

"Why not?" I asked.

"Because the ones we are going away from have their eyes on us. We have taken several measures for our whereabouts to remain hidden. Our credentials will remain secret. Until they become irrelevant."

"Should I go to the city for supplies? Alone!" Innok suggested.

"That will not be needed. We have people on the path that will provide for us."

"Are they members of the order?" I asked.

Her eyes commanded me into silence. "Affiliates," she finally said.

Our escort gave us a smile and got up, back at work, now putting our goods together into a tidy pile; the easier to prepare in the morning. His dish was clean, unused.

P eople were already awake and well into their business when we rode through the settlement that was supposed to be a city. There were more tents than houses, and most people seemed dirtier than their surroundings. Dust flew everywhere, and insects preyed around them and the produce of merchants.

Through the walking crowd, two or three walked much taller, maybe two times the height of the others. I turned to Chaa. She looked beyond the fabrics that covered the carriage on all sides.

"Giants. Remnants of a race long gone in our era. Their simple nature is usually taken advantage of by vultures." She shook her head.

It wasn't long before we left the busy roads and the tents behind us. Again, we rode alone. With an empty glance, I was almost asleep on the monotonous journey, until the horses came to a sudden stop that sent me, head first, dropping from my seat. I grabbed around just in time before hitting Chaa, while Innok, from the rider's seat, leaned back and whispered through the curtains.

"Nomads?"

Beyond him, in the distance, stood tall cliffs, like walls on the plane of sand. Men in black clothes waited at the only passage through the fortress wall whose mason was nature.

"No. Balluashir's men," Chaa said. "Keep going."

He turned to the front. Next to him, our escort whipped the reins, leading us towards the opening. Chaa sat up straight, closed her eyes, and opened her palms on her thighs. I rushed my focus to the centre of my forehead; I wanted to learn. I took my awareness beyond my forehead and out in the sky. She had expanded hers around the warriors.

They stood restless. They got on their horses and rode down to us; all but a very tall one who held his position. I opened my eyes in the flesh. Chaa kept hers closed. The sound of their horses' gallop in the sand got louder the closer they got. But they didn't slow down. They rode past us, at least five men, and circled the place we had stopped before. I turned to Chaa, still in concentration. Innok turned, wondering as well. Our horses kept their pace.

"They cannot see us!" I laughed out.

We reached the opening. The giant faced us but moved not. I closed my eyes again. I wanted to know exactly how she was mesmerising these warriors.

I moved my consciousness out of the carriage, beyond Innok and our escort. "No," the latter shouted. His eyes were on me. He could see me! "Come back," he said. Our interaction seemed to annoy the tall warrior. He blinked his blank eyes back to reality and shouted in another tongue; the riders from down the slope now thrusting their way up.

I got back in my body. Chaa was back in hers. Our escort, already off his horse, conversed with the giant. He urgently unwrapped the clothes around a small package to unveil a token.

"Do you know what this is?" He put the shiny emblem close to the giant's face. He repeated something in another tongue while the giant frowned and groaned.

Chaa sighed and got out. She headed to the back, overlooking the riders approaching. She shouted a word in another language, and the horses went wild, jumping violently until all men were thrown to the ground.

Our escort still mumbled to the giant. Some of the others tried to remount while some ran towards us. Chaa raised her foot and let it drop to the ground. The sand below the warriors now flowed like water from under them. Two were already knee-deep in the sand. Another backed off and stood still, not to get swallowed.

Our escort got on his seat and took the reins. "We move on," he shouted.

Chaa took a moment watching the helpless men before joining us in the carriage. In front of us, their comrade stepped aside, and we passed unencumbered.

With a deep inhalation, Chaa closed her eyes and clenched her hand into a fist. She then exhaled and leaned back. Behind us, the men finally reached the opening. One pushed the giant. Another spat on the ground while searching for us in the distance. Smiling widely, I fell in my seat; again, they could not see us.

It was dark before we arrived at a compound. We were received at the entrance of the small village and led to a house with two bedrooms, although it was the spring outside that grabbed my attention.

While the others remained in the house, preparing the food, I splashed water on my face, washing the dusty day from my skin. Cool droplets still fell from my hair as I joined Chaa and Innok, already holding their plates.

"He saw me," I told Chaa. "Our escort saw me when I followed you beyond the body."

She did not talk. She had withdrawn to her food.

"Aren't they going to talk?" Innok asked. "Give us away?"

She turned to me first, slowly. "Of course he did. Udenas is a part of... ours."

She looked up at the door as Udenas, our escort, entered. He nodded at her and joined us. Only then did she turn to Innok. "Do not worry. It is already taken care of."

Innok remained silent, unaware of the possibilities.

"What did you do?" he finally asked.

"Can they trace our actions?" I asked.

No one responded to Innok.

"No, of course not," Chaa said. "They do not possess such access to the records. But you need to be careful, for if you enter the planes they dwell in, they may know. And no contact!"

"What?" I knew what she meant. I had been planning to take my consciousness to Idhatora. "Why not?"

"You do not possess yet the necessary discipline. When you came to find me, your excitement almost drew you to the planes of mud. That is why Udenas warned you to go back. And remember last time? Even the lighter aspect of your brother swelled within you emotions that led you astray. You will only enter the higher realms with my guidance. Until you are ready."

I looked away and dropped my food on the plate as she continued.

"I maintain contact with your father. He is well aware of our whereabouts and wellbeing."

It was reassuring that Father knew. But my choice to leave the kingdom to train in the sacred sciences was accompanied by discontent from the beginning; now stronger, with her prohibition. And its source was my desire for Idhi; I already missed her. I kept her in my mind for long after we said our goodnights with Chaa.

Innok came into our shared bedroom and closed the door. He had been taking care of the horses and carriage.

"Do you know what she did to them? Could they really not see us?" he asked.

I did not answer. I lay with my back to him. I could still smell her neck and feel her skin on my lips.

Innok touched my arm. "You will see her again. Maybe not soon enough, but you will be back to her."

He didn't see the tear dropping from the corner of my eye. He could not know that we would return. He could not make any such promises. Neither could I when I promised Idhi. We would only hope.

Nothing else was said. My arm got cold when he removed his palm to lie down on the other side of the room.

T he light through the trees from outside projected Idhi's face in my eyes. The sound of her laughter became the chirping of the birds.

"Prince, get up," Innok said.

Reality came back to me and the sweetness in my chest dissipated as I turned away from the window towards Innok, tying his blade around his waist. Still dry from my sleep, I remembered.

"You should not call me that," I said.

"Aletheos, something's wrong."

He got out the room first. Neither Chaa nor Udenas were around. My heart pounded in my otherwise slow body. He kept me behind him as he inspected the house.

"Where are the horses?" I whispered as I looked beyond the open door.

The carriage outside was unstrapped, its curtains blowing in the wind.

"You are up!" I recognised Chaa's voice.

She came from behind the house with one of the horses. My shoulders relaxed with a loud sigh, trying to disperse our unnecessary fear. Udenas galloped from the other side with supplies.

"We wait here until the sun is down," Udenas explained.

"We rest. And travel tonight," Chaa added.

B ehind the house, Chaa was taking care of the second horse. I joined in assisting her.

"Where are the people who received us last night?" I asked as I grazed the head of the horse.

"They moved on."

"Where?"

"Back to their routines."

"They came here for us alone?"

She nodded.

"Who are these people?" I asked. "Why are they helping us?"

"I told you before. They are affiliates to the order."

I took a handful of hay and opened my palm for the horse to chew on. "What did you do to those men?" I asked. "What was it that was taken care of?"

"You shouldn't concern yourself with that."

"Why not? What did you do? Did Udenas kill them?"

"You think I would resort to that?" She raised her voice. "How dare you even think of it? Do you suppose I would be content with having men be done away with?"

"I don't know what to think when you tell me nothing!"

I stepped away before turning back to her.

"I took their memories," she exhaled.

I gasped. "You can do that?"

"I did it out of grave necessity. You should not interfere in people's brains."

"Was it not the same when they were blind to us?"

"That is different. Entirely! I restrained our image from making an impression on their brain."

"How is that not the same?"

"You should do well to find the distinction, Aletheos."

"How do you mean?" I insisted.

She sighed. "Whatever we do, my dear, has an impact on us. What I did was not right. And I have taken the consequences upon myself."

"What consequences?"

She finally turned to me. Her eyes looked different. I opened mine wide.

"You are blinded?" I cried.

I looked around. I wanted to run. I couldn't. My breath was shaking, and, in the heat, I was shivering cold.

"There is no escaping your actions, dear child," she continued, brushing the horse.

I went to her. I hugged her. And I stayed there, holding her tight.

RIPPLES

Travelling at night was cooler, calmer. The stars above danced through the folds of the carriage's curtains, together with the light of the moon. Innok sat next to me. Across from me sat Chaa, blind with open eyes.

It was Innok who broke the silence. "What did you do to those men?"

He would not let it go. She turned to him and then outside. He opened his mouth, but I interrupted.

"Innok, stop. We will speak of it another time. Rest assured, Chaa did nothing wrong."

I looked into his eyes and shook my head. He sighed, turning away.

"Should we stop? Take a break?" I asked Chaa.

She did not respond. I touched her palm that rested on her lap.

"Should we have some tea?" I suggested.

She smiled. Udenas was already slowing down the horses. I wondered whether he had heard us over the galloping and the wheels turning.

"Let's have some tea," grandmother agreed as we halted.

I took her arm and helped her down the carriage. Udenas built a small fire to boil the water.

"Innok. Come here," she said.

He had remained on the other side of the carriage. But he could but obey.

"You are right. You should know. I will divulge as much as I can. You will not enquire further. Agreed?"

He didn't have an option. He agreed by silence.

"I know, my boy, that your faith was taken from you."

He narrowed his eyes. She continued.

"I cannot change that, nor will I try, even though you have witnessed instances of higher sciences more than once. But I will tell you this. There is a natural law that commands balance. Each action causes ripples within us even before they reach the cosmic sea. Those ripples, according to the merit of their cause, can either raise or sink their creator."

Innok looked at me, as if for explanations. I said nothing and turned to Chaa.

"We all live within the effects of our actions, my dear, with no exceptions," she said. "The purer you become in all that you do, the more you are elevated. This is true of all people. And walking the path of transmutation is the true way, whose effects bring peace and knowledge of the true and sacred."

I didn't think Innok would refrain from pushing for an answer. But he did.

"I took their memories of us," Chaa admitted. "I did not want to risk our exposure. But it was not right, and you were correct in worrying. However, out of necessity, I decided to act. And I have accepted the ripples I have caused."

"Your eyes..." Innok acknowledged for the first time.

"Yes," she replied.

"Chaa," I intervened, "there are unspeakable actions taken by many. What little you did... and the memories you took would not serve them otherwise anyway."

"To see the truth of the realms, you must keep yourself clean. This is our way, Aletheos. And where does impurity matter the most?" She leaned and grabbed a handful of sand from the ground. She let it flow through her fist. "In the marbles of your palace or on the ground of this desert?"

I didn't speak. Neither did Innok. Udenas served our warm tea. We stood around the small fire with the quietness of the stars. Innok took a sip from his cup.

"Okay." He nodded.

KING OF SAVAGES

We had been travelling at night and rested when the sun was high. Innok was opening up with Chaa. Her outburst of honesty must have given him what he needed to see her for the person she was. Or his good heart would not leave a weakened woman unassisted.

Udenas kept to himself as usual, always one step ahead at our chores. And I... I longed for a moment to breathe alone. Every word they spoke sounded too loud for me, and every chore or nuance needed much more effort.

I was drained. We hadn't slept for a while, and my head was dry as my anger for the beast and his men, forcing me to leave my home and my loved ones, boiled in my blood. I kept bringing the image of Idhi and Father to mind, if only to console myself. *It's them I am doing this for. And the people.*

The sun was now high above the dunes of sand. Today, we hadn't stopped at dawn. We wanted to reach the capital of this state before resting. Just before noon, two enormous lions with human heads looked back at us from the distance; statues engraved on a great wall. Their height got more imposing the closer we got, standing tens of times taller than us. They had wings and oxen's tails, apparent only as we passed through the gates into fortified Khantara.

"What is that being?" I asked Chaa. I turned to her before I remembered she couldn't see. "The lion with..."

"A symbol of manifested life," she interrupted me. "The four elements of the cosmos and the four cardinal points, unified in an entity that can walk deep down into matter or fly high in spirit, thereby signifying the ruler of the six dimensions of space, itself being the seventh that unifies them all."

"I have seen it..."

She raised her hand to silence me. She concentrated, her eyes moving rapidly below her eyelids. Inside the great manned walls laid a big and structured city that resembled nothing of the small villages we had gone through. The first layer in the city reminded of the dirty tent bazaar. But as we moved towards the centre, the houses grew with gardens and ornamental statues.

We passed through them all and rode to the other side; again, filled with progressively poorer houses. We stopped outside a dusty house of mudbricks. A big man welcomed us with a cheer, loudly embracing Chaa. He then noticed her eyes and said something to her, still with a cheerful temperament. She laughed and told him not to worry as Innok moved inside with some of our bags.

Getting sheltered from the sun relieved the tension in my eyes. We settled around the table, and our new host brought food. Innok feasted on the dried meat. I set it aside and ate the yogurt with some bread, as did Chaa with some subtle assistance from our not-so-subtle host. Udenas had remained at the door, looking outside.

Chaa faced up and left her food fall from her hands.

"What is it?" asked Innok, standing up.

I rushed with him by the door.

"Calm down," she answered, "but keep your blade ready."

Two men rode in the yard. They pushed Udenas aside and entered the house.

"The king invites you to his courts," one said with a grim smile beneath his dirty beard.

Chaa sighed.

"There is no need for any unpleasantness," said our host.

The second intruder grabbed and twisted his arm behind his back. Innok drew his sword, but the grim-faced man raised his blade to Chaa.

"Drop your sword, boy. Now!" he said and stretched his neck, exposing a black tattoo of a lion on his brown skin.

Innok backed off. He looked at me and nodded. With a quick inbreath, I led my awareness out through my forehead to engulf the man threatening Chaa. He turned, angry at me, and I opened my eyes before I could establish any kind of grip on him.

"What is he doing?" he yelled at the room. "Reserve your tricks," he said, rushing towards me, swinging his sword on his way.

I pushed myself back against the wall.

"No," Innok and our host shouted.

I shut my eyes at the tip of his blade, only for a heartbeat. The sword cut through flesh, dropping a great weight on me which then hit the floor.

"Udenas!" I cried out.

His body lay before my feet. But it was no blood that dripped from his wound. It was sand! His last exhalation whirled through the house, smashing pots and throwing furniture to the ground. Udenas's body collapsed on itself, dissolving into sand in the wind.

Our host freed himself from the intruder who stood as stunned as me. Innok rushed to my side while the killer breathed heavily, turning to Chaa. Her eyes were now steady in his. The veil had lifted. She could see.

"What is this witchcraft?" he asked with a shaking voice.

She only gave him a smile that infuriated him more. He raised his sword, but her hand was already high.

"Enough," she said and sent the man flying on the wall.

He crawled to regain his weapon, but the sword floated away from his hand and banged on the back wall. We all ran by her side.

"Tell your king I accept his invitation," Chaa declared.

He got up, still searching for his sword. Chaa stood unmoved; he could not have it. He spat on the floor before grabbing his friend and leaving. And I ran, kneeled to what remained of Udenas's body, only traces of sand, moving my hand through them.

"What is this?" I asked.

She leaned over and picked up a chair from the floor. Then another. She sat down with a sigh.

"Udenas," she said, "he was a thought."

"A thought?" I asked.

Innok was almost in tears. Our host, hearing her words, began tidying up.

"Yes. Mine. A thought I created to help us on the way. You know the process. I taught you the process. Only this time, the idea I manifested was of a man. He rode our horses and set our fire."

"You can create men now?" Innok interrupted with his eyes still wet.

"Udenas was not a man. It was an outbreath of my will. Something similar to the time King Aletheos told you to meet me at the room of the mother."

"What?" Innok asked, panting.

"Did you not find it strange? That after I left the palace for days, I would come back only to give you instructions and then leave again?"

My mind was set at ease. But the weight on my chest refused to let go.

"Did you make him jump in front of me?" I asked her.

"No, Aletheos. My will was his destiny. You create something and set it free. It's true. All our creations remain partially connected to us until they carry out their destiny and find their way back. My will was for guidance and safety. And Udenas did just that. He carried out his reason for existence."

"Your eyes?" I asked.

"Udenas, took those warrior's memories. His actions burden me, of course. And for as long as I had suffered the consequences, he was my eyes. Now he has returned to me."

Innok sat on the floor, holding his head.

E ight guards led the way to the palace, surrounding the three of us, through
the gardens. Nothing reminded me of the beauty purposefully and carefully
attended to at our gardens. Between the dry bushes and overgrown trees, stood
proud, a gruesome sight. Something dead on two spikes.

"Is that their food?" I asked, covering my nose.

"That's meant for us," Chaa said.

I squinted my eyes to make sense of the masses. Beneath the bloody hair, a black
shape tainted the skin. It was a lion. My gut clenched me to a halt. My eyes widened,
and my stomach burned with acid. It was the two men who had attacked us in the
house.

"Take deep breaths and keep walking," she said without turning to me.

I shared glances with Innok. The guards at the door protested in their language,
pointing at Innok's sword. I looked at Chaa for translation.

"Innok will stay here," she said.

"No. What if they attack again?" he whispered.

"You saw their blood awaiting our arrival." She paused. "Stay here. Do nothing."

We found their king with his feet up the table. He swirled a knife on its tip,
scratching the arm of his chair.

"You called for us," Chaa said.

He got up and signalled the guards away.

"Do you not enjoy my company, honourable lady of the Five-Pointed Star?" he
said in an almost perfect accent of our language, laughing below his wild dark hair
and sharp beard.

Chaa walked closer to him. I followed, accidentally kicking a goblet that was on
the floor. Chaa picked it up and gently placed it on the table.

"Your brother was a man of order," she told him.

"Well, he is dead now, is he not?"

"And you thought you'd piss on his accomplishments?" asked Chaa. "How did
he die, really?" She looked around. "Where is your son?"

His mouth did a clacking sound, and he took a step back. He untied the cloth
around his waist and pulled his robe up. From below it, he grabbed his penis and
pissed on the floor.

"I knew you were troubled, Balluashir. Since you were a child, I knew you were
troubled. But I did not expect this," she said. "You invade cities and bring them to
the ground. You torture people and whoever manages to flee falls to wretchedness.

You have forgotten all you have learned. Your priests are selling objects from the temples to survive."

He hummed as he covered his penis. He walked to us and raised his arm close to her face. "And what of it? Whoever stands up to us is falling to the ground. No one will rebel if they are busy looking for food."

"What do you want, Balluashir? I have businesses to attend."

"Chaa! Always so serious! And why would I let you go?"

We don't have time for this. I haven't abandoned everything to engage with savagery.

"You think my people will allow this?" asked Chaa.

"Ha! What remains of your pathetic order is a mere nuisance. You have no reach here."

He moved his hand around Chaa's neck.

"You are wrong," I said.

He groaned. "What did you say, boy?"

"You are wrong," I repeated. "People rebel when they have nothing to lose. And you leave them with nothing. I have seen it. Only a few days from here. People sleep under ripped fabrics and pieces of trees. Merchants have almost nothing to sell. Their children are hungry. What fear do you think is left in them? Of hunger? Death? They are already there."

"You have turned them into wild animals," Chaa added. "And what do wild animals do when they are hungry?"

"They hunt," I said.

"Who is this boy you drag with you that dares speak to me?" he shouted.

I looked up at his dirty face.

"I am Aletheos. Son of the King Aletheos."

He looked at Chaa for a moment and brought his face close to mine.

"What are your plans?" I asked. "Keep hostage the prince of Erevos? Or hold his advisor against her will? Tell me now, what do you suppose my father's response would be towards treason from what used to be an affiliated state?"

"Is that a threat, boy?"

The foul smell of his mouth made me miss a breath.

"No threats," I said. "I am merely inviting you to calculate what lies at the end of this path you are treading."

He paced back to his table, throwing things on his way. "Get out. Get out!" he screamed at us.

"You will give us supplies and men to escort us to our destination. And none of them will know who we are," Chaa said.

"Get out!" he repeated.

We found Innok at the gates. He looked at me with enquiring eyes.

"Our names are no longer hidden," I said.
He touched his blade.

VULTURES

O ur fire threw light on the sharp cliffs around us, making the sky even darker by contrast. Innok joined Chaa and me around the fire.

"Our horses are taken care of," he said.

It was one of the very few times that only the three of us were in proximity. We had been riding with some ten of Balluashir's men for days. They were laughing and singing drunk at some distance.

"Can we trust them?" asked Innok.

"Of course not," she said. "But now we know exactly how many eyes we have on our backs."

"Will we let them arrive with us?"

She smiled. "No. They will return to the ruins of Balluashir where they belong."

A strange movement drew my attention to the rocks behind us. The light flickered unnaturally. The quivering shadows slowly formed transparent clouds, half my size, refracting the light.

One of them stayed still. The almost invisible cloud was something alive, an entity with two bony feet, a small trunk, and long thin arms. With an onion-shaped head and eyes the size of my fist, it stared at me.

I gave it a smile, and it approached with a gust that thrust sand around us. Innok was alerted by the sound. As he stood up, the small being stayed still, looking at Innok and then at me.

"He cannot see you," I said to it in my mind.

The little thing tilted its head and answered in a high-pitched voice.

"Sure?" I thought it said.

I nodded as more of these beings came closer. Innok's steps almost scared them away.

"He is okay," I told them. "Just stay away from those guys."

I pointed at the warriors, loud and imposing, playing with their blades and intoxicating themselves. Innok walked past them towards our carriage.

"Elementals," Chaa said with a cheer.

She already had some of them in her arms.

"These little ones are tricksters," she said, shaking her head at them with a smile.

Two were already pushing sand on our fire.

"Hey," I scared them away.

"There are many kinds of elementals," she continued, "some may cooperate with you, others are of a more selfish nature. Establishing a rapport with their realm is tricky but more than useful."

"I think I have seen some before. They looked like obscure versions of animals or a mixture of them and humans."

She nodded. From behind her, more elementals came running as one of the savages shouted at Innok. The mischievous creatures must have messed with them, and the men blamed him for it. They surrounded Innok, provoking him into a fight. One even drew his sword at him, with the others following. Quickly, I turned within and sent white force rushing through my hands, encircling my friend with protection. But Chaa was already between them.

"Put your swords down!" she said.

"No woman commands me!" the first one answered.

"Need I remind you," I shouted from behind them, "what happened to the men back in your city?"

They turned to me.

"They, too," I said, "failed to withhold their aggression."

They reluctantly lowered their swords. The man challenging Innok came to me while the others returned to their fire. He stood a few fingers away from me, glaring into my eyes. He stirred his jaw, keeping his lips closed. I moved not. Still looking into my eyes, he spat on the ground and walked away.

Innok, Chaa, and I gathered around our fire. The others resumed their drinking and singing. The elementals had dispersed.

T he rock formations around us separated the otherwise levelled plain into inter-crossing pathways. It was like travelling on the depths of the tributaries of a long-lost river. The cool air currents allowed us to proceed in their shadows during the day, with their sharp peaks threatening to collapse on us at any time.

Chaa was getting restless in the slow-moving carriage. Innok walked at the front, pulling the reins of our horses. Balluashir's men acted like prison guards more than anything else. And the further we travelled, the more they seemed to decompose and the less they cared about their ruler's orders. Half of them were quite ahead of us. The one who challenged us the previous night rode close with a smile below his slimy beard.

"What?" I finally gave in.

"You think you are better," he laughed, "you think our king wants to protect you. What you think happened to your friend back at the city?" he said, rubbing a cloth on his uncovered sword.

I looked at Chaa and back at him.

"What did you do?" I asked.

Chaa turned to him as well. One of his friends galloped back to us and shouted something in their language.

"Wait here!" he said through his beard.

All of them ran ahead and disappeared behind the rocks.

"Did they kill your friend?" I asked Chaa. "For taking us in?"

"I don't know, Aletheos. He was supposed to leave the city himself."

"What happened?" Innok interrupted from outside.

On the ground around him, moved emerging shadows. I followed their source up to the rocks, where men appeared left and right.

"Chaa," I alerted her to their presence.

She turned to Innok. "Get up and ride. Now!"

Innok rushed on the horses, whipping the reins.

"Keep a fast pace," Chaa said. "Don't stop until I tell you to."

"Chaa," I repeated as more and more men appeared on the rocks.

She didn't spare her attention. Innok turned to her again. She said nothing, merely looked onwards. He could but keep the horses' pace. And we reached Balluashir's warriors. Beyond them stood a line of men blocking any passage. Surrounded from above as well, they waited for a battle they could not possibly win. Innok slowed us down.

"I said carry on," Chaa shouted.

He tried to protest, only for a moment. Our horses ran fast. As we rode by our captivators, the bearded one jumped to catch the reins, but our horse hit and threw him to the ground. The line of foreigners raised their spears.

"Chaa!" Innok shouted, leading us directly on the spears.

Chaa calmly raised her head. "Keep onwards!"

He did. The men withdrew their spears and marched to the side. We passed unharmed.

"Stop," she yelled.

She got off the carriage and walked back to the foreigners who had regained formation. Innok and I ran behind her, as she walked through the barricade of men, meeting their leader. Now trapped, Balluashir's warriors dropped their weapons. I could finally breathe. I smiled. So did Innok.

"Go back to your wretched king," Chaa said. "Tell him that the order is grateful for his support. You are no longer needed."

"Remind him he is not welcome here," added our saviours' leader. "His army will be met with the wrath of the mountains. Now go."

The defeated tried to regain their swords. But spears scraped their throats.

"Be grateful you still have your horses," said the leader. "Now run back to your ruins."

They did.

"Thank you for arriving so soon," Chaa said to the leader as they walked back to us, adding something in his language.

LINEAGE OF MANKIND

The camp followed a calm pace. I sat with Chaa and their leader.

"I am glad Chohanatma's message reached you soon enough," Chaa told him.

"Yes, he sent a messenger as soon as he received your call for assistance. I hope you are comfortable here," he said in a broken accent.

She threw me a glance and answered, grateful. "Yes, we are fine. Thank you for your intervention. What are you doing all the way out here?"

"Chohanatma found a scroll and sent us to search for the ancient compound."

"You have excavated this area?"

"Yes, we did!" he said proudly.

Chaa furrowed her brows. She was searching for something in her mind. "What did you find?"

The man pointed at a hill nearby. "Caves carved in the mountain. Nothing leading further, though."

"Can you take us?"

The man stood up and nodded, expanding his chest. We followed him to the site, passing by men digging in the mountain, and reached an opening. Inside, the room was dark. She looked around in silence. She had turned within. She then focused on the walls of the cave, touched them while walking slowly around the room.

"This is it! You have found it!" she cheered out loud. "We have been reading about this compound, but I never thought I would step foot in it." She left her hand on the rock, and turned to him who led us there. "The whole mountain is a sacred area. It used to be a city; eons ago. It should be full of rooms carved on its sides. And if it is truly the place we think it is, you will find some great monuments."

"Where do you think we should dig first?"

She exited, and he followed. I remained in the empty space. *How old is this place?* How many years must have passed for a thriving city to fall into ruins in the rocks, at a place erased from history? *Could these ancient people tell anything of the beast?*

W e had finished our midday prayers, and I withdrew within, restless, eager to move on. But Chaa studied some scrolls, with the excavation site at a small distance from the camp. And Innok had already made acquaintances with some soldiers and was training in their kind of sword. He seemed to enjoy himself, more relaxed than I had seen him since long before our journey began. Indeed, he was the one responsible for our safety, and he was the one with the least knowledge of our circumstances; Chaa took care of everything while he was left worrying about an ever-impending danger. I never assumed he took this burden lightly.

The ground rumbled with a loud murmur. Behind Chaa, in the distance, the peak of the mountain had collapsed in a rockslide. We all ran through the thick clouds of dust at the excavation site. Four men, coughing, moved the rocks from one of their own. Only he was injured.

Chaa ordered for his transportation down to camp while she maintained her position. Beyond her, through the settling of dust, the landslide had uncovered something. It was part of a human head, itself alone, taller than us. I could not even imagine the size of the entire statue on the side of the cliff.

When we reached the infirmary tent, the wounded man already lay over some sheet to the ground; his wounds cleaned and patched with medicine. She signalled me to go to his feet while she stayed over his head. She uncovered the wound, and I followed her instructions. First, I gave violet energy for purification of the wound, lest it festered. Then, green to facilitate healing and beige for support.

"Now, just observe," she said, "and listen."

She extended etheric channels through her hands and expanded her consciousness through them and deep into the man's muscles.

"This is the part of the cells which activates regeneration," she said and sparked them into fast but meticulous activity. She then interlaced all we did with white light and grounded them, to work directly into the physical plane.

Outside, Chaa informed the chief that the wounded would be all right and led me to the river next to the camp. We both sank our hands, warmed by the force we used, into the cold water, normalising our blood circulation.

C haa sat with the others around the fire, and Innok must have gone to sleep. We were in a safe place now. I left their company and headed to the river that ran slow behind the camp.

I threw my clothes on the ground before walking in the cool water. Oh, it was wonderful. With my feet immersed in the water, I was overtaken by lightness. All my tension floated through my feet as if absorbed by the wet sand.

I ran against the water's resistance on my legs until I dived below, letting the sensation of safety sink deep within and turn into laughter. A splash of water from further into the river rained down on me. I stood up, alarmed. It was Innok, already wet and calm. I smiled and sat back in the water.

"Is she asleep?" he asked.

"Not yet."

He got up, letting the water drip from his body, and walked to shore.

"She is fine," I said. "You can stay. The place is full of soldiers."

He would not ease himself from his responsibilities; not for long. I threw some water back at him. He laughed, unleashing some quick blows on the river's surface that sent waves all around me.

"I will go check on her and come back." He got serious again.

He walked out of the water and dried himself on a cloth. I hadn't thought to bring one.

"Innok," I said, now serious as well. "Thank you."

"I will be back in a short while," he said.

The sound of his steps disappeared behind the bushes. I let myself fall back, get carried on whatever moonlight was reflected on the water, and closed my eyes into oblivion. Her face shocked me into wakefulness. I hadn't had the chance to bring Idhi in mind for some time. As if the brutality of Balluashir's men, escorting us since that barbarous city, was dangerous even to my thoughts.

I walked to shore, grabbed my clothes, and returned to the water. I rubbed and rubbed them, cleaning away all traces of the dry land we had travelled through. I did the same movement over and over, going through whatever had happened the past few days. 'No contact,' she had said. I could but obey her. But...

I finished with my clothes and walked out of the water. Innok had left some clean, dry clothes hanging from a branch. I didn't think they were for me, but I used them anyway, leaving mine to dry.

The others were still around the fire as I passed unnoticed through the camp and into my tent. I reached for a small bag of mine and made my way up to the excavation site. No one was around. I entered the empty room and sat with legs crossed and spine straight. 'Our creations remain connected with us,' she had said about Udenas.

I brought my consciousness through my heart, up to the centre of my forehead, and took Idhi's sandflower out of my bag. It was not created by her, but by the time my beloved gifted it to me, her intention and energy must have connected with it; hopefully. And, in accordance with Chaa's warning, I would not move through the realms, only sense her through it.

The sandflower took form in my mind's eye, and I connected with it through etheric channels from my hands. After a few moments of blankness, her flowery fragrance tickled my nose and filled my chest. My lips got bitter by a tear as a path of colours opened up in front of me. And I felt her; graceful and peaceful. That's all I wanted to know. My eyebrows dropped; my jaw relaxed.

As I let her image slip away, another invaded my mind; that man from the garden, wearing a white cloak, shining from within, missing his friend with the pearl gown shining yellow and orange-white light.

My eyes opened to a thump from outside. Someone whispered my name. *Innok.* But through the darkness of the cave, stared at me the glimmering eyes of a snake, now raised across from me. I kept my restless legs on the ground. And gathered myself, at least enough to focus on the centre of its head and make my intentions known. Innok kept calling for me from outside while the snake held my eyes. Slowly, the snake backed down, watching me closely until it slithered away, deeper into the mountain.

"Aletheos!" Innok repeated.

My heart pounded in my chest.

"Innok," I responded with a broken low voice.

"Where have you been?" he said from the entrance.

"Just here, for a walk."

"Come on, let's go back."

I nodded. I felt what I wanted to know. I was done here.

"Did she know?" I asked as we made our way down the hill.

"No, they went to sleep. I told her I would bring you back from the river."

"My clothes," I said.

"I got them. Come on."

Two soldiers guarded our tent. We greeted them and walked inside to fall on our beds. We could both sleep fine tonight.

GREENS OF CHANGE

O ur surroundings changed day by day. The dry lands of sand were succeeded by more and more greenery and dew. The cool days of the rising ground allowed us to proceed with comfort higher in the mountains. And as the leader of the camp had assured us, we were welcomed by many in our way. Every other village we passed through had a roof and food for us.

With the change of landscape came the change in appearances. People's skin got browner and their clothing more colourful. Everything changed as we moved on. We had stayed at four or five villages by now. And since the camp, a veil had been lifted from weighing on my head. I could think more clearly. I was lighter in my fear. And once, I had the chance to sneak away and revisit my connection with my beloved Idhatora through her gift.

T his morning was an especially quiet one. The usual sounds of the birds and in-sects and whatever other animals lived in these trees had disappeared. Maybe it was only more apparent because, once again, we prepared our horses and wheels. Some kids came to see us. They probably found our appearance much stranger than I found theirs' exotic.

Innok had left early in the morning. The woman that had accommodated us the previous night unloaded our carriage while I did the opposite. I smiled and tried to explain, but she talked in her language I could not understand and kept unloading and untying straps.

"She is right, you know." Chaa laughed from behind me.

A loud noise rumbled through the trees.

"Carriages will not serve us any longer," she said.

The noise was getting louder and closer. Only the children seemed to acknowledge it while the others kept on with their affairs. Someone yelled in the distance, and branches cracked before they broke. And there it was. I backed up, but only for a step. It was an elephant! An elephant, guided by a rider and mounted by Innok, who yelled in excitement.

I could not gather my smile. I had never seen one; they were driven to extinction in our kingdom hundreds of sun cycles ago. And there came another one, pulled by another man. The children ran and petted them, giggling. I got close as well. They were marvellous beasts. I respectfully touched one's side and then moved beyond his hanging ears towards his head, careful of the tusks. I looked into its gentle eyes. And then those of the other.

"They are amazing!" Innok said as he jumped off.

Indeed, our hostess was right. We unstrapped everything from our carriage and tied it to the big pouches hanging from the animals. Chaa went to the first elephant and touched the middle of its head as high as she could reach. She closed her eyes for a few moments and did the same with the other. They both kneeled, and we climbed on the thick rugs on their backs.

I waved goodbye to the children below and at our sweet hostess, showing my gratefulness by a gentle bow of the head. She did the same.

Two men led the elephants, and Innok followed with our horses.

T he two locals escorting us helped with setting the fire and the food and the tents. Chaa was very friendly with them. They, however, seemed a little distant, always bowing to Chaa and fast to attend our needs.

And the elephants did open our way through the jungle. Innok learned how to guide these kind beasts, the difference between riding them and a horse, and how to take care of them. And they would usually sleep around our fire, forming a fort around us. Tonight, I even leaned back on one as I had my evening tea, feeling her heartbeat on my back. *Idhi would have loved this.*

I nnok sat in front of me, leading the elephant as we made our way. The smells from the trees and the sunlight through the green leaves filled my chest with freshness. But every time I noticed feelings of contentment, they were soon followed by thoughts of those I left behind, my home. I could only hope that the beast left them as well.

"How was the island?" I asked Chaa.

We rode side by side; the density of the jungle now allowed us to.

"The Five-Pointed Star?"

"Yes. The place you used to live."

"Oh, it is charming. It is a big island but miniscule compared to the kingdom. And while small, it has a wild mountain range in its centre. Its people are rough, like the island itself. But they are decent and hardworking, always striving to survive."

"Did you grow up there?"

She nodded.

"The island emerged from the sea millennia ago. You can find seashells even on the highest peak of its mountains. I travelled all around it, but I spent most of my time next to the sea in a part of the island that sees south towards the kingdom.

"The temple?"

"The temple was simple, overlooking the horizon. Our shrine was only the big pot of white stone, cut from the same stone as the one we brought at the palace."

"Do you ever miss home?"

"My home?" she waited for more.

"I don't know. Where is your home? Is it the island? The temple you used to preside over? The priestesses? Is it at the palace with me?"

"My home, sweet prince... I never had a home on this earth. None of us does. True home, where we all truly belong, is not a place you can go. It is a condition of our true nature.

Sadly, that sense of belonging in oneness seems to disappear the instant we enter this earthly plane. And it feels as though we have lost a part of ourselves. We feel less of what we are. And out of that deep need for fulfilment, we create poor attachments to sand, trying to get a sense of connectedness.

But sand is sand and shall disappear with the next storm. The only thing that truly remains is the true home and the path that leads us there, always forged deep within us. And sometimes, just sometimes, the connection we form with some in the flesh is, truly, a reminder of home."

Idhi's image rushed to mind.

"As for my earthly attachments," she continued, "yes, my home used to be the island. I don't know that I will ever return... fully. But that path within us leads us to strange places. And now, here we are!"

We reached an opening. And I saw where my path had brought me. Our destination lay before us. A small city of stone appeared under the sun, with patches of greens livening almost every house. Streams of water ran in between them, full of violet lotus flowers. And above the houses showed tall an intrinsically majestic temple. Behind it, colossal mountains like pyramids of greens, greys, and whites disappeared high in the blue sky that was full of colourful birds.

"We are here!" I said.

I looked at her and then at Innok in front of me. Both of my dear companions shared my joy. "The feet of the mount," I whispered to myself. "We are here."

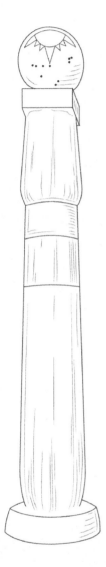

PART 3
MIDDAY

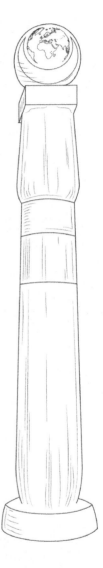

SHELTER

I woke up to a serene silence, carried by the small streams of water outside. A faint mist had not yet dissolved by the rising sun. Chaa was having her tea, leaning at the open door facing the garden. I joined her in silence. Her face, her features had softened.

"Good day," I said in a low voice.

She nodded with a smile.

"Is Innok asleep?" I asked, assuming as much.

We now had separate rooms, however small.

"Yes," she said softly. "Let him. The boy is exhausted."

I agreed. He had been on vigilance for a long time.

"Let's go out together," I proposed.

Her eyes were only half-open; her movements slow.

"I will stay here for a while," she said. "Go. Areteia is safe."

We are safe. We are free. I am... I looked up at her. My face relaxed, my stomach as well. I sipped my tea in her company for a little longer.

Beyond our garden, streams of water ran through pathways of grey stone. I took every turn I found. With no particular destination, I merely took in all the new impressions. The houses were part stone, part mud bricks; some with arched windows, all, at least partially, covered with plants. The water passed through their gardens before meeting the streams in the narrow streets.

People were already waking up to their lives. Whoever I crossed paths with greeted me with a warm smile. Some even stopped and offered a small bow that I tried to imitate. Their temperament was something new; calm, humble, graceful, living in a simplicity reflected in the architecture of the town.

At a crossroad stood a life-size statue of a woman, sculpted from the same grey stone and decorated with ribbons of flowers, red, orange, yellow, and white; some already dried, others fresh. Her face was real to every detail. Despite their grandiosity and colourful representations, our statues back home had never encaptured life itself so clearly.

I walked until I reached the temple at the heart of the town. The light of the sun shone on all its magnificence. Statues adorned its exterior as much as its interior, visible through the open spaces between its pillars. And they were all refined to perfection with a realistic resemblance of the sculptors' idea. Surely the imposing bulky structures of our temples were missing. But in its place stood a diorama that covered the entire building. The complex representation of the sacred entities seemed to hold their essence. I wondered whether the true meaning of each scene was known to the people of this land. Chaa had told me that the meaning of symbols would forever be kept by the initiates alone. How sad I had found it, how wasted all the beauty seemed, if no one could grasp it.

People were walking towards the temple, others coming out. All, reverent in their manners, quiet and slow. A hand warmed my shoulder. Chaa stood as calm as everyone.

"Let's go inside," she said.

My heart beat a little faster for a few moments. What if I was not welcome?

"Take off your sandals. No impurities in sacred spaces," she said.

I walked up the steps and into the temple, following Chaa, who passed by all the others and sat in front of the priest; a man with legs crossed on the floor and a small cloth covering only his genitals. He chanted in the deepest voice I had ever heard. I did not understand the language, but his words vibrated in my chest.

He held his eyes closed while Chaa and the others joined in his chant. They finished the prayer together before he opened his eyes to meet Chaa's. His features never moved. Both bowed their heads.

A necklace of jasmine flowers hung from his neck, filling the room with their fragrance. Next to him, incense was burning, and a bowl of oils still rippled with his voice. He dipped two fingers in the liquid and touched Chaa's forehead and palms. He then turned to me and bowed his head. I reciprocated while he anointed my forehead and palms with his wet fingers. The chanting then continued. I hummed the sounds of his tongue until my voice was bursting vibrations around my body.

The priest led the room into silence for some time before standing up. Everyone followed his example. He said something to the people behind us and nodded at Chaa. We returned the courtesy and walked towards the exit. On our way out, the people bowed to us as well. She gracefully responded while I clumsily tried to lean my head while walking.

Innok waited down the steps, calm with eyes full of light.

"You didn't come inside," I teased him.

"Well, you know..." He rubbed his head.

We walked back home. We were expecting visitors.

Chaa waited in the small garden outside while Innok and I threw a glance beyond the window every now and again. Before the sun was down, they arrived. A man of considerable build sat on his horse, straight and strong. He wore white garments and a turban above his black hair that curled down to his neck. Two others followed him, thinner, with dark clothes and swords around their waist.

The big one dismounted and entered the garden. He bowed to Chaa, and she did the same. They looked at each other for a few moments. Then, the man's serious face broke with a wide smile as he hugged her. Chaa, all strict and powerful, embraced him back and tenderly rested her head on his chest.

After exchanging some words in the tongue of this place, they came inside. He stood tall, eyes vibrant with will.

"This is Aletheos," Chaa said.

He looked deep into my eyes.

"Hello, Aletheos," he said in our language. "Welcome to Areteia. I am Chohanat-ma."

I was about to express my respect with the small bow that seemed customary in this place, but he came closer and touched my shoulders. His presence passed through me. I looked back into his eyes and let a true connection be established. When I blinked, he brought his hand to my cheek. His brows gathered into an inquisitive frown. He turned to Innok, cheerful again.

"I am well aware of your service, young man."

"Thank you," Innok replied with a tremor in his voice. "I am Innok."

"Now come," Chohanatma said.

We followed him into town to a big garden. Torches were lit, and tables prepared. People expected us.

"Tonight, we celebrate!" he said.

It was a feast with food and people and music! Wine kept filling our cups. And we danced with the kind people of this land, following their steps; Chaa with Chohanatma, myself with Innok. We danced free into the foreign rhythms. The black feathers were far behind.

WORDS

The following morning, I woke up a little dizzy. Chaa and Chohanatma were already in the common room, talking in a low voice.

"You should have told me, Chaa," he said.

"I believed it best for both of us. And her," she answered.

They silenced their argument as I opened my door. Chaa pointed at the water, boiled with local spices. I served myself and joined them at the table. The tea tasted a little too sharp for my habits. Across from me, a pile of scrolls mounted a wooden chest.

"Chohanatma brought them," she explained. "You will learn the language."

Shortly after our midday prayers, she laid the scrolls on the table.

"The most ancient of scriptures are written in this language," she said, unrolling one of them. "That's why it is of great significance to become proficient in it. And its pronunciation as well."

I looked at her and then at the scroll. "Is this truly necessary?" I asked. "Do we have time for this? The others..."

She never answered, only started teaching. With a sigh, I leaned over the first scroll. The figures were fundamentally different from our own. The written grammar and syntax were all different. I was accustomed to symbols and glyphs that corresponded to concepts, but this ancient language was more linear and specific; each letter was used to connote a sound, and their combinations formed words binding to their transliteration.

"You can practise by talking to the people here. But bear in mind that the proper pronunciation has been changed through the millennia. Don't confuse the common tongue with the proper science of sound."

L ater in the afternoon, we sent Innok away and resumed my training in the higher realms.

"Practice, practice, practice," Chaa said. "I want you to keep travelling between the different realms. Become able to distinguish the nature of each one, the impressions each gives, the way they register in your brain, how they correspond to your internal state. Only by experience and observation will you be able to lift the veils and see truth for what it is."

And so I did. I practised and practised.

"But, no contact," she repeated.

SOUND IN STONES

We took the afternoon to walk around the town. Innok and I were getting to know more and more of this peaceful town's little streets and passageways. Chohanatma had declared us honoured guests, and even in his absence, the people of this place provided for our needs. Chaa assisted at the local infirmary until midday, and we would usually continue with my education in the afternoon while Innok befriended our providers and assisted them in daily chores, reciprocating on behalf of all of us.

At the close of our excursion, we passed by the central temple. Chaa was there, sitting alone in the street facing the temple. It was one of the days she didn't want to stay inside and had sent us early on our walk. I assumed something had happened at the infirmary. We exchanged looks with Innok and split ways. He continued down the path to our house, and I approached her, sat by her and waited to open her eyes.

After a while, she seemed to emerge from a refreshing nap. But I knew she was anywhere but in sleep. She placed her hand on mine.

"Hello, my dear," she said.

I smiled at her. I wanted to know everything; where she was in her mind, how she saw things, everything she knew, all that she could ever tell me. But I never knew where to start.

"How have you been today?" I asked.

"I am fine. Did you have your walk?"

"Yes, we went around. Innok introduced me to some people. He is acquainted with a lot. He even picked up and tries to speak in their language. Maybe he could attend our lessons," I said.

"Yes, maybe he could. It will do him good to learn to express himself."

We took some time in silence, both facing the marvel that was the temple.

"Have you noticed how different the statues are here?" she asked.

"Yes, their craftmanship is magical."

"The people here are descendants of the most ancient. Their culture has been developing unhindered since the last of humanity's ancestors reached this place. And because of that, they have themselves developed a clearer vision of the unknown."

"Is that why we are here?"

"Yes. I insisted you come here as myself and your father did before you. But... Your father is naive for his family. He wanted to keep you close even amidst the darkness encircling us; or because of it."

"Naive?"

"Emotional, Aletheos. His love for your brother delayed his actions. And his love for you... He wanted to keep you protected under his wings and have you go through the initiations back home. I warned him against it. It was too soon. During initiations, we can only guide you, but we cannot protect you, for you face your own self. You need to transmute your lower self first; compose it into a developed personality that may be an appropriate vessel for your higher aspects to be carried out. It is you, the whole you, who weighs your heart. And development takes time and experiences for the ethics to take root in both your heart and mind. This is the one true way."

"Will I go through the initiations here?"

"Ceremonial initiations are meant to resemble processes we go through on our path. Most of them, you will consolidate through the development of your lower aspects and thereby initiate yourself. The rest, you will go through them when the time is right."

My chest warmed with anticipation. I wished myself ready, eager to return to Erevos, help the people against the darkness. But I remembered the black feathers cutting through my skin in that coffin.

"You both came here?" I finally asked.

"Yes. He was about two or three sun cycles younger than you, maybe at thirteen, when he came. Myself had arrived some sun cycles earlier. He came, as did I, driven by our thirst for truth. There is no other place to find water as pure to satisfy such thirst. Not the exoteric religion, that is one as many, but the esoteric knowledge kept in this place. And here we had bestowed upon us, as you will in due time, the ancient history and lineage of spirit, its fall into matter and the sacred sciences."

I thought of asking more about their past. She spoke first.

"You see all those entities carved in the stone?" She pointed at the temple.

"Every single one of them embodies a process or power underlying the universe or the sum of them. But as so many times happens, most people make of the symbol that which it represents. And thereby the birth of so many false gods are created in the minds of men."

I kept looking at all the complex characters depicted within scenes of fights and struggles, as well as scenes of beauty and serenity.

"You will learn of their meaning. That is why I want you to learn the language. Many scriptures to unveil them have been kept and guarded. Symbols, however, as words, mean a different thing according to the level you are focusing on. Keep that in mind in all cases, in your daily life as well."

"Father used to say this. Every teaching, he said, as everything in the world, has many levels of understanding."

"Exactly. Depending on the level you are looking at, you apply the symbol in the appropriate analogy. Take that wheel, for example." She pointed at a scene on the temple with a cycle as its centrepiece.

"In the level of most abstract ideation, it represents the Absolute in its plane alone; all differentiation still asleep. It thereafter becomes the symbol for space, or the female principle, within which all manifestation will occur. It can also represent the cyclic rhythm of involution and evolution, of birth and death within space."

I repeated her words in my mind. I wanted to absorb and make my own such noetic capacity.

"It is also the shape that stands for the Cosmic Atom or the Serpent that bites its tail," she continued, "the core of matter in its indivisible essence. And while a fundamental inner principle unites and pervades all that the wheel represents, its applications change according to the level of nature you lay your eye upon."

"I want to learn more," I admitted.

"You will. Have no doubt of that. One thing at a time. Your physical brain must advance gradually into the impressions and knowledge it receives, lest they overwhelm you and create effects similar to those of disoriented manifestation; obsession and suffering. So, learn the ancient language, make yourself able to study further, and practise your journeys through the realms."

I nodded.

GREEN LEAVES

I nnok and I walked into the jungle beyond the stone compounds of the city. He marched on towards the opening we had found, focused on sharing his swordsmanship skills. From above, followed us a family of monkeys, chattering amongst the trees and the colourful birds. The elementals were no longer hiding from us, but still kept their distance. I didn't always discern their exact form, but the vibrant colours of their energy mixed with the flowers and plants of the forest.

It was early in the afternoon when we reached our usual destination; an opening between trees on top of a small waterfall. Since Chaa divulged her wisdom only drop by drop, I wanted to prepare myself in all ways I could, wasting not the time I was away. After some time repeating the basic moves of the sword, he unleashed his wooden sword on me, breaking my defence in a display of his ability. He backed up and came at me again. And again, hitting the same spot on my ribs.

As he manoeuvred once more, the pain in my ribs rushed through my body. Before he hit me, I raised my hand as of instinct, and an invisible force thrust him on the ground. I laughed as he brushed the dirt off his clothes.

"Well, do you want to learn on not?" he protested.

"That was not teaching. You were showing off!"

He looked down, trying to withhold his laughter. I shook my head as a drop of sweat slid down my forehead and into my eye.

"That's enough for today," he said and walked in the shadows.

We sat across from each other with our backs resting on the trees.

"Let me show you something," I said.

He nodded.

"Close your eyes, and relax with your breath."

I touched the centre of his palms to activate his energy recipients and led force from my chest out in my hands.

"Can you feel this?" I asked.

"Umm... What should I be feeling?"

"Any change, any sensations in your palms."

"No, not really," he said after a while.

I grew my outpour stronger, much stronger than I ever had to with Idhi, and waited a few moments. He moved his head from side to side.

"Come, turn your hands towards mine," I said.

He opened his eyes and did as I said. I took my hands to his and established a connection. He looked at his hands and then at me. He didn't seem to register any impressions. But the connection was there. I saw and felt it, coloured with layers of blues and greens.

"It's not working," he exhaled and let his hands fall.

I withheld any response, wondering...

"Listen," he said, "I know there are things beyond the physical. I have been with you and grandmother enough to know as much. But it does not work with me. It's okay that I don't get it."

I neither agreed nor disagreed. My mind moved away from the reasons preventing him from experiencing the immaterial. I now wondered why could I.

"The sun is almost down. We should head back," he interrupted my thoughts.

He offered his hand and helped me up.

MERITS

A thunder broke out of the gentle drizzle. The rain whipped the wood covering the windows before calming back down. And the clouds had darkened the room earlier than usual, our language lesson now lit by candles.

My brain relaxed to the sound of rain. Innok, on the other hand, was sharp to ask questions. After a while, it was time for the teaching on proper pronunciation, and, as usual, Chaa sent him away. He would normally head outside, but not with this storm.

"I will be in my room," he said.

"Why do you do that?" I asked her when Innok closed his door.

She turned to me.

"Why do you send him away?" I explained. "Can he not study with me?"

"He is not ready to assimilate the higher knowledge," she answered, unravelling another scroll.

"Why not? He is a good person."

"He is. Absolutely."

"What made me ready, then? Is it because I was born to the king? That doesn't seem a criterion of substance."

"Aletheos, being a good person is a requirement, but it is not enough. Nor is the birth to a king. You are allowed to learn because of who you are. Birth rights are taken into account only by foolish priests and have no place in true education."

"Then what is it? How is it that I can learn and he cannot?"

"Remember the wheel Aletheos, remember the circular rhythm of evolution," she said and paused for a moment. "Humanity as a whole has its position in that circle. But each person, each individualised spirit, stands somewhere in that circle according to the merits produced by him in the flesh. Birth rights play no role for us because the position in the circle is constructed through many lifetimes, not the present one alone. You are allowed to learn as much because you have earned it through many lifetimes of hard labour. Each of us has. Careful, for this is no judgment to our brothers on the path. It is merely a law of nature, of the universe. We ourselves are responsible for our own pilgrimage, the product of the law of merit."

I sighed. "Can he ever learn?" I asked.

"Of course, he can learn. He will learn; whether he does it in this lifetime or a next one, it doesn't matter. The path is the same for everyone, and we shall all return to where we came from, which is Spirit and Fire. Kind as he is and loyal and trustworthy, he allowed the darkness to break his faith. His power of discernment has not matured in him yet. He alone hinders his development. But believe me when I say that he is mountains ahead of those who have not learned the value of kindness and, in their suffering, cause more pain than they can bear. Life has a way of bringing us back to our path, and he who has not learned the value of kindness has, sadly, not yet suffered enough."

"Why can't he not be with us even for this? It is only pronunciation."

"Aletheos, listen to me. Learning the value of words is not a mere way of communication. He is already learning that. Breathing out the words in a correct manner is a sacred science that causes effects. Sound makes light out of space; it shapes and informs it of its properties; it is creative. And it shall not pass to the uninitiated."

She never left room for negotiation.

"Is that a criterion for all of our sensory abilities?"

I thought of his inability to perceive our energy exchange.

"The ability to get impressions from other realms and create one's reality is in the nature of all men. The ability to be conscious of them and in all awareness, act upon and work through one's mechanisms, must be earned. Each aspirant must purify his lower aspects, his physical, emotional and mental natures. That way, the higher faculties develop naturally with no violent consequences on the person. I have met at least one aspirant whose impatience to proceed, impure, brought about his annihilation. Only with conscious transmutative work can one gain access to higher aspects of himself and be received through the initiations to accept the knowledge."

"Are names the same?" I asked, with my eyes steady on her lips.

She smiled and relaxed her tone. She knew she had already crossed the bridge.

"Names are words as well. They, too, are used carrying meaning and properties. What are words, if not names of thoughts, feelings, processes, whatever the case might be? From a feeling to a god, knowing its true name allows you a connection with it so intimate and transparent that facilitates an inner cooperation beyond all external influences."

I nodded and turned to the scrolls. She took a sip of her tea and proceeded with today's lesson.

GREEN LEAVES

I n the few moon cycles we had been in Areteia, Innok befriended almost everyone, greeting them on our way through town and exchanging pleasantries in
their language. Today, he also wanted to pass by the house of some of his friends
before going to our waterfall. He had promised to help with something, and I could
not make him break his promise, however much I wanted to.

The family welcomed us with milk, which I accepted only out of courtesy, and
took us out into the jungle to reach a small opening where they kept their elephants.

"What did you offer to do?" I asked Innok in our language.

He laughed and looked away. He removed his shirt and helped clean the small
shelter of the animals. *Oh, Innok, not today.* I forced a smile on my face for the sake
of the locals and all they have been offering us. But my arms and legs felt weak even
at the idea of helping. So, I resorted to petting the beautiful giants.

When he was done, we were again cheerfully greeted, and we moved on through
the usual route. The sound of the waterfall under the trees quietened my thoughts.

Innok grabbed the wooden sword from behind the rocks and threw one to me,
cutting through my absent-mindedness and grounding me to the present. I caught
it mid-air as he formed his stance. With a sigh, I did the same. His assault knocked
my sword off my hand. And again. And again.

"What's wrong with you today?" he said. "Pick it up. Stand your ground!"

I did. He came at me again. I pushed forward to hit him first, but he lowered his
body, and I tripped over his feet.

"What's bothering you?" he asked, helping me up.

I left the sword on the ground and walked towards the waterfall.

"Where did grandmother take you? You haven't said much since yesterday."

The trees below the waterfall were loud with cicadas. Green and blue birds flew
above them.

"Aletheos?"

"I went to the infirmary with her."

He nodded. "What did you see?"

"Pain, Innok."

I shook my head.

"But it's good that you are there, is it not? You help people."

"She does. I observed."

"Observed what?"

"The inner structures and processes."

I didn't assume he would know how to respond.

"Was it bad?" he finally exhaled in a concerned voice.

"Some of it. Very."

"But she can help, right? If she could create Udenas, she can surely heal a patient."

"Not soon enough," I said, abandoning my attempt to withhold the wave of sadness in my chest.

"Do you not want to talk about it?"

"It's just that... with all that power... I wish there were more that could be done."

I talked of matters beyond his knowledge. Still, he listened.

"They nurse the bodies of the ill," I said. "And those who deal with inner matters are looking into the true causes of their illnesses. It's just that... Neither she nor anyone can force healing on another. One must become conscious of the inner factors that led to the weakening of the body. And change them. But oftentimes, the damage of the physical body is so much that it cannot be reversed before it's too late."

He contemplated what I said.

"What about the other times?" he said.

I smiled. I didn't expect him, with all his lack of knowledge, to manage such a change of my heart. The fog in my mind was slowly washing away by the waterfall.

"You are right," I admitted.

"What about the other times?" he repeated.

"While their bodies are attended to, the causes of their suffering are found and discussed with them. And they are guided to become conscious of a way to change their behaviour or work through the emotional or mental burden that poisoned the body. Throughout the process, the inner bodies are attended to as well."

"And they become well?"

"They get better. If they make the changes permanent, their healing is solidified. Many times, though, the ailment returns because people are so much accustomed to their ways, to the ways their world makes sense to them, that they take refuge in them as soon as they forget the distress they had caused."

He stood up and walked towards the waterfall. He stood there, looking in the distance.

"Do you think that is what happened to my family as well?" he asked. "They couldn't change their ways?"

I went to him.

"I don't know. But it seems that many of our land's priests have also lost their way and attend to the physical body alone, if even; offering what merely resembles a healing ritual. Your family did not receive proper guidance nor assistance."

He nodded, apparently troubled, maybe saddened.

I was looking beyond the waterfall when Innok called my name. With my gaze still fondling the treetops below, I waited for him to continue. He didn't. He only whispered my name again. I turned to his unblinking eyes, pointing at the path behind us. From it, a beast walked towards us, a gorgeous beast of a tiger with bright orange and black stripes. We were already locked in her eyes.

"I don't have my blade," he said, trying to remain still.

His shaking voice sent a rush of heat around my body, disintegrating my admiration for the animal. The wooden swords were already behind her. I took a breath, trying to calm myself while she headed for Innok, slowly examining him. She smelled him and raised her paw.

"No," I shouted, extending my arm.

Hers froze in the air for two moments, and, with a swift twist of her body, she jumped towards me. Her head now stood enormous in front of mine, with fear rising from the base of my spine. I looked into her eyes, calculating my moves.

From behind her, I warm sensation filled the air. A glowing, winged white horse seemed to elongate the moment, with a fine white horn glimmering over its dark eyes. It only nodded as its calming temperament sank within me, and the moment resumed with its disappearance.

An elemental? The tiger's eyes still captured mine. I didn't have time to ponder the horse's nature, only focused on maintaining its aura, the sense of safety it bore, and let my whole body calm down, relaxing the tension off my muscles, never breaking eye contact with the tiger.

Innok reached the practice sword and came from behind the feline. I shook my finger at him, hoping he would see it.

"Don't," I whispered in a flat voice. "Just back away."

I gently shook my head at the tiger. She burst out with a roar that blasted drops out of her mouth and onto my face. With her warm breath on my nose, she stretched her neck and fondled my face. Her thick hair scraped my skin, but I would not disrupt her acceptance. Her whiskers brushed against my nose when she withdrew and vanished back into the jungle.

Innok shook pale. I got to him and touched his back until both our heartbeats were back to normal and my tension burst into laughter. He was vigilant the whole way back, now darkened by night. I looked around for the winged, horned horse. But it was an elemental that caught my eye, shining blue light from amidst the trees. It looked like a miniscule monkey. And, with a nod, it assured me the tiger was gone.

"It's all right," I kept affirming. "She is safe. Let's just go home."

Outside the elephant's shelter, their keeper waited with a bow at hand. His wife rushed from behind him, grabbing Innok's hand and bringing us to her husband. They told us that a tiger was found in the jungle and they feared for the animals.

"Can you help?" Innok asked me.

"The feline will maintain the sense of safety if no one threatens her," I said. "Don't worry," I told the couple in their language. "She will not harm them."

I turned within. That sense of safety we had shared in our momentary connection still tingled in my guts. I let it grow, fed it with my attention until it was substantiated, let it out of my hands as force, and walked around the shelter, drawing a circle with that energy of safety.

When I returned, Innok was tying his blade around his waist. He must have left it here when he took his clothes off to assist.

"Thank you for all that you offer to us," I said to the keepers. "The animals are safe."

They thanked us with the usual bow. I returned their gesture, and headed to our house. After dinner, we spent some time the three of us. Innok told Chaa what had happened, and she cheered at my actions.

When our faculties slowed down, I went to my room and closed the door behind me. Feeling lighter, I uncovered the sandflower from my bag and laid down, holding it to my chest. Mere moments later, I was with my beloved. When her essence revealed itself, I drifted into sleep.

DEMIURGE

I visited the infirmary with Chaa. It had become part of my training. But since the day I talked to Innok, I was careful to remind myself of all the 'other times' we had talked about; when it was not too late for the body, when people allowed for their healing in all levels and consciously bettered their lives. This made my observations more meaningful and the pain I felt more bearable.

When we left around midday, Chaa told me we would have no lesson nor excursions in the jungle today. We were to wash ourselves and wear some nice clothes. There was going to be a performance.

We arrived at the open theatre late in the afternoon. Chohanatma led the way through the town, which became more crowded as we got closer. Innok talked to some of his friends. I only greeted them while we waited to enter among the chatting locals.

The sky was still deepening its indigo as we joined the other spectators on the seven-levelled seating area surrounding the big square stage. When the night was fully upon us, the few lit torches around were all extinguished, and with them, so were all the voices. Chaa had explained that the performance was regarded more like a ceremony than a staged drama, and it showed in the venerating silence that now filled the air.

All was dark. From the central stage sounded the actors' breathing, coordinated into one loud rhythm. We still saw nothing. A drum broke the mesmerising breathing echoes, then another and another. On the seventh hit of the drum, a faint light appeared from behind the actors lying on the ground in dark clothes, moving their bodies like calm waves.

Then, at the hit of the drum, a torch was lit at the centre of the stage, probably by an actor whose clothes hid him, and its fire moved like a ray of light down on the dark sea of men. The light disappeared, and the actors trembled, exposing golden parts of their clothes.

A golden-winged serpent emerged from the centre and danced in a winding movement around the circle of laying men. The circle itself now broke into seven smaller groups of irregular shapes.

The winged dragon danced around the stage three times before separating into four entities. One kept the face of the serpent while the others bore masks of animals; a bull, a lion, and an eagle. Each of them lit a torch and slowly positioned themselves at the four cardinal points.

With another hit of the drum, the seven groups stood up and showed their masks proudly. Each one was distinct in colour, size, and resemblance; some beautiful, other scary, some similar to animals and others to humans, some a combination of the two. They danced around, coming together in groups, then breaking away to form others until they settled into seven spheres. The four animals overlooked them all from their corners, unmoved with their torches.

I watched carefully each step, each movement, all the while letting my mind search for the cosmic correspondences through the symbolism.

I exited the theatre with the quiet crowd, having lost my friends. Chaa appeared first, escorted by Chohanatma. Innok appeared soon behind, and we all followed the people's procession.

The streets were filled with locals who slowly broke the spell of silence. The path we took did not lead to our house. I didn't mind. I exchanged remarks with Innok about the gracefulness and complexity of the dramaturgy until we reached a great garden. Torches were lit, and tables prepared. It was another feast.

The place was livening up with laughter and music and people dancing with the light of fire. Chaa gave me a warm smile before resuming her talk with Chohanatma behind me. And Innok grabbed my hand, dragging me to the dancing company.

Some moon cycles after our welcoming feast, we now danced, not merely with locals of a new land but with friends, to rhythms I had grown accustomed to. Areteia was becoming a home.

DRY SAND

The following morning came sooner than I would have wished. The cheerful music still echoed in my chest. But my head was dry, as was my mouth. I turned in my bed, hoping to fall back asleep. I couldn't.

I got up and headed to the common room, where Chaa was already chatting with Chohanatma. I mumbled good morning as I filled my cup with warm, spicy tea.

"We are leaving in the afternoon," she said.

My stomach clenched, and a burning sensation rushed through my feet. "We are not staying here?"

"You will come live with me," said Chohanatma, "at the House of Lotus."

"It is very close," Chaa added.

"We are fine here! If we are leaving, it's back home we should be heading!"

"We will advance your training at the sanctuary," she said, giving an end to my objections.

My studies came first. I had to agree. She knew it.

"Does Innok know?" I asked.

"Innok will stay here," Chaa said.

"What? No!"

"The sanctuary is only for aspirants. Aletheos..."

"No!" I interrupted her. "We are not leaving him behind!"

"It's all right, Aletheos," Innok said from his bedroom door. "We have already agreed on it. I will stay here."

I looked at Chaa. "No. Why?"

"The sanctuary is very close," she said.

"Aletheos, I have been offered to live here by myself," Innok continued. "I never had a house of my own. And I will keep working with the community. I made friends here. And you will visit me often."

I sighed. I knew we did not have any alternatives.

"Are you sure?"

"Yes, I will be fine here."

I could not be certain he was saying the truth behind his kind eyes.

"Okay. But I will be coming here as often as I want," I said to Chaa to settle the arrangement.

By afternoon, we were ready to depart. Chaa mounted with Chohanatma while I took one of our horses, leaving the second to Innok. He stood by the door of his home and gave us a small bow.

"I will ride back soon," I assured him.

The sun was almost hidden. We rode beyond the jungle into a desert that appeared as of nowhere. I had never laid eyes on it during our afternoon walks. The House of Lotus was indeed close to town, a little further in the sandy terrain. It was four or five floors high, built on a rock. Only a few trees patched the dry ground; no ponds or lotuses anywhere.

Its interior was as simple as its exterior; walls of mudbricks and stone with no furniture other than the necessary ones. My room overlooked the jungle. Above it, in the distance, showed the top of the town's temple. And, behind it, gigantic as ever, stood the mountains.

I sat on the bed and looked at my half-open bag on the floor. I leaned for the sandflower and brought it up to my eyes, marvelling at the transparency of its petals catching the light. *My dear Idhi.* I intended to revisit my connection with her. But my mind ached, and my heart had all the joy from the previous night ridden away in the desert. With a sigh, I covered the sandflower, placed it in the bag, and hid it below the bed before throwing myself on the pillow, hurriedly to escape my body into sleep.

The Feet of the Mount

C haa led our way deep beneath the sanctuary. The narrow spiralling staircase was finally coming to a dark end. I took the last step into a long corridor that was dark no more, as if the torches had responded to our arrival and illuminated our way.

On the sides of the smooth stone floor, figures were carved in the rough natural rock. I tried to distinguish what they were and even stopped for a moment to touch one.

"Come," Chaa said, echoing in the hall.

At the end of the corridor, I could see an opening full of light. From within it came a man, meeting us halfway. He placed himself firmly still in front of us, holding some scrolls and some metallic instruments I did not recognise.

"Chaa," he said with a deep voice and a quick bow. "Chohanatma said you were back."

The old man spoke in the local tongue, dressed in simple white robes with hair and beard hanging well below his chest.

"Rajvidya," she named him. "How are you, old friend?"

"What are you doing back in the caves, child?" he responded.

"You should go out in the light more often, Rajvidya."

"I have a sacred duty here, child."

"So do I," she said and attempted to move onwards.

"I can let you proceed. But not the boy."

It took a moment to translate his words in my head.

"Rajvidya!" Chaa said.

"The boy is tainted, Chaa. How dare you!"

I opened my mouth to defend myself but had no words. Chaa was about to speak, but the old man stopped her.

"How dare you, Chaa, bring a killer amongst us! The child is tainted with darkness! No such man shall be allowed to the sacred knowledge. Leave. Immediately."

He pointed at the way back. I turned, but before I managed a step, my spine was shocked straight, vibrating electric. The crown of my head heavied. And I felt it opening; the weight dispersed, and so did any sensations. Instead, a blinding light rushed through me. My consciousness was displaced, or rather, its power was diminished. The light changed my appearance.

I was aware of what was taking place but unable to take back authority. I saw myself turning back to Chaa and the old man. I radiated with white light. And I felt taller, my body covered with a blue-white robe that was the light, beaming with violet symbols. And I spoke in his language, in an unmovable voice that made the rocks around us tremble.

"You believe me unworthy?"

He looked at whom used to be myself. His eyes were open wide. The scrolls and instruments dropped from his hands. And he was about to kneel.

"Stand up. You will allow passage," I said.

Chaa bowed. Even she, who seemed to know everything, was now astounded. I felt myself bowing back to her.

"Thank you," I said as our eyes met.

The vibrating sensation of the radiating light began to fade within, but only little by little. My consciousness gradually regained its position, still shaking with the light absorbed in my body.

The old man stepped aside. He kept his eyes on me as we passed by him, but uttered not a word. Myself, still numb, followed Chaa, with mind still scattered, unable to make sense of it all, and shivering with the loss of control.

She checked back at me every few steps. When I regained full authority in my body, I asked her, even if only with my eyes.

"I told you, dear brother, you have earned your place," she said.

We reached the end of the hall to a circular chamber with high ceilings. On the other side, two doors were open wide. To the left stood a statue of a man with a bull's head holding a hammer, and on the right, another statue with a bird's head held an axe.

Chaa took my hand and led us through the gate. A man stepped aside as we entered. He said nothing, only stared. The space inside extended many floors above and below, with balconies overseeing the entrance. Intricate carvings decorated its walls and columns, and innumerable scrolls rested neatly on rows upon rows of shelves.

"The library," she said, "our new teaching ground."

GREEN LEAVES

I found Chaa drinking her tea on the veranda of the common area, her resting space for the last moon cycle or so, ever since we came at the sanctuary.

"I will go into town," I said, covering my eyes from the sunlight.

"You should stay the night," she replied. "I will be going to the infirmary tomorrow. Meet you there."

I mounted my horse early in the afternoon, getting away from the dense scrolls of abstract symbols. Back in Areteia, Innok was attending the plants in his garden. Cheerful, he hugged me as soon as I stepped on the ground and led me inside.

"You are growing a beard now?" he said, teasing the short hair on my face.

I rubbed the back of my head. I hadn't shaved for a couple of days. Himself kept his appearance as always; clean, shaved face, short hair, and the Starani belt and sword around his waist. He was a keen reminder of life in the palace, our home.

He showed me how he kept the place in order, as he did the last time I visited, and insisted on preparing tea as I tried to ignore the image of Idhi in my mind and the ache in my chest.

"How have you been?" he asked.

"I am good," I said. "Mostly studying."

"How about Chaa?"

"She is okay. Working at the infirmary. When she is at the sanctuary, she is either studying or fighting with Chohanatma." I changed the subject before he asked for more. "How about you?"

"I am well here," he said. "Working with some friends. They are coming over tonight!"

I had hoped to visit our usual spot in the jungle, but he was too excited about a night with friends. Two girls and two boys arrived later in the afternoon, and we prepared dinner earlier than usual, boiling vegetables into soup.

Stories and laughter soon filled the house, and I could but withdraw in my thoughts. I sat there, enjoying myself, in a city moon cycles away from home, while father tried to keep the darkness from taking roots in the kingdom. And Idhi... *Will I be able to bring this peacefulness back to you?*

I shook my head, together with the sense of shame away, and forced a smile towards Innok's friends. It wasn't too late before our guests had to return to their parents, lest they were seen with people of the opposite sex.

"I don't get it," I told Innok when we remained alone.

"It's just their customs," he said, already busy with tidying up the house.

I joined him. "I am glad you are having a good time here. You know I did not want to leave you behind."

"I am not left behind, Aletheos. I knew there would come a time I would be by myself."

"What do you mean?"

"She told me; as soon as we arrived. And she gave me the choice of staying here, knowing that you would move on, or go back to the palace. She even said that if I went back, she would arrange for me a new place to stay and money to build a life of my own."

"And you chose to stay?"

"I chose to stay. My duty lies with you. I may be useful here."

Why would you sacrifice all that? "I am glad you are here," I said. "As long as it remains your choice."

He nodded.

Not long later, we said our goodnights. I still had my bedroom there.

STREAMS

The infirmary had many rooms of different sizes, and patients lay even in the yard, all separated according to the needs of their physical and subtle bodies.

"Today, I want you to follow the structures into the patient and separate the physical from the emotional and mental aspects of the illness," Chaa said. "Try to translate the impressions you get into words or images to understand the underlying causes. Use the main disks of force aligned with the spine as a point of reference."

I had found certain scrolls back in the library that enumerated the different centres or streams of force within man and distinguished them according to their functions.

"Okay," I said, already preparing my state of mind to connect with that of others.

"Usually, we do this when we carry out the healing, but I want you to place yourself within an egg of beige light and violet energy. This will protect your subtle bodies from attaching to themselves energies and issues you find in the patient."

I closed my eyes and did as told. She approved, and led the way into the room.

"Work in silence," she whispered. "We shall discuss your findings later."

I stayed a few steps behind as she addressed the patient, the only one in there; a pale woman, weak and cold. I could not assume her age. Her muscles had atrophied, and shadows of her bones showed below her skin, full of wounds that smelled festered. Despite the warmth of the room, her legs were covered with blankets. She had just released her excrements, and an attendant came to her. As soon as the nurse touched her, she screamed in pain. I stepped back. Her outburst tightened my chest with sadness. I tried to breathe, despite the smell, back to a normal heartbeat.

I closed my eyes and focused within. I expanded my consciousness beyond my body and connected with that of the ill woman. It took a few moments to make sense of what I found. Her body felt dry and utterly disconnected from her consciousness, which was hidden somewhere deeper. Instead, she experienced her body, her life, only through instinct. The energy that aligned with her nervous system was misplaced; she no longer had awareness or control of her lower body. The layers of colour that should be around her were but faint and dirty greens and browns. Her lungs were barely working and full of fungal black dots. Her head was covered in shadows.

I tried to keep myself composed as her subtle bodies yelled her painful story. After a few short breaths, I took her centres of force one by one to locate the causes of suffering. A sense of fear caused by abandonment screamed in desperation. She had no sense of safety nor stability; her needs were never met. Her mother was cruel to her. Through the violence, her feelings never became conscious.

She had no sense of self and, therefore, no power; she was sold, by her mother nevertheless. She was treated like an object, dried out for the satisfaction of others. She was grieving; for herself, her life, for all the love she had never experienced. Her light was sealed away, her consciousness had withdrawn long ago.

I retrieved my consciousness and saw her whole again. *I am so sorry.*

"I am sorry too," she answered in my mind.

Above her body stood an aspect of her consciousness. She had the form of a woman unaffected by the physical afflictions, albeit her light was, too, burning low and faint.

"Are you in there?" I pointed at her body.

"An aspect of me still holds me prisoner," she replied.

"Can you escape? Can you try to break through?"

"I am too tired. And my body is weak."

"That's not true," I said. "I heard your voice before. Loud as a drum!"

She smiled, exhausted. "I am so sorry I tire all these people here."

"No, no! Everyone here wants you to get better! They are here for you."

Chaa looked at me from across the room. She did not say anything. I turned back to the woman. She went closer to her own body; touched it tenderly.

"I think I should just go," she said.

I tried to understand what she meant, but in a split of a moment, she disappeared, and her body shook uncontrollably.

"No, no!" I tried to reach her wherever she was.

I opened my eyes in the flesh. The nurse was already upon her while Chaa stood back in sadness. The woman stopped shaking. Her arms locked bent in the air before slowly dropping. Her last breath was slow and deep as if the air had escaped from a shelter buried deep within.

Chaa touched my shoulder and led me outside while I kept my eyes on the body. She took me to the garden and had me sit below a tree. She remained silent while my thoughts crashed on each other, banging in my mind, drowning me. With a gasp against the flood of emotions, I looked at her through wet eyes.

"Did I do that? Because of what I told her?" I asked with a broken voice.

"No, my sweet prince," she said in a low voice that carried all her love. "She finally felt safe; safe to let go of her suffering."

Her words were comforting to my ears but not to my heart.

"Is there anything else we can do?"

"There is," she said.

She led me to the land of mud, the realm that corresponded to the woman's consciousness. We traced her in the misery plane she had placed herself. She was looking away, her hands gathered close to her body.

"Hey, it's me," I said.

She walked around me, still looking away.

"It's okay," I said. "Do you remember me? We talked before."

She raised her head and turned her ear to me, staying still. Next to me, Chaa raised her hands, dispersing the murky clouds in the brown sky for a pillar of light to pass through, reaching us from the higher realms. Orbs of light emerged from it, swirling around us.

The woman turned to me. "It's okay?" she asked.

I nodded. With a deep breath, she closed her eyes, and let go. She collapsed, but before reaching the ground, the orbs burst with light, enfolding her, now floating in the air. From the pillar came beings of light.

"They are responsible for assisting in passing," Chaa said.

They took her and disappeared together in the sky, rising to the higher planes.

"Shall we follow?" I asked.

"No. She will be shielded from outer interventions now. She has all the help she can get."

We returned to the flesh. Before I opened my eyes, Chaa's warm embrace was upon me. Above us, the sunlight glimmered through the trees. She never let go of my hand as I dragged myself to Innok's house. His smile disappeared when he saw me. He brought me inside and helped me bathe in cold water.

M y dreams were coloured with death, my brother and the woman from the infirmary. It was early in the afternoon when I opened my eyes. The bed was comfortably warm on my body. Until voices found their way to my ears.

"Did you know she was going to die?" Innok asked.

"I knew she was weak, but no, I was not expecting Aletheos to witness that today."

"Should he be coming with you? Maybe you shouldn't have him deal with the heavily ill. It took days for him to feel better after you took him there the first time. And now this?"

"Innok," she stopped him. "Aletheos needs to learn the art of healing. In the process, he will understand that death is merely a change of state."

"He cares too much."

"Exactly. That is what will make him a great healer and a great ruler someday. It's his duty. And because he cares so much, it will be good for him to fully understand the process of healing and that of death. He can help many, affect even more."

They both remained silent for a while.

"What is it?" Innok then asked.

"Innok," she said with a sigh, "I will need to advance his training faster than I would." She paused. "Back at Erevos... The dark priests are gaining ground. Aletheos's future won't be easy. It is paved with darkness and death. Without proper understanding, his sorrow will swallow him."

I took a deep breath and stood up. I pulled the half-opened door.

"What can I do?" Innok asked before he saw me.

"I am fine," I said.

I joined them. None spoke. I turned to Chaa. And described what I had seen before the patient died. I discussed it all in detail with her, who further explained the impressions I got, expanding on every aspect as we went through them. Innok prepared our meal. We both stayed the night and returned to the sanctuary the following day.

ARCHETYPES

I had been in the library since early in the morning and, in the absence of natural light, lost track of time. I focused on some scrolls describing the descent of men into matter and the forms their monad went through, from ethereal being to androgynous entities until they reached the separation of the sexes and the human form we now had. Each form had their own era, separated in geological epochs, almost completely separated from each other. Only a few of each preceding phase survived and passed the sacred teachings to the new eras.

"What are you reading about?" Chaa asked.

I hadn't heard her coming.

"About..." I cleared my throat; I hadn't talked for a while. "...about the last in our line of ancestors and the monument they built to commemorate our lineage."

She smiled. "I read about that for a long time. Your father, Chohanatma, and I searched this library for every scroll we could find that could give us any hints of its location."

"The description reminds me of the site we visited near the camp."

"Yes. Chohanatma hopes that we have finally found it."

"Have they unearthed more? Are we going?"

"Maybe. When the time comes."

"Are these the same people that formed the cave back at the kingdom," I asked, "below the Black Temple?"

She smiled and nodded as she sat next to me.

"Any news from home?" I asked. "Are they okay?"

"Have trust in your father, Aletheos. He has been doing this since long before you were born. Back then..." She sighed, looking at the empty halls of the library. "This place used to be alive with aspirants. Look at it now. Only a handful of old, bitter initiates that drag themselves around."

"At least we serve the most high!" Old Rajvidya walked from behind us with scrolls at hand. "We are not murderers." He glanced at me and then away. "Nor self-serving beasts like your friends."

"Altazadeh is long-gone, Rajvidya," Chaa responded.

"Is he?" he said as he walked away.

"Who's Altazadeh?" I asked.

"An old friend." She shook her head at Rajvidya. "How about of symbols?" she asked. "Have you deconstructed the ways of symbolism?"

"I have read a lot," I answered, reserved.

"Okay." She leaned back. "What do you make of Water and Fire?"

I took some time to gather my thoughts and put them in order. She only nodded as I gave my answers.

"And what of the Serpent?" she asked. "The serpent is in some aspect the circle or the wheel. It is lightning that infuses life with electric vitality. In that level, it is similar to the Fire. It stretches from the boundless Absolute down to physical matter and becomes the path for consciousnesses to descend and ascend. In its higher aspects, it is Divine Wisdom, the Blazing Winged Dragon. In its lower aspects, it is the slithering serpent that is suffering, caused by ignorance and pain."

"And how do you reconcile its two aspects?"

"Since we, men, have hidden our true nature from ourselves and came in the worlds of existence to slither on the ground, unconscious of our connection to the Absolute, suffering and pain are all that we know of. But through the suffering and separation, we shall learn our true self and emerge again into our spiritual nature, thus becoming the Flying Dragon."

"Very good, my dear. Does this symbol remind you of another, from back at the kingdom?"

I searched my brain.

"It's the crocodile!" I exclaimed.

"Indeed. The two are meant to signify the same. Both become the Monad of man that can live and connect the worlds of water and fire."

"My father once told me that the crocodile is my guide and guardian."

She nodded. "Its nature, twofold as it may be, is upon you," she said. "Now, let's go above."

We left the library and climbed the stairs up to the veranda. It was early in the afternoon. The cicadas were still loud on the trees around us. We sat close to each other, and she drank her tea while mine was still hot on the table. Eager not to let a moment go to waste, I brought my hands close to each other, playing with energy, observing the magnetising force between them.

She took a sip from her cup and placed it down as a cicada flew towards me. I immediately raised my hands, and it stopped mid-air before falling to the ground. It wasn't hurt. By the time I went close, it flew away. Chaa laughed.

"This happened before," I said and returned to her, taking a sip of my tea.

"Your father sends his regards," she said.

My stomach stiffened and a crackle, whose source I could not place, caught my ears. I sighed. The sun reached me through rustling leaves as my chest sank with images; Father, Idhi, my hill, my mother's room. I swallowed through a dry throat.

"Are we going back in time?" I asked.

Hot drops wet my lap. I jumped up. It was my tea, dripping from cracks in the cup.

"Focus on the now, my dear," she said. "You are well on your path."

GREEN LEAVES

W e had returned from the infirmary around midday. Chaa and I did our prayers together and separated ways. I needed to rest.

I turned in my bed for some time. I had been helping people for some moon cycles now. I had learned about treating the physical body and incorporating the causes of misery into the treatments I was authorised to attempt. And the more I helped, the easier it became to understand the impressions I got from the subtle planes.

But today had been different. Early in the afternoon, I gave up on any attempt to sleep and headed for the common room. Voices caught my attention before entering. It was Chaa. And Chohanatma. They were arguing again.

I shook my head. As I walked away, a resident of the sanctuary crossed paths with me.

"Would you tell Chaa I will stay the night at Innok's?"

He nodded.

I arrived at Innok's place to shut doors and windows. I did knock to make sure, but there was no answer. His horse was around the house, so I assumed he was close. I sat in his garden, allowing my mind to set my thoughts free, if only to lose their grip on my consciousness. I watched them all scream in my head until they faded out. I don't know how long it took. When I opened my eyes, the sun made the flowers far more orange than when I sat down.

Innok was startled to find me there. He seemed tired, still sweaty, probably from helping around the city. He welcomed me with a cheer, but his face changed when he truly saw me. We went inside and opened all the windows; I needed the air.

He prepared some tea and washed himself.

"What's wrong?" he kept asking.

He wouldn't give me the time as Idhi used to; his concern overtook his patience.

"Let's walk," I said.

He nodded, and we soon moved through the jungle towards our usual spot above the waterfall. The birds creaked above, but I spared not a look. Nor did I open my eye for any elementals; only headed for the opening.

I let the crashing water calm my mind, and Innok could but wait. After a while, he came next to me on the rock.

"What happened?" he asked gently.

"I... I treated a patient today."

"Okay... you've been doing that for some time now. Was Chaa there?"

"She was. She guided me. It was something new."

"Did you talk after?"

"She was arguing with Chohanatma."

"Again?"

I nodded.

"You can come here whenever you want. You know that," he said.

"He was possessed, Innok!" I burst out with it.

"What?" He tilted his head and stiffened his brows.

"The patient I treated. He had the consciousness of another inhabiting his body."

He jumped up. "How does that even work? Where did his own go?"

"He was in there as well."

He uttered not a single word.

"He turned into a lunatic, Innok. His brain was taking impressions from two separate entities, and they hammered his mind into torture. There was a schism in his subtle bodies. I had to guide them both out and keep guard between two spines in his neck until his consciousness, alone, could return."

"And is he well now?"

"He was. But it will depend on his actions. A schism in the subtle bodies is usually facilitated by intoxication. That's what Chaa said. I don't know if he can refrain from poisoning himself again. And if he retains actions of bad consequences, he may reattract entities of malevolent nature to solidify his suffering."

Innok kept quiet for a while.

"I am very sorry you have to see all that pain," he finally said and brought his arm around my shoulders.

I turned back to the river, crashing below. The sound of the water filled the jungle.

"Innok... I am tired... I miss home."

He pressed his lips together and softly brought his forehead to mine, with his hand on my back.

"We will return," he said, "soon."

He moved his face away; his eyes locked in mine. My heart beat with longing. I stayed with his caring eyes and sweet features that reminded of home. He leaned and kissed my lips, a quick kiss that caught my breath. His face lingered close. He was about to turn away. With another heartbeat, I kissed him back.

The jungle was dark by the time we clothed ourselves and turned back. We spent the rest of the evening in calm interaction, with only the warmth of the candles around us. I didn't sleep alone that night.

THE MOUNT

C hohanatma rode first on the narrow path up the mountain, then Chaa, then
me. The sun was about to dive below the horizon, no longer protecting us
against the chill in the air. My tailbone hurt; we had been riding since before the
sun was up.

"A little while longer," Chaa said from up front.

"Easy," said Chohanatma, raising his arm and signalling us to halt.

A tiger blocked the path, unmoved, evaluating us. Her roar trembled in my chest.
But it was my horse's chest that I cared for, bringing my hand to calmly graze his
neck, still careful of the reins as I waited for instructions.

Chohanatma slowly moved his hand to the side, and, a heartbeat later, the tiger
walked out of the way. He marched on, and we followed. The big cat sat down, her
tongue wetting her whiskers as I rode by her.

Further among the trees, rocks had crumbled on each other, creating a den for
another tiger, laying down with four cubs sucking on her breasts. Chohanatma
nodded to the mother, who looked up for only a moment.

"There," said Chaa, pointing at a cabin on the next hill, our shelter for the night.

Chaa had explained that Chohanatma had commissioned several such houses,
manned only by one, to care for the pilgrims on their journey. Indeed, a man was
bringing logs of wood to the door as we arrived.

"This is Paradchi," said Chohanatma, embracing him.

"Hello, old friend," said Chaa as she walked into the house.

I gave him a smile and followed Chaa towards the fire inside. The two men joined
us soon thereafter.

"Is he the one Rajvidya talked about?" Paradchi asked Chohanatma.

"He is..."

I turned to him, but Chaa raised her hand, interrupting them. I sighed.

"Will you not ever tell me then?" I asked her.

"Tell you what?"

"Who was that who came over me and demanded entrance to the library!"

"The personality of a former lifetime," she said, as if she didn't know I wanted more.

"You already said that. Will you not..."

"No. As I told you countless times, coming in contact with former lifetimes is dangerous. You will find out by yourself when it's necessary."

I turned away.

"Chaa is right, you know," said Chohanatma in a sympathetic tone. "You may bring forth issues from a previous personality that do not fit your present. Even worse, the old might overtake you, mess with your brain with past actions and regrets. Distinguishing the two needs great restraint and maturity. Even I don't know all my former lifetimes; only those that are relevant, brought forth by spirit and circumstances to work through."

His words, still unsatisfying, were more settling than Chaa's.

"Fine," I finally responded.

T he following morning, we left our horses at the house and continued on foot; the path was too narrow for horses. By late in the afternoon, snow began to whiten the landscape, but most melted into small streams of water. Chohanatma and Chaa led the way to a cave, the designated shelter for the second night of the ascent.

In its centre, there was a small circle of intermingling sharp stones, shaping a cross where they met. I left my bag on the floor next to the entrance and, by the time I changed into dry clothes, Chohanatma had lit a fire on the stones. There were no branches, no dry leaves. He merely raised his hand and uttered a word that sparked a fire floating above the stones. The flames revealed the walls of the cave, all engraved with reliefs of entities and sigils.

We sat around the fire. Chaa unpacked some dried fruits and nuts and water. Beyond the cave, the sky had cleared with the stars shimmering in the indigo sea of space. After a while, Chohanatma walked outside.

"The Great Seven are upon us," he said to Chaa with a smile, as we joined him. She got closer to him and touched his hand.

"Aletheos, come," he said.

"Do you see those stars that shine through all the rest?"

He traced their formation with his finger. But I already knew them well; my mother's favourites.

"They are the Crown of the Cosmos," he said. "Within them lay the spirits of the Builders of our universe."

I marvelled at the bright orbs.

"You may know them as the Thigh constellation," Chaa added, "named to signify that through them, the world is born. Or the Plough, for with it, the land of matter is fertilised."

The builders of the world. "Did they emerge from the Absolute as well?" I asked.

"Yes," Chaa answered. "From that plane, or state, within which, the Absolute Be-ness is but Itself, the Parentless Parent, always moving but always unchangeable, where the All is One, endless, boundless, where separation cannot be."

I looked at the night beyond the stars, thinking of such a place, or state, where my consciousness would merge with the worlds and the all.

"When the Law commands," she said, "the all emanates from that blissful one-ness to which they shall return upon the end of each great cycle of existence."

Even the idea of such a state calmed my face.

"First comes Space, the Great Mother of the Universe," she continued, "the dark sea of abstract matter, latent with the potential to exist."

"Space and matter are one," I said. "And the Male Principle?"

It was Chohanatma who answered. "Remember that the Female and Male Principles are but aspects of the Absolute. And with the existence of one, the other follows.

"Imagine a circle horizontally cut in half," Chaa said. "You see, while drawing a line to distinguish the bottom half, you unavoidably create the upper half as well."

I let that take its place in my brain.

"And when these two aspects come in contact," she continued, "when male Spirit impregnates female Space, their Son, the thunderous Dragon, being in the image of the Absolute, continues to create in the same manner, and Cosmogenesis commences."

I brought forth all my noetic capacity and all I have studied so far, so eloquently summarised in a few moments under the stars. And I could feel my mind shaping my brain, changing what structures it should to fully comprehend this.

"With every subsequent contact of the two principles, down through the worlds, man, the dragon the youngest, is born. And man, in the likeness of his parent, carries those potencies within him, and carries them out, in analogous measure, within his reality."

"Is this the Truth?"

"It is; the uttermost part of the truth that we as men can ever know," she said.

I found comfort in knowing that. Now it was up to me to understand it. In silence, we remained looking at the seven stars.

"Let the rays of the light work their way into your consciousness," Chaa said. "You are here."

We were up with the waking of the sun. Chohanatma took three wooden staffs from the cave, one for each of us, intricately carved with spiralling snakes.

"The road ahead is steep," he said.

We travelled through a clear but cold blue sky. Small bushes and trees aligned with our path, covered in snow. We took many breaks on our way, mostly for my benefit it seemed; I needed more effort to breathe as we got higher and higher.

We headed up another slope, reaching an opening. Pine trees filled the plateau with sparks of light bursting in between them. Maybe the altitude and exhaustion messed with my sight. I needed another break. I shut my eyes for a few moments but it didn't help. The lights were now almost solid, shaping sigils in the air around us.

"The light is impenetrable to the uninitiated," Chaa said.

With her confirmation of their existence, I stopped resisting.

"I have seen these kinds of symbols before," I told her. "They are similar to those engraved on the library doors."

She nodded. "The sigils protect the library from psychic attacks."

"And what do they protect here?"

I leaned on a tree to catch my breath, never receiving an answer. A warm sensation filled the air, calming my chest with safety. *Familiar.* I let the sensation guide my eyes to its source. And there it was. Across from me, through the dense greenery and snow, shone the white winged horse, observing us, its horn catching the sunlight.

"Do you see it?" I asked my companions.

They both turned towards the trees, and then at me with vacant looks.

"The winged horse," I explained.

The looked at each other with a smile.

"No," said Chaa, "but do pass our regards, together with our gratitude."

The horse nodded, staring with dark eyes. Its light now fading, it became one with the shimmering sigils in the air. And we walked again.

"Have you seen it before?" I asked.

"Only once," said Chohanatma, "back when your father and Chaa were still here with me. There was an incident back then. And the horse appeared to us, helped us with the purity of its light to make this place safe again. And accessible."

Chohanatma suddenly stopped and raised his arm.

"Connect to the realms of Fire," Chaa commanded me.

I took my consciousness to my heart, up the spine to the crown of my head. Above it, as always, shone the golden pillar of light, and through it, I connected to the appropriate realm. I opened my eyes in the flesh, as did the others, maintaining connection with the higher aspects.

I followed Chaa and Chohanatma through the trees that now extruded light from within them; every leaf on every tree, every stone on the ground now radiated white light. We walked until the light engulfed us in a bliss of milky white mist.

Slowly, the light dissipated into new shapes and forms. When the day cleared, we stood on a great white square against the blue of the sky. At the centre of this marble stage stood a stone fountain, overflowing into four streams that floated from it like a cross.

One of the streams ran by us towards the plateau we came from. But there was no plateau behind us anymore. No trees, no rocks. The water just poured down from the edge of the square.

I followed the stream to the edge. And my tailbone tingled hot; the trees and mountains were far below us! The square stage floated in the middle of the sky, the rivers splashing in the air into miniscule droplets long before reaching the ground.

I dropped in all four to regain balance against the sight. Mere moments later, Chaa touched my shoulder, dispersing the dizziness in my mind and grounding me in my body, before leading me back towards the centre.

Small structures around the stage faded into sight; each made of four red pillars with a pyramid roof above them. Two men sat with legs crossed in such structures. Another walked to the other side.

What is this place? My thought was heard without voicing it. Chaa turned to me. She didn't open her mouth. But her voice was clear.

"Be aware in remaining silent," she said, tapping on my forehead.

With every step towards the fountain, I became more attuned to the space around me. Chaa dipped her hand in it. A sense of knowingness rose from within. She brought water to her mouth. And extended her hand for me to drink from; crystal clear water that was cool to my lips and soothing within me.

My questions were replaced with a sense of certainty. I needed no further instructions. Each of us walked to one of the structures. I took my place between the four columns, crossed my legs, and rested my palms on my thighs, facing upwards.

With closed eyes, I became one with the golden pillar of light, the connection between all aspects of me. I was one with all of them. My sense of self expanded, and the more it did, the more it faded.

The all that I was, the light that I was, now became darkness. I became space, nothingness. Time was not. I and the all was not. Then a heartbeat gave the signal. Currents of white electric fire spiralling around me emerged like dragons, circling my legs and torso and hands. Clouds of cosmic matter and milky rivers of starry dust were born within me. The centre of consciousness focused in the head. I was nothingness, and I was the all, the serpent and the dragon, and I was conscious only of it, and of it all.

The dragons flew within me and disappeared into a miniscule golden sphere in the head. From it, dropped a single ray of electric fire through all dimensions of space, to fall amidst the threefold flame in my heart and blossom outwards into a sphere of a thousand golden petals. And from it, all the wanderers thrust into existence. The sun was born; the earth was born.

A multifaceted diamond appeared above my brows, and from it emerged two rays of violet light that encircled my head, crossing at the back. I opened my eyes in the flesh.

In front of me shined a circle of light in between two wings, with a dot at its centre. It faded as we all emerged from our small temples at the same time. We walked towards each other and bowed. The pillars of light above our heads touched each other, and, in that moment, I knew all of Chaa and all of Chohanatma; and they of me.

When we went through the milky light again, out to the mountain we came from, thunders ripped space in a cloudless sky. My mind was in pieces. Some focused on our descent, others were still scattered in the dimensions of space. We exchanged words only after the second day, and by the time we were back in town, I had almost recomposed myself. We didn't stop; it was too crowded. The energies of people swayed me dizzy. We rode back to the sanctuary and sheltered ourselves in solitude.

C haa had arranged for food to be left at my door. I couldn't go outside. The voices, thoughts, and feelings of those around me were too loud, making my heart boil in my chest. My stomach got irritated if I wasn't slow with food. And when I wasn't dizzy, I felt the substance of whatever object I focused on, solid in my mind, as if my thoughts and the object were made of the same material, occupying the same space.

On the third day, I attempted to go outside again. As soon as I left my room, one of the residents passed by the other side of the hall. His loud green energy flooded the corridor, and I got nauseated. I rushed back to my room and dropped onto my bed.

His turbulence still reached me. I looked back at the door. I hadn't closed it fully. Before I pushed myself up, the door slammed closed.

T he window was open. I still hadn't been outside, and I needed the fresh air. With legs crossed on the floor, I practiced imposing my will on objects. In front of me floated a scroll at the height of my eyes.

It's done, it's done!

The scroll shook and dropped to the floor. I groaned. It was so easy for my emotions to sway my mental forces and will.

Chaa knocked on my door. She was the only one that I could bear. The door opened, scratching the ground with a broken plate, one of the objects I had practiced on.

Chaa smiled. She inspected me for a few moments.

"Tomorrow," she said, "you should be okay coming out. Just proceed with care."

RECORDS

C haa found me inspecting the glyphs on the doors to the library. I felt their power, and I almost deciphered their meaning. She stood a step behind me.

"They protect against more than psychic attacks. They are like seals," I told her, still wandering in my mind to place their function.

"That's correct," she said. "If the doors ever close, the sigils will keep them closed."

"Oh, that's what it is. But I can't seem to trace within the sigils the way to open them back."

"That's because the key to them is three secret words; each word known only to one of the highest initiates. Them alone can pass the key, and they do so only before they depart the physical world."

"And there is no other way?"

"Because there are many dangers that we want to be protected from," she said.

I turned to her, waiting for more.

"This library holds the records of the ages and the keys of initiation," she said. "Such knowledge is sought after by many who would have it drown in the mud. But the contents of the scrolls are invaluable to humanity, and the doors must remain open for those whose path of self-discovery brought them here. We needed a way to balance the risks and the benefits; thus, the order crafted this measure in place. The doors can be sealed to any intruders, and only the keepers of the words can judge the time to safely open them."

"Why three initiates? What if something happens to one of them?"

"The three initiates were voted by the order, back when its members were many, to avoid having the wisdom of old at the hands of only one. Such power could twist the mind of many."

"How old is this place?"

"This sanctuary is of the most ancient."

"And the words have indeed passed on?"

"They have."

"Do you have them?"

She closed her eyes for a moment and headed within. I turned within in as well.

I let my scroll on the table. She read from another.

"Grandmother?" I called her for the first time.

Even her eyes smiled as she drew them away from the scroll. "Yes, my dear?"

"How did humanity end up like this? That state I experienced high in the mountain; how do we fall from that into misery?"

"Ignorance, my dear. Our ignorance of the true self and nature leads us to the one true sin that is separation. And separation, be it from the spirit that we are, the world around us, or from one another, the sense that we, as individuals, are alone and disconnected from everything else, creates within us fear.

And through that fear, we suffer and cause suffering. Through the longing for connectedness, we create attachments to dead objects, and when they fail to satisfy, we create more and more, until we come to realise their empty nature in the hope of finding our own."

"How do we find our true nature? And even if we do find it, how do we manage to carry it out?"

"Yes, you are right. Finding it and carrying it out are two fundamentally different processes. The pilgrim must desire and will that which is good and pure. He must name his afflictions in honesty and discriminate the true from the empty, the flame from the candle; see and learn himself and will his purification, the shedding away of all of his burdens. Layer by layer, he finds what is true and pure and good within him and learns to see it without. Then the shadows disappear, and the light remains. It always remains and guides to liberation."

"The way to liberation..." I repeated, trying to mentally construct the image of a liberated Erevos.

She turned to her scrolls.

GREEN LEAVES

I concentrated on some stones on the garden below the veranda. I expanded my etheric channels, growing like roots to reach and engulf the objects of my focus. It took a lot of effort to reach them and numerous attempts thereafter. The first merely shook the stone for a few moments. Then, I accidentally sent it flying further. I also dropped them many times midway. But finally, one reached the veranda and was almost in my hand.

"You are getting better," Chaa said from inside.

The stone dropped to the ground. She came outside, past the translucent curtains flowing in the breeze.

"Am I ready to go back?" I asked, hoping.

"Matter is matter," she said, ignoring my question. "Energy, intention, all the worlds above this one, are all of the same matter. Only their attributes change. Realising that allows you to handle it through more means than the physical. But of course, it needs time for the ability to be refined. It is like a small baby learning to take control of its developing body. It is clumsy at first, but you will soon learn. It's only natural."

I picked up the stone to continue my training.

"Come inside," she said.

I nodded. We had our prayers.

I leaned below my bed and dragged my bag out, smiling at the small package inside. I unfolded the cloth that protected my little treasure and brought Idhi's sandflower close to my eyes. I hadn't visited my beloved since before we settled in the sanctuary.

"My dear Idhi," I said.

I imagined her voice, her arms around me. She had been in my thoughts often, but her gift, I had safely put away. With a sigh, I drowned my shame.

"Have you also found warmth in the arms of another?" I asked, looking at the stone.

I shook my head and sat on the bed, facing out my window. The stone's energy mingled with mine as I led my consciousness to her. She felt calm, charming as always, more mature and centred.

I arrived at Innok's house before sunset. He ran from inside and hugged me.

"Where have you been? I thought something might have happened!" he said.

"I am sorry I haven't visited for a while. Studies... and Chaa."

He smiled. "Come, come inside."

We had some tea and hurried to visit the waterfall before the sun was down. He told me about his days in the city since we last met. There wasn't much I could actually share with him. But I was content hearing about his simpler life.

"Want to practise?" he asked, pointing at the wooden swords.

"Let's just take a dive," I said.

I threw my clothes on a rock and jumped down the waterfall. The cold water of the lake below grounded me to the present moment. My thoughts, my studies, Idhi, all but dispersed in the water. Innok joined me with a splash. The greens around us intermingled with the pink and purple of the sky.

We returned to the house just before dark. He lit the candles and prepared a light meal. And, as he served my dish, he leaned and kissed my cheek.

FLOOD

T he flickering candles sent dancing shades of orange around the room. Innok
lay asleep next to me. From his neck, hung a pendant. Its metal was warm to
the touch; an upside-down cone dangled from a gold sphere with six wings. *A gift
from someone?*

I let the sheet slip from my hips and walked to the open window. The crickets
still chirped despite the cold breeze of the night. With quiet movements, I took my
clothes from the bed, dressed up and went outside.

Above the trees of the garden, rivers of stars sparkled in the dark sky. The seven
great stars shone supreme among the myriads of earths lighting the milky sea of
space.

Innok's warm breath touched the back of my neck as he spread his arms around
me. With a soft outbreath, I leaned and rested on his chest. Clouds covered the stars
before I could show him. And an insect flew close to my eyes, disturbing the sweet
calmness with annoyance.

"What is it?" he said, half asleep.

"Nothing. Just an insect," I said and readjusted in his arms.

Another insect floated by me. And another landed on my cheek. I gently shook
and wiped my face, but a dusty sensation remained. I rubbed my blackened fingers
and sniffed the dirt. With a gasp, I pulled away from Innok's chest.

"It's ashes!" I looked up in the night and the rolling clouds of black smoke.

A woman shouted in the distance while Innok ran inside, re-emerging dressed up
with his blade in hand. Ashes fell down around us. The screams were now many,
accompanying a roaring blaze.

Beyond his garden, a horse almost scraped my nose as it galloped past me, forcing
me to throw myself to the ground. Innok pulled me up while the rider marched
on with a bloody sword in one hand and a torch in the other. Houses were already

ablaze along his path. Innok ran towards them while something floated down with the ashes in front of me. I squinted; a big black feather.

My spine stretched electric. "Innok," I shouted.

A flaming rock flashed through the night sky and towards the House of Lotus. "The sanctuary!"

Innok brought our horses. He turned one more time towards the yelling town. "We will come back!" I said, hoping I wasn't lying.

We rode away from the fires, away from the people in their fate. I led the way through the burning jungle, with birds and monkeys and elementals running from the flames and dense smoke.

I tightened my legs around my horse and leaned close to its body, breathing through its hair. I pushed and pushed until we got beyond the fire and into the desert. I coughed, trying to take in the clean air. In the distance, flames were already swallowing the sanctuary. Above it, another flaming rock burst into pieces against an invisible shield. Another made it through, smashing its walls.

I looked for Innok behind me, only in time to see a torch flying at me and several riders coming at us. I clumsily pulled the reins, bewildering my horse, who dropped us both in the sand. Innok jumped in front of me and caught the rider's blade with his own.

"Go!" he shouted.

The horse pulled us up and rode towards the sanctuary. Innok now fought against three. Without stopping, I pulled whatever power of concentration I had and focused on him. My mental reach stretched in the sand until it hit the three warriors in a burst that threw them away. Innok got back on his horse when I marched on.

Chohanatma's men were already in close combat. Flames and men roared. I jumped from my horse and ran towards a broken wall, amidst men of both sides falling to their death. One of the intruders dropped in front of me, cracking his skull on a brick. The blood ran over a lion tattoo on his neck. *Balluashir's wretched men!*

With a burning stomach, I jumped above him and headed for the spiralling stairs. Innok was fighting his way to me. I turned at the end of a hallway and slipped on wet floor, banging my head on the ground. All went silent, but only for a moment. With pulsating head, I raised myself in the puddle of blood that still spilled through the guts of Chohanatma's guard.

They are already down in the library. "No, no, no."

A shadow of a figure emerged in the hallway. I grabbed the dead man's sword.

"Aletheos!" he spat out, leaning on the wall.

"Innok!" I exhaled. "Down below!"

I almost tripped running down the stairs. But I never slowed down, not until I reached the bottom. Men lay on the ground across the hallway, and clashing blades echoed from the other end, almost as loudly as my pounding heart.

We jumped above the bodies, down the engraved hall that dripped with blood. Men had surrounded Chaa and Chohanatma and old Rajvidya, who stood guard at the chamber before the library gates.

Around them stood our guards, deterring the intruders. Among the swordsmen, some stood still. They wore masks, the same worn by the conspirators back at the palace. One's raised arm held an invisible grip on a guard and, with a twist of the hand, the guard's neck cracked, collapsing on the ground.

Chaa and Chohanatma and Rajvidya fought with bursts of light and invisible forces, trying to keep the dark priests and the warriors at bay. My boiling anger gathered in my hands and unleashed a gust of force that threw many of them on the ground. I ran to my friends' side as Innok, a step behind, slashed with his blade whomever he could.

Our men fell one by one as we struggled among the blades and dark forces to protect what we could. I raised my sword and blocked an attack on Chaa. Innok grabbed the aggressor and pushed him down with a swing of his sword. I looked around. So many dead.

"Close the doors! Close them!" Chaa commanded from behind me.

Old Rajvidya raised his hand and traced a symbol at the doors, which moved at his will. Before they could seal shut, a sword passed through his back and out his chest. With another small blade, the warrior slit his throat. He had not uttered the final words.

My chest beat relentless. I took an inbreath; kept it. It vibrated electric. I opened my eyes; counted as many aggressors as I could. Eight. Nine. Thirteen. More. I yelled out my anger, and with it, lightning blasted out of me and struck them.

One, masked, raised his arms in defence. My outburst nailed those around him to the ground. He still stood. He responded with a cloud of rolling dark smoke, swaying away all on its way; his friends and ours. His mask was solid in my mind as the cloud stormed towards me. I clenched my eyes, and so did the mask bend on his face, the metal crushing in on his head. With his screams, vanished his attack, and he groaned, pulling away his mask with bits of flesh still on it.

"Valsaris!" I roared.

He stared at me with bleeding face. Others fought in between us. But I moved my gaze not. He panted below unblinking eyes, now observing the chaos, his lips shivering as if with terror. I took but a step towards him and, in a heartbeat, his weakness disappeared. He stood up straight and swung his arms around, sending his men and ours flying. With a last scream, he disappeared in a gust of black smoke.

From behind me, Chaa yelled the words, and the gates sealed with a bang. The cave trembled around us. Rocks and dust rolled from cracks in the ceiling. The statues beside the gates moved, bringing their hammer and axe in front of the doors.

Innok threw me to the ground before stones landed in my place. The chamber echoed, commanding our silence. An intruder came from the hall, walking among the rest of us on the floor.

"Balluashir!" I called for him through my teeth.

He raised his sword through Chaa's ribs. Time ceased as my eyes widened and breathing stopped. A grin slowly appeared on his face as he twisted his sword.

"No," cried Chohanatma.

Time resumed. Chohanatma raised his hand and threw the murderer on the wall. He reached Chaa before she fell. With her in his hands, he ran above the fallen men and into the hallway. With a fast-beating heart that urged me to live, I pulled Innok up and rushed behind him. Only we remained.

He kneeled, holding grandmother on one hand and raising the other as the intruders reclaimed their feet and Balluashir came for us. The glowing sigils of the gates now faded into darkness. Chohanatma uttered a word I did not recognise. The earth shook. The dark chamber between us and the library trembled before collapsing on the murderers. Balluashir locked his eyes on mine and raised his sword before he vanished forever. Dust flooded the hall and extinguished all torches.

Silence followed. Darkness followed. We did not move. We did not utter a word. Chohanatma held my grandmother in his arms.

DROUGHT

I sat on the ground with my back to the wall. To my left lay the ruins. The
voices of dying from below the rocks had long ceased. To my right, the spiralling
steps reflected whatever glimpses of sunlight reached them through the broken walls
above. In the hallway's darkness, I could still hear the cracking of the neck; I could
see Valsaris's eyes, Balluashir's grin, Chaa.

I rubbed my eyes dry. The wall engraved with the actions of the gods and our
sacred lineage was now stained with dried red patches. Slow steps descended the
stairs.

"Aletheos," Innok said, coming close.

I didn't answer. I didn't turn. I fixated on a flower carved on the wall. Dirtied.
Corrupted.

"Aletheos," he repeated and crouched next to me. "We are ready."

He gently touched my arm. I turned to him with burning eyes.

"Let's go," he said.

My eyes struggled to adjust to the light of day. Mudbricks were everywhere.
Parts of the sanctuary had collapsed. Only half of the veranda remained,
where we had our tea a few days ago.

The smell of smoke was numbing. I tried to balance myself through the piles of
bricks, if only to get a little closer. Innok walked next to me.

"Did you find it?" I asked him.

He pointed at a bag already tied to his horse with all that remained of my belong-
ings. He pulled out a small covered package; Idhatora's sandflower. I nodded.

"Go get some rest," Chohanatma said. "I will let you know when we are ready."

I didn't answer. I wanted to raise my hands around him. He was suffering too. But my heart ached. Before I turned away, he pulled me into his arms and close to his chest. He smelled of ashes. I, effortfully, raised mine enough to touch him. With wet eyes, he turned to Innok; nodded as he let me go.

We mounted. Around us laid men and bricks and stones, and we rode amongst them. Men were half sunk in the sand, unconscious. Parts of them were disfigured, their skin turned to wood-like masses. Chohanatma's wrath had awakened the desert. After our ordeal underground, he had run upstairs and finished the battle we had already lost. I looked away from the horror, straight ahead, and into the jungle leading to Areteia, scorched. Trees still burned from within them.

We rode into empty streets. Houses had burned down. The greens that kept the town alive were now black. People lay amidst the ashes. And the statue of the serene lady was in pieces; the ribbons of flowers from her neck, scattered on the ground. Only one survived, white. We proceeded around it.

From a ruined house rushed out a man. "Where were you?" he cried.

Innok got off his horse with the man falling on his shoulder.

"They brought fire and blood," the man said. "They tied the statues of the temple on horses and brought them to pieces."

He turned towards his house. He said nothing. In his garden, where we had danced and feasted with friends, now lay his wife and child. Burned. My heart filled my eyes. *This can't be happening.* I kept shaking my head.

Another man came from behind us. "You are alive," he shouted. "Are there others?"

He froze when he saw the eyes of the stricken husband and father. With a glance at the garden, he rushed to embrace him, tears flooding his eyes.

"You have survivors?" I said with a broken voice.

The second man turned to me but said nothing.

"Check with the infirmary," I said. "Have them send for me if there are wounded."

He nodded and turned to his friend.

We made our way home. Houses around the street were still in smoke. Innok's house still had some greens on it. We headed inside. I let my bag fall on the floor as a breeze slammed the door behind us. With it, I heard the cracking of the neck. I saw Valsaris's eyes, Balluashir's grin, Chaa.

My head throbbed with pain. It pulsated, expanding to my eyes. It kneeled me. I brought my hands to my temples. I saw the sword that slashed through Chaa's flesh. Pots crashed around me. Dust and pieces flew around. I saw the masked men. Innok's table broke into fibres and splintered on the walls.

The pain pressed on my head. Innok's touch was excruciating. My scream sent him flying on the door. I kept my head down while a burning sensation charged through and all around me.

Innok came again. He threw himself on me and held me tight. His touch was like sharp stones cutting through my skin. My body stretched in shock. He kept his hands around me.

"It's okay," he kept saying with tears in his eyes.

My body loosened; his touch was bearable. He kept me close. My face burned wet. But my eyes were now dry. My fists were clenched. And I kept the masked men in mind.

MARCHING ON

I applied ointment, yet again, on the scarred skin of my patient, if only to ease his mind. His wounds had already healed.

"The pain?" he kept asking. "It burns at night!"

I shook my head. It was not his skin that kept him awake. With my arms close to his temples, I led pink and green light around his head, hoping it would gradually help him go through the pain.

His voice became deeper, now grounded in reality. "Will it go away?"

I forced a smile on my face, only for a moment.

"I don't know," I said with a heavy chest.

"Can things go back to normal?" he insisted.

I closed the vial of ointment and tidied it on the shelf.

"Maybe we can find a new normal," I said. "With time."

He sat in silence for a few moments. He only nodded before leaving and I dragged myself below a tree, still alive with greens. At least the infirmary with the ointments and substances had escaped the fire.

With Balluashir buried deep beneath the sanctuary, together with countless others swallowed by the desert, the face of the enemy was now Valsaris. *Are there others?* I couldn't assume the beast was buried as well. I laughed at my thoughts, breaking the charming hope and feeding my rage against all the beasts. *If only we were done!*

"Her death then, would have at least meant something," I said to myself with flaring nostrils and clenched fists.

A man joined me from the threshold, almost naked, cutting through the fuming forces around me.

"Do you need assistance?" I asked before I realised; it was the priest from the temple.

I hadn't seen him since the invasion. I jumped up. The customs were different in this part of the world. But he knew and had been instructing his disciples in the ways to preserve and prepare the body according to our tradition.

"Is she ready?" I asked.

Chohanatma answered from the door.

"We are ready."

W e set camp below the excavation site, the ancient city of our ancestors. Our men dug holes to bury the bones and cracked skulls we found upon our arrival. Balluashir and his men had passed through here.

I turned away; towards the statues, already visible from a great distance. The giant head we had seen with Chaa on our way to Areteia now had its entire body unearthed. Others stood next to it, somewhat resembling the ones engraved in the great hall to the library.

One of them was almost as tall as the mountain. *The first step.* The first of our progeny, the great fires that shaped our earth, sexless and formless. The second held almost half its height. *The androgynous beings, the etherial, manifested.* Then the third, considerably shorter. *The separation of the sexes, the fall of man.* The whole monument was built by the fourth, Chaa had said, the one before our humanity, whose kingdom sank in corruption and brought annihilation to themselves.

Innok sat next to me, dirty from burying the dead.

"She wanted to see them," I said, pointing at the carriage that held her body.

He touched my hand. But with a sigh, I walked away from his affection. I kneeled next to the river, flowing indifferent, burbling cool and life-giving.

K hantara stood proud in the desert. But its great walls and winged lions at its gates were now black by fire. Men hung from the walls, some scorched, others still dripping red.

My jaw clenched as we rode through the open gates. It reeked of death. Bodies piled in the streets and the houses seemed abandoned. Only a creaking sound broke the silence of degeneration, answered by our archer's stretching bows, all aiming at a door. A man came through, dragging a body. Without a trace of fear, he just let it fall to the ground when he saw us.

Chohanatma nodded at the archers, who lowered their bows, and coughed before speaking. "What happened here?"

The man said something in his language.

"Does anyone speak the tongue?" Chohanatma asked us.

"No need," said another, carrying a body down the street.

He left it on the pile and turned to Chohanatma.

"Have you come to marvel at the splendour of my father?" he asked.

"I am Chohanatma, the keeper of the records. Balluashir was your father?"

"By blood alone. You slayed a monster in that cave."

Innok came close to me with his sword already in hand.

"I am Meneir," the man said.

"What happened here?" Chohanatma asked.

"News of my father's defeat came fast. His men's loyalty to the nation disintegrated even faster. I tried, with whomever still held on to hope, to take away their power and throw them out. This..." he raised his arms at the bodies and houses, "...this is what came of it."

Doors and windows were broken. Blood stained the walls around us. Swords and arrows paved the streets. I liked to think that Khantara deserved this, but my thoughts would not align with my heart, saddened by more destruction and death.

"Where did they go?" asked Chohanatma.

"I do not know. They left what remains of us. The city alone is my one concern."

The savages will probably drink themselves senseless, and fall to die rotting in the desert. As they should!

"Are you travelling to King Aletheos, revered Chohanatma?" asked Meneir.

Chohanatma did not answer.

"I apologise. I mean no indiscretion. My uncle had great respect for you and your order. And they were friends with King Aletheos."

"I am aware," said Chohanatma.

"So were our nations." Meneir shook his head. "Before my father killed his brother to take his place. Please, we need the king's help if we are to revive our civilisation. Please give him a good word on our behalf."

"Your uncle had good relations with Chaa as well," I said.

Innok touched my hand. I pushed it aside.

"The lady of the Five-Pointed Star! Is she with you?" Meneir asked.

"She is," I said.

He smiled and raised himself. "Can I see her? She must remember me! She will speak good of us to the king."

"Your father pushed a sword through her chest," I said.

His smile vanished. He looked around and up at the sky, and brought his arms to his head.

"There is no hope," he said. "I cannot fathom what demon walked through my father. When I found out he had travelled to your sanctuary... I never thought... I should have known..." He let out a quick burst of laughter. "Of course, I should have known."

His knees dropped to the ground.

"There is no hope," he said. "King Aletheos will never..."

Chohanatma looked at me.

"King Aletheos is a man of honour," I said and turned my horse away. "I will speak to him."

O utside Khantara, our camp was ready. I rode close to Chohanatma.

"He is brought to ruins," he said through a cough.

"He is," I said, void of the satisfaction I wanted to feel.

I moved on.

"Aletheos," he called me. "Come with me."

He tripped as he dismounted outside his tent. I helped him up. His hands were covered with white clothes, and signs of blood seeped through them. After a resting breath, he, slow-moving and heavy, dragged his legs inside. I followed and sat across from him. No one spoke. Night was upon us.

"Did she give you the word to the library?" he finally asked.

"No."

"She intended to pass it on to you when... when the time came. I will tell you mine. Just in case. Although without hers, I don't know there is a reason anymore. With her..."

He did not finish his sentence.

"So, the library is gone as well? No way to open it without her word?"

He shook his head. All that we held dear, all that I yearned to achieve, brought only pain and darkness. I exhaled a wave of sadness into a short laughter. And I returned to silence.

"I will give you mine," he said.

"Why did you argue with her?" I responded.

He looked into my eyes and exhaled deeply. "Your grandmother and I... we had a past between us."

I kept my eyes on him.

"I loved her, and she loved me. We were together. But we hadn't seen each other since she left. She... she never told me. I didn't know."

I leaned back in my chair, looked outside, beyond the guard at the entrance.

"She was pregnant when she left. I never knew. Our customs do not allow for pre-marital relationships. And a child... Chaa thought it would ruin me. I never got to know her. And I never will. I did not know about you either. That's why we fought. When I saw you... I would give everything up to have spent my life with my daughter."

I closed my eyes, still facing away.

"I should give you the word, my wise boy."

I pushed back my chair, screeching, and stood up.

"I loved her," he said.

"I did, too," I whispered, leaving his tent.

The sun was relentless. Sweat heavied my eyelids as I walked next to my horse, the dry sand shifting too much below our feet. Amongst the blinding light, I tried to get a sense of direction. But something hard caught my foot and brought me down in the sand.

I stayed there, inspecting the obstacle that looked like a statue. Innok ran to help me up.

"Dig," I said, sweeping the sand around the statue.

We uncovered a small wooden hawk connected to something big below it. We kept digging until we reached a wide surface.

"Innok! It's the four houses; the first ones we found on our way!"

"We are close to home," Innok said.

I looked around for any signs of life. All was hidden in the sand. *What happened? Did they never return?*

Our men set camp. It was too hot to continue, and frailing Chohanatma needed more and more rest as we proceeded.

The night was unbearable as well. I sat up in my bed and swiped the drops off my forehead. With an outbreath that did nothing to cool me, I went to the last remaining candle and blew it into a thick stripe of smoke. In the darkness, sounded whispers. But the tent was empty. I headed for the exit.

"Aletheos," someone said from within the tent.

I turned around, trying to locate its source. A man came from the shadows.

"Valsaris!" I took my sword from the table and raised it to his neck.

"Aletheos, please! Listen to me."

My hand shook. His face was scarred by the bits of flesh he'd ripped off with the mask down in the library. All I could do was keep my sword from slashing across his throat.

"They are coming," he said in a beaten voice.

"What?" My blade scraped through his skin.

He hissed in pain but moved not.

"Who's coming?"

"The priests. Khantara's warriors."

I kept searching in his eyes for a sign of honesty, of malice, something. A man shouted from outside as the bells rang. The camp was waking up to an ambush. I kept my eyes on Valsaris, his scars, his mouth, the drop of blood running down his neck, my unyielding blade. I released him. And ran to the clashing of swords outside.

"Innok!" I yelled.

An intruder held one of our men. I swiped my blade across the back of his leg, and our soldier overtook him.

"Innok!" I shouted again.

"I am here!" He came from behind a tent, already scratched.

Around us, men swung their swords. A masked man walked slowly among them. He held fire. No torch; only a flaming orb floating above his hand. Innok looked at me with wide eyes. The dark priest raised his arm and spewed fire around, but before reaching the tents or trees, the flames dispersed and vanished. Chohanatma already had his mind on it. He stood in the middle of the camp, his face twisting as he raised his arms. The clothes that covered his palms had fallen to the ground, unravelling his deformation; his limbs had turned wood-like.

A loud clatter surrounded us. Horses galloped towards us and men marched through the camp. Innok held his sword, looking around for the new enemy. A rider headed for us. Innok grabbed my hand, but before we could take cover, the horseman slashed the masked priest, who fell down in his fire.

"The Starani!" said Innok and stood tall among his fellows.

With their arrival, Chohanatma lowered his arms. He stood still, breathing. Through the fires, swords, and spears, I ran to him. His eyes were shut. And blood flooded his mouth.

"Chohanatma," I pleaded.

He opened his eyes. His cheeks relaxed. His shoulders dropped. A small smile formed at the corners of his mouth. I caught him right as he collapsed and helped him lay on the ground. With all my might, I gathered my breath into a soothing voice.

"What can I do?" I asked, holding his misshapen hand.

Irregular masses grew from his neck as well. He only smiled.

"Be wise, my grandson," he said with his last outbreath.

The Starani men soon ended the battle. The first light of day counted our losses yet again. Chohanatma lay on the ground. The masses had disappeared from his body and his face was now calm, as if in sleep. A hand warmed my shoulder. With it came a ray of hope. *Father!* He was cut, his clothes were bloody. But he stood, alive.

THE FIVE-POINTED STAR

T he great sea waved free. Splashes of mist cooled my face over the bow of the ship. My father sat next to me. I had so many things to tell him. But our reunion was filled with sadness. His face had a few more wrinkles than I remembered, and his temples were now silvered below his intricate golden crown. We said nothing, only held hands.

S tone white pillars stood bright on the hill, marking the temple against the blue sky. Below it, cypress and pine trees greened the land among patches of yellow weeds and red flowers.

Boats received us from the ships, now almost at shore. I stepped off and into the water, knee-deep, with the foam of the waves magnetising me in place. The pulse of the sea dragged the blur of my sensations down through my feet, where the turquoise waters met with acacia trees, sparse across the coastline.

Eight priestesses waited in two rows to ceremonially receive the coffin. Behind them stood my father's friend, Galias, and his sons, Cyrus and Mythus, together with other officials. I stepped out of the water and reached a platform of beige rectangular stones. My grandmother was now on land.

The temple hid beyond the steepness of the hill. At its base, the agora was quietly busy. A few people came close, some merely curious, others to pay their respect. From the distance, watched a woman with a white flower in her hands; her long black hair waving in the wind around her vacant look.

Galias approached and greeted us in a low voice. His sons followed. While the priestesses prepared the body, we went into the agora. We sat around a table with fruits and nuts, water and wine.

"What happened?" Galias asked.

"The priests." I spat the words.

"And Balluashir; his men," Father said. "They have found something to gain."

"Did she not stand guard in the higher realms to see them coming?" Galias said with a small laugh.

I banged my hands on the table, at whatever he insinuated, as I engulfed Innok's sword with my mind and threw it on Galias, keeping it floating mere fingers from his eyes. Father stood up and lowered the sword with his hand.

"Enough," Father said. "Sit down, Aletheos! No phenomena!"

I stared at Galias with flaring nostrils. With Innok's gentle touch on my shoulder, I sat down, and looked away.

"Balluashir?" asked Cyrus after a few moments of silence.

"Dead," said Innok.

"What is left of his men left Khantara, but not before massacring its people," said Father. "They now rage at our villages."

I turned to him. "They attack the kingdom?"

"I was informed when we arrived," Father said.

"I want to help," Cyrus exclaimed from the other side of the table.

Horns sounded. The procession had begun.

"We shall talk after," said my father.

We went around the merchants, up the slope, and into a cave. Innok kept close to me while Father stood in front of us.

"Until we meet again," he whispered.

The priestesses, facing us from the other side of the vessel, sang their prayers in their language. They removed the body from its container and laid it in the ground. With a few more words, they emptied a ceramic bowl of water in the grave, which they then broke, dropping its pieces around my grandmother. They covered her with branches of wheat, bay leaves, acacia, and sand.

I stayed behind and sat with my back to the burial chamber amongst the red flowers and weeds. Innok had offered to stay, but I sent him off with the others. I watched them as they descended, remaining with the sense of earth below my hands and the sea of blue on the unbound horizon.

The scent of the sea blended with the soft but sharp fragrance of the flowers as I kept thinking of the first time I met grandmother, back at the port palace in Dessha, in her long white gowns.

Soft steps touched the ground behind me. It was the woman from before, with the long black hair, exiting the cave. She leaned on the rocks, sobbing. She let out a cry, and, after some deep breaths, wiped her tears. By the time I stood up, she was already on the path up to the temple.

T he ship moved with the calm sea while I kept turning in my bed. Galias had insisted we stayed with him on shore, but I much preferred our ship, away from the burden of royal courtesies. And so did my father.

The dense humidity made it hard to relax though, and I finally retaliated and walked outside. In the distance, the island was asleep while the moon cast its silver path, shattered in the water. I leaned on the ship's wooden rails and stayed with the sound of waves.

Father touched my hand. I kept with the rhythm of the sea until I was soberly in my head.

"Can't sleep?" I asked.

"She was a great woman," he said. "A force equalled by almost none."

I smiled. "She was."

"She is already proceeding through the realms," Father said.

"And Chohanatma?"

He nodded.

"Father?" I sighed. "Why is this happening?"

He pressed his lips together. "The root of evil is one. Its branches, unaccountable. Ignorance makes beasts out of men, that soar aimless and senseless."

"How do we crash them?" I asked.

"We don't," he said, looking in the distance. "You don't crash weeds. You uproot them. But it cannot be as direct as it should. Not with all the innocents amongst them. Not with all the balances we must keep for the sake of our people and the kingdom."

A gentle breeze cooled the humid night, together with my anxiousness to return. *So much to do!*

"I met Chaa many years ago," Father said. "The order was strong; the halls of the library were alive with students eager to learn and help humanity see. That was soon destined to change. But for us, our paths beyond apprenticeship were revealed clear. Chaa's wisdom made her keeper of the sacred female and high priestess to the temple. Chohanatma served as guardian of the records, as his father did before him. And I... I was to make of Erevos a beacon of light. But I returned to a kingdom swayed by demons born of ignorance.

I called a convocation of the chief priests and proposed that all temples should revere the one Spirit above all gods, even if alongside to them. But the different cults had already gained power over the desperate minds of men; they would hear none of it. Dark practices were sought by many who wanted their needs met in unnatural ways. And they were found."

He shook his head and sat on a bench.

"One day, the head of the Starani men had received some grave reports and called me to a house. It seemed abandoned, but it was not. I went inside; a filthy room. A foul smell led me further to a rotten body lying in the darkness; a woman. She opened her mouth and yelled, drooling in pain. On the other side of the room, a set of eyes was wide upon me. It was a boy hiding below the table.

The poor woman was ill, and she had the most rotten of rituals performed on her. Her body was kept from falling apart, but her consciousness was poisoned, kept prisoner in a decaying body. I tried to untie the dark knots within her. I worked and worked on her for days. But her pain was too much. Her consciousness had already decided; she could not take the suffering. I took little Innok into care and helped her free herself."

Innok's mother!

"How about the father?" I asked.

"We don't know. The mother had no husband, only lovers."

I furrowed my brows. *Innok knew his father. He had mentioned a father!*

"A few others had been found in a similar state," Father continued. "With her death, I issued a decree prohibiting dark rituals. Such practices had no place in our kingdom. Meleethos advised strongly against it. And he was right. Whatever malformed knowledge and power the dark practitioners retained had already earned them followers. And the prohibition fuelled their devotion. They infiltrated the cities and the temples, maintaining that true power places man above the laws of nature. And they were against all that the order held dear and sacred, all that I had taken upon me to accomplish.

The dark arts were no longer in hiding. But their corrosive energies began to manifest as illness. First, it was them who fell sick. Then, it spread to the people. The effect of their practices took hold of my mother and the queen's parents."

"The plague," I said.

He nodded.

"With whatever few initiates remained, we agreed to open the temples we still had power over, for the shadows to disperse and let people walk through the invisible forces within them. Even unconsciously, receiving impressions from the light could make them more sensitive and receptive to the higher truths. And I had copied several scrolls from the sanctuary to fill the library anew; teach new ways to the mysteries.

Understanding was vital. But we were met with resistance. The more we shared the light, the more darkness roamed the streets; until the attack in the palace was made possible. I was then forced to agree with Meleethos's proposition. We traced and exiled all priests that we could find in the shadows. At least to separate them from the innocent. They could practise alone in the abandoned villages. But, evidently, their ignorance still leashes their aims."

"How much suffering have they caused? So many people died of that plague. And Favar, Chohanatma, Chaa; and so many others. For what? They have taken over the temples and our cities. The library is lost. What can we hope to accomplish? How may we uproot such darkness?"

"We have lost a great amount, my son. But do not despair. The library will open when the time commands it, as it did again and again. Rest assured that light and truth always remain untouched by acts of men, only hidden for a while to be rediscovered. Not all is lost."

We returned to shore in the morning. My father had matters to discuss with Galias. Myself, went up the hill to the tomb, now sealed with a rock, and sat in front of the cave. Red and white ribbons hung in the trees around.

I sighed, reminiscing about her strong-mindedness. All were to be carried out according to her will. And she was always right. I smiled. *Almost always.* And I thought of her love and kindness, our journey, all that she was and had accomplished. And the last day I heard her voice in a dark cave so far away. I touched the rock, all that kept me away from her. I repeated the words of my father, wishing them true with all my heart.

"Not all is lost."

I slowly made my way up the hill. I wanted to see her legacy. The temple compound consisted of a few small buildings, three or four rooms to accommodate the priestesses and two or three spaces that made up the temple. The depictions of natural scenery on the walls and columns were playfully colourful, but made of strict lines. In no way did they resemble the artistic complexity of Areteia.

A little girl ran out one door and towards another. *Idhi must have been around the same age when she was here.*

Surrounded by the buildings, raised on a small stage, stood a big pot of white stone. In front of it kneeled alone a woman; her long black hair covered her face. She was immersed in grief. She placed fresh flowers below the pot and whispered a few words.

I remained with her voice; it struck a chord within me that awoke sparks in my heart and mind. I tried taking a step, but my feet insisted against it, heavy on the ground. My mind had uncovered her identity, but I refused to accept it. My heart boiled within. Until I finally cried it out loud.

"Mother?"

CRESCENT MOON

T he swollen waves tossed me up and pulled me down, halfway between our ship and the shore. I kept diving below the surface. The heaviness of the water smoothened my sharp thoughts until I needed my next breath.

She had fallen, she said, away from the light. She was prey for the priests of darkness, she said. And I knew nothing. I was a small child. I could not have protected her. Why didn't my father? I pulled my head above the waves. I took a sharp breath and let them carry me under again.

She would either stay and die or leave and live. She had hoped that leaving would draw them away from me, she said. And that by hiding, they would lose their grip on all of us. But she was wrong! She could have been there with me, for me. We could have found a way.

My stomach burned with a throbbing pain. I bent my body around my gut. I needed air. But my hands and legs locked close to my chest. My lungs emptied with a last orb of air escaping my mouth. I was sinking. I closed my eyes. For a moment, I did not struggle anymore.

Flashes of light invited my eyes to open. Blurry, three mammals swam around me. They looked like seals, but they were made of light, one pink, one blue, and one yellow. The playfulness of the elementals called mine from drowning. And as their light touched me, each drop of water revealed its inner structure. And in that revelation, an intimate connection was established.

I could feel the water around me, solidly, as an extension of my body, which was still bent locked. Instead of moving my arms, I moved the currents of the water. I was finally above the waves, and my lungs rushed to draw vitality in.

T he three colourful elementals stayed close in the dark waters below our anchored ship. They remained looking at me, passing the secrets of the sea in
wordless communication. Behind them, at a small distance, slept the island. So close
she was, my mother, and yet so far. Maybe I should have stayed, forgiven her. But
her explanations were not enough, not to excuse her disappearance.

I moved my hand around, and the waves followed. Like the stones back at the
sanctuary, them too accepted my mental direction. Effortfully, I let all thoughts fade
with the fluidity.

Until Father spoke from behind me. "Your mother became the object of their
attacks."

The waters I held high, splashed back into the sea. Father inspected the waters,
now calm, before turning to me.

"The order stood in their way," he said. "She was my wife and the daughter of
Chaa and Chohanatma. And she was your mother. Hurting her would wound us
all greatly."

"Why didn't you help her?" I asked.

"She had a vision of her death; in the open room you so adore and in front of
your eyes. She was afraid they would use her to corrupt you. Soon after her vision,
she suffered an attack out in the streets. They had caused an angry crowd, and they
grabbed her amidst the chaos. They dragged her to the river, ripped off her clothes.

She managed to run towards the water; she had no other route. But they reached
her. In her despair, she called upon the elementals. And they answered. The waters
soon swallowed them all. But the men still held her tight. And in the water, it was
crocodiles that saved her. They devoured the aggressors while she swam out of the
bloody waters. I found her crying in the red mud.

What she had caused hurt her more than the attackers. In her guilt, she renounced
her powers, and she came to doubt all that she was ever taught. But in doing so, she
had renounced a great aspect of herself, and it rendered her prey. They could reach
her now. Her fear and guilt allowed them so.

And indeed, many nights, she came, certain that the attackers had invaded her
sacred space. Even Muttiya tried to console her. But her fear was not for herself. She
only cared about you. And she was inconsolable."

"Why didn't you do something?"

"I could not forgive her on her behalf. She had to do that alone. Instead, she came
to me with a decision. She wanted to leave to set you free. It would break her heart,
and it did. But she was adamant about protecting you. She returned to the island
and regained her position in the temple, trying to heal and regain herself. And she
asked her mother to come to you, help you when she couldn't."

The anger inside burned with my inability to change the past. Until it locked on its source; the dark ones, the masked priests. *They have taken so much more from me than I knew. They should all burn!*

"This is the whole truth," he said. "And you should do well to know that your mother did all she could for you."

I left our ship with the first daylight. The small town was still asleep when I stepped out of the small boat and into the water. She waited on the shore. With shaking legs and a yearning heart, I was rooted unmoved in the wet sand.

For a few heartbeats, we only looked into each other's eyes. She then burst into tears as she ran into the water to enfold me in her embrace. Her touch, her scent of flowers... I was her little boy again, back in the sacred room, listening to her stories about the stars and wanderers. She was my mother.

I spent the entire morning telling her as much as I could. All her presence was with me. I assured her I kept going back to our room, bringing flowers. I told her about the nan who had returned, strict as ever. And about Idhatora and Innok and the jungle and the elephants and all the people of Areteia. And Chaa.

"My mother was a good woman," she said with a sigh.

The waves kept crashing to shore.

"She was difficult," she said, "but she always did what she thought was right. She told me all about you and your studies and how you grew into this strong, handsome man."

"She contacted you?"

"She kept coming back here. She had asked me to take her position as high priestess, but I couldn't, not yet. And I would wait for her here, next to the sea, to hear all about you before we went up the temple to carry out our duties."

"She kept creating a vessel to project her consciousness here!" I laughed. *Of course she did.*

"Until a few moon cycles ago. When she did not appear, I knew my dear mother had left this world. And I kept hoping that in whatever might have happened, you were safe."

She touched my cheek. Oh, how much I had missed her.

"When I first arrived," she continued, "I didn't want to go back to the temple. I didn't even tell Chaa I was back. My faith was broken. I stayed with my great-grand-father instead. He had been a father to me when Chaa was away on her spiritual duties. Until one day, she came through the door. Udenas knew me well."

Udenas! I smiled but said nothing.

"He knew he could not help me. So, he called her. And she comforted me and took me back to the temple. I stayed with the young ones, training them in the ways of the Mother. And through them, I was reminded of the sacred teachings."

"Mother... I... I have met your father. We were staying with him at his sanctuary."

"Chaa did not speak of him. Not of her own past either. Her only response when I insisted on learning about my origins was to give me seeds of the violet lotus."

"Areteia is full of them! Where they all came together."

"Your father did say that he was a good and noble man with a sacred duty."

"He was! He took care of us and protected the records of wisdom. And he was kind to his people."

My smile faded.

"Is he...?" she asked.

"We were on our way here..."

She looked down for a moment and then at the horizon. She took my hand, and we walked into the sea. The waves foamed around us, soothing the wounds. The three water elementals surfaced at the distance. Their light reached us with every wave.

W ith the sun now behind the hill, the sea in front of us turned purple.

"Will you take Chaa's place in the temple?" I asked her.

"I will have to."

"You are not coming back with us..." I looked away, at our ship in the sea.

"No, my love," she said. "I will have to keep the flame of the Mother."

"Maybe I can stay!" Even as I said it, I knew it, the absurdity of my words. Oh how lovely it would have been, for our lives to had unravelled otherwise. It was but a dream, staying at this haven of an island. I couldn't. Not with all that happened. I wouldn't. Not with all I had to do.

She smiled, almost in tears. "My dear beloved son... You will always have a home here. But you have a path to build of your own."

"Maybe I will make the kingdom safe again. And maybe you can teach another to lead the temple."

She turned to me with eyes warm with love.

"Yes, my sweet prince. Maybe. And I will be here, waiting."

A round the ship, men prepared for battle. My cousin Cyrus had joined us, leading the attacks. Father discussed tactics with him and Innok. And I remained with the sense of my mother's embrace, holding my heart together. I was heading back home. And I was heading into war, one where the enemy was everywhere and nowhere.

PART 4
SUNSET

THORNS

I finally walked on land, but my stomach still moved with the rhythm of the sea. We headed for the port palace of Dessha where we, some sun cycles ago, had received Chaa for the first time. In the yard, troops formed amidst their camps, spears and swords already at hand, raising clouds of dust as the soldiers marched in rows to meet their commanders.

Stepping on Erevos land after almost three sun cycles was a sweet sorrow amongst the fury of war. I had returned home, a man of eighteen, and I couldn't wait to present myself to Idhatora at the capital. So close she was! But, for now, war.

Those of the highest ranks received my father and briefed him on their numbers while an official waited to welcome us into the palace before the enormous monument my brother had commissioned. With stone severed hands piling on high at the feet of a warrior king, it was a grim reminder of Favar's lost ways.

"Bring this down," I said to the official.

He looked up at me with his scribbles at hand. "Excuse me, my prince. What should..."

"Bring this atrocity to the ground," I repeated and walked inside.

Father and his commanders soon followed. They stood in the middle of the room, around a table engraved with the map of the kingdom. I observed from some distance with my back to the wall; I was not to join the battles in the fields. The king assigned each commander an area.

"This is where their leader should be," said one of the seasoned warriors.

"Then it will be my honour to lead our men there and bring him to you!" Cyrus said.

Innok leaned next to me on the wall.

"I told you, you shouldn't do this," I said without looking at him.

"This is my duty, Prince Aletheos," he said.

He took a step to the front, bowed to me, and walked away.

You are an idiot for doing this!

I couldn't wait to get off the boat. For good this time. We floated up the river for days. We had just passed by the Black Temple, and now, Eos was visible under the dazzling sun. I kept my hands busy, weaving knots. But my consciousness was beyond my body, far behind, into strange battlefields, ravaged villages and bloody grounds. *Where are you?* Innok was engulfed in darkness and pain, keeping his consciousness out of my reach. *What happened to you?*

With a deep inbreath, I returned to my body and, as of instinct, touched his sword hanging from my waist. He had left it in my bedroom back at Dessha. At least I could still feel his presence on the metal. I drew it and cut the last threads that hung from the weaving. I tied Idhatora's sandflower into a pendant and placed it around my neck, the stone touching the centre of my chest.

"May you be safe," I wished for Innok looking at the sun, and went inside to my father. "We are almost..."

Father was not alone. The stranger had his back to me.

"Yes, my king," said a familiar voice in a shaking tone.

Innok's sword scraped its sheath as I brought it to the visitor's neck.

"Valsaris! What are you doing here?"

He didn't speak.

"Please, lower your sword," Father said.

I walked around Valsaris, keeping the blade on his throat. "What is he doing here?"

"I was wrong," Valsaris said. "Gravely."

"Yes. You are!"

"None of this was supposed to happen. Altazadeh..." He sighed. "We wanted the scrolls, the library. Not death. I was wrong."

"You wanted Father's death! Your king's! Your sister's husband's!"

He kept shaking his head.

"Father," I pleaded, "you can't trust him!"

Father raised his gaze. "No one spoke of trust, Aletheos. But, he did help us. He is the one who informed me of the attack at your camp. That's how we got there in time."

"This is a trick," I exclaimed.

"He saved your life, Aletheos," Father said. "I will hear what he has to say."

With unmoved eyes, Father nodded at me.

I exhaled through flaring nostrils, and moved the sword away from Valsaris's skin. "Why did you warn my father?"

"We came for the library; all the hidden knowledge that the order kept away from us. Not destruction. We never meant to... I never meant to hurt anyone. What happened down there, your eyes... It was as if a veil had dissolved and I could see the reality of my actions."

"I will never trust you, Valsaris," I said.

He only looked at the floor.

"How did you know of the library?" I asked.

"Altazadeh," said Father. "He was one of us."

"And the beast?"

The boat stopped before I got an answer from the murderer.

"Ashore," yelled a guard from outside.

"Are they waiting?" asked Father.

"They are here," said Valsaris.

Ten, no, thirteen masked men waited on the river bank. They stood in a row, blocking our passage. I ran off the boat and through the guards who already pointed their spears at the dark priests. Between us, the sand was moving, black. Myriads of scorpions split the land for as far as I could see, keeping the masked men several steps away.

"You are not welcome here," said their chief in the middle.

"This is my home," I declared.

"Aletheos, get back," Father said from the boat, keeping his loud voice as calm as possible.

"What do you want?" I asked the dark priest, the leader of cowards who hurt innocents and hunted my mother.

"Your rule here is done. These are our temples, our city," he replied.

The scorpions moved like a black wave. I turned within and then at them. I found the subtle plane through which the priests exuded dark smoke and reached a hold on the arachnids. With a half-smile, I penetrated the dark smoke with a ray of light. And I stretched my arms, willing the light to expand and dissolving their reach.

I approached as the priests stood still and arrogant. The scorpions moved away from below my steps, and I stood amidst the black wave. The masked men turned to their chief.

"Remove your masks," I commanded.

He shook his head. And I led the scorpions onwards. The priests raised their arms, trying to regain power over the creatures. But I stood guard in the realms beyond, blocking their hold.

"Stop this," the chief said.

"Remove your masks," I repeated.

He took a step back. He raised his cloak and twisted his body. When the cloth fell, he already held a blade at a girl's throat.

"Back off, little prince!" he mocked me.

From the boat, screamed Valsaris. "No!"

I insisted. "I said, remove your..." The girl's eyes caught mine. "Idhatora!"

A burning wave of emotions swallowed my mind, breaching my hold on the scorpions. They ran, uncontrollable. They covered the men, stinging them to the ground, all except the captor. At his comrades' cries, he pushed Idhatora in front of him and ran.

The scorpions now surged for Idhatora. I breathed within. Before I could find a mental equilibrium, she raised her hands with a smile on her face, projecting a sphere of light around her. The scorpions moved around her light, bringing the last masked priest to the ground and dispersing in the desert.

Everything else faded. I only saw her. And I went to her. She withdrew her shield as I raised my fingers to her cheek, keeping her eyes on mine. With soft movements, I removed the sandflower from my neck and placed it around hers. Then, I leaned and kissed her lips.

"You are home," she said.

"I am home."

NEW GROUNDS

T he veranda of my new chambers overlooked the marvel my father had created
during my absence. Around the new palace stood only temples to the gods
of death whose true meaning, I knew now, was rebirth beyond this world of sand.
Below, a great rectangular lake was constructed in harmony with the cardinal points.
In it, the sacred crocodile was celebrated.

The humid night was bearable only by the breeze captured by the architects of
this place. Over the silent waters of the lake, I could not but wonder about our old
place on the other side of the river, surrounded by our enemies on the side of the
living, or rather, of that which they, in their ignorance, took for life.

In my mind, rushed the screams in the fire; of the people we had left behind when
we ran for the sanctuary. I wanted to end them all, all masked evil, free the land from
their rambling plague. But Father was right. Now that I was home, it was clearer
to see. There was no simple way to uproot the weeds of darkness. The dark priests
moved amongst innocents who praised them. And defeating those few men that
waited for us out in the desert meant nothing against the vastness of their ranks.

"My love." Idhi placed her hand above mine, interrupting my burning thoughts.

With a blurry smile, my beloved Idhatora met me in my worries, ones she probably could not comprehend but cared for all the same. She leaned and pulled me in
her embrace, grounding me in her presence with a kiss.

"Where does your mind wander?" she asked.

"The fires," I said, "and Innok. I still cannot reach him clearly."

"He is back," she said.

I stood up. She nodded.

"They are receiving them at the palace right now."

I passed through the gardens that separated my apartments from the palace and rushed through the gates of the new throne chamber, engraved again with the winged beetle. The structure was the same as before; three sections, the middle one taller with windows on top, leading to the throne stage. The two side sections, separated by columns, were darker. But the walls here were painted alive. Greens, blues, and reds flickered under the torches, with natural scenes of waters, animals, and trees. Each column looked like a bundle of reeds with a lotus flower on top, opening up to support the roof over our heads.

Father and Queen Muttiya sat on the throne stage. Her face was thinner than it used to be, making her look even more serious. Old Meleethos stood by their side. New signs of age didn't even show on him anymore.

The horns sounded and the gates opened. The commanders entered victorious. Cyrus marched in behind the seasoned warriors. It was with him that Innok had gone. He should have been close. *Where are you?* All men were already inside; without Innok. Horns sounded again. As each commander gave their report to my father, I paced towards the exit and into the hall; empty, with the outer gates already closed.

"Is it me you are looking for?"

I stood tall. My shoulders dropped with a sigh of relief before I turned around. Innok was behind me, leaning on the wall. I ran to him, hugged him. He responded with a groan and readjusted his position.

"Are you hurt?" I asked.

He had garments falling from his shoulders, covering most of his upper body. He pushed my hand away before I could check if he was hurt.

A maiden served our tea. First mine, Idhatora's, and then Innok's. Whatever light reached us on the veranda came from the torches inside and the stars above.

I took a sip. So did Idhatora. The maiden went inside.

"What happened?" I asked.

He looked away.

"Innok..." I said and left my cup on the table.

"We freed the villages," he finally said.

"Balluashir's men?"

"Gone."

"And our people?"

"We lost some soldiers. As for villagers, there weren't many left to save when we arrived."

He took his arm out from below his cloth and took a sip of his tea. He spilled some as he brought it back on the table.

"Innok..." I said in a low voice. *What happened?*

He stood up and removed the cloth from around his shoulders, uncovering his trunk. I said nothing. I didn't even blink. He had lost his arm. He stayed still; for us to see his present condition.

You idiot, I told you not to go! I went to him. Idhatora stayed seated.

"What happened?" I asked as I observed his wound.

"We freed the villages," he said with wet eyes.

I let my embrace enfold him, careful to avoid his wound. In my arms, he let go, bursting into tears.

"You freed the villages," said Idhatora.

Innok rubbed his eyes.

"You saved many people," she continued. "You rid the kingdom and its people of Balluashir's men."

"Now what?" said Innok. "How can I serve? How can I protect anyone?"

Idhatora came close as well. She took his left arm.

"This one is also strong," she said and looked into his eyes.

"You know the ways of the Starani," I said. "You've been learning their ways since you were a child. And you've learned the ways of Areteia."

"Your mind, dear Innok..." said Idhatora and touched his temple. "You have enough knowledge and enough hands to carry it out. You can train yourself again. And you can train others of your swordsmanship ways."

Innok looked at his left arm, stretched his fingers, turned it around. He raised his head. He nodded.

STEPS

I dismounted my horse outside the closed gates of the Black Temple. Idhatora got off her horse as I unloaded two straw-woven bags from mine.

"Is anyone inside?" she asked in a low voice.

The complex reminded nothing of the busy affair that took place here at every solstice. The gigantic white statues were full of sand, the air was silent, and no people chanted aloud under the sun.

I left my bags on the floor and knocked on the gate three times. A priest opened and bowed as we passed through.

"Is it safe?" Idhatora whispered.

I nodded. *Dare they interrupt my ritual?*

The second set of statues, half the height of the ones outside, and the even smaller ones around the third gate, reminded me of those excavated up in the mountains. The symbolism must have been the same; the story of our progeny, the lineage of mankind. The truth was always here, had I the eyes to see it.

"Shall I wait here?" asked Idhatora before the third gate.

I nodded and readjusted the bags on my shoulders before carrying on in the large courtyard. The plane of sand around the stone path was now almost dry since the last flooding. Only when I reached the black spheres with the names of those taken by the plague did I halt.

A few steps past them, towards the temple, I let the bags down. I pulled out two spheres of gold, destined to lie here and be blessed by the waters of the river as it flooded the complex. One was engraved with the name of Chohanatma, the great keeper of the records, the guardian of the library; my grandfather. I placed it on one side of the path. The other sphere was for Chaa, the high priestess of the Great Mother, wise, powerful, and loving; my grandmother. I placed it on the other side of the path. I stood between them, looking at the temple, the sacred space built above the cave of origins, our origins, the sons of the Sun.

Father rested his hand on my shoulder while Idhatora took my hand. I didn't hear them approaching. We stood in silence for a few moments. And in that silence, I could almost see Chaa and Chohanatma above their spheres, calm and smiling, as they deserved to be.

"Are you ready?" asked Father.

My chest was light. I nodded. Innok waited for us at the third gate.

"We will work on your arm again tomorrow, okay?" I said.

"Yes, yes, of course," said Innok.

"You should stop that," Idhatora whispered in my ear as we headed back to the new palace.

The palace halls were noisy, with servants preparing for the celebration, a custom of old that marked the thirty sun cycles of Father's reign. Meleethos overlooked everything. Through the colourful depictions on the walls, officials now engraved ancient symbols accurately to the tenth of a degree.

Polished metal mirrored the light from the high windows around the throne chamber. And behind it, in his private apartments, Father recited prayers in the ancient language of Areteia in front of the amethyst crystal that held his crown.

I waited for him to finish and join me around the table.

"I am not doing it, Father."

"This is the day for both of us," he said.

"I will not be crowned. Not unless you do it with your crown." I pointed at the amethyst altar.

"That's not happening," Queen Muttiya said as she emerged from their bedroom. "That cursed thing almost blinded Favar."

Because of his inner condition! At least, I assumed as much.

"I will not be taking the crown then." *Not if I am corrupted.* "You can name Hetta your successor."

"You are not king yet, and you will not be one today," she said. "That crown is your father's."

Don't twist my words.

"Go prepare, Aletheos," she said. "This is an important day for your father."

I let my chair drag on the floor as I stood up. Father nodded.

"My king," said Commander Harapi of the Starani from the door.

Father invited him in. Innok followed, wearing the Starani black uniform.

"We expect no retaliation. All gates are guarded, and each guest will be searched," said the commander.

"Thank you," Father said. "Is everyone at their post?"

"Yes, my king. Guests are already arriving."

Innok looked at me from the corner of his eyes. They bowed and left.

"I will go prepare," I mumbled and exited behind them.

Innok waited around the corner in the hall.

"So?" I asked.

"I believe they are okay. The Starani are deeply loyal to their duty."

"Keep your eyes on them."

He nodded.

T he warm water infused with oils of lavender, rose, and frankincense loosened my muscles. Orbs of water flew around me. With my mind, I brought the big one to my face, observing the light as it refracted through it. I took my awareness in it, travelled through each drop to find the most miniscule unit of matter. And even further, in the immaterial structures, successively dissolving each one in my mind until I reached the innermost element, the most primordial unit of matter I could find. The one that, if I was correct, would be the same at the root of everything.

I leaned back and freed the orbs of water from the grasp of my will. Some splashed on the floor, others in the bathtub, rippling around me. I closed my eyes at the candles in the empty room, and stayed with the fragrances, soothing at the tip of my nose.

From amidst the warm sensations, Idhatora's lips touched mine. With a smile, I touched her hair and moved my hand below her ear. Her jasmine scent opened my eyes before I pulled her close. She leaned in with a kiss and backed up.

"Not now, my love. It's almost time." She smiled.

She wore a long white dress of thin linen, with sleeves almost touching the floor, golden at the chest with peacock feathers woven like scales above her breasts. Her neck was adorned with gold and hanging aquamarines. And she wore her sandflower I had made into a pendant with thin rope.

"Come on," she said.

She got a towel and came close. She put her hand in the water and coursed the tip of her fingers over my body. I hopped up to catch her, but, with a laugh, she unwrapped the towel between us. I got out, letting the water drip on the floor. She covered my back with the towel, tenderly rubbing me dry.

"Is it safe? Tonight?" she lowered her voice.

I sighed.

"I think it is. Innok is on guard."

I took the sharpened seashell and shaved in front of the mirror while she leaned on the wall, smiling.

"What?" I asked playfully.

She gave me a kiss on the cheek and went outside. In our bedroom waited my garments; white, cut to measure, with golden sigils around the chest. The refined textile was light and soft on my skin. I checked myself in the mirror and patted the clothes to position. From behind me, Idhatora put a pendant around my neck. A lapis lazuli disk inlaid with golden dots, surrounded by six golden wings.

"It's a map of the sky," she said, "with all the wanderers you so adore."

I put my hand on the pendant over my chest. The thought of the wanderers brought mother's scent of safety to my nose. But in a breath's time, three knocks opened our door.

"Ready?" asked Innok, waiting to escort us to the throne chamber.

T he crowd in the throne chamber opened up for Idhatora and me to pass. Whispers were exchanged as we walked to the front. My sister, Hetta, all grown up and adorned, stood under the attentive gaze of frail nan.

The lights faded out. The chamber was silenced into darkness. The horns sounded, and the doors opened. A single blue flame floated above the crowd. In a manner of reverence, everyone moved to the sides. The flame reached the front of the room and flickered before the steps to the throne stage.

Below the flame now stood three men where there were none before. They chanted together.

"Hear the Voice of Silence, see the Light in Darkness. From it, we emerge. We, the chiefs of gods, who guide and oversee the path of all pilgrims. Walk the path and join us as One."

Three bangs echoed in the room. My father stood at the gates.

"Who is it that wishes to pass the threshold?" the three men asked.

"It is I, the pilgrim on the path, the child of the One who has travelled in the seas and reached the shore," the king declared. "Who is it that receives me?"

The words they exchanged took me back to the first reception of Chaa.

"It is we, the sons of Sun, who await your return and that of all the brethren pilgrims on the path, from the first day to this day, 'be with us.'"

"I shall pass the threshold and rejoice with you!"

"We shall receive you and rejoice with you as One!"

Father took a single step through the gates, before the horns accompanied his path through the crowd. All torches in the room flashed with light, and the three men who performed the ceremony were now clear to see. One was Meleethos. The others were not priests of our tradition. One had brown skin with white attire similar to Chohanatma's and a turban covering his dark hair. The other had dark skin with green garments wrapped around him.

The horns quietened. Father bowed before them.

"Do you accept me as one of your own?" he asked.

"Proceed, receive the flame and be reborn as the undead, the eternal, the One," they answered together.

Father walked to the middle of them. He opened his arms to the floating flame above him. The flame sent sparks around the room as it spiralled down in front of his chest.

"I am the Flame!" Father declared as he absorbed it into his heart.

With a deep exhalation, the flame burst through him, engulfing his whole body in fire that burned him not.

Queen Muttiya came from behind the circle of Meleethos and his companions, holding Father's crown. "I, the first from the All, accept you as my equal and give you again this crown. Bear it, no more as king of men, but a god amongst gods."

Father kneeled for his queen to pass his crown. He then turned to the crowd. The three gems glimmered on the heads of the golden snakes that made the crown.

We, the people, bowed before him, and so did the queen and the three men. Father ascended the steps and sat on his throne as the flames faded around him.

Meleethos and the other two were the first to present him with gifts. "You are the fire," they said together.

Meleethos proceeded. "May you rule over the earth," he said and placed a cube of gold on the floor.

Then the second. "And the waters," he said and left a bowl of sandalwood oil.

"And the airs," said the third man with a pyramid of frankincense.

The queen proceeded to present her daughter. "And may you rule the people in kindness and wisdom."

My stomach burned. The foreign kings now went to him, in their turn, to give their gifts. I took a step. Idhatora held me back for a moment. I took another as she let go.

"And I," I said, interrupting the kneeling rulers of kingdoms. The queen stared from the back.

"And I, dear father, give you myself. May I, as all brethren on their path, become one, as you. May your light lead the way as I embody the Fire as well."

Father's eyes sparkled. I bowed my head and turned. Among the crowd, Innok had his eyes wide on me, signalling. In front of him stood Valsaris. With much restraint, I slowly walked to Idhatora, as did Innok.

"How did he get inside?" I whispered.

"Queen's orders," he said.

The queen, on the other side of the room, stood tall with her hands around her Hetta. Next to them stood Valsaris's wife and daughter, Cereena.

"Innok," I said.

"I know," he replied and returned to watch Valsaris.

Another ruler proceeded to the front. It was Meneir, the son of Balluashir. I wondered whether he recognised me from back in the city. I hadn't introduced myself back then.

"I kneel to you, magnificent king," he said. "Our states' affiliation runs as deep as the course of history. We bring gifts of whatever remains of our city. Perfumes and spices and medicinal herbs of the highest order. And the blade of my uncle, who so adored you. And I bring you my sister, Savghana. May the prince accept her as his wife and so unite our nations again. May it be enough to heal the wounds of our recent affairs."

My chest contracted at the proposition. Idhatora took my hand while Savghana bowed to the king. She wore a sand-coloured dress with a light blue chest plate. Her hair curled above her shoulders and, like her brother, her skin was bolder than her clothes. Father stood up.

"The girl shall stay here if she so pleases. She will be protected and provided for. But my son, I believe, saves his heart for another. As for your father... He is gone now, Meneir. Let his course in the sand be washed away by our great river."

Meneir bowed again and backed up with his sister.

Father now turned to the crowd. "I am honoured by your presence; revered members of the order, daughters and sons of this land, and leaders of nations."

"Commander Harapi of the Starani men, proceed! You and your troops have served us well. New estates and gold may keep your men strong."

"Commander Hapshu, Commander Meferin, Commander Shetemut, your king is proud, the land is free..."

I turned to Valsaris as Father presented gifts to those who carried out their duties.

"Cyrus," Father called. "You came from afar, forever loyal to our nation. You may stay. The palace at Dessha is yours to reside and be the face of your king to the north..."

Valsaris merely watched the affair.

"Innok!" Father said.

Innok looked at me from behind Valsaris.

"Come, my boy. You have served greatly," my father continued. "Your duties were of immense significance, albeit less apparent. It is my wish, as that of an exceptional woman we both knew, that you will be rewarded with a house and land and gold. And you may live your life as you wish, away from hardships and servitude."

Innok looked back at me. I only smiled. He turned and bowed to my father.

"Thank you, great king of men. But I will never abandon my post. I will continue to serve if you will have me, as a humble man of the Starani."

"Your devotion is touching, my boy," Father said before looking for the next fortunate man.

Innok walked towards me.

"Thank you," he said.

I patted his shoulder. He winced. I must have hit his injury, now covered by a hanging garment to hide his missing arm. He said nothing of it and looked for Valsaris instead. He was gone. We only exchanged uneasy glances before Father spoke again.

"Let us celebrate," Father said and pointed at the gates.

People exited towards the gardens. I walked with Idhatora and Innok, still looking for the queen's brother amidst the crowd. Cereena reached us, and whispered in Idhatora's ears.

"I will join you in a while," Idhatora said to me.

Innok asked Starani guards to escort my beloved and Cereena while we joined the others in the songs of the night.

The music in the gardens was fading out. Most of the feasting men and women had dispersed, a few lay asleep on the tables or on the ground. Meleethos and the two men who performed the ritual led me and my sister out to the rectangular lake. Idhatora and Innok followed soon behind, together with a few others close to the family and the higher chiefs of the region.

A blue flame appeared from the other side of the lake, while in front of me, Hetta hummed in ceremonial rhythm. The flame was approaching over the lake. And in the darkness of the night, showed Father and his queen, floating on a small boat. With a raised hand, it was Father who held the flame flying.

The ripples around the boat glowed from within them, as if myriads of stars danced in the water against the dark depths of the lake. And through the myriads of lights, the sacred crocodile swam from one side of the boat to the other until the king and queen reached us ashore.

Father sent the blue flame high above us. From it, dozens of flames were born and illuminated the space around us.

"My son, the son of Suns," he said. "Let it be known that you and you alone shall lead this land upon my deliverance."

I bowed my head while he removed his crown. The queen clenched her jaw but said nothing.

"Will you take this crown upon you?" he asked.

I kneeled with my heart pounding at the memory of wounded Favar. I held my breath as the cold gold touched my head. It remained steady, solid. A heartbeat later, I let my lungs empty and my shoulders drop.

The queen ran closer as I stood up. The snakes now shook around my head. Their grip tightened. My stomach burned. My heart raced. *No!* I took a sharp inbreath and turned within. Heart. Spine. Head. I focused on the light above, the pillar connecting me with the higher aspects. I brought them all into awareness; the dragons that flew within me up in the mountain with Chaa and Chohanatma, the thousand petals flower that blossomed in my heart, the diamond at the centre of my forehead. And the serenity of being space and the All.

I opened my eyes. All but Father bowed before me. Light extruded from my skin. Father held a chest with the three gifts from before. He took the gold, let it slip in between his fingers, moving like liquid. The sandalwood oil moved in the air as well. The frankincense burned with thick smoke. They all blended together into a small, thin snake that flew in circles in between his palms. The golden snake shaped scales out of the oil and grew wings of smoke. The golden dragon now raised himself, looking at me.

Meleethos stepped closer behind me, removing Father's crown from my head. From my father's hands, the dragon flashed like lightning, circling around me. Its waving movement and intricate wings solidified through my hair as it raised its head above my eyes.

"A dazzling crown for the rising king," said my father.

My consciousness expanded, far and wide. It enfolded the city, the river, the deserts. The entire kingdom and its people, all were within my light.

"Your path is one," Father exclaimed. "And it is forever entangled with that of your people."

The sun was almost up when I lay in bed as crowned prince. *Crowned prince... of a kingdom in disarray, of a nation that corrupts itself by choice.* I had spent entire sun cycles away only to become able to help my people. But how do you help those who do not wish to see their suffering?

Across from me, Idhatora stood naked. She removed her jewellery, bringing only her sandflower on the bedside table. The rope I had used to weave it into a pendant was now replaced with threads of gold.

"Where did you get that?" I asked.

She joined me in bed and kissed my lips.

"A gift," she said and laid on top of me, pressing her lips against mine.

FALLEN LEAVES

I excused myself and left Father and his advisors. Finances could wait. The sun was almost right above us. I rushed through the gardens, overwatched by the Starani. A guard opened the door to my apartments as I approached.

Innok waited inside, next to another closed door. Behind it, Father had built a replica of my mother's room. He had brought her pot here and built a narrow pond behind it, connected to the river, open on one side overlooking the gardens.

Inside, Idhatora was taking care of the lotus seeds in the water. I couldn't wait to see them bloom; violet, like my mother's. We had brought them from Areteia.

Idhi and Innok went to opposite sides of the pot while I stood on the edge of the open side. I raised my arms to the sun shining over me. With a deep breath, I took my awareness within and then at the light from the great sun disk; let it connect with me, fill me, my body, and consciousness. I turned to the room and breathed out the light onto the stone pot. The white stone absorbed and emitted it back in a milky white mist. We remained quiet with the mist of light, coloured with rainbow refractions.

Many moments after the mist had dissipated, Idhatora broke the silence in a low voice. "Innok, will you please excuse us?"

He, of course, left.

"My love," she said, "I think you are making a mistake."

"So you've said. But what am I supposed to do?"

"Let him move on. You have been trying since he came back. You cannot regrow his arm."

I looked away and swallowed my words. She was probably right.

"Is his hand's etheric structure even alive? How are you going to build the physical arm back?"

"I need to try, Idhi. I am trying to recreate his etheric counterpart as well."

"You are causing him more pain. For as long as you experiment, he clings on to hope where there is none."

"You don't know that."

"My love... I trust in you. And you told me yourself..."

"I have to keep trying."

"Why?"

I kept silent.

"Aletheos, as long as you don't accept what happened to him, he won't either. Let him move on."

She kissed my cheek and headed outside. Innok, waiting on the other side of the door, now returned.

"Shall we?" he said.

I pressed my lips and nodded.

He sat on the floor. I joined him, focusing on his subtle bodies, all invisible to him. Channels, like roots and branches, spread throughout his physical body. I had healed many of them in our previous sessions. But those that used to hold his arm had dissolved. I created new ones, but they kept disconnecting from his own and atrophied into dissolution. I put my hands where his arm would be and pushed out different kinds of force.

"Can you feel any of this?"

"My wound hurts."

"But not on your arm?"

"I have no arm!" he said, capturing my eyes.

I turned back down and focused again. I led the energy from my hands to recreate the etheric structure. Again. Hoping it would hold this time. My chest tightened with a burn in my heart. It wouldn't. With a sigh, I let my hands drop. I stood up and walked to the open side of the room.

"Where are you going? Continue!"

"I can't, Innok."

"What?" He stood up. "No! Continue!"

"I can't! Whatever I do, it doesn't hold!"

"Then do more!"

I looked into his eyes, and shook my head, gently.

"No," he said. He sighed at my silence. "Well, this is nice, isn't it? I almost died for you!"

With one arm, he pushed and twisted until he managed to get his shirt off. My breathing got fast at the scars filling his chest and back.

"I fought for you!" he said. "I kept by your side!"

"No, Innok, you left," I said with wet eyes. "You should have come back home with me!"

"Why would I? To keep guard at the door while you spend your life with your beloved? Why would I..."

"What did you expect?" I interrupted him. "You knew I loved her!"

He froze. His shoulders dropped. He closed his eyes.

"I don't know what I expected. We should have never left Areteia," he said.

"That wasn't a choice, was it?"

"There is no place for me here."

My chest tightened. *You promised. Your duty lies with me.*

"Then go," I yelled. "You have a house and land now. Go. Leave. The king released you from your duties."

He clenched his jaw. He said nothing. He grabbed his shirt from the floor and slammed the door behind him.

ROUND TABLE

B irds chirped in the waking garden, now cleared of all tables and drunk guests. Two Starani men escorted me to the throne chamber, where Father waited with Meleethos and the two men who had performed the ritual with him.

Father nodded at the man with darker skin and clothes. "This is Manasatas," he said, "the order's high priest in the South."

Manasatas came close and bowed his head, keeping his hands close to his chest. I returned the gesture.

"This is Paradchi," said Father, of the man with attire similar to Chohanatma's. "He has taken charge of the sanctuary in Chohanatma's absence."

"Do you not remember me, prince?" he said.

I took a good look at his face. Nothing.

"You stayed at my cabin on your way up the mountain."

Oh, yes. "I..." I coughed. "I thank you for your hospitality."

"Shall we?" said Meleethos.

We proceeded behind the throne and into the assembly room. The queen was already there.

"My honourable lady," Manasatas said to her and bowed.

"It's been a long time, my friend," she said and touched his shoulder.

Paradchi went to her as well.

"Hello, Paradchi," Muttiya said and went around the table.

The king removed his crown and placed it on the amethyst altar. I forgot to wear mine again. He sat first, and we joined him around the table. Father smiled, looking at us.

"I am happy to see you all," he said. "And that my son is now part of our own."

Paradchi joined in Father's sentiment while Manasatas maintained his rigid look.

"Paradchi," said Father, now serious, "have you enforced measures?"

"Concerning what?" I asked.

"We have terminated access to the town," Paradchi answered. "The paths to the mountain are now inaccessible as well."

My neck stiffened.

"You expect more attacks at Areteia?" I asked.

"Laypeople now know of our sanctuary; warriors and dark priests. We won't allow another sacrilege," said Paradchi.

"The library?" I asked.

"We reopened the tunnel. But Chohanatma," he looked down for a moment, "may we meet again, refused to give me his word. And we don't know to whom Chaa gave hers."

"The town?" I asked.

"We rebuilt what we could."

"And we," continued Manasatas in a dry accent, "have closed the school and restricted access to the mysteries."

"That's not what we should be doing!" I proclaimed.

Father turned to me. Meleethos faced the centre of the table, blind as he was.

"People need understanding, "I said. "Closing the gates to wisdom will serve no one, only drown us in darkness! Chaa said it herself. The library used to be filled with neophytes. For the sun cycles that I resided at the sanctuary, only old Rajvidya and a couple of other old men studied the scrolls. The library is gone, the paths are gone. And you decided to withhold access to the teachings as well?"

"Knowledge must survive. The order must survive!" Manasatas responded.

"So, you decide to hide?" I asked. "That's your answer? Hiding! And hiding the truth with you?"

I looked at my father. "You once told me that the order oversees traditions. Is that what you meant? Hiding as silent observers of the towering darkness?"

"Our work is still carried out, Aletheos," Father said. "We stand as guides to humanity."

"But choose not to teach them how to guide themselves," I responded.

"The order must survive, young prince," said Paradchi.

"The men that make it are not the order," I said. "The order serves the highest of knowledge. And knowledge survives only in the minds of men. Not in inaccessible libraries with keys lost. Wisdom is cultivated in men's consciousness. How do you assume the order's survival if not by laying the seeds of wisdom wherever we go? Otherwise, what's the survival of a few old men supposed to achieve?"

"We don't know how they found us, young prince," said Paradchi. "We can, therefore, do nothing to stop another attack. Unless you will give us the army we need to protect ourselves."

"We can spare none!" Muttiya exclaimed.

"We have a sacred duty," said Paradchi.

"And I have mine," the queen responded. "The safety of my people, my family! We have already suffered enough because of your duty."

Father glanced at her next to him. She kept looking at us.

"You can have a dozen men each," Father said.

"Aletheos!" Muttiya protested.

Father placed his hand on hers. "But they must volunteer. I will order none of them to follow you."

Surely none would leave their posts if not as part of their duty. Father knew that. *Would Innok?* I shook my head at the thought.

"I don't need them," said Manasatas. "Our army is loyal and strong."

"What can a dozen men do?" said Paradchi. "We still don't know how they found us!"

"Altazadeh," said Father.

"Altazadeh?" asked Paradchi with a burst of laughter. "Where did you go unearth such echo of a man?"

Father said nothing.

"Besides, Altazadeh had his memories wiped clean before being expelled," Paradchi added. "He is probably dead somewhere, drowned in his madness."

Father hit his fist on the table and stood up. "You took his memories?"

Paradchi widened his eyes and withdrew his smile. His mouth moved, but, for a few moments, uttered not a word. "Taking his memory of the House of Lotus was a precautionary measure!" he finally mumbled.

"You cannot meddle in people's brains!" Father said. "Who authorised this?"

Paradchi stared at Father's outburst.

"Surely not the council!" Meleethos said.

"And who do you assume made away with the council?" Paradchi stood up as well.

Father remained silent. So did the rest of us.

"While you, Chaa, and Chohanatma took over the order..."

"Elected!" said Meleethos, who sat unmoved.

"While you prided yourselves on reorganising the order after the elders were murdered, I ensured our survival! You should thank me!"

"He was already expelled. How do you assume he got to the elders?" asked my father.

"Those old, stubborn men you so admired... you think they had no weaknesses. But what was Altazadeh's talent?"

Father sighed. "He was a healer."

"What does that..." I asked.

Meleethos interrupted. "A good healer is one who can connect deeply with others, find their ailment, and bring it to their conscious mind."

"And...?"

"A twisted mind can use such talent in many ways," Meleethos said.

"He found their weaknesses," I said.

"He used them, drove them mad," said Paradchi. "One's heart couldn't take it. Nor the other's brain. The third, in his despair, took his own life." He turned to Father again. "And none of you thought to check the records to find out why! You just assumed they died of old age. How very convenient it turned out for you three!"

"How dare you, Paradchi? Convenient for us? Master Avalais was Chohanatma's father!"

Meleethos took a deep breath. His eyes, blind as they were, rapidly moved from side to side. He sighed as his eyes came to stillness. "It's true," he said.

Father looked out the window of the assembly room. He brought his hands to his head, hid his eyes, rubbed his neck.

"Father?"

"Altazadeh had been in the sanctuary long before I arrived," he said. "The order was strong back then, accepting students from all over the world. He helped train me. He was a good man. But he was impatient. And our teachers refused to pass the sacred words to him. He distanced himself; from me, from Chaa and Chohanatma, from everything other than studying. He was always in the library. Until, to his dismay, he found some scrolls that indicated parts of the words. He became obsessed. And resorted to incomplete rituals that brought destruction. He used forces in forbidden ways, and he was expelled for it. The doors were sealed for him."

"Chaa mentioned him back at the library," I said.

They all turned to me. It was Father who spoke again.

"After the loss of the council, we worked fiercely to keep its fire alive. And, there came a time for us to carry the flame beyond the sanctuary. Before I left, I went to give my farewells to my friends and patients in the city. I found Altazadeh in the infirmary, fallen into lunacy. His attendant told me he had been living in the streets close to the temple. He would attack whoever tried to assist him with food or water. He ate rats and leaves from the trees."

He turned to Paradchi. "You did that to him! You don't dig in people's brains!"

"I did what was right for the order! You didn't see what he did to those people...his very patients."

"That's why Chohanatma never gave you the word," I said. "And sent you away to man that cabin."

His nostrils flared. Father looked at Meleethos, who remained silent.

"I stayed a few days and helped him stand on his feet," Father continued. "He was getting better. He was opening up to me, gradually showing glimpses of his old self. But he never talked of the library. Nor of our past together."

"What did you do, Aletheos?" asked Manasatas.

Father took a deep breath. "I brought him back with me. I gave him a house to live in and land to cultivate."

"He is here?" Paradchi asked.

"I met with him a few times. He was getting better. But after a while, he distanced himself again. Then, he came to see me. He was different. He had been dwelling in the temples, losing himself into obsession again. He wanted to come into the palace and preside over the temples. He was convinced he could teach the nation of true power, introduce us to a new god. I let him go. I didn't see him again. Until the dark days of the plague, fuelled by the growing numbers of dark practitioners. When I ordered prohibition, he came to see me. I explained the effects of his rituals to him. I thought he would understand; he had taken much of the training we had. Instead, he threatened that my family and I would break at the fury of his god."

"His inner demons twisted his mind again," Meleethos said.

"That was the last time I heard of him," said Father. "Until Valsaris told us it was him behind all of this. The plague. The death of my mother. Chaa's parents. The corruption of my late son. The invasion of the library."

"How did he know of the sanctuary? If he did not remember?" asked Manasatas.

"You can keep telling yourselves that," said Valsaris as he entered the room, "but it won't make it true."

I jumped off my seat. "What are you doing here?"

"Has your father not told you that you need me? Certain memories of Altazadeh may be scattered," he said at the assembly, "but your friend here only confused him for a while. I assure you; his knowledge is all there. And his god gave him plenty of power."

"How dare you speak to us in such a manner?" said Manasatas.

"You have been ignorant of his doings for so long..." Valsaris said.

"Silence, Valsaris!" Father intervened. "Mind your words!"

"You have been allowed back in the palace," said the queen, "but your deeds are not forgotten, dear brother!"

Valsaris clenched his jaw at his sister's words. He said nothing more, merely turned away. I ran behind him into the empty throne chamber.

"Valsaris!"

He looked back before he reached the gates. I expanded the force around me and banged him on the door, keeping him still.

"If he had his memories, why did he wait for so long to attack the sanctuary?"

He struggled to carry air out of his mouth. "He didn't remember how to get there."

"Then how?"

"He followed you!"

My hold on him broke. He bent, gasping for air.

"Listen, boy," he got up and grabbed my shirt, "you do well to keep in that pretty little head of yours that you need me." He pushed me back and went for the exit. "For the sake of all of us!"

SEVEN RIVERS

The mist in mother's room had already dissolved. Idhatora sat with crossed legs close to the white pot while I stood at the open side of the room. I held my hands high, evoking out of air that primordial substance at the root of all matter. I thought of a form, a small amethyst stone; the dust, the elements, the conditions that would have made it. The invisible matter took the shape of the amethyst crystal, the mental form. Now I needed to infuse it with the desire to exist. I turned within and searched in my body and emotional planes for how to direct emotional force into my creation.

Sparks flew from the invisible mass. I held my hands still, trying to focus on the emotional material that came through. I needed to concentrate. What is this feeling? How can I tap into it? Anxiousness took its place, whatever it had been. My worries rushed out and united with my creation, melting it out of existence.

I dropped my hands and breathed in the view from outside. The orange sun of the afternoon smoothened all it touched. The river ran with the pinks and purples of the sky. Three distinct lights flashed in the river, one pink, one blue, one yellow. I slowly made forms of them, seal-like creatures looking back at me, the three water elementals I saw on my mother's island. I smiled at them, wondering whether they were the same three or just of the same kind. They remained still in the middle of the river, whose water reached the pond of this room.

"Where is Innok?" Idhatora asked from behind me, as if she didn't know.

"Gone."

She pushed her lips together. "Is he coming back?"

"I don't know." I shook my head and pushed my thoughts away. "Shall we?"

She rested her open palms on her thighs, took a deep breath, and closed her eyes. I took my awareness within and spoke out loud the path I followed.

"From the sacred chamber of the heart," I instructed, "to the spine, into the brain..." I waited for her consciousness to shine at the right place. "... to the crown of the head. Above it, there is a pillar of light. Take a deep breath and go into it."

She did. With ease. We met beyond our bodies. *She must have been practising with Meleethos.* I smiled at her while still talking in the flesh.

"This is expanding our consciousness beyond our bodies, while still focused on the physical realm, the lowers of the worlds."

She nodded.

"Now, come with me."

Our consciousnesses floated upwards, each in our own pillar, as our surroundings changed into masses of muddy and faded colours.

"This is the emotional world, the world of waters. As the physical world changes with our actions, this world changes according to the emotions of each incarnated being. It, of course, has different levels, beginning with the densest of emotions and ending with those of kindness, loving, and caring."

She looked around.

"Each colour is an emotional state," I said. "Together, this world is the accumulation of the emotional experience of us all."

I looked upwards. We moved on into drier clouds of colours. Each one was more clear, more specific.

"This is the world of mind; the lower part of it. This is the aggregate of our thoughts, which we call the realm of men's fire. Its higher planes are the intermediate between the lower worlds, those of human experience, and those above us, of spiritual truths. Beyond us, we have the worlds of Fire."

I pointed up. We floated upwards as a white flare burst above us. She slowed down before entering the higher realms.

"What's wrong?"

"I... I can't move." She looked around. "I... I can't!" She was sinking. A black cloud weighed on her legs.

"Idhatora! Look at me."

She looked into my eyes.

"It is okay," I said, calm. "Take my hand."

She reached out, but missed my hand as her emotions dragged her down. Calm, I took and brought her close.

"My love," I said in a deep voice. "Look at me."

She panted. I looked into her eyes until her breathing slowed down.

"It is okay," I said with a smile. I held her in my embrace as we moved on. "Take a look," I said.

The currents of white flames flew free around us.

"As Meleethos told you," I said, "from here onwards, we have four more worlds. This one is the realm that embodies the spark that is the individualised spirit of man. Itself, the individualised man, is in the realm above this one. The sixth realm thereafter is the collective plane of all individualised sparks, from which all individualities emerge. And, the seventh, is the manifested Absolute which will absorb our consciousness during the nights of our existence."

Her eyes rapidly moved around, the knowledge restructuring her mind.

"Allow the light of this plane with all the wisdom it embodies to fill your consciousness."

She nodded as she absorbed what she could.

"Are you ready?" I asked.

She took my hand as we moved back into our bodies and mother's room. I opened my eyes at the violet lotuses in the pond. Tears slipped down her cheeks.

"It is so beautiful," she said.

"Our true nature," I responded.

I slowly stood up, still smiling, and turned away with the image of the dark cloud around her feet.

OFFERINGS

T wo guards rushed to me as I stepped outside my apartments. I pointed at them to stay at their posts, and proceeded alone. Further into the garden, Idhatora enjoyed the company of Cereena and Savghana, the sister of Meneir. The foreigner must have witnessed a couple of sun cycles more than the rest of us, probably twenty-one or so.

I smiled at Idhi as I walked away, but she fixated on the cloak hanging from my back. She excused herself and came to me.

"You are going?" she asked.

I nodded.

"And without guards? Aletheos!"

"I will be fine."

I pulled the hood of my white cloak above my head.

"There is nothing to see," she said. "Nothing changed."

I had already made up my mind.

"Okay," she exhaled. "Take this off at least," she said and took away the lapis pendant with golden wings. "Don't let them see you."

She adjusted the hood around my head.

S mall boats were tied to poles in the ground along the river bank. I set one free and pushed it into the water as I jumped on. Moving faster than anticipated, the current spun the boat sideways. With one hand on the sails pole to keep my balance, I closed my eyes and expanded my consciousness to the water.

The boat slowed down. I had established a hold. I opened my eyes to the three water elementals looking at me. I gave them a nod and moved my hands to mark my intended course until the water aligned with my will.

I hadn't been in the city since before I left with Chaa. I wondered what changes were brought about during my absence and after Father moved our palace west of the river.

I guided the water, carrying me to the other side, all the while away from some fishermen. With an exhalation of a push, the water brought half the boat to the sand.

The roads were busy as ever; merchants with their customers, smiths with their craft. Priests were now in the streets as well. People had gathered around one in particular, leaving food and money at his feet.

"Only the gods' favour can deliver us through false prophecies," he preached, "the teaching of those who would have you defile our traditions and spit on our nation's history!"

Some people raised their fists, shouting in agreement. Others just watched, as if mesmerised. I turned away from the nonsense while a couple bumped into me, trying to lay their eyes on the priest. I pushed them aside and passed through the small crowd.

Rectangular stone altars filled the main road. 'For the favours of the Gods,' the inscriptions wrote above the relief of the father of gods.

A woman ran and kneeled next to me. She placed bread and wheat on the stone and closed her eyes in prayer. *For the favours of the Gods! Ha! People think Spirit cares for offerings. And the order thinks it's time to refrain from teaching!*

I shook my head and moved along the stone altars, all of them overflown with food and herbs and flowers, leading to the temple that, apart from the offering altars, was always closed to laypeople. Only priests were allowed to enter the sacred spaces. And the royals, as first servants of the gods.

A little further, at the end of the main road, stood the old palace with two guards at its gates. The walls around them were dirty with paint. 'Death to the snake king.' Below it, in strokes of black, a bird devoured three snakes.

"Ay! You! Move along," said one of the guards.

I turned away beneath my hood. I took a turn. Then another. I remembered Altazadeh's fluttering robe. Left. Right. Left. Left. I reached the quiet alley, closed on all sides, and walked to the house at the other end.

'Turn away,' Chaa had said last time.

The door was clumsily painted with three black feathers.

'Turn away,' she had said.

The door creaked open against my hand. Rats ran away from the light; their excrements crackling below my sandals as I walked inside. The dark room echoed with whispers from upstairs. With quiet movements, I went for the staircase, received by a rotten smell on the second step. I followed it to the upper floor. What little light came through the closed windows showed the space even dirtier than the one below.

A baby's cry broke the silence. In a heartbeat, I rushed into the room it came from. It stank like a festered wound. My eyes adjusted to the darkness as dark silhouettes moved around. Unable to make forms of them, and certainly outnumbered, I went to the window and pulled down the dark garments that kept the light outside. Dust spiralled around in the sunbeam that came through, and landed on many faces in the corner of the room.

They all stared at me. With dirty faces and torn clothes. One of them held a baby.

"I am not here to hurt you," I said.

They were all children. The one in the front held a rusty sickle.

"Get out!" she said.

I showed her my empty hands. "Are you alone here?"

"What do you want?"

The children behind the brave girl looked at me with bulging eyes. A little one had his hands around her waist, hiding his face against her clothes. Another had tears sliding down his muddy cheeks. One lay on the floor amidst the dust and rat faeces.

"Is she sick? I want to help," I said with my arms still high for her to see.

"Give me your sword," she said and shook her sickle towards me.

I touched the cold metal on my waist; Innok's.

"I am sorry. I cannot do that."

"Why not?"

"It was a gift from a friend. Please. Let me help."

"How?" she asked, lowering, just a little, her weapon.

My ears pounded. I skipped every other step on the stairs and pushed the door open. I stood tall as I paced through the narrow streets and into the main road towards the palace. Only when I reached the temple did I stop. Its stone altars overflowed with food. I grabbed two loaves of bread. No, I could hold a third. And grapes and dates and figs and nuts. I stacked them against my chest.

"Ay!" A man's voice. *Dare he challenge me?*

By the time I turned around, a small crowd had gathered. And the preaching priest stood proud, quiet, expecting the gullible to do his bidding.

"Sacrilege!" said one.

"How dare you steal from the gods?" said another.

"How dare you ruin the poor offeror's favours with the gods?" yelled a third.

A fourth came with a fist. I leaned away as his punch landed on my chest. The food dropped in the street.

"You are all idiots!" I yelled.

The crowd grimaced into silence. With flaring nostrils, the priest now took a step forward. He raised his arm and opened his mouth. Before his next outbreath, I let my hood drop, showing my face. He didn't utter the words he intended, only stared at me.

I climbed on the altar. "You are all idiots!" I said, looking down at the priest.

More priests gathered to defend the gods.

"The gods don't care for food!" I declared. "The gods care for mercy and kindness."

The guards of the palace ran to prevent a fight. One raised his spear at me.

"Get down, young man," he said.

The other guard stayed back with narrowed eyes.

"Do you know who I am?" I asked the second guard.

He nodded and rushed to lower the other's spear. He said something to him, and they both kneeled.

"Stand up, right now! And bring me a kart!"

I stepped down from the altar as the guards arrived with the kart. And I filled it with food from the altars. The crowd protested. The priests did nothing.

"Follow me," I ordered the guards.

More guards cleared the way through the crowd.

A priest stayed close. "You think Maya will accept this? You will regret defying us," he whispered as I passed by him.

I stopped. "Tell your high priest this," I said and turned back, jumping on the altar. "Listen, everyone! I am Prince Aletheos. And I am telling you! The gods don't need food. Only the priests do. Count your priests. There will remain one altar for every two priests. The rest of your offerings will feed your poor neighbours. This might actually mean something to your gods as well."

The priest's face was red. He said nothing.

T he children came out in the sun. The kart had everything. Some filled their bellies with bread and nuts. Others munched on the sweetness of figs. All of them drank water. The brave girl, the tallest of the children, had nothing. She took the food out of the kart and only passed it to the others.

"Have some as well," I said. "There is plenty."

She looked at me, hesitant.

I turned to the guards. "You! Please make sure the kids will have food from the altars."

They bowed.

"About the sick girl," I said, "let me take her to the palace. She will be nursed."

"We won't go to the land of the dead," she answered.

"That's not..."

She stood unmoved, but her eyes were wet.

"Okay," I said. "I will send for her tonight, as soon as I get back."

She exhaled in relief.

I pushed my boat into the river. The three elementals moved cheerful, as if in a dance, as if with the beat of my heart.

My house was empty. Idhatora was out again, more and more it seemed. I went into mother's room, moved towards the open side, and looked at the city beyond the gardens and the river.

"You are back," Idhatora said from behind me.

"Where were you this late?" I asked in a low voice.

She gasped, staring at my clothes, now stained by food and dirt.

"I did good today," I said with a light heart and big smile.

WOUNDS

"**Y**ou did what?" Father asked.

"It's about time the temples lose some of their power," I said.

Only Meleethos sat at the table. Father paced around the assembly room and I leaned on the wall next to the window, waiting for Father to explain his objection.

"There is a balance to be kept, prince," said Meleethos.

"Balance? We have left our people at the mercy of beasts!" The word fumed within me. "Balance?" I repeated. "If we were to bring balance upon them, they would have their heads floating down the river!"

"I understand your intentions, my dear son. I do. But this will bring more disorder. I made the same mistake when I prohibited dark practices. It became fuel for those who still hid within our own, a fuel that helped burn down our connection with religion. Now they have taken over, almost completely."

"How about the initiates? Aren't they still in the temples?" I asked.

Meleethos spoke again, slowly. "They are afraid for their lives. They are asking for refuge."

Father rubbed his eyes as the queen entered the room. "Have you found him?" Father asked her.

She nodded, followed by Valsaris a few steps behind.

"Why did you call for me?" Valsaris asked. "I can't be seen coming and going from the palace."

"Are they planning to retaliate?" asked Father.

"Altazadeh has appeared at their call. All he said was that the priests should protect the faith of the people. He will not instruct on ill deeds. Nor did he say to refrain from them."

"He needs to maintain a facade," Father interrupted.

"Yes. He presents his intentions as concern for tradition and the spiritual state of the people. And the priests will justify their actions to that effect."

"As you did in the library," I said.

He sighed. "He said that you held the knowledge hidden," he said to justify himself.

"And commissioned savage warriors to find it," I answered. "What did you expect, Valsaris? That Balluashir cared for spiritual truths? Or that his men would kindly ask for scholarly enlightenment?"

Idhatora opened the door, gasping.

"I am sorry, my king. Aletheos, come!"

I walked up the cobble pathway just outside the city. Idhatora was a step behind, together with four or five guards, while a maiden led the way.

"Thank you, my king," she said.

Prince.

"But I didn't know what else to do. I am so sorry."

"You did well to come for me," I said.

"I knew you two were close. Thank you," she said.

"How is he now?"

"A priest keeps visiting. He is mostly asleep afterwards. But when he wakes up... he is in pain."

We passed through vineyards and reached the mansion. The maiden took us upstairs and opened the door to a dark, dump room.

"Innok," said Idhatora and ran close to his bed.

I stayed at the door. "What's that smell?" I asked.

"Mandrake oil, my king," said the maiden.

Prince.

"And sedative incenses," she continued.

"Where did you get them?"

"The priest brings them. Every time."

"Remove the curtains. Open the windows," I said and walked to Innok.

He sweated under his sheets. His eyes twitched as the sun touched him. He opened his drooling mouth for a deep breath. And screamed! With a cry that pounded on my heart, he stretched his body in agony. My neck tightened as I swallowed, and I took another breath trying to keep myself composed as I leaned over him.

"Innok!"

I held him down as he turned and screamed. He finally opened his eyes, even a little.

"I am here," I repeated.

He looked into my eyes.

"Help me," he said.

"What happened?"

He screamed and swung around in his bed, pushing me away. His sheets were wet with blood. I pulled them away. Red masses had grown below his right shoulder, abscessed, seeping blood. It was an arm! No skin. Only muscles; bloody. And grey bones. Black patches stained the arm with little worms wiggling through them.

I didn't do this! I panted. *That's not me! That can't be me!*

"Cut it off!" he yelled in tears.

I pushed my hands on his forehead and chest, thrusting his consciousness beyond his body.

"He fainted?" the maiden asked, eager to help.

Idhatora kept her back while Innok and I moved beyond our bodies.

"What happened, Innok?"

He looked around and down at his body. "What is this?"

"Innok! What happened?"

He rubbed his eyes and forehead; he had both his arms in this plane. He stretched his neck.

"I left." He looked up at me. "I messed up."

"Innok! We don't have much time before you are drawn back to your body!"

"When I came here..." He looked around again, as if trying to remember. "He kept visiting. He said he could help with my arm. He said he could help where you failed."

My stomach unclenched. I didn't do this!

"Dark magic, Innok? You know about this!"

He frowned.

"What do you mean?" he asked.

"Your mother, Innok. Dark magic is never a solution."

He sighed. "He said it was your father's fault it didn't work back then."

He shook his head. He knew now, this was a lie. His right arm suddenly boiled from the inside with blood bubbling through. With a scream, he opened his eyes in the flesh. I opened mine as well.

"Cut it off!" he screamed. "Cut it!"

A cool breeze made the almost transparent curtains wave in the room. And out. In again. My bed was comfortably cool, with Idhatora asleep behind me. She had left her arm around me, warming my chest with her palm. Outside, the stars faded with every passing moment as the sun neared the horizon for a new journey.

I should be working on Innok's wound. No. He should be resting now. Maybe after the sun rises.

My stomach burned with acid at the memory of his worm-infested muscles. I could still smell the decomposition. My heart ached at his cries as the healers took off his decaying arm.

I let out a warm outbreath. I could get no sleep. Carefully, I got away from Idhatora's embrace, threw some cold water on my face and walked out on the veranda overlooking the gardens.

My stomach still burned. And it went into spasms, pushing the acid upwards. I barely stretched my neck beyond the pillars as the bile left my mouth. I leaned there for a few moments, waiting for my stomach to either push out more or calm down. And I breathed; slowly.

After a while, I stood up, still focusing on each inhalation and exhalation. The leaves on the trees now captured the orange light of the rising sun, moving with the breeze in an almost imperceivable rhythm. The flowing river burbled beyond the gardens as the sun's light stretched on it.

The city was waking up. The light on the eastern banks of the living though, uncovered more than reeds and boats. Several wooden poles rose high. People hung from them, facing me and the palace. Many wore the uniform of the Starani with spears coming out of their chests. Others, shorter, had no uniform. They were children. One had a sickle hanging from her bowels.

SCARS

We buried them all. With manners and glory of kings. The images of their faces as we took them down from the poles kept flashing to mind. I kept pushing them away, replacing them with the children's laughter under the light of the sun, as they munched on the goodies I had brought them. Father made sure the priests performing the funerary rituals were all initiates; none of their killers would contaminate with darkness their death as well!

When the ceremonies ended, we headed to the city. Idhatora and the queen stayed at the new palace while we proceeded across the river to the old one. Father wanted to address the people. And I wanted to see the faces of murderers.

Our guards cleared the way through protesting crowds. Priests yelled, preaching in the streets. Invisible to them, dark smoke flared around; a testament to their sentiment. How insignificant they seemed, mere shells of men. Yet they roared like monsters. Only if the people abandoned them, would the desolation of their promises truly show. But only at the sight of their true nature, would people abandon them.

On a raised platform stood the priest that threatened me when I took their altars away. He looked down on us with sunburned cheeks above his grin. *How do I take their power from them?* The thought ground my teeth. *How do I make the people accept the effects of their choices and see their suffering?*

From behind us, ran a man, pushing the guards away, crashing on me, and pulling me to the ground. It was Valsaris. "Get out. Go back!" he whispered. "I am sorry, my prince," he yelled as he got up for the crowd to hear.

He passed by Father and walked away, calmly to disappear amidst the people. From them, flew a pomegranate, landing on my chest before breaking on the ground. Father turned to me.

"There're your offerings!" a man shouted with cheers from the crowd.

Others followed. The guards gathered around us, forming a wall with their shields. Above us, an arrow pierced the air and landed deep in the chest of the smiling priest. People stopped yelling. All was silent. Only for a moment. Then their anger burst. They surrounded us. Stones now rumbled on the guards' shields, scraping the metal. They were everywhere.

Father missed a step. He brought his hands to his head, turning red with blood. I ran, put Father's arm around my shoulders to keep him from falling. Guards came out of the old palace and pushed people away. They cleared a path for us towards the palace, with their shields now hiding the sky.

I carried father towards the gates. 'Death' and 'fury of gods' I read on the walls; only a few of the slurs painted in black and red. The doors closed behind us. I sat Father on a bench in the yard and raised his head.

"Are you okay?"

He didn't answer.

"Father?"

He merely looked at me with hazy eyes. His hair dripped with blood through his delicate crown.

Father sat inside, holding his head. Beyond the balcony, fires burned through the night. People shouted. Some tried to climb the walls, but met with the wrath of the Starani.

"We need to get you home," I said. "We need to have your wound treated."

"Shall we clear the roads?" the Starani's commander proposed, standing tall and unmoved.

"No, Harapi," said Father with a broken voice, covering his eyes from the flames of torches. "Violence will get us nowhere."

I raised my voice. "How do we deal with this, then?"

"We listen to them," he said.

"Listen to them? They want us dead!"

"No. What they want is to feel they have a choice."

"The wrong choice! They demand their own demise!"

"Son, I took their choice away twice by now; prohibition and exile. People need to learn. Let them practise what they want. It seems to be what they need."

"It's not a real choice if our ways are not available to them as well."

He took his hand away from his eyes and looked into mine.

Valsaris joined us. "Are you okay?" He rushed to my father.

I narrowed my eyes at his supposed concern. "How did you come in?" I asked.

"I sneaked in. Aletheos, we need to have your injury looked after."

"How did you come in, Valsaris?" I repeated.

"The passage from the cave in the desert." He turned to Father again. "We can escape through it."

I helped him raise my father.

"No one knows about that passage," I said.

"Innok told me," he said. "We need to move fast; the wound must be looked after."

SCALES

I nnok lay awake in the infirmary. It was almost morning. Meleethos and Savghana brought special ointments while Valsaris and Muttiya helped Father up. I went close.

"No, my son. It's okay," Father said. He could barely hold his head up. "It's okay," he repeated. "I will go rest. You do the same."

Idhi held my hand as Father left with the queen and guards.

"Shall we?" she said, touching my shoulder.

"You go, my love. I will stay a little," I said and looked at Innok.

She kissed my cheek and nodded at Innok before leaving with Savghana, escorted away by guards. I was now alone with him. From next to his bed, the window showed the blue of the sky. The sun had risen. I couldn't imagine he got much sleep either. His eyes were swollen black, and the sheets were dirty, either by the ointments or the rotten pus still dripping from his patched shoulder.

Why would you allow dark rituals to be performed on you? Your mother's state must have been gruesome to witness.

"What?" he asked.

"I am very sorry if I wasn't clear enough," I said.

He narrowed his eyes.

"Back in Areteia, I mean. Being close to you was nice and comforting and fun. I am sorry if I have hurt you."

He sighed. "You were right before, Aletheos. I knew your feelings for Idhatora. But somewhere in between the closeness and the fun, I got overtaken. But I did know your spirit was raised by her alone. And it's true. I see how you look at her. And she, you."

"I am sorry either way."

"We were friends. Everyone has friends before they are committed to one. I've had others before," he said, as if it was I that needed comforting.

"How about now? Cereena? Or Savghana? Or one of the guards, your old mates?"

He shook his head and shrivelled with pain. He looked outside.

"Innok, will you come back? We have work to do."

"If you will have me..."

I dismissed his insecurity with silence and sat by him.

"Innok, remember the passage underneath the old palace? The one we used when we left the kingdom? Have you mentioned it to Valsaris?"

He narrowed his swollen eyes. "No. Why would I?"

I nodded and pressed my lips together. "He said we led them to the sanctuary. Could they have followed us?"

"Not possible!" he said. "Even if they tried, they were never close enough."

"How can you be certain?"

"We were always careful. Chaa scouted our surroundings every day in her... mind. And we took extraordinary measures. We kept changing our guides and took false routes. None of them knew where we headed."

"What about Balluashir's men, those who took us close to the camp?"

"Even if they somehow survived to find their way back, no one there knew of our plans for Areteia."

I took a deep breath.

"I am certain!" Innok said.

F ather sat with one hand on the table of the assembly room. He held a small bundle of herbs that helped with his pain; leaves of blue lotus, cumin, and some other high-quality herbs. His head was still bandaged and too swollen for his crown. He leaned towards Muttiya, who held his hand and whispered in his ear, words that made him laugh. How peaceful they seemed. No crowns, no fancy dresses, no official facades. Just a wife comforting her husband.

I let my hand slide over the engravings in the wood. Flames formed the outermost circle of the table. In the middle, a plain cycle. Muttiya's gaze wandered in the assembly room as I leaned back, looking away from their intimate interaction.

Above us, the ceiling was painted with an animal on each corner; an ox, a lion, an eagle, and a serpent. They reminded me of the performance we attended in Areteia. The four animals held a lapis blue disk depicting the constellations of the celestial sphere. Heroes, animals, symbols, all looked down on us; our work, our discussions, our decisions.

Meleethos entered the room with Commander Harapi. Father tried to push himself up but gasped and brought his arm to his head. With a gentle touch on his shoulder, the queen stood up and welcomed the two men. Meleethos took his position around the table while Harapi stood guard.

"Sit, Harapi," said Father.

Harapi pressed his arms against his sides, his dark skin almost matching the black uniform of the Starani. He looked at me and then at Father.

"You are the commander of the Starani," Father said. "You lost men. Sit down."

He obeyed.

Father spoke again. "Do we know anything about Altazadeh's position?"

"Valsaris has no news for us," said the queen, "and he confirms the arrow was shot by one of their own to bury us in people's anger."

Yes, but Valsaris is a liar.

"No, my king," said Harapi and clenched his fist. "And people will say nothing to us."

"No," said Meleethos. "I can find his auric impression on many people and priests. But I can't trace it back to him. He has veiled himself."

Meleethos's words revealed another potential of the realms beyond, even if unsuccessful at this instance. *Brilliant.*

"The people are angry," said Father. "And they have committed crimes. But order must be kept. And I ask you," he looked at each one of us, "what course of action do you propose?"

After a few moments of silence, Meleethos spoke first. "Reconciliation."

Father looked at Harapi.

"I agree," said the commander. "A violent response will drown us in blood. We will keep working in silence to find the murderers of the children and my men. But we should reconcile with the people."

Father turned to me. My chest boiled. "They killed children!" I said. "And tried to kill us! Will we just give them...?"

"And why did any of this happen?" asked the queen.

I held my breath. Only for a heartbeat. "Your insinuation being that it is my fault? Because I cared to feed the poor children?"

"My insinuation being that you are now a crowned prince. I don't know how things worked where you hid for all that time. But you are back now, and your actions have consequences! And you'd do well to consider all of them before declaring war on the power that holds the kingdom together!"

"You think I was hiding? You think I wanted to leave? And what did you do during my absence? What did you do to keep those children from starving in a dark, abandoned house?"

"Enough, both of you," said Father. "What do you propose, Aletheos?"

I breathed, gathering my anger and composing my thoughts. "I want to open a school. It's the only way I can think of to help people see. Hopefully, by gaining understanding, they will withdraw from the dark priests, diminishing their power. You said it should be the people's choice. So, let's give them one. Beyond the confines of the order. We will share what we can at the old palace."

They all looked at me in silence.

"This will not go unanswered either," finally said Muttiya. "They know of your incentives."

"What's your solution?" I asked her and looked at Father. "After all this time... We still know nothing of the beast. And Altazadeh stays hidden. We can only do something about the priests. It's how their darkness finds expression in the kingdom. They can keep their altars and offerings. I want a list with all surviving initiates, all who can help share the wisdom. And I want copies of all our scrolls to take with me. The originals should stay protected here."

Father turned to Meleethos, who nodded. Harapi had no input on the matter. The queen laughed and leaned back in her chair, shaking her head.

"Agreed," said Father. "But you will divulge as much as appropriate. Let them come close to the light, but keep them safe from the burning fire. If their eyes are not accustomed, the light will consume them like it did to Altazadeh. There are secrets that will remain hidden. Understood?"

I could but comply. He continued.

"Harapi, keep looking in secrecy. Meleethos, talk with the initiates, see if they are willing to help. And call upon all scribes."

DROPS OF INK

The shelves of the library were mostly empty. Several scrolls laid on the floor, others on the tables. Scribes worked in silence, copying every word and symbol among piles of parchments.

I walked around the room, looking at the process. The strong oily scent of black ink forced me, every now and again, to push a gush of air out my nose. There was nothing much to do there. But it was my cause. So, I took another walk around.

Through the empty bookcases, a chest showed in the back of the room. The symbols on it were familiar. I passed by a scribe to get to the chest but stumbled on one of his scrolls on the ground, knocking over his ink palette and ruining his work.

"I am very sorry," I said, picking up the reed brush from the floor.

He said nothing. He didn't even look up. He threw the ruined parchment on the floor, drew another piece, and began anew. I didn't ruminate on it either. I went for the wooden chest in the back. With my hand, I grazed over its engravings. Symbols and words; in the sacred language. 'For my grandson.'

My chest warmed. *Chohanatma. He must have put it together before we left.* I pulled it open. Scrolls piled within it. One about the sacred disks. Another about the subtle planes. The flames, the lineage, the state of absolute, all had their own scrolls. *Excellent!* I put them all back and called a guard from outside.

"Please, help me."

We each got a side of the chest and carried it out in the garden. Another guard saw us. He insisted on taking my place.

"Thank you. To my chambers," I said and followed them there. I would go through these scrolls alone, translate and copy them myself.

"My love," Idhi said before I entered the house. "Join us."

I hadn't seen her on my way. She was with Cereena, enjoying the beautiful morning between the bird-inhabiting trees of the garden. *Translations can wait.* I halted when Savghana greeted me from behind them. Her narrow eyes reminded me of Balluashir. I approached my beloved, resting my hand on her shoulder.

"Aletheos," said Cereena.

Savghana acknowledged my presence with a nod.

"Have you seen Innok today?" Idhi asked.

"I did. Earlier," I replied, still looking at Savghana.

"Savghana has been treating him! She says he is getting better, fast."

"We didn't have the chance to speak, Savghana," I said. "What developments from your nation?"

"I haven't heard from them in a while," she said, "but reconstruction was well on its way when we left. I am sure my kingdom will rise to its former glory."

"What did that look like, really?" I asked.

I stayed with her eyes. She stared back at me. *What is it that you want?* Her subtle planes unfolded in front of me. *Sadness. What else?* Idhatora stood up, interfering with my connection with the foreigner.

"Are preparations moving along?" she asked.

Savghana looked away. I wouldn't get more from her.

"They are," I said. "I should go."

Chohanatma's scrolls blurred under the warm light of the torches. I hadn't moved for most of the day, and the scribbles no longer made sense. I shut my eyes for a moment. An image flashed strong in my mind; as if it had been waiting for my mind to withdraw from external activity. It was the dark cloud around Idhi's feet that weighed her from ascending into the realm of Fire. I still hadn't traced it to its source.

She had a rough childhood. I sighed. With her experiences, the burden of fear or anger would not be unnatural. The image of the cloud came closer and closer, expanding around me. Each of the cloud's particles held an experience of hers. One projected her capture from the island, amidst the red flowers. Another held a fight with another priestess there. I only drifted with them; my brain was too exhausted to translate them all.

A knock on the door brought me back to wakefulness. I cleared my throat but the door opened before I invited them in.

"My love," said Idhi, "is everything all right?"

I nodded.

"Are you busy?"

I left the scroll on the table as she leaned and kissed my cheek with her arm around my shoulders.

"It's from the library," I said, "I need to translate them for the school. Where have you been all day?"

"With Cereena. Can I help?"

I smiled at her, pulling her onto my lap. She giggled as she lost her balance and fell in my arms, my face close to hers. Her dark eyes sparkled with the flames from the torches.

"You are beautiful," I said.

"You are not so bad either," she teased.

I leaned into a kiss while tickling her. Her laughter filled the room. And I let my hands rest around her waist and legs.

"Will you help me?" I asked.

"Always!"

"I want to teach people. Help them understand."

"I know," she said. "We will do it together."

"You are great with people. People admire you. I admire you. I don't have your charm with people, I don't think. I don't know if people will want to learn from me."

"They will if you let them see you, my love. You are charming, more than you know. But your beautiful mind," she touched my temple, "holds so many mysteries that secrecy spills out and hides you in it."

My cheeks warmed.

"Cereena says you were always like this," she continued, "even as a child. She never knew what was going on in this handsome head of yours."

"You do know, though. Right?"

"Only because you tell me." She kissed my forehead and got up. "What happened with Savghana today?"

"How do you mean?"

"What were you looking for in her subtle planes?"

My chest lightened with joy at her ability to see that. But I hid my smile from her.

"I don't really know her. How come you are so close?"

"She is a young woman in a foreign land. I know what that feels like."

"Right."

"She is smart and funny. You will see when you get to know her."

"It's just that... Maybe it's because she reminds me of her father."

"She is a nurse. She cared for her people. She is nothing like her father."

I sighed. "Maybe you are right."

Fear and anxiousness were taking over me again. I hopped up, away from them and my seat, and took Idhi in my arms. She laughed as I teased her. I kissed her lips, her jasmine fragrance rubbing on me. She wasn't laughing anymore. She looked deep into my eyes and kissed me back, bringing my shirt over my head.

GLIMMERS

T he yard of the old palace was already loud with people. Guards were vigilant, staring down from the high walls surrounding the yard, as we had asked them. I turned away from the window.

Father left his analgesic bundle of herbs on the table and gently placed his new crown on his head. I could tell it was a fake. It was not as delicate as the old one, and no gems sparkled on the three snakes. But his injury was still swollen and couldn't fit the old one.

"Ready?" he asked me.

My heart pounded in my chest. Idhatora adjusted my crown and patted my clothes. She then stood still, looking at me. After a few deep breaths, my heart slowed down. I stood tall. Innok nodded from behind her.

Father went first, limping on his way. I followed a few steps behind, through the curtains out to the balcony. The crowd taunted us. Beyond the balcony rails, threads of black smoke danced in the air.

"My dear citizens," Father exclaimed. He grimaced in pain but swiftly composed himself and continued. "I am your king! You have been heard!"

Their agitation quietened.

"I am not here to dictate your lives! We are here to help you navigate them. And keep you safe while doing so."

People's anger rose again, swinging their fists, shouting. *Do they really want a choice? Do they really understand what is at stake?*

In the back of the yard, a little girl struggled to climb a statue. She held on with one hand while she pressed on her chest with the other. She looked up at us. Her dirty face reoriented my focus. *She wants a choice.*

Father took a step back and invited me to take his place. I stood on the edge.

"You have a choice to make," I said. "You can follow the priests of old tradition. Let them speak for you to the gods. Or! You can learn about spirit yourselves! I want nothing from you. True spirit wants nothing from you. But offers everything! And first of all, understanding."

The people mumbled but soon silenced themselves.

"The choice is yours and yours alone! There will be no judgment or discrimination against whatever you choose. Not from us! To live freely, you need a choice! And we hereby give you one!"

People were already leaving the yard. They were not interested, not in taking authority over their lives. I sighed. It was easier this way. They had someone to blame for their mishaps. No need to assume responsibility.

Father came next to me, pressing his lips together. He touched my shoulder, he expected this. We walked downstairs and out into the yard. Innok came close.

"Have you seen him?" I asked.

He shook his head.

"Let me know if you do."

He grabbed my arm before I left. He leaned close and whispered. "What do you want with him? Isn't he dangerous?"

"Valsaris is lying, and I need to know why. Stay with Idhi," I said as she approached.

I left them and followed Father. Not one-tenth of the people had remained. But they smiled with hope. Women, children, some men, cheered close to my father.

OPEN DOORS

N o guards stood outside the old palace gates, lest they intimidated people who wanted to join us. They would protect us, the people and us, from more discreet positions.

I sat on the steps leading to the main entrance of the palace. *First day accepting people, pilgrims on their path.* My leg shook against the ground as I waited.

"They will come," said Idhi next to me, overlooking the empty yard.

I only sighed.

Innok joined us from the city. "Priests are preaching in front of the palace."

I jumped up and paced to the main gates under the vigilant eyes of the guards. People had gathered in front of the palace. But all crowded around the priests.

"... our tradition!" a priest yelled.

Others were a little further, shouting their words of fear and control.

"...the gods give us life on this land, providing our glory! Do we dare abandon them? Provoke them with ungratefulness?"

"They are threatening the people," I said.

Idhi leaned close to my ear. "Look." She pointed at the steps leading down to the river.

The dirty face of a little girl stared from behind a tree.

"Go," I told Innok. "We will head back to get the eyes away from you."

He blended with the crowd until Idhi and I were inside, and soon returned with the little girl.

"She is hungry," Innok said.

"Don't be scared, little one," said Idhi. "Come, we will get you something to eat."

She opened her hand, waiting for the girl to accept the invitation. The little one looked at me. I nodded with a smile. So did Innok. She scanned the yard before finally reaching for Idhi's hand. Together, they went up the steps and inside the palace.

"Does she have a place to stay?" I asked Innok.

He shook his head. "The streets."

"Even with the Starani men staying here," I said, "there are tens of empty rooms in this place. Let her stay the night. Will you take care of it?"

"I will ask one of the servants to watch over her."

"Thank you. Let's go home. No one is coming."

We climbed the steps into the shady halls to find Idhatora.

"Prince Aletheos," a man said from the shadows.

I turned towards the voice. Innok had already drawn his sword. A young man emerged from behind the columns. He raised his hands.

"Please, my prince, I am Zurath," he said.

His face was wet with sweat. He kneeled.

"Valsaris sent me."

The library of the old palace was full with scrolls again. The little homeless girl never let go of Idhatora's hand. And the young priest kept pouring water down his throat.

"How did you come in?" Innok asked.

"Valsaris told me of a passage in the desert. There are others who wanted to learn, to walk on your path, my prince. But we are afraid. The priests have threatened us. The others were scared to try. You've seen them out in the streets. They will come after any one of us that reaches out."

Valsaris did good to show him the way. Why?

"There are others?" I asked.

"Yes. I have friends who feel like I do. Trying to remain honest in their pursuit of higher, sacred knowledge. I am a priest, I have devoted myself to the divine. But it is nowhere to be found in the temples. I have read the theology. Countless godly names. Countless stories of selfish, arrogant, and vengeful gods. Where is the truth?"

"The truth is there," I said. "The stories and symbols must be deciphered and applied in the appropriate measures to reveal their secrets. But the keepers of the keys to analogy have either lost them or keep them to themselves."

"All we do is carry out routines and rituals and meaningless preaching," the priest said.

"Immortalising blind faith," I responded, "in the name of tradition, power, and money." I felt sick hearing one from their own ranks say these things. "Get the others, Zurath," I said. "Those that you can trust. Lead them through the passage in secrecy. Let us spread the flame in these dark times."

NEST

The white mist sparkled in mother's room. I breathed it in. The flowery scent, the tickling of my nose, all reminded of my mother, now carrying out her duty beyond the sea. Her image solidified in my mind, slowly filling the room. She was talking to a few girls who sat on the ground around her. Some seemed to listen carefully. Others whispered to each other. One was drawing in the sand with her finger. But mother continued sharing her sweet words, like she used to do with me.

I went closer, observed her. Silver rivers ran through her rich black hair. Softly, I brought my hand to hers. With my touch, she extended her neck and expanded her chest. She stopped talking and took a deep inbreath that turned into a wide smile. She turned to me, looked into my eyes.

"My son," she said without moving her mouth.

The image dissipated, and I was drawn out of it. I opened my eyes. The mist had faded. *I am late.* I rushed out of my house and down the river, hoping that Idhi wasn't late as well, wondering off again with Cereena. With my mind, I moved the currents of water and carried my boat.

Across the river, the city was quiet. Priests no longer preached out loud in front of the old palace. Maybe sometimes. Not today. With a nod, I greeted the guards at the gates and entered the courtyard of the old palace.

Innok called from behind me in the street. He was not alone. He paced towards me, carrying something, holding it with his only hand. A child! Others followed, children. And Savghana with Cereena.

"He is sick," he said, with the child's head resting over his shoulder. "Should I take him inside?"

"I can help," said Savghana.

My stomach clenched at the sight of her. But Cereena looked at me with wide eyes, waiting. And around us stood only guards. None of them or the servants inside knew of the healing practices.

"Yes, yes, take him inside," I said.

They all climbed the steps in a hurry. *I couldn't say no.* I pushed my worries away with the thought of Innok's presence. *He will know if something...*

I walked through the hall and into the library. A few more people had gathered today. Twelve in all. They all sat, listening to Idhatora at the front. She was so gracious in her movements, taking her time to answer every question, calm, gathered. She saw me as I sat behind her students.

"Why does this matter?" one asked, demanding her attention. I hadn't seen him before. "We came here for the spiritual truth, and you speak of rules of conduct."

My presence had disrupted her line of thoughts. She didn't answer. She turned to me.

"What is your name?" I stood up and walked to my beloved.

He raised himself. "I am Lohar."

"Welcome, Lohar. Sit down. What spiritual truth is it you seek beyond ethics?"

"Tradition is filled with little myths and parables. And we already serve that tradition," he said. "Why risk ourselves coming here if we are only to get more general rules of how to live our lives?"

"I understand your thirst, Lohar. I do. But tell me, what do you think a mind that is not rooted in morality will do with the sacred sciences? What if I tell you that you are gods yourselves? And teach you how to carry out as much of your divine potencies as possible? In what ways would you practise those powers if you have not realigned your earthly planes, your emotional and mental aspects, to correspond to their divine counterparts?"

He said nothing.

"Turn to those you fear," I continued, "to those who pose a risk in your coming here. What do they do, those who have not realigned themselves, trained to hold ethics as an essential part of their lives? Those who do hold some mutilated aspects of the higher knowledge?"

He thought for a few moments.

"Fear," he said. "They evoke fear."

I nodded.

"Training ourselves in self-awareness is the ultimate capacity of human nature. And as we, through personal effort, refine our inner aspects, our behaviour, our emotional and mental planes, there will come a time when during our introspection, we will recognise the divine, the spiritual true nature of us and the all!"

The room filled with silence. I turned to Idhi. She had nothing to add.

"I think that is enough for today," I said.

The students stood up, preparing themselves before going out in the desert.

"We need to go," I told Idhi. "There is a child..."

Zurath interrupted me. "My prince?"

"Yes, Zurath?"

"There are others who want to learn. But they are scared."

I sighed.

"You did well, bringing all that would follow you." I forced a smile. "Carry out what you learn here. We may need to proceed in other manners."

"Thank you," he said and bowed before he turned away.

I pushed the door open. Savghana shushed us. She stood over the child on the bed with wet linen strips and a used mortar and pestle on the table next to her.

"He is okay," she said. "Let's give the boy some time."

Innok and Idhatora, along with the children, the boy's friends, walked towards the door. I stayed looking at the sick boy.

"I will see how I can help," I said.

Savghana placed her hand on my chest. I held my breath at her intrusion.

"There is no need for your magic," she said. "He is malnourished. He will be okay."

She moved away her arm and waited for me at the door.

"My prince?" she insisted.

I went to the boy. His subtle bodies were weak. But no dense issues showed in his organs. She was probably right. I focused within me and brought green, red, and yellow energy out of my hands and into the boy.

The white stars pierced through the dark, moonless sky. Idhi leaned on my shoulder as I contemplated all the time we had spent in this garden of the old palace. Ages could have passed since then. The trees around us seemed less alive, void of their old vibrancy.

"What's on your mind, my love?" Idhi asked in her sweet tone.

"The boy." *And Savghana.* "And the people. We need to do more. The school was meant to diminish the priests' power while Altazadeh and his beast lurk in the shadows. I don't know that we are achieving anything."

"My love, the school, you, all that we do, is meant to help the people. And we are doing just that. Even if it's one person at a time."

"This is too slow, Idhi. I can't have the priests scaring people away from the light."

"Let's go home, my love," she said. "Let's rest for a while."

Savghana finally came outside, accompanied by Innok.

"The boy will be fine. Your magic must have helped. He is doing much better; he gained a good appetite. But he needs rest."

Innok nodded from behind her.

"Okay," I said. "Let's go home."

"I will stay," Savghana said, "to make sure he is okay during the night."

I turned to Innok, who surely knew my worries.

"I will stay as well," he said.

"Thank you," I whispered as we passed by him.

GRAFTS

L essons had finished for the day. I sat in the garden, practising with primordial matter, that innermost unit of matter I had discovered in the water. It was everywhere. All that I could see and touch was made of that matter. I moved my hand around, gathered, and infused it with my will. A small stripe of water manifested, sliding between my waving fingers. I closed my hand around it; changed my thoughts. I opened my palm with a small flame that disappeared with the span of my breath.

Idhi leaned on the wall, looking towards the courtyard in front of the old palace. Beyond her, the children, now residents of this place, ran around in the yard. Their laughter raised my spirit. What a change did it make for them, some food, some water, and a shelter to sleep safely at night. How fast the hardship on their faces had turned into tender innocence.

"They are here," Idhatora said.

The weight on my chest had returned.

"Remember," I said, "beige and violet before connecting to him."

She nodded. The children's laughter now eluded my awareness. Innok led the way as two guards carried a sick man, with Savghana a few steps behind. They passed by us, helping the man inside. We followed.

"Savghana," I said, still walking, "did Zurath tell you what the priests did to treat him?"

"He did. Medicine that makes no sense for his condition," she said, pushing open the door to the old infirmary, vacant and dusty. "I already asked the servants to bring me what I need."

"Ready?" I turned to Idhi.

She closed her eyes for a moment. She brought beige and violet force around her, and focused her consciousness above her eyes, now shining outwards like a beacon. I brought her hand close to the patient.

"First, his subtle planes. The quality, the colours, and intensity of his energy. Get a general idea of his condition before we contact his consciousness."

The light from her forehead expanded towards the man on the bed. She gasped and tightened my hand when her force connected with his.

I rushed out into the garden, my chest constricted with all the things I wanted to scream. Idhatora, Innok, and Savghana soon followed. Innok sat on the ground. Idhi hugged me tight.

"He was too far gone," Savghana said.

She was right. But she was right!

"They caused this!" I finally exhaled, pointing at the temples beyond the palace walls. "That man was just sick! We could have helped if they let him come earlier."

"My love," said Idhi, concerned.

"He died!" I interrupted her. "He died! Because those people, those wretched ignorants, like to play gods! Because they decided to grow fear into men instead of helping them! And for what? This man and countless others died because of them! Because they cared more about their status than others' lives!"

They looked at me in silence.

"What can we do?" said Savghana.

"My love," talked sweet Idhi, "you are doing all that you can. You opened this place to teach and heal and help the people. We are doing all that we can."

My anger froze inside me as I thought of Zurath's eagerness to help this man, scared of his superior priests, those who would walk the temples of stone forgetting that they themselves are made of sand.

"No," I said with the centre of my forehead pulsating. "But I will."

I walked behind the throne chamber as Meleethos finished treating my father's subtle planes. They both stared at my abrupt visit. Father's eyes were half-closed with dark circles around them, and the linens on the bed were wet with sweat.

"Send Maya away," I said.

"The high priest?" asked Meleethos.

I nodded. "Find a pretence. Tell him he is needed at the temples of Dessha. I need a few moon cycles with his absence."

"Why?" asked Father.

"Send him away. No more hiding. People need to see!"

GOLDEN THREAD

The students sat silent in the library. I unwrapped the long scroll and let them see. Most of them frowned. They were probably expecting more of a revelation, a comprehensive explanation of the greatest mystery. Instead, the scroll had a handful of symbols drawn in black ink, with a number below each one.

I smiled and let them observe the mystery, waiting for a reaction. Nobody. I turned at the scroll. A blank circle with the number zero below it.

"The Absolute Be-ness, the unmanifested, eternal, unchangeable, and unlimited," I said.

Next to it, the same circle had a dot at its centre and the number one below it.

"The potential emerges when the time strikes seven."

Next, above number two, a circle was cut in the middle by a horizontal line.

"The one becomes two," I said. "The Absolute differentiates itself into the Female and Male principles. Here, we have the great Triad; the Absolute and its two aspects."

The fourth circle had a cross in it, with the number four.

"Then, the two principles unite and manifest the one god, the manifestation of the Absolute."

"The dragon," said Idhatora in a low voice.

"The dragon," I smiled. "Together, the parent, the two aspects and the manifestation make four."

The priests looked at the scroll as if to extrapolate more from it than the plain circles in black ink.

"The fifth circle?" asked Zurath.

"The cross in the circle," I said. "Only now, the upper line of the cross is replaced by a circle. This is the dragon the youngest, manifesting in our round of existence as man, whose upper principles are reached and carried out. These higher principles are represented by the smaller cycle; still a cycle, the same as that representing the absolute, only smaller, microcosmic."

Lohar spoke. "So, which one is the god we worship in the temple?"

"You tell me, Lohar. Our tradition worships many gods. Do they have attributes? Do they carry out certain processes? Do they possess an individualised consciousness?"

He brought his hand to his head with nervous laughter and said nothing. Innok entered the room and nodded. It was time.

"Contemplate these abstractions," I said. "And remember that the parent is absolute in all conceivable ways; no attributes, no restrictions. We will see you outside."

Zurath stood first. "My prince, what will happen to us?"

"Our school shall continue its function for those who wish to join us. And the infirmary here will keep its doors open. You did well to bring more patients."

I glanced at Savghana, sitting next to Idhi.

"Savghana has volunteered to stay here, to take care of them. And Idhatora and I will help as well, and train you in working on the inner levels of the ill. And there will always be room and food for the children of this world."

"Thank you," Zurath said. "You have gifted us with hope and purpose!"

I smiled. "Take the passage into the desert, Zurath. We will see you in a while."

My feet were heavy on the floor. My breathing was fast and short. Time slowed down as I rested my gaze on the closed doors, and my spine vibrated electric, with the weight of the palace on my shoulders. I turned within, brought my awareness above my eyes, and pushed the doors open.

I paced through the empty courtyard and out into the street. On my left ran the river. The three water elementals were close by. I expanded my consciousness to them and the water that now slowly waved to shore.

To my right, Meleethos waited at the steps of the temple. He touched my chest and forehead, clearing my mind with his warm hands. Behind him stood Idhatora and Innok amongst the people who made their offerings and asked for the help of higher forces.

A guard held back one of the priests. "Maya would never accept this," the priest protested.

"You forget yourself, priest!" I spoke. "Your chief has no authority on me!"

"Is that why you sent him to the water temples? I will send for him; he will return faster than you wanted."

I gave him a short laugh and left him with the guard. I raised my arm to my beloved. She took my hand as we climbed the steps to the temple.

"Your father?" she asked in a low voice, looking straight ahead.

People faced up from their prayers, turning to us.

"He is not feeling well. It's better he rests," I said. *He wouldn't approve of this anyway.*

"Can't you help him?"

"My feelings for him cloud my perception. Meleethos will help him best."

We reached the gates where Maya, the high priest, would stand and preach the words of gods. We faced the people. Our students were in the crowd. The few initiates that remained were also there.

"We have promised you a choice!" I said. "But it was again taken from you through threats and fear by the priests who claim to speak of the goodness and mercy of gods. For far too long, we have worshipped false gods, personified processes of nature, and given them our devotion. For far too long, entities of the world of mud have passed themselves as the sons of the sun, as the sons of Fire! No more! My beloved wife and I stand here, amongst you, so you may hear clearly, free of fear. No more hiding. Let it all show under the light of the sun!"

People got closer. Above them, in the distance, danced glimpses of darkness. Out of them burst the black beast, floating high above us. *It's about time you showed up again!* He said nothing. Did nothing. Only stared down at me, holding his sceptre, with big black feathers around him. Nobody else seemed to be aware of him, not Idhatora nor Meleethos.

I focused on the sacred chamber in my heart and the threefold flame, let it burn through me and outwards. I was not the same as the last time he came for me. I stood straight, bright, looking back at him.

"What have the gods done for you that you haven't brought upon yourselves in ways of effort and merit?" I exclaimed. "The gods are dead! We devote ourselves to empty bodies, carcasses in the sand! Only one is; nameless, the causeless cause of all. It, which gives birth to itself; It, which is life Itself. And It lives in all of us; the people, the animals, the trees, and the earth! Knowing It is knowing ourselves! Let us shed away our blindfolds, throw them in the sand and bury them with the empty promises of the dead gods!"

A small stream of water flowed up the slope from the river, making its way upward, step by step. People began to notice, getting out of its way.

"Hear now the Voice of Silence, see the Light of Darkness. From it, we emerge," I declared.

The stream of water reached us.

"I am the daughter, the sister, the mother," Idhatora said. "Naked and alone, I am the firstborn." She let her gown drop to the ground as the water enfolded our feet.

"And I am the son, the brother, the father," I said, letting my clothes slip away. The rays of the sun warmed my skin. I raised my hand towards the stone altars, and, with a twitch of my palm, flames sparked out of them. "In the image of my parent who remains parentless."

We spoke as one. "Together, we birth the will of the One!"

She brought her hands to her belly, slightly swollen.

"The will of the Absolute," she said.

Her eyes stayed on mine with a smile. My brows rose with a wave of joy flooding my chest.

"A child?" I managed to exhale.

I hugged her tight. Below us, Meleethos's face warmed with a smile. Above him, the beast stared in silence.

INUNDATION

I pushed the paddles into the water. Our small boat floated through the lake that the annual flooding formed in the Black Temple. It was almost time for the solstice celebrations. But today, all was quiet. Alone, Father and I travelled on the still reflections of the afternoon blue sky.

Father pulled his leg with his hands. His face stiffened with wrinkles around his eyes as he managed to stretch. He then leaned back, looking up.

"Does it hurt?" I asked.

"Just a little numb," he said.

"Your head?"

"Let go of unpleasantness, my son. Look around. The silence, the beauty, the harmony."

A golden spark came from below the lake. I pulled the paddles up and let the boat slowly drift to a stop, close to the submerged golden spheres of Chaa and Chohanatma. Water dripped from the paddles, sending ripples through the mirrored white clouds. Above us, birds crossed the sky.

"Have the initiates in the temples answered your call? It will be good for the young priests to see that there are still people to learn from in the higher ranks."

"Son..." he exhaled.

I leaned back, letting him enjoy the marvellous landscape. It was as if we floated through the sky. Only the black walls in the distance created a sense of distinction between what was above us from the below.

"Twelve men and women already came to us." I broke the silence again. "But they are always worried they will be discovered. If the initiates come..."

"Son..."

"They can come through the passage in the desert! Have you explained it to them?"

"Things are out of our hands, my young prince," he finally engaged. "It's up to them now."

"The initiates?"

"The initiates, the students, the people. We can never force someone to learn. Nor serve. Nor heal. We can only create the appropriate conditions for them. And you have done that. Now it's up to them. Don't take their power away. And don't assume their responsibility.

You need to respect their choices. Remember, my son, we don't rule over people. We don't control them. We serve them. It may not look that way to others. But our duty is to create the necessary conditions for people to carry out their lives as they please, as they choose."

The water was coloured with purples.

"Can we truly be safe? Can the people? Can Mother ever return?"

"Harmony. Balance. Look around you. Everything is in perpetuating balance. People must indulge in reflecting the balance of the all in their lives. Only then will we, and everyone else, be safe."

He looked up again. And took a deep breath. His face relaxed, and his shoulders dropped. He didn't seem in pain anymore.

"You will be a father," he said.

"I am going to be a father," I repeated with a burst of laughter.

"I am so happy for you," he said. "But if you allow me, let me say this. Be careful with your child. I know you are determined to carry out what you think is your duty. But you will have more duties now. I do not believe I was successful in mine. But I do hope you will forgive my shortcomings someday. It was never my intention to hurt you, even when I did just that."

"Father, I... I know you have been doing everything you can. You..."

He raised his arm. "That is enough for me."

His eyes relaxed. He seemed at peace. The sun met the horizon, and pinks and oranges mingled with purples above and below us. I leaned back. And I rested with my father.

BURNING VEILS

I sat on my balcony, overlooking the city across the river, quiet under the warm veil of the night and thinking about our students. Were our words truly touching their minds?

"What is your mind at?" asked Innok.

I sighed. "They backed off, Innok. The initiates won't help me."

"They won't teach with you? Why?"

"They are probably too comfortable in their positions to bother helping others. They forgot their cause."

Open letters covered the table. All saying the same.

"But they will sponsor us in silence," I said and flipped the table that banged on the floor together with their words.

"I am sorry, Aletheos."

I looked back at the city. *I promised them.*

"Why won't the people give refuge to the truth?" I asked.

"They are scared, Aletheos. Their beliefs have been central to their lives. Changing them would mean changing their worldview. Where would that leave them? Where do they stand in a world they know nothing about?"

"It doesn't make sense, Innok. Why stick to a false teaching when you have a chance to learn the truth?"

"It's not about sense, Aletheos. It isn't about logic and mind. People are emotional. You yourself have said many times that emotions can cloud your perception. Imagine what emotions can do to people whose mind is not as developed as yours."

I swiped the sweat off my forehead.

"Look at me, for example," he said and pulled the table back in its place. He sat next to me, looked beyond the river as well. "That priest that did... whatever he did to my arm. I didn't let him because I thought you had failed. Nor because I was angry at you." He kept swallowing his words. He wouldn't face me. "I knew about the dark forces. I have seen them, in Areteia, with Chaa, all this time I have been with you, and even back then, with my mom... I have seen what they can do to people."

"Then why..."

"That man. He was the same who worked on my mother."

I stood up. "And you still let him..."

"He is my father."

My eyes trembled.

"I thought he came back for me. He said he loved my mother. And that he did everything for her. But the king stopped him before he could manage... But I know the pain now. The king was right to release her from it. He didn't come back for me. He used me as an imposition on you."

"Innok..."

The river murmured with the song of cicadas. *No priest should have the power to regrow an arm. Even if not successfully.* One by one, the city lights went out. In the darkness, my eyes widened, and I turned to him, scared to ask my question.

"Master Meleethos is here, my prince." A maiden came from inside. "He requests your presence."

"I will be right there," I said, still looking at Innok. "Stay here," I told him as I left.

Meleethos waited at the bottom of the stairs.

"What's wrong, Meleethos?"

"Can we speak? In private?" he asked in a low voice.

I led him to the chamber of the mother, where Idhi carried out her evening prayers. She sat next to the violet lotus flowers with one hand on her big belly. She smiled at me, but only until she saw Meleethos behind me.

"Would you excuse us, my love?"

She turned to the open side of the room, finished her thought in prayer, and left us.

"Is it about the initiates?" I asked. *I can't tell him about Innok's father.* "I know they backed off!" *He might send him away.*

"No, my boy..."

"I don't need them!" I paced around the room.

"It's about your father."

"I will do it together with Idhatora! You taught her well."

I stopped moving as his words and tone found their way within me. He spoke before I enquired more.

"I haven't been teaching Idhatora. She kept coming to me after you left for the sanctuary but only for a short time. I haven't instructed her since."

But she is practiced in guiding her consciousness! At least through certain levels. And she knows how to... I gathered my thoughts. *Later!*

"What's wrong with Father?"

"His wound. I treat him every day, but he is deteriorating instead."

I sighed. A reality that long lingered over my head, was now sinking in my chest.

"Does he know?"

"He does."

A knock on the door interrupted us. Idhi leaned inside.

"I am sorry. The king..."

I ran into his room. Muttiya held him as he threw up. Blood splashed on the floor. Maidens rushed inside as well, brought water and prepared his bed.

"Library," he yelled.

He pushed everyone aside and limped through the throne chamber. I followed. Before I touched him, he stopped to catch his breath, leaned down, and threw up again.

"Father." My arms were now around him.

His eyes were wet.

"I can't breathe," he said between his teeth. "Love, love!" He pointed at the door.

"Father, you need to lie down," I said, fighting back the tears that insisted on blurring my eyes. He was burning up. "Let us take you back."

He didn't protest. He couldn't. He closed his eyes with tears dropping on the floor. It was Innok who helped me pull him up.

"I told you to stay home," I whispered.

Together, we carried him back. Father mumbled something before his body stretched, his neck bent backwards, and collapsed on me.

"Everyone out," I said as we lay him in bed.

Muttiya leaned close to Father.

"What are you doing?" I asked Meleethos. "Do something!"

He stood unmoved. I took a breath and headed within. Tension in my legs; fear. Stiff stomach; I was worried. *I see you all.* I took another breath to raise my consciousness above my feelings, lest they coloured my perception. I let violet and beige force enfold me according to Chaa's instructions. And I opened my eyes to Father's inner condition.

Bright colours filled the outer layers of his aura. Greens, yellows, whites. The disks along his spine moved fine. But their colours were darkening. Most so, the yellow disk in his stomach. It sparked with browns. I connected with that force. *Anger... Guilt? Why?* Favar came to mind. Father felt his death was his responsibility.

I searched for more. His stomach was twisted. He hadn't been eating normally for a while, so that was expected. The kidneys. They seemed rotten, as if they had begun to dissolve. The liver was sore with lumps. Black speckles passed through it. I concentrated on them. They shined all around his body, travelling with every breath up to his head.

I focused on his head injury. The column of light above his head was like a waterfall of white light coming through him. But there was a hindrance around his injury, like a rock blocking the flow of the water. *Is that it? His wound blocks the flow of energy, slowing down his recovery?*

"Go deeper, my beloved grandson."

My heart warmed. It was Chaa across from me!

"You came for us!" I told her in my mind, almost in tears. "I looked for you! I couldn't reach you!"

"Look deeper, Aletheos, always!"

So many things I wanted to say. No time. I focused on my father again. I went further into the injury. His brain was swollen as well, pressing on his skull.

"Chaa, what do I do? His brain!"

She slowly walked outside. I opened my eyes in the flesh and followed her into the assembly room. She was gone. I looked at the round table engraved with flames, the ceiling with all the heroes and animals and symbols looking down at me.

"What? Chaa!"

I turned back. The amethyst altar. His crown. The three golden snakes stood proud, with raised heads and gleaming gems, with open mouths and sharp teeth. I grabbed it and returned to Father. I raised it above him, slowly placing it on his malformed head.

"What are you doing?" Muttiya protested.

Meleethos raised his hand at her. I waited. My eyes were now wet, as were my cheeks. The snakes vibrated, barely. All together then, turned and pushed their teeth through Father's wound, cracking through his skull. Muttiya rushed to him, but I held her back. She cried and yelled.

"I know," I said, crying, "please, please wait."

The snakes raised themselves out of the skin and solidified back into their delicate composition. Blood dripped down the side of his head.

"No," the queen shouted.

She fought herself out of my hands, grabbing the sheet on the bed to cover the wound. Father opened his eyes before the cloth stopped the blood. He was serious, angry almost, as if just awakened by a tormenting dream. He didn't speak. Just stared back at us. Unmoved.

Muttiya embraced him, crying, holding his head.

"My beloved family," Father said from behind us; his consciousness.

He radiated with light. I exhaled with relief.

"Father! It's poison! Your liver... We will heal your body!"

Chaa and Chohanatma stood next to him. They were all calm, with warm smiles and sad eyes. *No.* My cheeks burned with tears.

"My beloved wife, my strength, please don't be sad. Our bond never breaks."

"No, Aletheos, please," she said, still embracing his body on the bed. "Isn't there anything I can do?"

Father looked at her with a smile.

"Please," pleaded the queen.

"Please tell our Hetta I love her. Don't let her see my body like this."

She leaned her head on his body, shaking.

"My dear Meleethos, my wisdom," Father said, "thank you."

Meleethos kept still, calm as always. He merely nodded as tears slid out of his blind eyes.

"My son." Father turned to me.

I shook my head, trying again to hold back the tears and stand strong for him.

"My love," he said, "my light. You are the sun in this dark world. Don't fear your light. Find it. And let it burn through you; bright for all to see. You are all that remains now to guide and protect this world."

"Father," I exhaled.

He and Chaa and Chohanatma looked at me, serene, content. Father kissed my forehead as all three of them faded from this dense, visible world of misery.

The queen's eyes were dry. She lay with Father's body, resting her head on his shoulder, holding his hands. Meleethos sat silent on a chair. I was on the floor with my back to the wall. Muttiya had removed the crown from Father's head. The gems on the snakes' foreheads glimmered no more. They had darkened, fallen into the mundane. It was now a plain object; gold, cold, dead, resting on the table next to the small bundle of leaves and herbs.

I jumped up. I took hold of the analgesics. I brought them to my nose.

"What is this?" I asked them both. I knew what it was, leaves of the blue lotus and cumin. But it smelled of something else.

"What's in this?" I repeated.

"Blue lotus," Meleethos finally answered.

"What else?"

"Cumin."

"Meleethos!"

He turned to me. With blank eyes. He brought his hands to his face.

"Meleethos," said Queen Muttiya with a dry, low voice. She sat up on the bed. "What is it?"

"Herbs," he answered. "Meneir's gifts."

My heart pounded with my breath.

"Who prepared this?" I yelled.

Meleethos faced the ground.

"Savghana," he said.

I threw it on the wall and rushed outside. Nan waited in the throne chamber, holding my sister's hand, with eyes already locked on me. I only shook my head. She pressed her lips together and hugged Hetta. From the other side, approached Idhatora and Innok.

"How is he?" asked my beloved.

Seeing my eyes, she brought her arms close to her chest, around her pendant. I touched the golden chain holding her sandflower, rubbed it between my fingers.

"Where did you find this?" I asked.

She caught her breath as I looked into her eyes.

"And where did you practise if not with Meleethos?"

"I..." She said nothing.

"Idhatora!"

"Valsaris," she exhaled.

The dark cloud in her finally took shape; Valsaris.

My chest boiled. "All that time you said you were with Cereena... You were with him?"

She nodded. I turned to Innok.

"What is your... What was the priest's name?"

He furrowed his brow, trying to understand. I waited.

"Altazadeh," he answered.

My stomach burned. My feet almost gave way as all the waves of emotion spilled through them and into the ground. I was empty. Dry. I burst out with a short laugh. *My child.* I looked at Idhatora's belly. My heart ached for my child. I took a breath and passed from between them.

"Aletheos, please, I..." Idhatora said from behind me. "You don't understand... Valsaris is my father."

I stopped. My body burned from within. I shut my eyes. My thoughts disappeared. The storms of pain ravaged around me. I turned to the guard at the doors.

"Bring me Savghana!"

DUTIES

I climbed the steep side of my favourite hill below the heavy, clouded sky. I hadn't ascended to my high place since before I left for the sanctuary. But now I had nowhere else to go. Father was gone. Idhatora and Innok were...

A cold drop landed on my forehead. The grey-blue clouds above were releasing their burden; calm, sporadic drops of water nurtured the hot, dry landscape. I reached the top. Whatever light passed through the heavy clouds made the city indistinguishable from the sand around it. The colours of the busy roads and imposing temples had flattened and fused with the desert.

I inhaled the smell of wet sand. My throat remained tight with the grip of my truth. Muttiya was right. I should have never come back. The darkness of the beast was following me. None of this would have happened if I hadn't come back. How many people died because I did? Yes, I was trying to help. And what did that achieve? How many more will disperse in the sand? My child! My unborn child. How can I ever hope to protect it?

My mind was loud with conflict. Rain now fell heavy on me. "Show yourself, you cursed beast!" I yelled over the cliff, my chest aching. "Show yourself and face me!"

The clouds responded with lightning and thunder over the city. And then, silence. The cold water that dripped from my face, took with it my tears. I couldn't go back. I couldn't go anywhere. What is this path I walk on?

Another lightning ripped space behind me, and the hill rumbled, bashing sand and stones all around. I covered my face until all rubble fell where it would. The storm was getting stronger with gushes of wind pushing the rain around before thrashing on the ground.

From the middle of this plane, came light, warm and soothing. *The pillar of glass!* I persevered through the relentless storm. Father already stood close to the thin crystallised tube, extruding light from within. His surroundings were calm, as if the storm could not touch his light. I entered his space. Embracing.

"My son," he said.

The pain in my chest kneeled me.

"I am sorry!" I yelled, "I am so sorry! I was wrong! All I thought I knew…"

"Do not cry for me, my son. I am awake. I am conscious. You haven't lost me."

I shivered with his words.

"And you haven't lost your friends," he said.

I looked beyond my tears.

"It does not matter where they come from. All that matters is what they are, who they have become. What did it matter for Favar where he came from? And you have a child to take care of!"

My child!

"Stand up," he said. "Stand tall. Don't let your demons hold you from the truth. People need you. Your loved ones need you."

The flames in my heart burned bright. But I touched them not; I was too angry. But they were there. Their existence was enough. For now.

"Do you have to go?" I asked.

"I do. The higher planes await. I need to refine myself as well."

"Are Chaa and Chohanatma with you?"

"They received me. But they go through their own levels, as one must do upon leaving this plane. But don't despair. Our connection runs deep. We may not be able to reach each other, but we remain forever intertwined within the light."

I gave him a smile beneath my wet eyes.

"Before I go," he said, "I need to share a burden and a gift with you."

I nodded before he approached.

"Remember when you were crowned. Your consciousness expanded to connect with that of our people, as is mine. When I completely withdraw from this realm, my force will withdraw from around the kingdom as well. Be aware of that. This is now a burden for you to bear. Be prepared. Muttiya can help you."

Muttiya?

"She is a good person, Aletheos, a great woman and a capable ruler. Let her help you."

I said nothing.

"And my gift, if you will allow me, is to help reawaken another part of you; one that lays dormant like a scattered dream. It may not be pleasant, but your past can pave your path with understanding. Please take some comfort in that."

He came close. He leaned and kissed my forehead as he vanished with the wind. His protective aura disappeared as well, and I was hit again by the storm. The pillar of glass across from me radiated from within. The white light coming from the tube vibrated with a sound that shocked waves up and down my body.

I was drawn closer, magnetised even. I brought my hand around the tube. The buzzing light masked the splattering of the rain. Close to the glass, the light was hot; and the pulling force now changed, pushing my hands away.

I pressed with all my weight. My hands finally touched the glass. As I grabbed it tight, its light gathered at its centre, and disappeared altogether. The storm now rampaged on me. Only for a heartbeat. Then, the light re-emerged, shattering the tube into an explosion of shards and dust that scraped my skin. A miniscule piece struck my forehead, enfolding space with white silence.

A man walked towards me. Taller than me, short fair hair, with a bright blue-white robe radiating violet symbols. I knew that man. I had met him before. More than once. He approached. His eyes were steady on mine. Kind. Rigid. Certain. He was close now but didn't halt. I stepped back, but he never stopped. Before I could protest, his body passed through mine, taking hold of my consciousness.

I was in his body, separated but one. His consciousness slowly fused with mine. He had done this before, demanding my entrance to the library. But it was different now. His body, his knowledge, merged with mine, unlocking a forgotten part of my brain. He was me. And I walked as one with him through white space until the light dispersed and a new world appeared.

L ight became mist. And out of the mist emerged colourful crystal-like structures. They became the walls around me, the floor below my feet, coming together to form a high temple with narrow pillars and pointed arches, all ornate with vine-like engravings on the otherwise straight, strict architecture.

The composition of my surroundings was almost immaterial, like dense white crystals of smoke or water that never quite solidified into glass, permeated by the light of the sky outside to fill the entire space and overflow the pyramidical vault with refractions among its starry patterns. Blues and yellows and pinks glimmered through them, depending on the angle of my gaze. And, when I focused enough, I could see miniscule symbols engraved on all surfaces.

In front of me stood a three-legged pedestal with a white iridescent flame floating over it. I sat with crossed legs and hands open to the side, under the electric influence of the flame. My heart was calm, with a sense of power and wisdom and love.

Before I was ready to let go of those attributes, my legs unfolded and touched the ground. I had been floating at some distance from it! And I walked. I had no authority over myself, as if all that took place was preconditioned, experiencing a life that had already played out.

I passed below the grand arch of the open gates and out to a small stage in front of the temple. Around me stretched the endless blue sky. The whole temple stood mid-air! Down below, an entire city of the same immaterial composition, intricate, crystal-like, coloured the ground amidst clear streams of waters and gardens. All was vibrant with colours and force. All but a small area that was dark, muddy green, rotten and twisted in shape. Surrounding the entire city, was a gigantic stone wall, raised almost as high in the sky as this temple.

Beyond the stage, steps floated in the sky, one by one. They led me down to another temple, similar to the previous one, but slightly more yellow than blue. Thereafter, more steps led lower, to another temple and another and another. Seven in total, spiralled from the sky downwards around the city.

At the second temple, waited a woman. She shone from within, as if her body was not completely physical. She wore a pearl gown shining yellow and orange-white light. Even before I approached, the forces around us were already connected. She extended her arm and met mine, mingling her essence with mine in a familiar sense of togetherness. My heart sparked with the recognition; Idhatora.

A piercing sound that invaded the peacefulness, drew us both to the edge of the stage. Another area of the city was losing its vibrancy. Its material twisted and mingled with the others around it, dissolving in parts and scorching in others.

"Another one," she said in disappointment.

I turned to her. She was not there. The temple seemed different, cracked, as was the stage below my feet. It was another time. The city was in turmoil. Most of it was already overtaken by rotting dissolution. Idhatora ran up the steps to meet me, her force now filled with fear.

"It's time!" I said. "The flames!"

Entire areas were collapsing to the ground; their state spreading with dark smoke that dissolved all that it engulfed. She touched me, demanding my attention.

"What do we do?" she said.

I spoke, still having no authority over this body. "Go."

I stayed unmoved. Masses of people swarmed the floating steps as flocks of big, colourful birds flew by me and beyond the walls surrounding the city. From this second temple, returned Idhatora, with the flame of it floating between her hands. Another man joined us with the flame of the third.

"The others?" I asked.

"They went for the flames!" she said.

With loud bursts, the dark clouds rose high, dissolving the steps below people's feet and throwing them to their dismay. *No!* I extended my arms and let my will manifest as light where the steps used to be, pushing the darkness away. People saw. They ran for them.

"Go. Go up," I told her.

"The other flames! I am not leaving you! And the people!" she said.

People were trying to reach us, pushing one another over the steps to survive the corruption.

"Go!" I said.

She came next to me instead. So did the other flamekeeper. They raised their hands and guided their light, protecting people from being swallowed by darkness. My shoulder now twitched with sharp pain. Behind me, a crack had burst the wall, an enormous piece of it sliding down and crashing in the city. The pain grew stronger, as if my body connected to the walls. Water now poured in from the cracks. I turned one arm to the wall and kept it solid in my mind.

My efforts were split. Steps were falling again. By focusing on them, the wall cracked more. And by addressing the wall, more steps disappeared. Below us, the flamekeepers stood proud outside their temples, helping sustain the steps with their force.

I let them. I held the wall, whose cracks burned within me. The lowest temple was overtaken by darkness. One by one, the steps dissolved. Our power did nothing for them. The sixth temple fell. The fifth. The fourth.

"Go!" I yelled to Idhatora and the other keeper, pushing as hard as I could against the collapsing walls.

The third temple fell. Corruption was coming for us on the second. A few people had reached the steps to us. From between them came a man in dark robes, holding a gold sceptre engraved with a jackal's head. Everything dissolved as he walked past them. People lost the ground before their feet, screaming as they fell.

The keeper went for the steps upwards. But Idhatora came for me. She placed her hands on my back, her force raising mine. The wall steadied. And we went for the steps. From behind us, the dark magician hit his sceptre on the floor. Darkness emerged from within the clear crystal stage, growing, taking down this temple as well.

Corruption spread towards us. I pushed Idhatora on the steps and stood still. With one hand, I held the steps in place, for her and the other keeper to ascend towards the temple above us, the last one. With the other, I created a sphere of light around me that kept me and the floor within it safe.

"What do you hope to achieve?" I asked the corruptor.

"The black flame is at the root of everything!" he exclaimed. "It is time for the dissolution of the corrupted!"

"You still understand nothing! You are feeding the corruption! The black flame is part of mine, the white flame. You cannot maintain the darkness separated from the light without it consuming you!"

"Yet here we are," he said with a grin.

"Here we are," I responded.

My friends had reached the temple. The steps that would lead me there were now gone. And the corruptor's muddy energy rose over my sphere of light. From below, a black bird flew to his escape. With my next outbreath, I expanded the sphere around me, its light bursting to ward off the darkness. The dark cloud, reassuming its position, headed for me. In an instance, I turned within, and moved my consciousness into the bird just before darkness could consume me.

I flew towards the temple above, leaving all behind, the city, the people, the other keepers. My stomach burned with blinding pain; the magician had tossed his golden sceptre, piercing me in the bird. Before my vessel's brain ceased its function, I freed my consciousness from it, throwing myself next to my friends while the bird plummeted down in the city.

Idhatora's touch helped me up. Below us, my beloved crystal city was now flooded by darkness. And from that darkness, the magician stared up at me with flashing eyes. I searched in them, trying to understand. I found nothing. I shook my head at him and turned my back, closing the gate of the temple behind me.

The three of us gathered around the pedestal, ablaze with all three of our flames. I composed myself. And my forces. We touched the flames and spread our hands towards each other in a circle. Through the transparency of the temple, the city walls now crashed down with the force of the ocean just as a pyramid of light appeared around us and the flames, hiding the gruesome affair behind its white force. We were safe. The flames were safe. At least the three of them. But the other four could re-emerge from ours. Hope was not lost. Existence would carry on.

The light of the pyramid was fading. Beyond it, a sphere of whirling white fire carved space for us to emerge. The pyramid slowly dissolved from around us, extending its light down to each of its sides to create steps. The sphere of fire dissipated as well, having created empty space in the otherwise dense material; a cave, with no exit.

We were alive. The three of us. Alone. I kneeled on the platform. The three flames burned bright.

Each of us absorbed their flame and descended the platform. Idhatora and I touched the walls of the cave. Bending to our will, pillars of light appeared in the stone. Above them, we each willed an orb; one for the sun, the primordial father, and one for the moon, the abstract mother. The third keeper touched the space between the pillars. The stone gave way and shaped steps upwards. Light now reached this dark cave.

WILL

I opened my eyes down in the cave of forefathers, with the sense of loss weighing on my heart. My hands were warm with sparks of force. I brought them to my face. I moved at will again. My consciousness was back to my body and current lifetime. But the cave felt strange. Oh, it was the light! Rays of sunlight came through the narrow staircase. They weren't supposed to; the Black Temple above kept this place hidden and protected.

I stretched my body as a deep inhalation cracked my spine and neck. And I made my way through the two pillars with the orbs and up the stairs. Small currents of air warmed my skin. On the corners of the steps, piled sand, more and more as I approached the light at the top. I covered my eyes against it, and stepped out in the sun.

My eyes needed a few moments to readjust to this reality. The air was strong, needling my skin with sand. As the light dissipated into the environment, my heart pounded in my chest. Around me stretched the desert. No temples, no city. Only high cliffs rose in the distance with but a small passage through them. The mountains shaped a crescent moon that almost met the river in front of me.

I ran down to the banks. No rafts or signs of a village. Only boundless desert followed the river in all directions. Life was only the scattered acacia trees next to the river. I was many days away from home. No food. No way back.

I kneeled in the water as the sun shone relentless. I pushed all thoughts away, even for a moment, to stay with the cool water flowing in my dry mouth. My eye though, twitched with a sense of danger, breaking the oasis that was the moment. I pushed myself up as the open mouth of a crocodile thrust towards me. I dropped back, rolled on the ground, and found my feet. I reached for my sword around my waist; Innok's. I had left it at the palace. No matter. The calmness of power rushed over me. I raised my hand at the great reptile. Its aggression ceased midway.

"No more," I said and swung my hand to the side.

The crocodile returned to the water. I looked around, at the dry, inhospitable landscape. And I turned within. Heart, spine, head. I raised my consciousness high above the mountains. No signs of settlement for as far as I could see. But sudden movement drew my attention. A man walked by me down in the flesh. I returned to my body; moved my fingers and toes to ground myself and opened my eyes. The man headed for the cave.

"Hello," I yelled.

He paced onwards. I ran to him, pushing my weight through the sandy terrain. I called for him, again and again. He stopped right before the entrance with his back to me. I caught up.

"Hey, are you from around here?"

He didn't answer, only looked down the steps while a white feather drifted in the air and landed on the sand below him. The sun was getting closer to the horizon on the other side of the river, and with its fading light, the man seemed to fade as well, as if his white robe and body were made of dense smoke. I walked around to see his face.

It was me from before, the vessel my spirit occupied in the city of crystal. I put my hand on him. No solid substance. Just smoke. I retrieved my hand and followed him down the cave and onto the central platform. With his mind, he imposed his will on the walls, carving symbols deep into the stone. The sigils told of his story, of his origin and the origin of those before him, ending with a sigil that looked like a man.

He brought his arms to his chest. "My dear friends," he said. "Fellow keepers of the flames. May you be reborn and re-join us in this new round of existence. Forms already exist here. The forces must have been transferring for a while. The new race has already commenced. And they need our guidance."

He looked down. I could feel his heart beating in mine, burdened with sadness from his past and an immovable sense of duty towards the future.

"I will have to move on now," he said, "away into these gross lands." His gaze moved around the cave. "May we meet again."

The symbols on the walls extruded blue light as whatever sunrays reached us down here withdrew. With the setting sun, disappeared the vision of my former personality as well, like an outbreath in space.

The symbols got brighter with every passing moment, and warm air rushed through my nose. I turned behind me, expecting to meet another. I closed my eyes, inviting it. It did come. Its presence was already upon me. I opened my eyes to myriads of flames floating in the cave. In front of me stood the winged lion with the face of a dragon and the tail of an ox. We breathed together in harmony. Our outbreath shook the cave. Our inbreath brought silence.

My mind illuminated a hidden memory; our last encounter. I spoke. "You had warned me. You said I would forsake you. That I would be corrupted."

The creature stared back, breathing with me. Silence.

I continued. "Is this what you meant? Have I been corrupted? That's why I caused the death of so many?"

It talked. Its mouth never moved. "The will of One is known to the two alone."

Its voice, male and female as one, echoed loud and unyielding. In its eyes laid the mysteries of the world. And I looked at them. With all my presence.

"Don't forsake us," it said. "We are in the middle point. Open your eye and see; yourself and Life. Will you?"

Its outbreath burst out to capture me whole. Its inbreath drew me to it, closer and closer, until I stood in its place; itself vanished. My consciousness expanded in all directions, filled the cave and beyond. As I passed through the walls, the illuminated sigils projected their light outwards, creating a dome of force that went up to the mountains and down to the river. And I grew bigger, bringing within me our entire earthly sphere and all the wanderers and space. Spiralling dragons of electric fire circled my legs and torso and hands. Rivers of cosmic dust spanned in all directions.

And then I saw him in the night, with his dark robes and golden mask, standing on the crescent cliffs and overlooking the desert from beyond the projections of the sigils. I focused on him, drew closer until I positioned myself behind him.

"Altazadeh!" I yelled.

He turned to me. He no longer wore the mask on his thin face. He let his hood drop, showing scars on his bald head, and, with a grim smile, burst into dark fire that flew towards me.

His attack hit my raised hand with an explosion that turned me into white flame. He came again. I met him with equal force. And again, spiralling around each other in the air and coming back to a strike that pushed both of us away until the next hit. His force became stronger, and so did mine. The more we came for each other, the further we were pushed. He stopped for a moment, his darkness flaring up. And we bashed each other once more.

When our forces joined, I thrust myself beyond my light and into his darkness. I touched the middle of his forehead, imposing on his consciousness and bringing us to the ground. His essence was on my hand. Through it, I could feel him. His eyes opened wide at his fall.

"What do you want, Altazadeh?"

He stood up, composing himself. "I want everything!"

He swung his arm, already ablaze with dark flames. I caught his wrist right before it reached me, and threw a final blow on his chest that knocked him over the cliff. As he fell, he became dark fire again, and banged on the light of the sigils that pushed him away in the air.

Darkness turned back into man, floating over the dome of sigils. From behind him flashed lightning, revealing the shadow of the beast in heavy clouds. In an instance, clouds and shadow vanished, together with the lightning. Altazadeh looked at me from beyond the mountain. He smiled.

"Everything!" he said and turned back into a black fire that flew away.

I came to the river. The way down of the cliff left me scratched and bruised. The crocodiles on the bank didn't scare me. Only the thought of Altazadeh burned my mind, at my city, with my people, Idhatora, Innok. I focused within, trying to emulate his power, pull out that white fire again to move on air. In vain.

My scream at his threat blasted on water and sand, scaring the sleeping reptiles that crawled away. With a sigh, I started walking next to the river, up against the stream, following Altazadeh's direction, and hoping that I was going the right way.

DRY SOIL

I woke up to the scent of rotten fish. With hands numb below my head, I opened my eyes to sharp yellow teeth. The crocodile never left my side, and I petted its coarse skin, alerting her to my wakefulness. The pain in my muscles needed extra stretching before I could sit up.

In the desert's silence, the crocodile growled and pushed her jaw forward, almost catching a hyena from behind me. I stayed down, surveying for more scavengers. Two or more hyenas waited in the distance while the crocodile fended off the one close to me. With another attack, my companion threw the hyena to the ground, her teeth now stained with red. The wounded animal withdrew, and left with the others.

With warm blood now coursing through my body, I went in the water, splashed it on my face and in my mouth. The float of crocodiles dared not defy the grunting of my companion. It had been so for days.

The sun was almost setting. I should resume my route up the stream, but my stomach growled with hunger. Knee-deep in the river, I let my awareness enfold the body of water and all that went through it, the basking crocodiles, some leaves on the surface, the muddy ground. I coughed. I lost my focus. My force was not as strong as back in the cave when I manifested my crocodile guard. I was now hungry, sunburned and tired. I took a deep breath, trying to rise above the weariness and enfold the river again; no fruit or nuts around.

There! A fish! I opened my eyes, gripping it tight with my mind. I got it. I raised my arm and drew it out of the water.

"I am so sorry," I said before smashing its spine. A swift death.

I walked out of the water with the fish floating next to me; cut some branches and piled them on the ground. With what remained of my mental strength, I sparked a fire to cook my prey.

I dragged my feet through the sand. I could still feel Altazadeh's force on my hand from touching his forehead. I shook my hands and wrapped them around my chest. The desert was getting colder, as cold as it was hot during the day. And my crocodile guard was sustained from sucking on my force. Chaa had said that the thought of Udenas was connected to her. Maybe I needed more skill to achieve the appropriate equilibrium. Surely, my physical condition didn't help.

In the distance flashed a tiny light. *Fire? People?* I pushed my pace. A few steps later, I stopped for a breath. *No reason to waste energy.* I continued slowly; steadily.

The fire went out after a while. But I kept onwards. It was almost morning before I reached the spot. A small house, a room really, with a vegetable garden and an ox tied to a pole with a cow. I halted and turned to the loyal crocodile.

"Thank you," I said and touched its forehead.

Its body dispersed into floating grains of sand before fading altogether, and its vital force returned to its source in my mind and body. A rush of blood went through me. My brain pulsated hard in my head and my stomach was empty with acid. I knocked on the door. It squeaked open as my eyes rolled back in my head.

H ands shook me awake. I gasped, pushing myself up. A little girl ran away from me, screaming outside. A moment later, she returned with her parents. They said nothing, only smiled and brought bread and milk.

"Thank you," I said in a hoarse whisper that could not contain my true gratefulness.

They sat across from me on a mat of reeds. The room didn't have much else.

"Who are you?" asked the man.

"Aletheos," I said, still munching on the bread. "Thank you!"

"Aletheos? Like the royals?" asked the woman.

I nodded. "Yes. Like the royals."

"You come from the capital?" asked the man. "Are you a fancy man? A scribe or something?"

The woman gently touched his arm. "I am Caitty. What my husband, Terran, meant to say was, what brings you to this forgotten part of the kingdom?"

"Strange paths," I answered and got up. "I will need to move on."

"Where?" asked Terran. "Nothing lives around here. Not for days of sailing. And our raft wouldn't even take you there."

No. I walked outside, past the girl and down the river. They did have a small raft, patched and tied all over. I turned to them, standing at the door.

"How about ships?" I asked. "I have been walking for days next to the river! Not one boat passed by!"

The woman smiled. It was the man who answered. "This is not the main river. The hill across the water... That's an island!"

My heart sparked with hope. And I dived in the water.

"You are wasting your time, city boy!" Terran yelled from behind me as I splashed onwards.

With all the breaths I had in me, I reached the other side. I rested only for a moment. My legs burned as I climbed up the hill. Two ships sailed upstream. Three or four were already far ahead. I called to them. Waved. Screamed with all my might. A passenger heard me from the ship closest. He waved back.

No! "Take me with you," I yelled.

He leaned forward.

"Take me with you!" I repeated.

He stood straight. He looked around him. Another passenger joined him, bursting into laughter. He waved, grabbed his genitals and shook them below his clothes.

"You idiots," I said.

No more boats followed behind for as far as I could see. I sat on the ground with my back against a cypress tree, watching the river. Over to the other side, reeds moved with the wind around a black stone cube.

I knocked on the open door. No one was inside. I followed the girl's voice to the other side of the house. They had lit their fire with a pot boiling on it. The girl teased her father while the mother inspected the content of the pot and sat back down.

"May I join you?" I asked.

"No ship for the city boy?" Terran said with a rigid voice.

"Come," Caitty said.

The light of the flames was like a sweet embrace to my skin, and the boiled turnip made a nutty soup that soothed my stomach. Across from me, the girl was soon asleep on her mother's lap. Caitty kissed her cheek and touched her tenderly.

"Hanjya, let's go, my little one," she said, waking her up and heading inside.

Terran got up. "Listen," he said, "the house is small."

"I know. I am already grateful. You have done enough."

"I will bring you a rug. It's not much. But it will keep you warm when the fire is out," he said and went inside.

Whatever small flames remained, danced in my eyes, as I led my consciousness within and up high. I thought of Idhatora. Her betrayal burned my stomach. I let it be, its grip on me diminishing with the memory of her embrace. Her sense of safety drew me to her. And there she was, sleeping in our bed. Her belly, much bigger than I remembered, shined bright with the heartbeat of our child. I went closer. The little one's heart pulsated in my hand. *Oh, how I long to meet you.* I looked at Idhatora, unconscious, yet with lines of concern on her forehead. *I have missed you so much.* With a sigh, I leaned and kissed her forehead.

She opened her eyes. "My love! Is that you?" she said and sat up.

I waited for her to wake up, hopeful she would bring her awareness to my level. She rubbed her eyes and adjusted her belly to leave the bed. For a few moments, she paced around the room with a hand over her stomach, before the light in her forehead was ignited, stronger and stronger. She could now focus. With her next blink, she opened her eyes at me.

"My love," she said again, with tears running down her cheeks.

I hugged her tight, taking in her jasmine scent.

"Where have you been?" she asked.

"I will explain everything as soon as I am back," I said.

"Where are you?"

"I don't know. I think I'm down the river towards the sea."

"How?" She shook her head. "Are you safe?"

"I am. Don't worry."

"Meleethos has been looking for days. He couldn't reach you. He didn't know whether you were alive or not! Why didn't you contact us sooner?"

"I was... somewhere else. And a little weak. I will explain everything..."

My eyes opened in the flesh, with the crackling fire next to the small house. My brain was tired, drifting off to sleep. I closed them again and employed all capacities I had left. I was with Idhatora again.

"Please be careful," I said. "Altazadeh knows I am away. Tell Innok and Meleethos. You can trust Muttiya. Father promised."

"When will you be back? Should we come searching?"

"No. Stay safe. You can't search the entire kingdom up and down the river. I will find a way."

I touched her hand before I was drawn back to my body. *They are good. They are safe.*

A rug was already on the ground, as Terran promised.

AGAINST THE STREAM

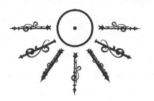

T he family was already down at the river. The sun barely shed any light above the horizon. They all spoke words of pray, facing the river. Then, a moment of silence, and they returned. I raised myself. Caitty went inside with little Hanjya. Terran came for his hand plough.

"Do you not pray?" he asked.

"To what gods?" I responded, looking away.

"I am not learned in theology. My wife is more interested in that stuff. She knows the names. I don't care. I pray to a general god; that being, if there is one, that gives us the light of the sun and the water of the river to grow our crops and survive."

"I saw the black cube across the river," I said.

"Then you know. You must have been a baby when this happened."

I nodded.

"I was probably around your age back then," he said. "I remember well. We lost neighbours and friends and family and parents. Do you know what they did during the plague? They prayed. To each and every name they could find in scriptures of old. Or to gods proposed by priests for something in exchange. Do you know what they got? A black stone cube. So, no. I pray to no god in particular. I just speak my gratitude to life. For being alive. In the hope of keeping my family alive as well."

"You know, Terran, my friend, you are more learned than most priests and scribes I know."

T he river was quieter today. I went high beyond my physical body. No ships, no boats. Time passed with only birds flying by. Until a shadow eclipsed the sun's reflection on the water. I moved my consciousness close. This was a big ship, heavy and ornate. I circled a passenger standing next to the rails, hoping he was sensitive to any impressions from beyond physical matter.

He didn't seem to react. I called upon his consciousness beyond his body. It shook its head. I went to another. And then a third and a fourth. None was open enough to hear me, even subconsciously.

The ship was getting closer to the small island where the river separated into two. No other vessel showed in the distance. Only the light refractions sparkled in the water. Of course! I could try the currents of water, call upon the elementals. Or, maybe, the wind in the sails carrying the ship.

I searched for the elementals when another man came from his cabin. His clothes were fine; white linen with a golden belt and a decorated sword around his waist. Maybe he was more receptive. I floated in front of him. A familiar face of a strong warrior.

"Cyrus!" I exclaimed.

His eyes moved around, reacting to my voice, searching for its source. I touched his forehead to alert him of my presence. He took a deep breath and opened his eyes.

"Cousin!" he said.

"Cyrus! Oh, you can hear me. Please! Turn the boat to the left of that island. I am stranded. I need you!"

"Stop the ship!" he yelled with no explanations needed other than my plea. "Left!" he declared. "Left!"

CURRENTS

T he wind sprinkled my face with water as we sailed closer to the city. Cultivated land now carved the banks around us. Cyrus joined me at the bow of the ship. "What are your plans?" he asked.

"I don't know that there is much to do," I said. "Every time we unveil part of the light, the shadows seem to get stronger." I brought my hand to my face, my palm fuming with Altazadeh's essence. "But I think I have a way to trace the enemy now."

"Whatever you decide, I am your soldier," he said.

"Is Maya still playing at the water temples?"

He furrowed his brow. "I wrote to you. How long have you been gone for?"

"What happened?" I asked.

"When your father sent him down at Dessha, we told Maya that he was needed for the ceremonies at the stone quarries. We kept him busy for a few moon cycles, collecting materials for new constructions. But when your father..." He looked at me with the corner of his eyes. "When news of your father reached us, he disappeared."

"From the temples?"

"From the city. I have troops searching for him. But nothing yet."

"Okay... Maybe he stays away."

"Do you believe that?"

I looked away. "No."

Behind him, a big black structure showed above the mudbrick houses of the farmers.

"We are making a stop," I said and pointed at the Black Temple.

T he stone tablet, carved with prayers for safe travels, was thrown overboard, anchoring the ship close to the Black Temple complex.

"Wait for me," I said as I marched on.

The flood had withdrawn, leaving cracks in the dry mud. The path through the yards was not cleaned yet. Neither was the silent interior of the temple. I climbed up the seven steps to the stage. After a quick glance, my eyes narrowed and pressure pulsated on my forehead. *I don't understand.* The floor was solid. I kneeled where the hole leading to the cave of forefathers used to be. I scraped the stone with my fingers. No marks told of any additions or alterations. The stone was unmarred from one side to the other.

"It was never here, my boy," Meleethos said from behind me.

I stood up and hugged the old man, my first encounter of home. And a coarse reminder of Father's absence.

"How do you mean?" I asked.

"The cave was never below this temple. Not in the physical plane. Your father guided your mind there once; and you kept going back to it. Unconscious of your travels in other dimensions, you must have thought it natural for the cave to be here."

All those times I came here, going down the steps in my mind. How was I not aware?

"I saw him," I said. "I touched him. I think I can reach him now."

I rubbed the fingers of my hand, awakening Altazadeh's essence on them.

"That's good," Meleethos said. "But we need to be careful. If you open a route to him, he will see you too."

I nodded. "Understood."

"Did he say anything? What does he want?"

"Everything!"

He sighed.

"Have you been safe?" I asked.

"Muttiya oversees the funeral preparation; never left my side. And Idhatora and Innok have been restless. I kept searching for you every day. But you were out of reach. Until Idhatora said you re-emerged."

My face must have given away my confusion.

"Do you know how long you've been gone for?" he asked.

"A few days," I said, "maybe eleven, twelve?"

"Ninety-nine days."

STAINS IN THE SAND

I crossed the dark river with Idhatora and Innok; they insisted I didn't go in the night alone. Through the quiet city, the guards stood proud and alert at the gates of the old palace. I only greeted them with a nod, and paced through the yard, conscious that my beloved carried the weight of our unborn child.

Innok drew his sword as we entered the old palace. It was Zurath, waiting in the shadows.

"My king!" he exclaimed. "You are back!"

"Good to see you, my friend. What are you doing here this late?"

"Some of us are treating patients with Meleethos. He needs some medicine from the new palace."

"How about the children?"

"All well and asleep," he said.

"Good. Go bring the medicine, Zurath. I will come find you at the infirmary later."

"Welcome back, my king," he said with a small bow before leaving.

Our steps stroke the stone of the ground as we marched in the hall and down some forgotten stairway to reach a heavy wooden door. Innok pushed it open and moved his torch around the dark, reeking room.

And there she was, sitting in the corner, Savghana, with her tangled hair hiding her face. I expanded my consciousness on her. She looked up at my invisible touch and threw herself towards us. The clanging chain on her neck almost choked her before reaching us, throwing her to the ground, gasping for air.

I walked in the stench and leaned to touch her forehead. With her scream around me, I coursed through her mind. I saw the herbs, taken from the jars Meneir brought as gifts. Her attention on preparing them into oils silenced my mind. She mixed the extracts with other oils and let them sip through leaves. She then used a small stick of reed to transfer the drops on my father's bundle of analgesics. Her own heart rotted with every drop she poured.

I withdrew from her mind and back into my body. She laid with tears on the ground.

"Why?" I asked, unmoved and dry.

She burst out with laughter.

"Savghana," pleaded Idhatora.

"Tell me this," I said. "Are there others?"

She rolled around. I narrowed my eyes at the brown force that heavied her body. The energy moved like smoke and unravelled into the golden mask, the same worn by the dark magicians. I swung my arm, trying to remove it and unveil her influences. Nothing laid behind it. *She was under the influence of darkness on her own volition.* The mask dissolved. Through the muddy energy, I traced her brother, Meneir. He had his back to Savghana. *He had no part in this.* With my next outbreath, I let the images fade away.

"Okay then," I said.

Innok already opened the door for us. Idhatora, with tears in her eyes, leaned close to her former friend, softly touching her dirty cheeks and hair. Savghana stopped laughing as I was about to exit the cell. She grabbed Idhatora's dress.

"Idhatora," she said, looking up into her eyes. "Please, don't tell my brother."

"What did you see?" asked Idhatora.

"Her pain consumed her," I said, walking straight ahead in the dark halls.

She touched my arm, stopping me. "My love…"

I turned to her.

"I am so sorry," she said.

I sighed. "We will talk. Later. We all need to talk," I said, turning at Innok. "But no more secrets. It's us now."

We moved to meet Meleethos and our students at the infirmary. The door was already open. No voices came from within, only dripping. And the room around the sleeping patients was lit only by a half-dead candle.

Innok grabbed a torch from the hall while Idhatora pulled up the arm of an old man, hanging from the bed. She brought the sheet up from his legs to cover his trunk, and I moved to check on the next one.

"Aletheos," said Innok.

Idhatora screamed. She turned to us with bloody hands as the stained sheet dropped in a puddle of blood.

"It's everyone," yelled Innok.

He moved his torch around; its flames reflected on the blood that slowly covered the ground. In their beds, the patients lay with slashed throats and hanging guts.

"Stay with her," I told Innok as I ran back into the halls. "Guards!" I screamed. "Guards!"

I halted at the sight of red liquid flowing from around a corner. Not a sound reached my ears. I approached, one step at a time. A guard laid in his blood. And a scream broke the silence. *Outside.* I ran, jumped over steps and splatters of blood to reach the main gates. Meleethos was on the ground, leaning against the wall. *No, no, no!*

I put my arms around him. "Meleethos, no," I said, trying to pull him up. "You will be..."

"My sweet boy... The children... He took their innocence," he said through bloody teeth together with his last outbreath.

I gently laid him on the floor and rushed in the cool night beyond the doors. A guard extended his spear towards an approaching child.

"No, go back," he repeated, himself stepping back.

Another child came from behind him, stabbed the guard below his ribs. Two, three, four times. The guard dropped to the ground. Others laid dead around him, in priests' uniform and guards' attire. The walls around the yard were red with our guards hanging from them.

Children ran around with knives in their hands. Our children; those we took in to feed and shelter. They jumped over their victims and out the open gates. *They killed everyone!* I gasped for air while looking amidst the massacre for a sign of life.

In the starry night, Zurath came back with the medicine. He hummed a melody with the song of the cicadas. He halted at the sight past the gates in the yard. From behind a column emerged a man, shaking with fear. It was our student, Lohar. He jumped at Zurath's next step with a dagger.

"No!" I yelled, raising my hand.

My mind grasped the panicked man, freezing him in place before, in his instinct to survive, mistakenly murdered his own friend. Zurath's glass vials shuttered on the ground. From behind the outer wall came Altazadeh. He drew his sword and slit Lohar's throat before I could release him. He stared back at me as the lifeless body collapsed in front of him.

I ran towards him. "Go inside!" I shouted at Zurath, never moving my eyes off Altazadeh. "Find Idhi and Innok!"

"Father!" shouted Innok as he came outside.

"Everything!" said Altazadeh with a grin and dissolved into a black cloud that flooded the yard. I raised my arms with a wall of light that blocked his attack. And I let the light fall down on it, crushing and drowning the clouds.

He vanished together with his darkness. Innok ran among the dead. He grabbed my hand.

"Idhatora!" he said. "She is in labour!"

PENDANTS

I dhatora held our baby, Volitia, humming to her while breastfeeding next to our
bed. I closed the door behind me and sat across from them. My chest fluttered
with light through my sadness.

"How was it?" she whispered.

"The ceremonies were carried out simultaneously. Both were raised to face each
other, and all amulets were placed properly. And we farewelled them both; Father
and Meleethos, each in his own ornate tomb. Close to each other. As in life."

I sighed.

"And how are you, my love?" She extended her free arm, waiting for mine.

"I will go wash myself before touching you or the baby, wash the morbid energy
away."

She nodded.

"And I have to keep working on tracing Altazadeh," I said, waking his essence on
my fingers.

"Meleethos advised against it," she reminded me, as she did many times before.

"I know. But what else is there to do? I can't wait for another attack. He comes
and goes as he pleases, taunting us for how long now, while his priests are doing his
bidding in ways that we can't prosecute."

"The Starani?"

"Harapi's men search for him in our cities, in secrecy as I have asked them. But..."
She pressed her lips together. "My love, what does he want with you?"

"Everything, he said."

"Yes, but, what does he want with you? Why didn't he come for us while you were
away? It's like he wants you to suffer, you personally. Yes, he corrupts the kingdom.
But every attack, every abomination he inflicts on the people, is meant to hurt you."

"I know..." I said gazing outside, at the trees and the river, the city across from us. *It was always personal. And I am counting on it.* "What I saw in the desert... There is a connection there I don't understand."

"With Altazadeh?" Her eyes widened but kept her voice low, shaking our Volitia in her arms.

"With Altazadeh, his beast... I don't know."

None of us spoke. We only stared at the baby girl, her little innocent eyes. Oh, that innocence... The most precious of things.

I sighed. I had things to do that would keep me away from her. "Valsaris insisted on seeing you," I said as I removed my clothes.

"Are you okay with this?"

"You are his daughter. I get it. He has been asking to see you and his granddaughter for a while now."

"No secrets," she said.

"No more," I responded. "I will be out in the afternoon. Cyrus wanted to talk to me and Muttiya."

"Is he leaving?"

"I suppose he is. He came moon cycles ago for a funeral and stayed for two. He will probably want to go home now."

W e laid in bed with the sweet afternoon light fondling the room and our sleeping baby in between us. In the subtle planes above her head, a small white-blue flame burned fierce.

"Are you seeing this?" asked Idhatora.

I nodded.

"I should go," I whispered.

Idhatora got up as well, with soft movements for the sake of the baby. She reached for one of her formal dresses and went to the mirror. I approached from behind her, gently moving her long hair to kiss her neck.

"You are always beautiful," I said.

She kissed my cheek before I reached for my lapis pendant, the one she gifted me with, and went down to mother's chamber.

I kneeled and sank my hand in the narrow pond of violet lotuses. After some blind movements that shattered the surface of the water, I sensed the sharp cold edges. I grabbed and brought my crown out of the 'waters of life,' letting it drip over the lotuses, with the dragon of golden threads looking back at me. Innok knocked on the open door.

"Can I speak with you?" he asked.

"Come in," I said and placed the crown on my head with a few cold drops flowing through my hair.

He removed a gold pendant from around his neck and held it close to my face. "This is yours," he said.

A small upside-down cone with six wings around it, hanging from a sphere of gold. *I have seen this before. Back in Areteia!* He placed it in my hand. A sense of warmth filled my heart. It was not a gift from one of his friends as I had thought back then. I closed my eyes with a smile, staying in the invisible embrace.

"It's Chaa's," I said.

"It is. She used to visit every once in a while, back when she worked at the infirmary."

I smiled at the memories. "It almost feels like another lifetime."

"She said that I should give this to you when both your father and herself were gone."

I could not imagine the purpose of such a condition. Nevertheless, her energy was calm to my chest. I looked into his eyes and then the pendant.

"The dent?" I asked.

The cone was damaged.

"I don't know," Innok replied. "Actually, that's not true. I found it like this after a certain visit from Altazadeh. I think it had something to do with derailing his magic on my hand. As if it protected me." He sighed. "I don't know how these things work. Maybe it was a dream. I just thought that maybe the grandmother wished to protect me as well."

"That's very probable," I said.

"Excuse me, my king," said a maiden from the door. "Master Valsaris is here."

"He is not a master of anything," I said. "Let him in."

"Are you sure about this?" Innok asked.

"I need to go. Call for Idhatora. And stay with her." I touched his chest, holding his eyes in mine. "He does not touch the baby!"

He nodded. Outside, Valsaris waited amongst my guards.

"Thank you," he said.

"One more misstep, Valsaris... Just one!" I raised my finger and walked away.

"Is that a threat?" he asked.

"A kindness," I responded. "If I only had the luxury of knowing the consequences of my actions..." I turned back to face him. "Oh, and you do not lay a hand on my child! Understood?"

I walked behind the throne. The door to the assembly room was open. Muttiya talked with the chief architect, Gnomnas, who took over after Meleethos. I knocked on the door.

"Come in," said Muttiya, sunk in her chair.

"Is everything okay, Gnomnas?" I asked.

"Yes, my king. I was just telling the Queen Mother that construction of the new temple is well ahead."

"How about the city?"

"All according to plan!"

"Good. Have you instructed the sculptors of the new paradigms?"

"What new paradigms?" asked Muttiya.

"From Areteia, the clarity and devotion to realism."

"Okay," she said, looking away.

She didn't really care.

"If that's all, Gnomnas," I said.

He bowed and left the room. Muttiya leaned back in her chair with a twisted body, looking out at the afternoon sun.

"Are you okay?" I asked.

"Queen Mother..." she said. "Is that my title now?"

"I don't think Gnomnas meant..."

"I am not your mother," she said.

"I... No one is removing you from your position as Queen Mother, Muttiya."

"I should have been... Your mother, I mean."

"What?"

"I don't mean replacing her. No one could replace the loving priestess of the Goddess." She let out a gust of laughter that turned into a frown. "But I should have been better to you, for you. I was trying to be the best I could for my dear husband..." Her eyes filled with tears. Her voice broke. "And now, he is gone... and I am left with you, the constant reminder of my greatest failure."

I went close to her, sat by her side.

"Your failure?" I asked. "It was my mistakes..."

"Your actions... You are leading a revolution. However dire the consequences..."

I turned to her, ready to defend myself. She raised her palm.

"I understand, Aletheos," she said. "I have been harsh on you. But I understand. And if you let me, I want to help you."

"You are experienced in this Muttiya. And seasoned in diplomatic affairs. I need you."

She let her hand drop on mine in an awkward attempt at affection. Cyrus knocked on the door. Thankfully. Muttiya withdrew her hand and swiped the tears away from her face.

"Should I come another time?" asked Cyrus.

"No, no," answered Muttiya. "Come in."

He joined us around the table.

"More bad news?" I asked.

"No," he said, "pleasant news, I hope."

I raised my brows with a smile.

"I wish to take your sister, Hetta," he said and turned to Muttiya, "your daughter with me. Take her as my wife."

Muttiya composed herself and sat straight.

"We have been writing to each other since my last visit during your coronation," Cyrus explained. "If you let me, I will be kind and loyal to her, keep her safe; always."

"My dear Cyrus," I said, "our fathers were like brothers to each other. And I have known you since we were children. I am certain you would make a good husband for her; if Hetta so wishes."

"What does my daughter say on the matter?" Muttiya said in a heavy tone.

"She wants to... I would never force her to have me."

"Mom, it's true," Hetta said from the door. "I want to go with him."

"You want to leave home?" Muttiya responded.

"Mom, I don't want to leave you, but Cyrus... after Father... Cyrus makes my heart dance with life."

"Muttiya," I said, "if they want to be with each other, we can't..."

She walked to the window, looking away. "I will miss you so much," she finally said, with tears drowning her voice.

I exhaled with relief. Hetta fell into her mother's embrace.

"I will miss you too," Hetta said. "Thank you!"

"On one condition," Muttiya said.

We all stared at her lips.

"I want to always know that you are fine!"

"I will keep writing to you!"

Muttiya shook her head. "I will have your uncle Valsaris make a pendant for us. He can't say no, not after all his bad judgment."

"A pendant?" asked Hetta.

I listened very carefully.

"Yes," Muttiya said. "He had created one for me when I first moved to the palace. Through it, our forces remained connected, and he knew of my wellbeing. It will keep us connected." She placed her hand on her chest. "And it will comfort your mother's heart knowing that you are good and safe."

My stomach burned, as did my mind.

"Excuse me," I said and ran outside and through the gardens.

Outside my house stood the Starani men, as always.

"Valsaris doesn't leave this house," I told them and pushed open the door.

Innok stood inside, watching Idhatora and her father from some distance.

"Anything strange?" I asked him, whispering.

"All good. What's wrong?"

I walked to the side of my wife.

"Hello my love," she said and took my hand.

"Can you please hand over your pendant?" I asked her.

She said nothing, merely went with the tone of my voice. Valsaris locked his eyes on me as Idhatora brought the sandflower with its golden chain over her head and placed it in my hand.

I held the sandflower high, its golden chain swinging from my hand. I blew on it, awakening its energy that vibrated around it like grains of sand. Most of them were coloured with the force of Idhatora; violet, yellow, orange. A few others reflected mine. But there was another one, almost hidden by the vibrancy of ours, a black one. I extended my finger to it.

Valsaris got up as I touched it. The room around me froze in position; Valsaris with his arms in the air and mouth open, Idhatora pressing on the chair to get up, and Innok entering the room with his sword halfway out of its sheath.

I focused on the black spot. I breathed light through it and let it project its records around me. It showed Valsaris holding the rare sandflower in front of a younger Idhi, back in the old palace. The image switched. I saw myself at the excavation site, connecting with my beloved from the cave. In the background, Valsaris overlooked our connection. Behind him, a black chord extended in the darkness. Then, I saw myself again, connecting with Idhi from the jungle, the elephants sleeping close by. Valsaris still watched. The final image showed me at the sanctuary; the last time I used the sandflower.

I drew all projections back into the pendant. Time resumed.

"No," yelled Valsaris.

Idhatora was on her feet. Innok came next to me with his sword in hand. I placed the pendant on the table and dropped on the chair. Valsaris' eyes pleaded in silence.

"Have you told her?" I asked him.

Idhatora brought her arm on my shoulder, looking at her father. "Valsaris? What did you do?"

He sat back in his chair.

"You said I led them to us," I told him. "But that's a lie, isn't it?"

He shook his head. "I tracked you through this," he admitted, nodding towards the pendant.

"You used your daughter's love against me," I said, "and burned it all to the ground."

"You used me?" cried Idhatora. "And all this time I thought you were misunderstood, somehow! I hoped!"

"Do you even care for her?" I asked. "Manipulating her past fears and birth darkness in them..."

His eyes widened. She grabbed the pendant from the table and threw the vibrant sandflower on the wall, shattering it to dust.

"No more lies, Valsaris!" I said. "Are you truly trying to make amends? Are you truly on our side?"

"I am!" he said with tears in his eyes.

In his chest shone a light with his truthfulness, however faint.

"Is he still with you?" I asked Valsaris.

"I don't know. Sometimes I feel him. Subtly. Lurking."

I turned to Innok. "Take him outside."

Innok grabbed Valsaris's neck and twisted his arms, dragging him out the door and throwing him out in the night. Valsaris pushed himself up. But I reached him before he stood straight. I touched his forehead and chest, thrusting his consciousness beyond his body.

Floating at a small distance, he looked around, startled. I maintained a grasp on him, his consciousness. I swung my hand and moved him to the side. Behind him, a black chord disappeared into a swirling black cloud.

"Keep him steady," I said in the flesh to the guards, who grabbed his arms and bent his waist, exposing the back of his neck.

My fingers grazed over his neck to find the appropriate spines. And I pressed.

"Valsaris," I spoke loudly, "come back! Anchor yourself in your body!"

At my will, flames of invisible light burned the chord from his back as he floated closer. From behind him though, erupted the dark cloud, swallowing his consciousness before he reached us and his body.

"Idhatora! Protect the rest!" I yelled.

She breathed out with light that sheltered Innok and the guards. I moved my fingers, leading my force deep into the cloud. *I have you!* I twitched my hand, and, with it, my light shined outwards, bursting the cloud from within itself. Valsaris's consciousness was free again.

"Now!" I told him.

He rushed back into his body, and I released his neck, enfolding it with light. He fell to the ground as the guards let go of him, gasping for air. I didn't wait for him to calm down, only pulled him up and inspected his centres of force, one by one, the colours of each as bright or as dirtied as the attributes he carried out. With a deep inhalation, I withdrew my examination.

"Take care of your shame and self-pity, Valsaris," I said, "lest you draw him back in!"

He still struggled for air. But I was done. I walked back in my house and up the stairs, to my child.

"She is awake," said the maiden in low voice.

"Thank you," I said as she placed her in my arms.

My innocent little girl looked into my eyes. And gifted me with her first smile before grabbing with her little fingers Chaa's pendant, hanging from my neck.

KEEPERS

"What is the meaning, Altazadeh? What are you doing?" I asked.

"I am supposed to assist in bringing harmony," said the being of light, "but I lost my way in the flesh."

"Can you tell me where you are?"

Altazadeh's consciousness shook its head. I moved away from its silence, bringing my consciousness lower in the worlds, following his pillar of light that connected the spiritual levels of his consciousness with his personality. I anchored myself in the realm of men's fire. Below me stretched the city with a black force lingering over it and the people, the same black force that isolated Altazadeh in the flesh from his highest aspects and hid him from me and his own true self. As if it sensed me, the black cloud expanded towards me. I backed off, covering myself with mist of light. And I opened my eyes with Idhatora's touch, back in our house.

"You have been up there the whole morning," she said.

"I need to go again. There must be a way."

"You need to rest. Your brain needs to rest. You will lose control!"

I sighed and walked to the window. "This is futile. I can't connect to him without him connecting to me. Not at the levels of his personality."

"Then stop."

Couldn't I break his connection if he does indeed sense me?

"Meleethos warned you for a reason," she said. "We will find another way."

She brought her arms to my temples and kissed my forehead, helping me ground my consciousness back into my body.

"Volitia?" I asked.

"She is with Valsaris."

"Any changes?"

"No," she said. "He refuses to leave the palace. He is too scared he'll draw back the darkness."

"But I explained it to him. Staying truth to morality will keep darkness away."

"My love, consider his position. He was one of them. And he betrayed them, telling us of their plans. And now, with your intervention... He is scared to go back."

"I don't think Altazadeh's grip was a conscious one," I said. *But still, the dark priests would be done away with him if they found out he had been warning us.*

"It's good for him, spending time with Volitia," she said.

"I agree. But he can't hide forever. Are you okay with this?"

"It will take time to forgive him. Have you?" she asked.

I shook my head. She brushed my neck with her fingers. "Innok is complaining," she said, smiling.

"I know."

We headed downstairs. Under Innok's unmoving gaze, Valsaris stood attentive over Volitia's crib. He had let his beard grow. I took my daughter in my arms, carefully adjusting her position and assembled with Idhatora and Innok in mother's room.

"He just stands and looks at her!" Innok said as he closed the door.

I looked at him, waiting.

"You made me his bodyguard!" Innok protested.

"You are not his! You are my daughter's, Innok!" I said with an even tone; not to upset the baby in my arms.

"You are one of the very few people we trust," Idhatora said.

Innok said nothing. He must have realised his concern was misplaced.

"Idhatora, can you perform the ritual?" I asked of her. "My brain needs more rest."

"Yes, of course."

She walked to the edge of the room and raised her arms towards the sun.

I let my daughter breathe in the mist of light from around the room. It was a little denser than when I did the ritual, but Idhatora hadn't practised it a lot. I usually liked to take over the midday ceremony as a tribute to my mother and Chaa.

"Shall we go?" Idhatora asked.

I sat on the steps, cuddling with my little incarnated spirit. Volitia yawned and stretched and opened her eyes wide awake. I brushed her brows and cheek with my finger, and, with a nod at my friends, we left the room.

Valsaris sat looking beyond the windows.

"You can't hide forever," I told him.

"What are you suggesting, Aletheos?"

"Why don't you come with us to the new temple?" Idhatora proposed.

"No! I am not ready. They will see me."

"You can't stay in the twilight of apathy," I said. "Show yourself. Act on your choice; if your choice is light. For your granddaughter, if nothing else."

I caught his attention.

"You need to raise yourself up, Valsaris; practise, trigger your light aspects into wakefulness. Come. You were a high priest. You can teach Zurath and the remaining students about the hidden meanings in religion's myths. Give him some peace about the life he has chosen in the temple; the same life that cost him his friends. And he can train you in healing the subtle structures of man. Let his kindness transmute your darkness."

He stared at Volitia. Then at me. And then away.

My consciousness floated above us, grounding light on our path as we walked through the city, pushing what faint clouds of darkness distorted my view. Innok mumbled down in the flesh. I returned fully in my body, dry, as if awakened from a deep sleep, while Idhatora smiled at Volitia, tied below her chest.

"Are you all right, my love?" I asked. "Want me to carry her?"

Idhatora cheerfully shook her head.

"Why the temple?" Innok repeated.

"People of this era; It's not easy for them to carry out their spiritual nature. But they will mindlessly devote themselves to structured constructions of dogmas to hold those aspects of them for them, a place they can turn to when they don't know how to turn within, people to listen to when the voice of their spirit is drowned by emotions and thoughts. So, we do that. We will be the keepers; act as keepers, but take none of their devoted efforts. We will keep reminding them of their true essence until they can carry it out themselves. Keepers of each person's flame."

Priests threw glances at me and my companions as we walked by their temple of corruption. The guards, following our every step, marched on. White limestone shaped the path in the sand as we passed behind the old temple towards the east. In the distance, the new structure shone white. Twelve pillars, maybe five times our height, encircled a square courtyard. Each pillar was engraved with different scenes, starting at the bottom with rivers, flowers, and trees. Above them were depictions of animals, birds, humans, and people within the high spiritual flames. On top laid the stars and wanderers. Each scene, each entity, was sculpted out of the stone to jump in space in as a realistic representation as our sculptors' abilities would allow.

"They are like the temple back in Areteia," Innok said.

Idhatora looked around, taking in the marvellously delicate and intrinsic new art style. We passed through the gate and into the square courtyard. No ceiling hindered the light of the sun from reaching us. A statue of a winged lion with a human head and tail of an ox waited in the middle, in front of a small stage held for Idhatora, our daughter, and myself. We took our position on the stage, looking back at the entrance.

People soon appeared on the white path beyond the gate. Zurath came in first, with Valsaris just behind him. And Muttiya with Harapi. Others followed, gathering in small groups. Laypeople, children, women, men. Even some priests with their official clothes, a few with leopard skins, signifying their higher ranks.

I took a step forward on the stage.

"I welcome you all," I exclaimed, "as people amongst people, equals amongst equals. Let me be very clear. There are no ranks under the sun! We learn from others. We teach others. Our lives, our suffering, all matter the same. We walk together, even if the steps we take on our path are ours alone.

And I am glad to see priests of tradition among us. I cannot and I will not tell you to withdraw from your tradition. None of you. You may do as you will. Pray to the gods that you choose. What I will give you, however, is understanding, so that you yourselves can discover and experience the true nature of yourselves and of the gods you pray to. So that in your mind, each aspect holds the significance it deserves according to that aspect of reality it embodies."

People's tension turned to gentle nods and even some smiles. But my eye suddenly twitched and stomach burned. I took a step back and looked at Idhatora. I didn't have to ask. She took my place on the front of the stage and welcomed the people, while I brought my awareness beyond the physical realm.

Several gusts of dark smoke flew towards us, as if catapulted from afar, bashing against the invisible shield I had placed around the temple. Idhatora carried on with her speech, giving me space to resort within and high above. I brought all of my higher aspects into awareness, functioning as one. I brought light around my daughter, my beloved and our temple, solidifying it as much as I could.

Darkness struck hard but did not infiltrate it. I focused on the clouds themselves, dissolved them as they came. And I followed them back to their sources, several priests in masks. I forced my light into their hands, out of which the darkness emerged. Their hands burned bright, disrupting their attack.

I didn't listen to Idhatora's words. Instead, I forced myself to stand by her side, but my eyelids kept dropping and eyes rolling back in my head.

"You need to rest," Idhatora said.

She must have finished some time ago. She kissed my forehead, somewhat gathering my mind.

"Let's go home," she said.

I kept smiling at the people around us who never knew what took place. Zurath approached, almost hopping towards us.

"This is great," he said. "People really listened."

"You did good... bringing them..." I mumbled, but before I spoke my thoughts, my weight dropped on his shoulder.

They helped me down the river; Zurath and another, maybe Innok or Valsaris. They sat me in the water while Idhatora wetted her hand to cool my pulsating forehead and temples.

"Too much, Aletheos. Even for you!" she said as she kept wetting my face.

Grinding Blades

I faced the city from higher in the realms. I kept dissolving dark clouds around
different areas. It was like healing. But as in healing, the issue laid deep in people's
consciousness. After a while, the clouds returned, again and again.

I called for Altazadeh's aspect of light. He did come, and I followed his pillar of
light downwards, to where his storm interrupted the flow of light and hid him from
me. His darkness reacted as I got close, expanding towards me. I backed off; tried
another side. Again, the clouds moved around me. I kept searching for the centre
of his storm, a way to reach him. I approached while his darkness rampaged above
me. *Where are you? What lays below this dense, gross smoke?* I floated closer, slowly,
as if magnetised. I wanted to know. Above me, the light was almost sealed out by
the clouds.

She grabbed my arm. I opened my eyes in the flesh, blurry in our bedroom. Idhi's
hand almost scraped the skin.

"Think of Volitia!" she said. "What happens to her if you get lost?"

"She has you," I said with a dry throat.

"I would die for her, Aletheos! But I don't think my death would be enough. And
neither would yours!"

"Who do you think I am doing this for?" I protested. "This is the first time I get
why my mother left! If I thought my absence would protect Volitia, I would remove
myself from her as well. Even if it shattered my heart. But it's not enough. Not now.
Not for her. So, I am doing all the best I can, the best way I know how."

"My love," she came close, "I know. But I worry about you. We can't lose you
again."

She leaned close and hugged me, her warm cheek touching mine. My shoulders
relaxed.

"Isn't there a safe place for us? For her!" she asked and looked at our baby crawling
on the floor.

So innocent. So vulnerable.

"There is," I said with a spark of hope. "One. The temple is not the only construction I commissioned."

Volitia grabbed Chaa's necklace, whose thin chain hung from the table. Idhatora jumped and caught it before falling on the baby's head.

"This thing is sharp," she said and observed it up close. "The craftmanship is extraordinary."

"Chaa was a woman of great taste."

"It was very sweet of her to gift you this."

I shook my head. "Things were never that simple with Chaa," I said.

She placed it neatly on the table, took Volitia in her arms and sat close to me. "Where is this safe place?"

"I am building us a sanctuary. One that I believe is impenetrable to Altazadeh."

Innok pushed the door open, hitting the wall. The baby started crying in her mother's embrace.

"Innok!" said Idhatora.

He panted.

"We've found Maya," he said. "He has started a war!"

T he assembly room buzzed with the chatter of commanders. Others were silent, those who had more to think about than the gruesomeness of war; Idhatora, Muttiya, Valsaris, Harapi, who filled the seats around the table. Innok brought another man in the room. A young soldier with dusty black skin and clothes.

"Silence!" I commanded the room.

"Nubis, of the South-eastern towers," the soldier introduced himself and bowed.

"Speak, Nubis," I said.

"The nations beyond the towers have joined forces and, by now, they must almost be at our doorsteps."

"Should I call for Cyrus and his soldiers?" Innok asked.

"When did you leave the Towers?" I asked the weary soldier.

"Thirteen days ago," he said.

I turned to Innok. "Tell Cyrus to hold the North safe and send all troops he can spare here in the capital. And stay here as we march South."

"Do we know what they want?" asked Muttiya.

"My queen..." he talked.

"Queen Mother," Muttiya corrected him.

"Queen Mother, I..." He looked around and then at me.

"You may speak Nubis," I said.

"Our informant says there was a traitor from the capital, an old priest."

"Maya," said Valsaris.

The soldier nodded. "He told them that the capital is in unrest after the king's death. King's Father?" He tried to be appropriate with titles. But moved on to the important matters. "That our kingdom is unstable. An opportunity for a strike."

"He would have the kingdom burn to the ground before losing his power," Muttiya said.

"Arrogance is a dangerous advisor," I said, "self-destructive."

"Do we meet them in the open ground?" Innok asked.

"Yes," I answered, "before they reach more of our cities in the South."

I turned to Harapi.

"Agreed," he said.

The palace was quiet after the meeting. I held my daughter on my lap, looking at her big eyes, trying to convey all that I wanted to say, promise her with a nod that I would be back. I broke the silence in the mother's room.

"You haven't said anything during the meeting."

"You are really going?" Idhi asked.

My chest contracted. "It's not really a choice, my love."

"Is it not? They don't need you down there. Harapi is more than capable of leading them!"

"I can't send them to fight for us. People will die down there. I can't stay back, hiding behind walls."

"They are not fighting for us! They are fighting for their homes."

"Do you think they will see it like that? Do you think I want to go to war? Leave you? Leave Volitia?"

"There is another war here! One that only you can fight. What happens here when you are gone? And who will protect us? Your daughter?"

I sighed. "Idhatora, please stop. Don't you think I know that? There is nothing I would rather do more than stay with you. Always. But I need to go."

She looked away. I walked to the open side of the room; watched the sweet colour of the sand and trees and river with the setting sun.

"You are more than capable of protecting our daughter. Your skills in commanding the light are almost as good as you are a mother. And Zurath and Valsaris should
stay close, keeping an extra eye on you two."

"How about the kingdom? I can't rule alone."

"You are new at this," I said. "So am I. We have Muttiya on our side."

"The sanctuary you are building?"

"It's not ready yet. But, my love, you are needed here. Maya was not wrong. Our
nation is unstable. You are the queen! If we both leave... We cannot abandon our
people."

She stayed in silence.

"I know," she finally said.

Innok opened the door to join us. "Is everything all right?"

We didn't give him an answer.

"Muttiya is here," he said.

Idhi pushed Innok out of her way and left the room.

"What's going on?" Innok asked me.

"She wants me to stay," I said.

He didn't respond.

"Let Muttiya in," I said.

"He doesn't have to," Muttiya said, entering the room. "I brought you this."
She gave me a small pouch.

"Meleethos gathered them after your father left."

I carefully let the contents of the pouch slip into my hand. One, two, three small
stones. The gems from Father's crown.

"I think you should have them. He was probably saving them for you, anyway."

"Thank you, Muttiya. I..."

She didn't let me express any emotions.

"And this," she said, giving me an ornate dagger. "Lettani's. Balluashir's brother
was a friend of your father."

I drew it from its sheath. A blade of black metal.

"What time do you leave tomorrow?" she asked.

"Before sunrise. Move a few days up the river, as far as we can before we meet them
on land."

"Please be safe," she said, all the while looking away from me. "Okay?"

"I will. Will you stay with Idhi and Volitia?"

"This is my kingdom, my nation. I will do anything for the good of the people."

"Of course," I said with a smile that was absent from my eyes.

I put the gems back in the pouch and slowly sank them in the pond, together with
my crown.

"**L**ast bath for a while," Idhi said.

The candlelit room relaxed my body. My mind was not so easily calmed.
"I have washed myself in the river before," I said.

She sat next to me on the bathtub. "You will come back, right?"

"I would never leave you willingly."

She brushed over my cheek.

"Is Volitia asleep?" I asked.

She nodded and removed her clothes. She leaned close to my face. Her outbreath warmed my neck as she brought her lips on mine, her tongue moistening the tip of my lips. She sank her hand into the water, between my legs. I sat up in the tub as she raised her leg to join me.

HORNS OF WAR

T he walls of light around the palace and my family stood strong and bright.

"Every day?" asked Innok.

"And night," I said as I returned to my body and the ship.

"I don't get it. But at the sanctuary, you surrounded the elephants' yard with light only once. And you were certain the tiger would not infiltrate it."

"Animals are simple, Innok, innocent. Unless the beast is particularly disturbed, frightened, or hungry, it will sense the light and calm down. Humans are a different kind of beast. Their feelings and thoughts fester with chronic beliefs and issues. They may sense the light and calm down. But they may also be triggered into their destructive behaviours."

"The priests don't seem to have a problem using their force to manipulate people. My father..."

"Using people's darkness for your own gain is even worse. Your father is a twisted man."

He paced around the room; halted in front of the small table that held my crown.

"Was that always there?" he asked.

He pointed at the diamond below the dragon's head. I smiled.

"No. It's father's gems, one of the three. Muttiya brought them to me the day before we sailed."

"When did the craftsmen put it in?"

"They didn't. I placed the gems in the water together with the crown. When I pulled it out, the diamond was already in place."

"Does this mean something?" he asked.

Harapi entered the cabin. "We are ready," he said.

Outside, beyond the anchored ships, our army lined up in full armour; on foot and horses.

"How long?" I asked Harapi.

"We should be in battle within a day."

I mounted my horse that waited on the bank and galloped to the front of the soldiers; men and women, young, children almost, simple farmers and craftsmen from our cities and villages, all who answered the call to protect our kingdom. I raised my sword in the air, the one Innok had gifted me. I kept it high and rode on. The earth trembled with my army's march.

I was out of my tent with the first light. I couldn't sleep. I splashed my face with water from a pot and washed my mouth. The silence of dawn was deafening. I walked to the edge of the hill. The plain below was about to turn into a lake of blood. *So much loss, so much suffering; for what?*

The camp behind me woke up with the sound of metal; swords, shields, spears, and bows. The commanders lined up their battalions.

"Our tracker is back," said Innok as he approached. "The enemy is about to reach the plain."

"They are marching into certain death, Innok! Why?"

"This is the only passage from the Towers towards the kingdom. Harapi said it would take weeks for them to go around the mountains."

"I know the topography, Innok. That was not my question."

I returned to my tent. My armour shone with the light of the torch; small bronze hexagons lined up into a dragon embracing the trunk amidst the otherwise shaped scales on leather pelts. The dragon even had wings in the back. My shield had my sigil on it, a circle in between two wings with a dot in the middle; the first time it would be used in public.

"I am suiting up to commit murder," I told Innok, who extinguished the torch.

"We are defending our kingdom, our people."

"We are. And, how many mothers will cry tonight?"

The horizon beyond the plain was now black with incoming hordes of soldiers, both on horseback and foot. I, alone, showed myself on the hill. Their first commander saw me and stopped the stampede.

I raised a horn. "No man who surrenders will be harmed," I echoed in the plain.

My army revealed itself on top of the mountains surrounding the aggressors. Innok stood by my side.

"You still insist?" he asked. "You can end this war before it begins!"

"Do you remember what happened to Chohanatma when he unleashed his power to defend the sanctuary?"

"You might save lives here!"

I looked as far as I could see, at the young faces prepared to die for our kingdom. I raised the horn again.

"I only ask of Maya," I said. "The traitor is ours to deal with. You may leave your swords on the ground and return to your sweet homes!"

The foreign army was still. But their rage for blood was boiling.

"Just scare them," said Innok.

"Maya," I yelled, "come out! Don't take them with you!"

Their commander raised his sword. At his howl, the army galloped again towards me and the passage. With a quick glance at Innok, I tossed the horn on the ground and took a deep breath. I expanded my awareness over the plain amidst the mountains, each hoof beating at the base of my spine.

Everything slowed down as I concentrated on the movement. I now held them in my hand; the anger, the noise, the rumbling deep beneath the surface. And I magnified them all, let them soar beneath their feet. The horses tripped and fell. The pedestrians kneeled, trying to balance themselves. The earth shook. My hands shook in response, trying to contain it.

Hissing through the air, an arrow pierced my armour and bashed me to the ground. The disturbance was no longer under my command. The earth rumbled. Our armies rained arrows on the plain and marched down to clash their swords. But part of the cliffs collapsed, taking our men within the landslide that drowned much of the enemy.

Unable to move, my heart pounded deafening under the weight of my people that was now in my chest, still not covering their cries. With all my might I pushed and pushed, until I stretched my arm to regain control of the earth. The arrow though, still deep in my chest, sent shocks around my body and cries out of my mouth.

The battle came closer. Swords crashed; shields hammered. Innok was surrounded. *No!* I needed to help, but my burning body kept me pinned to the ground.

"My love," sounded Idhi's voice. "There is an army marching towards the city!"

My eyes opened wide as a blade was raised high above me. And forced down. It stopped midway. With a push, I twisted my sword in the stranger's guts. Innok pushed him away.

"You will be okay," he kept saying.

"The city! They are attacking Eos," I managed to exhale.

Iron and Fire

T he battlefield glowed with spilled blood. My chest flashed with pain, my
wrapped wound burning with every move.

"Treat our injured," I told Harapi.

"Should we start hand counting?" he asked.

Hundreds lay amidst the mud of blood and rocks below the cliff. Favar's monument down at Dessha rushed to mind, together with the grip it had on my stomach.

"No. Find another way to count the fallen enemies. We are not mutilating them."

"But..." he tried to protest.

"I need to go back. Give me half of our unscathed men. You lead the others to
the Towers and hold our ground. Proceed to the rebels' nation. Make sure order is
kept."

W e galloped through the desert. We carried as little as possible; we wouldn't
set camp. I wanted to reach our ships before sundown.

"Behind the hill," said Innok.

We were almost there. I pressed my legs as hard as I could. The horse pushed
forwards. I didn't care about my burning wound, only about reaching the banks.
But, beyond the last hill, I pulled on the reins and stopped. So did the few dozens of
my companions. In the river, our ships floated ablaze. The soldiers protecting them
were dead on the ground.

No way back! The city! My wife, my child!

A cry anchored me to the present. Warriors attacked from behind us. They
slashed through our numbers, coming for me. What men still stood, fought back.

I fought back, my wound already bleeding through the linen wraps and out my armour.

Screams approached from behind me; a horse on fire galloped with his now dead rider amongst us. At the flaming fury, my horse twisted uncontrollable, and threw me to the ground. I pushed myself up and sword high to catch another assault, avoiding another, trying to make sense of the enemy that towered around me.

Behind the ceaseless battle of horses and men, stood on high rocks the traitor. "Maya!" I yelled.

I swung my sword and kicked a man away. I had to reach him. But my men fell, one by one. I let go of Maya, I had to, and turned towards my people. With all effort my mind could conjure, I gathered my force on my hand, and swung my sword around, its reach now expanding beyond its blade and bashing away the enemy from over my friends.

I turned as fast as I could, striking invisible hits again and again. Those of us who stood alive were now free. *Maya. This must end.* But he wasn't on the rocks anymore. I turned and turned, trying to locate him amongst the roaring battle, until a blade met my throat. I followed it up to its wielder. His shoulders extruded dark smoke circling the blade.

"Maya!" I said through grinding teeth. "You treacherous leech!"

Below his arrogant smile, his blade made its way through my skin. My pain and urgency thrust my consciousness beyond my body in a ravaging white fire. And I passed through him. His consciousness separated from his body. It looked around, facing his actions, crying, screaming, holding its head.

His body suddenly stretched, neck twisted to the back, and fell to the ground in spasms. Innok had landed his sword in Maya's chest. Maya gasped and opened his eyes wide as he exhaled for the last time. His forehead and palms were scarred by fire, my invisible fire.

Innok pulled his sword from him and came by my side. All remaining five of us gathered close. At least a hundred men charged towards us. I surged to get a hold of the ground beneath them. Their blades were almost upon us. My channels had not yet reached the sand.

My chest expanded, counting the moments. *Idhi. Volitia.* I had to reach the ground. But I lost it altogether at a deafening bang. A stampede of soldiers crashed into the enemy from the side.

The chaos lasted mere moments. The intruders piled on the ground. The man leading our saviours approached with a smile. I narrowed my eyes, my eyelids heavy with sweat and sand. *Cyrus!*

"Cousin," I cried, "the city!"

"Our troops are there, my king!" he said, touching my shoulder.

Earth Shaking

C yrus's ships floated fast down the river.

"What's that?" Innok asked from the door. "What are they doing so far out in the desert?"

"People?" I asked and moved outside.

Days had passed with no sight of people or houses, only the sun and winds ravaging the desert. Cyrus waved at them; his troops set camp here. They dug deep holes in the sand. Dead masses mounted wooden sleighs, our enemies, waiting to become again one with the earth.

The soldiers abandoned their posts, stood straight and bowed as our ship floated in front of them. I bowed back to them. In the distance appeared the city.

"Cyrus, give them our supplies," I said.

"They are set," Cyrus answered.

"Give them everything," I repeated.

T he air around me was cooling to the senses as our ships floated into the city; probably just my relief to be home. Small broken houses welcomed us back. In the sand around them lay scattered enormous stones.

I squinted. They were carved, colourful with depictions of the gods. One of them had crushed through a house. Beyond it, a temple laid in shambles. The gigantic pillars had fallen, bringing down the walls of the courtyard and the inner sanctuaries, exposing the sacred altars.

Destruction unfolded as we floated towards the palace. Houses to rubbles, temples half-standing, the old palace missing walls and rooms. We threw anchor while people silently picked away at the ruins. Some rested on rocks holding their children, attended to by Cereena and a few others with fruit and nuts.

I stepped to shore. Before I could join the people, Idhatora fell on me, spreading her arms around me.

"You are back," she said with tears in her eyes.

My wound pulsated in my chest. I waited for it to dissipate in her embrace, and took her face in my hands, absorbing all her beauty, all the joy of seeing her safe.

"Volitia?" I asked.

"She is fine. Home with Valsaris."

A small house collapsed behind us, raising a cloud of dust. No one was hurt.

"How did they do this?" I asked.

"This," approached Muttiya, "was not an act of man."

She handed another basket of food to a little girl. "This was the earth. She brought destruction at her awakening."

I looked away. Something chiselled on my mind. I could not make sense of it yet. My gaze wandered in the distance. I gasped. The Black Temple! A stable in the background of the city. Gone.

I reached for a horse and galloped through the city. People pushed mudbricks out of their houses and into piles. Some treated wounds. Zurath was one of them, pouring water on the arm of an elderly woman before wrapping it with linen soaked in oils.

I halted. "There is food and nursing at the harbour," I yelled.

A young man nodded. He pushed a couple of his friends up, making their way for help. Zurath saw me. He pressed his lips together and let his shoulders drop, shaking his head.

"My wife!" cried a man.

He stood on the ruins of his house, holding his head at the sight of a woman's foot buried underneath the pile of bricks. I jumped down from my horse and joined him together with a few others. We pulled and pulled the bricks away. My wound pulsated hard. I took another brick, threw it behind. And the woman's face appeared, covered in layers of dust. I reached down to her, touched her face and expanded my awareness into her body. Nothing. No heartbeat. No faint light. No life.

I backed up, moving with the sound of my heavy breath as the others went to her.

"Here!" another man shouted.

He had uncovered a hand. Others helped remove the bricks to save the man. I threw myself close, gripped the hand. Again. Nothing. More cries filled the air.

"Oh, my daughter! Thank you, gods!" one said.

A man held his daughter in his arms. He had dragged her out of the rubble. Her eyes were open. She moved her hand. I turned within and pleaded I'd be enough as

I touched the girl, passing as much as I could; green, red, yellow light. Zurath did the same.

Help had arrived. The three young men had brought others from the harbour; soldiers and nurses. Innok was with them.

"You are bleeding!" he said.

I got up and pushed myself up my horse, rode further. The Black Temple now laid in masses of black stone in the mud. The falling pieces must have crashed the canals that safely flooded the complex. Now, water, sand, and stone, all mingled. I slowly rode above what used to be the outer walls and towards the inner temple. The commemorative spheres of gold and stone were swallowed by the mud.

I tried to sense them, hard, metallic, in the otherwise malleable ground. I kneeled and dug with my hands. Handful by handful, I threw the mud to the side until I uncovered a black one. The sound of horses flashed in my brain, together with the crushing hills that brought death, back in the plain.

I kept digging. The dead woman's dusty face was projected on the ground. My wound burned. Around me shone, sad, several beings of sand. The elementals' force cried with me as they watched from amidst the ruins. I held one hand close to my chest, and kept pushing through the mud with the other.

"Aletheos!"

A silhouette hid the sun. He crouched close.

"What are you doing?" asked Innok.

"Help me," I said, panting in the mess.

"Aletheos, you are bleeding. You need help!"

"I told you there would be consequences in using higher forces in wars of men!"

His eyes widened as the realisation took shape in his brain.

"We... We were trying to save everyone!" he said. "More would have died if you hadn't shaken the earth!"

I looked down at my task. Dirt was everywhere. I kept digging. He said nothing more; just kneeled in the mud.

"There." I pointed where I sensed the other spheres. "There, there, and there."

SEVERED CHORDS

Maya's body floated in front of me, in one moment frozen in my mind. Around me, deep dark blue was space. I inspected his body. It was just before Innok's blade had landed in him; Maya's consciousness was already pushed beyond his body by my fire.

I focused on the burn marks on his forehead. His skin was malformed, swollen. The channels of force in his wound seemed like snapped roots or branches. Several such snapped channels appeared red throughout his body, the crown of his head, forehead, throat, chest, stomach, and even lower below his waist. And at the centres of his palms. All major centres of force had been scorched. I brought my hand to his chest, grazing over the scar.

The projection moved backwards in time, now tracing the moments before my fire had passed through him. He stood straight with a blade in hand, next to our burning ships. Dark tubes of smoke were anchored in his centres of force, filling him with power. The image of myself appeared at the tip of his blade, amidst whirling white fire. The fire passed through him, pushing his consciousness out of his body and dismantling his centres, severing their connection with the dark tubes.

I opened my eyes in the flesh and sat up, slowly focusing on my bedroom around me.

"You fever is up again," Idhi said. "But your wound gets better."

She leaned and placed her lips on my forehead before placing a cold, wet cloth on it. I touched her arm and kept her close.

"The fire," I exhaled. "The electric fire. It takes away their power!"

She stood up with widened eyes.

I told her! Somebody knows. I can fall back to sleep.

I did.

ROOTS

With a sigh, I left Altazadeh's higher consciousness and returned to my body. He was still unable to help locate his dark counterpart in the flesh. I took a deep breath, raising my mind above the potential consequences of my failure to find him, and turned towards the sun.

My wound still stiffened my chest when I raised my arms. But I didn't stop, let the light from within me, soothing and healing, shine on the stone pot and fill the room as a mist.

With the ceremony done, I sat on the open side of mother's room, receiving the rays of the sun from outside, yet still immersed in the mist inside. A glimmer drew my attention back into the pond; a spark amidst the colourful refractions.

I sank my hands in the water, and smiled as my fingers gripped the metal. My submerged crown must have caught the light at a weird angle. I pulled it out, dripping over the lotuses and sending ripples throughout the stripe of water.

My finger slid over the delicate lines of gold that formed the dragon and its wings. A spark of red flashed in my eyes again. And I saw it. It was the ruby, my father's second gem. It had attached itself to the crown as well, a little lower than the diamond.

I rubbed the ruby to make sure it was secure in the polished metal and awaken its energy. Idhatora joined me in the room. She walked slowly, letting her shoulders drop and eyes close. She hummed relaxed and approached through the mist, sitting by me and resting in my embrace.

"The ruby attached itself," I said in low voice.

Her warm cheek and forehead leaned softly on mine. I let the crown sink back in the pond. She, slowly, took my hands and placed them on her belly. I wondered for a moment. Then looked up into her eyes.

"Are we?" I asked.

She nodded.

"Another child?" I wanted to make sure.

She smiled. I hopped up, drew her into my embrace and danced around the room. One, two circles, then stopped. She didn't meet me in my sentiment.

"What's wrong?" I asked.

She sighed.

"I am worried, my love. Volitia was born in a field of death. We were lucky enough to survive that night. I am always worried about her. And now…"

"The sanctuary is ready!" I said with joy fluttering in my chest. "Our children will be safe. I promise!"

NEW HORIZONS

"To the right of that tall island," I told Idhi.

The bow of the ship did slowly turn. Volitia patted my leg. At the age of two, she was now very clear about her demands. She had both her arms open, waiting. I pulled her up, helped her sit on my shoulders, her little feet bouncing on my chest. I kept her secure with one hand, as she took in all the new sceneries, and wrapped my other hand around Idhi's waist, my palm resting at the side of her big belly.

My daughter kept innocently bouncing her legs. And my wife leaned on my shoulder. All else faded away from my mind. My heart was at ease. *A new beginning, at a safe place.* And, if I was correct, a new chance at victory.

My palm got warm, pulsating on Idhi's belly; not at the rhythm of my heart, but that of our unborn baby. I let my heart join its pace. Both slowed down. A third joined the beat, calling at my consciousness. Two little hearts beat with light.

"Twins," I said.

"What?" Idhi asked.

I took her hand, gently placing it above her navel.

"Listen," I said. "Listen through your hand."

She closed her eyes, remaining silent for a while. Her concentration shaped wrinkles on her forehead.

"Twins," she smiled.

"Pad," Volitia cried for my attention.

"My love?"

I brought her down to the floor. With confused eyes, she held her stomach, probably nauseated.

"Come my little one," Idhi said.

She took Volitia's hand and sat down. The child crawled on the bench and leaned on her mother's lap with her knees close to the chest. Idhi slowly rubbed the child's stomach.

"No wonder you find it hard to stay focused in the realms above," I told Idhatora. "You have two more consciousnesses using your channels!"

We floated away from the main course of the river, behind the island. I expected to greet Caitty's family at any moment. Behind some trees, their garden was half the size it used to be, mostly dry. The door to the small house was shut.

"Maybe they left," said Idhatora.

"Maybe," I replied as we floated away.

"Are we close?" she asked.

"Do you see those mountains? Behind them, protected from all sides."

The shore got greener the closer we got, until the mountains no longer obstructed the view of my oasis. Acacias, cypress and palm trees captured the psithurism of the wind, welcoming us to our new home. Gnomnas, the chief architect, waited to receive us at the dock. I held Volitia's hand on one side and Idhi's on the other, as we left the ship to join him.

"My king, my queen," he said with a small bow and exchanged a nod with Innok behind us. "Welcome to Esperos. All is according to your plans!" he said.

"I know, Gnomnas," I replied. "I have been observing your marvel from up high."

We walked up the stone passages. In between the green trees laid houses, mansions, and big storage facilities, vibrant with pink, violet, and white bougainvilleas. Ponds and streams of water ran on the side of the streets.

Gnomnas escorted us through a long beige wall of stone. "Across the courtyard," he said, "is the administration complex."

The walls surrounding the great square yard were ornate with colourful scenery of nature's beauty and delicate statues that resembled all that my memory still held from Areteia's temple.

"This is..." Idhatora mumbled. "This is extraordinary! Peaceful."

"Behind this building is the infirmary and the library," I told her.

She took a good look around, smiling with satisfaction.

"Our chambers?" she asked.

"Across the street," I said. "Come."

Gnomnas walked first. He took us through a bridge overlooking the main street and into the gardens of our house. A path of white stone led us to the main entrance. Maidens waited inside, having prepared the premises for our arrival. Above floors of lapis and walls of white stone, waved delicate fabrics in front of the windows.

Volitia let go of my hand and ran into Cereena's embrace, who had arrived earlier to overlook the work in our house. Idhi hugged her half-sister as well.

"My love," I said, "I want you to see this."

I took her to our bedroom and through the curtains to a small private garden. Trees filled the circular space around a square pond with violet lotus flowers. White rectangular stones created a narrow path through the pond, leading to my mother's pot in the middle. The golden spheres in memory of Chaa, Chohanatma, and my father were already submerged in the water. Behind the pot, the narrow path continued to a clear quartz pyramid about the same height as us. The pyramid vibrated with force, and, several streaks within it captured the light from different angles, giving it back as rainbows.

"What is this?" she asked with her palm open to the vibrations.

"Below it lies the cave of our forefathers," I said, "from where emerges the light that will keep us safe."

Her shoulders dropped with a smile.

"We are safe?" she asked.

"We are safe!"

She turned back to the pyramid, moving her arms around and connecting with its force. Myself, looked up at the invisible dome of sigils and the blue sky above it. *Come Altazadeh... Leave my people... Follow me.*

PART 5

DUSK

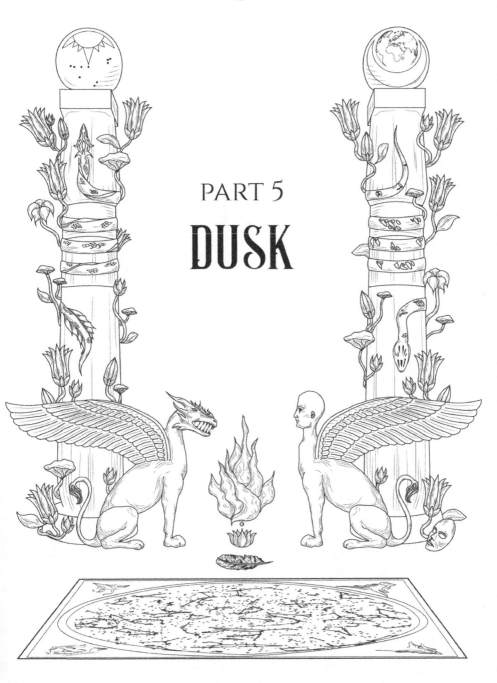

SANCTUARY

M uttiya was dry as ever, albeit less confrontational.

"Upheaval seems to have left the capital with you," she said, pacing around the assembly room of the capital palace. "No riots. But we cannot account for some of the priests. They abandoned their temple a few days ago."

"Are they associated with Altazadeh?" I asked.

"I don't know. Low ranks."

She sat down, alone, below the indigo illustration of the sky and its constellations.

"My temple? Auffia?"

"Your student teaches unencumbered. She is guarded by the Starani, as you requested. A few people do visit."

"The people? Is reconstruction moving along?"

"All is as we talked about. Supplies and construction materials are provided to those affected by the earthquake."

I nodded.

"Muttiya, thank you for acting on my behalf. Esperos is always open for you when you decide to join us."

"I know. But who will maintain order here?" She kept looking away from me.

"I will see you tomorrow," I said. "If anything comes up, please do reach me."

"Goodbye, Aletheos."

I let the old palace burst into light around me, and light reshaped the small garden in the new city. I leaned back on the pyramid of crystal. Across from me, on the narrow path in the pond, sat Idhi. She was doing her work in the invisible planes, her vibrating force rippling in the water. Innok watched us in silence from the door. I hadn't noticed his arrival.

Idhi opened her eyes in the flesh. I gave her my hand and helped her up; her twins-carrying belly restricted her flexibility.

"Gnomnas said the obelisks are ready," Innok said.

I patted his shoulder and kissed my wife, a quick kiss on the cheek. With a wide smile, I left my house and got on my horse. Twelve white obelisks with crystal quartz pyramids on top of them marked the boundaries around the city, just below the natural borders that were the mountains, and all the way across the river to create a perfect circle. I inspected them all; the right size, at the exact location, with the correct symbols on each one.

Satisfied, I rode back. At the harbour, ships unloaded supplies. People carried chests with scrolls for the library, others jars with food and seeds for storage. Livestock were also lined in the streets while guards sorted their arsenal.

"King Aletheos!" someone yelled from the different groups.

He ran to me.

"Zurath, my friend!"

I hopped off the horse for a welcoming embrace.

"Are you settled? Are the other students here?" I asked.

"Yes, Master Gnomnas sorted us. My house is enormous. And it has a yard. Too much!"

"Enjoy, my friend."

"Thank you for this," he said, pointing around at the small city.

"I am glad you are here."

"I will go sort the scrolls and devices at the library."

"You do that. Tomorrow, I will show you and the others around the temples," I said and made my way to my house.

Valsaris sat in the garden with his daughters around him, both Cereena and my wife.

"Welcome," I told him.

"My son," he said. "What you have done here is idyllic."

"There is one more thing to do before I join you," I said. "My love?"

"It is time?" she asked.

I nodded and gave her my hand.

I raised my arms and connected my force with the crystal pyramid in the secret garden. It moved, uncovering the passage into the dark cave below. I went first, just in case my pregnant wife needed support or lost her step down the steep staircase.

She moved slowly. Not because of her belly. Her eyes moved rapidly, as if she was hit with a thousand images on every step. We passed through the two columns and entered the spherical chamber with the square platform in the middle.

"I have been here before," she said with eyes that glimmered, even with the absence of light.

I let her hand go and stepped up onto the stage. I took a deep breath within and found that aspect of me that encapsulated that former lifetime, when we had first created this place. The white electric fire burned strong within me. With a heavy outbreath, it flooded the cave, activating the symbols with blue light. And I expanded my consciousness. With it, the sigils projected their light outwards, anchoring it in the obelisks to enfold the entire city.

When the light's vibrations stabled, I withdrew my consciousness back into my body, gradually, to see whether the light would retrieve as well. It didn't. It stayed in a sphere that stretched from the mountains all the way across the river. My shoulders dropped with a sigh of relief before I opened my eyes in the flesh. Idhi had tears running down her cheeks. She remembered.

"The crystal city, the temples, the flames, the people," she said, serious and calm.

I went down the platform and took her in my embrace. "I know, my love. But we are here now. And we will do all that we can to prevent it from happening again."

She tightened her arms around me before letting go. I helped her upstairs and, with my mind, sealed the cave with the pyramid. The sky above us glimmered with the light of the sigils. *So beautiful. Maybe someday everyone will be able to see it.*

"Aletheos!" cried Idhatora. She leaned on a tree, arching her body. "The babies are coming!"

WHEAT

Volitia inspected the babies, as did I. Above her head sparked the powerful white-blue flame, invisible to the physical eyes. Fiave and Noees slept in their cribs. They, too, had small flames above their heads. Fiave had a yellow one that burned slow and kind, almost magnetising, while Noees had a pink flame that sparkled fast and playful.

"Our little flames," Idhi said, resting her arm on my shoulder.

I turned and kissed her hand.

"Will you be late?" she asked.

"I should be back by midday," I said.

I stepped back, but I could not find it in my heart to leave the babies' side. And neither did Volitia. Idhi kissed me with a gentle push.

"Go. And come back early."

"Goodbye, Volitia. I will see you later, okay?"

My first born didn't even spare me a glance. I leaned and touched my lips on the crown of her head while she remained devoted to observing her sisters.

I dismounted my horse outside the single room that served as a house to Caitty's family. The small vegetable garden laid dry. From the river came Hanjya, with an empty basket. She was taller than I remembered, skinny, with sharp bones on her face.

"What do you want?" the girl asked.

"No fish today?" I responded, pointing at her basket.

She frowned. "Leave," she said and went for the door.

"You have grown."

She tilted her head. "You don't know me!"

"But I do," I said with a smile. "Hanjya, you and your family were very good to me some time ago."

She inspected my face, focused in my eyes. Slowly, her features softened. She dropped the basket and fell into my embrace. I thought she laughed, but it was cries she exhaled.

"Hey, hey, what's wrong?"

She took my hand and opened the door to her house. Her father, Terran, laid on a rug with his back to us.

"Father?" she said in a sweet tone.

He responded with a groan.

"Terran?" I spoke.

He moved his head. I got closer. He stank. I pushed some air out and away from my nose.

"Terran, it's Aletheos. Do you remember me?"

I laid my hand on his back. He swung his, pushing me away. "Get out of my house!"

"Terran, I want to help. What happened?"

He jumped up and grabbed my shirt.

"Get out of my house," he said and threw me out, banging the door shut.

With a heavy heart, I stayed looking at the door for a few moments before going for my horse. I untied the baskets of reed, filled with nuts and fresh produce, and left them on the side of the house, where we had sat around the fire so many nights ago to enjoy Caitty's turnip soup.

I took my horse's reins and led her down the river to quench both our thirst. On the island across the river, stones covered a burial area. *Oh, Caitty.* I sighed, swiping water drops from my mouth and chin.

"He's been like that since then," Hanjya said from behind me.

"When did..."

"A few moon cycles ago."

"And your father?"

"He doesn't get out of the house. He barely gets up from the floor."

I hugged her tight.

"I am so sorry," I said.

She merely shook her head.

"I left some supplies there." I raised her head with a gentle touch for our eyes to meet. "But there is much more from where that came from. I will send more supplies in a few days. If you need something else, just let the rider know."

She pressed her lips together with wet eyes.

"And listen, there is a city nearby. You can come with your raft, just float down the river. You are both welcome to stay there. Always! Just tell them to bring you to me."

I held her gaze. She nodded through her tears.

SEVEN BEACONS

Zurath waited in my front garden, together with the six students that had survived Altazadeh's attack in the old infirmary. They all observed me with a smile on their faces. *So eager, so truthful!*

"My initiates!" I exclaimed. "It is time for us to stand for all to see."

They stood around me, waiting for my words.

"As you know, I have asked Auffia to stay in the capital, teach at our temple there. She graciously accepted. It is now our time to light the path."

They all nodded.

"We have constructed different spaces," I said, "for people to gather and connect with their subtle planes; seven in total. Each space will be a temple for a different plane and its corresponding force. And I need each of you to maintain the light there and guide the people on their path."

I turned to the first one. "Gaos, the energy of the builder is yours. You may guide all to feel secure, safe in their bodies. Your energy will sponsor all construction workers, farmers and cultivators of land."

"Thank you, my king," he said in a heavy voice.

"Nera, the energy of the artist is yours. You may guide the people into their emotions, help them utilise their creative energies. You will sponsor the artists, the sculptors, the musicians. And the cooks."

Nera agreed with a small bow of her head.

"Phir, you shall teach discipline, conscious effort and strength, guide people in mental restrain. The energy of the soldier is yours."

He stood straight.

"Pathia, you are a natural healer. Guide people with kindness and acceptance!"

She smiled.

"Each aspirant must pass through education in all the temples. You, Erios, will teach people of truthful expression and literacy. You hold the energy of the scribe and you will be the last safeguard before people approach esoteric knowledge."

He nodded.

"Noina," I turned to the sixth initiate, "you will hold the light for the aspirants and shed the veils of illusion into the realms beyond."

Noina's forehead sparked with light over her blind eyes.

"And Zurath..."

He held his palms together, eager to receive his duty.

"You, Zurath, will teach of Spirit in the great white temple of the Dazzling Sun, where Idhatora and I will address our people as well."

I stretched my arms and gathered them all in a circle. With a deep breath, our energies ran through each other's hearts.

"We stand together," I said.

Silent Feast

I floated high above the mountains overlooking Esperos, my sanctuary of a city. The stars sparkled around me and the moon shone a path on the river, connecting the eastern and western lands. On the side of the living, further east, my tomb was being prepared deep in the mountains while across the river, on the west land of death, the seasonal flooding had already fertilised the soil for our crops.

Nothing showed in the distance. My search for Altazadeh through the higher realms still proved fruitless. From down in the flesh, my name was called out. I opened my eyes among the glowing sigils in the cave.

"Aletheos!" Innok kept calling for me.

I cleared my throat and slowly brought myself to the surface.

"Everyone is here," Innok said.

"I will be right there."

The streaks in the crystal pyramid sealing the cave sparkled with whatever blue light they captured from deep below them. I took a deep breath and dragged myself behind Innok, through my house, all the way to the front yard.

Torches lit the night around long tables, mounted with food and wine. The trees rustled with a slow wind and friends had gathered, some already sitting, others chatting around the garden. Innok moved along, close to a young man with brown skin and trimmed hair in Starani's uniform, who held a second glass for him. Volitia ran restless around my wife and Cereena, who each held one of the twins.

I inhaled the jasmine scent that flooded the night and brought a smile to my lips. "Dear friends," I exclaimed, "welcome to my house. Welcome to Esperos, our city. Thank you all for joining our cause. Each and every one of you is valued greatly. Together, we stand guard of the records!" I raised my glass, filled with wine. "Here is to our new beginning. And what best occasion to commence our celebration, than with the birth of my twin daughters!"

People raised their glasses, cheering and proclaiming their blessings for the future of the city and that of the children. Their joy didn't echo for long in my chest. I sat down, letting them feast with their companions. I stayed still as their voices faded from my perception. Innok was alerted, focusing on me. Idhatora touched my chest.

"My love?" I heard her saying as if from afar.

My focus was elsewhere; far above the city. Over the torches and food and wine. Over the pleasantries of companionship. Over the dome of light projecting from the cave. In the dark background of the sky, two enormous blank eyes stared down at me.

The Way

"Muttiya, you should join us at Esperos," I said.

The light from the assembly room windows reached Father's empty seat, while next to it, Muttiya sank in hers.

"You don't have to be alone here in the capital," I continued.

She softly placed one hand on the arm of my father's chair. "We all have our own duty to carry out," she answered, fondling with the other hand the pendant around her neck that connected her to her daughter.

"Muttiya... I want you safe."

"How old are you now?" she asked. "Twenty-two, twenty-three?"

I nodded.

"And you have already attempted more to rid us and the people of this darkness than what your father and I did in dozens of sun cycles. You mother would be proud."

Mentioning my mother brought a sweet warmth in my chest, though it lasted mere moments. *I have made many attempts, but not yet achieved victory.* I could only hope that grounding the light in the people would work. At least we were doing so in a safe place.

"It was another time, Muttiya. You have nothing to prove."

"I know," she said. "But, each where we belong, Aletheos. I am staying here."

Her frown seemed all the more permanent with every passing day.

"Just think about it," I said and let my consciousness be drawn away from the assembly room and back into my body at Esperos.

The leaves of my garden rustled with the wind.

"Pad, come!" Volitia barged in our garden.

"Ma says it's time," she said loudly, demanding I follow her.

She took my hand and never let go as we, together with Idhi, made our way through the tree-shaded pathways, interspersed with the small streams of water. Each of the twins was wrapped around our chests.

Outside the temple, Valsaris stood among the people. Zurath waited at the white pillars that shaped the doorless gate, together with the six initiates. He welcomed us with a big smile as we proceeded in the first courtyard, followed by the initiates and the laypeople.

Hundreds of black stone cubes laid in rows on the sides of the main path. On top of them laid seeds and dried fruits. No part of the temple had a ceiling that would keep the sunlight from reaching us.

"Offerings to the god?" asked Valsaris with furrowed brows.

"Yes," I answered and walked towards the next gate.

I turned to face the people.

"My dear friends! These black stones are pieces from the Black Temple of old. Each cube is carved out of the old sacred space in memory of our past, for it led us where we stand. And in memory of all those we have lost during the plague that ravaged our kingdom so long ago, the one we never truly healed from just yet.

I ask of you to bring your offerings here and place them on the stones. These offerings are for the god. Not that unknown god that shines its light down on us, for it needs no offerings, but the godly planes that lay dormant in each one of us, the spirit that expresses itself through our bodies. They do. They need our offerings; food, water, kindness, love.

So, as you make offerings, you may also take whatever you need. As we open our city to more people, let no one worry about the sustenance of their bodies. Food will be provided to all that don't have it. And seeds to cultivate in the blessed lands.

Make it known to all!"

I proceeded through the second gate all the way to the front of the third and final gate. This second section was smaller. Black cubes contrasted again, the white pathway and walls.

"When our bodies, our emotions and thoughts are taken care of, safe and composed, we stand in the middle ground. Where we may, in full awareness, choose between the light or darkness. These are the only true forces in the cosmos. One leads to unity, the other causes separation. And here we stand between the white and black, the right and wrong, still amidst the grey of our experience. We may fall, choose the wrong. That is okay. Make those loving offering to yourselves as well. Bring light into your darkness and try anew."

I took a step into the third section, alone with my family in a small space of white stone. Only a sphere of marble emerged from a round pond.

"Until the will of the one is known," I declared to the people back in the middle section. "Until the whole of our consciousness is fused with the will of the One, and light and darkness are one again, in harmony with the all."

Idhi and I went to opposite sides of the small round pond and opened our hands to the light of the sun above. With a deep breath, we projected that light from our hands onto the marble sphere. The sphere gave back the light, caressing the water of the pond below it and turning into a white mist that filled space around us and expanded throughout the whole temple, enfolding each person with its spiritual warmth.

T he sunlight was heavy on my head. We were finally on our way home. Cereena walked next to us and Innok had met a friend of his midway.

"Do you really think people understand the abstractions you talk about?" Idhi asked in kind tone.

"Only through experience will they consolidate these abstractions into understanding. There is no other teacher than grey experience," I responded with weary eyes.

Cereena offered to help with the babies as we entered our yard.

"Thank you," I said and gave her small Fiave from around my chest.

Volitia ran inside. I kissed my wife and Noees in her arms.

"Excuse me, my love," I said, "I will go rest for a while."

Behind our bedroom, the light was calmer through the green leaves in the small garden. But I floated above it, far above, into the afternoon sky. I called for Altazadeh's higher principles and followed his pillar of consciousness down to his dark storm in the lower planes.

I breathed out white light on his clouds, as I did so many times before. And in the usual manner, the clouds moved around the light and reassumed their position.

Where do you get this power, Altazadeh? Where, if not from your higher aspects?

I threw light again, on the dark clouds. I clenched my fist, observing them as if time had stopped, floating around them and searching for anything that could spark a sign in my mind. Nothing. I let time resume, and the clouds smashed back together before swirling around into a sphere for the first time.

I turned to his higher aspects for an explanation.

"He sensed you," his core of light explained.

I drew back, higher in the realms, watching him from a point he could not reach. The clouds became a whirlwind around him. An opening appeared on top of the tornado.

"No," warned me his higher aspect.

An opening! The only one so far! I slipped down and close to him, rushing towards the opening. The darkness quickly flooded space, giving form to the enormous black beast. He looked at me with blank eyes above his beak, his black feathers surging around his wingless body. He swung his sceptre from afar, filling my chest with an invisible grasp of fear. I turned to the three flames in my heart, expanding them around me and set myself free.

"Why are you helping him?" I yelled. "What are you?"

The whirlwind around Altazadeh's lower aspects closed above him, hiding him from any contact or reach. The beast disappeared. I opened my eyes down in my body and jumped up with a scream that moved the trees around me.

Idhatora ran outside together with Cereena, Innok, and another.

"My love!" she said, concerned.

Innok had his sword in hand. His friend as well.

"I almost reached him!"

SEEDS

People still arrived at the docks. Gnomnas commanded the guards to escort each family to their houses as they descended from their ships.

"Are you sure about this?" Innok asked.

The people were weary, but looked around the new city with a spark of hope in their eyes. No dark clouds lurked above them.

"Are you sure he can't get in?" asked Idhatora from my side.

"The sigils will keep the city out of Altazadeh's reach."

"Can't someone bring them in?" asked Idhatora.

I kept searching for dark energies around the crowds.

"The darkness in these people is born out of their personal issues. When they are within our dome of light, Altazadeh cannot use and manipulate them. As long as they haven't practiced dark magic."

"What then?" asked Innok.

"His essence would reside within their bodies, hiding, able to pass through with them."

Innok furrowed his brow.

"No," I said. "The dome will not keep people outside, but might deter them subconsciously."

"Like the tiger," he said, "moving on, only if receptive to the light."

I nodded, smiling. He did get it.

A few shouts caused unrest amidst the people coming up the slope. It was a girl, pushing through as the guards tried to maintain order. A guard reached her, pulled her aside and brought her to me, gripping her shoulder. The girl pushed her hands through the air to break free from Innok's friend.

"My king," he said, trying to hold her still.

"Hanjya! Come, my dear!" I responded.

The guard looked confused. Innok nodded at him to retrieve.

"I told you I knew him," Hanjya said and pushed the guard aside.

"Come, my dear, what do you need? Is Terran okay?"

She stayed quiet, glancing at the people around me.

"Give me some time," I told her. "I want to see the last people arriving. Then we can talk."

She nodded and positioned herself between Innok and me.

I walked Hanjya into the temple. Abundance itself laid on top of the black cubes.

"What is this place?" she asked.

"This is where we gather and speak about the invisible forces that underlie the physical cosmos."

She kept looking at the offerings.

"People here help each other," I said. "I want everyone to feel secure and nurtured; their physical needs provided for."

She grabbed some nuts and threw them in her mouth. "Why the crown? Are you like a king or something?"

"I am," I said with a smile.

She stopped chewing.

"I am sorry," she said, with crushed nuts spraying out of her mouth.

I laughed and grabbed some nuts myself. "Don't worry about it," I said, munching.

The girl stared at the great structures as we proceeded further into the temple.

"Why are you here, Hanjya?"

"I have nowhere else to go."

"Your father?"

"He kicked me out. He didn't appreciate the food you kept sending us. He said I should learn to cultivate the land if I wanted to survive; gifts are for the weak. And when I told him we could come here, he punched the wall and ordered me to leave."

"I am very sorry, Hanjya. Terran is a good man. I know it. It's his pain talking."

"He used to be. I am not so sure anymore."

"Come, meet my family. Cereena will sort you out in my house."

"I don't want to live in a palace. Despite what Father said, I know how to cultivate the land! Just put a plough in my hand."

"Come, my dear. You may have your plough."

Idols of Old

G nomnas sat silent at the back of the throne chamber. He had already made
his report on the constructions' development; an almost daily task since we
arrived in Esperos. He now listened, as did I, to our chiefs of storage facilities and
land cultivation. Numbers upon numbers of the harvest quantities for each kind.

"That is good for now," Gnomnas said. "But people keep coming. We will need
new areas to fertilise with seeds."

"Agreed," I said. "We should start preparing the lands beyond the obelisks before
the next flooding."

"Yes, my king," he said, and led the other officials outside.

I turned to Innok, who stood by me with red cheeks and heavy eyelids.

"Wake up," I said.

He moved his jaw around and smiled.

"Let's go."

Z urath and Valsaris were already in the library. I stepped down into the centre of
the compact stone amphitheatre while they finished tidying some scrolls. The
light from the gardens passed through engraved panels of wood, projecting lotus
flowers and starry patterns on the ground.

"Idhatora?" asked Valsaris.

"She is not joining us today," I responded. "She will be addressing the people at
the temple while we proceed on our esoteric path."

They made their way down the steps and sat across from me. Innok stayed away,
always on alert.

"The others?" I asked Zurath.

"At their temples. Some people have come."

"Good. What have you been working on?" I asked them.

It was Zurath who answered.

"Valsaris has been teaching me the true symbolism in the myths of tradition," he said. "It's all there! What you have been teaching us... it's all there; hidden in plain side."

"It is," I said.

"Why isn't the truth laid out clear for all to see? Out of what need did our forefathers hide it?" asked Zurath.

"I don't believe the intention was to hide it, Zurath," said Valsaris.

"I agree," I said. "If our forefathers intended to conceal the sacred knowledge, they would not create elaborate stories filled with coherent symbolism. They would use nonsensical enigmas instead. Symbolism ensured that only those who have developed the necessary capacities through personal effort may have access to the secrets. And this protects both the knowledge and the unprepared men from using it; for one who uses such knowledge in selfish ways condemns himself to a fate that he is not equipped to deal with."

"I understand that," Zurath replied. "But hasn't this brought more disorder in the world? Our own priests have been using the symbols and their potencies wrong."

"Personification of the divine principles, being the fallacy that it is, has nevertheless been a way for the higher sciences to survive in the minds of simpler men for millennia. And you are right, my friend. As of consequence, there has been a lot of confusion. But that is the nature of the powers laying in men. No one can prevent or protect them from using them in such ways. And that is what brings the fall of spirit into illusion, again and again."

"The disorder that would fall upon our world," added Valsaris, "had everyone had conscious access to the higher sciences, is unimaginable."

"As evident by the condition of the realm of mud," I said, "the collective emotional state of our world."

Zurath pressed his lips together, nodding. Behind me remained open the scroll with the five circles, each minorly differentiated from its preceding one, denoting the unfoldment of the Absolute down to spiritual consciousness.

"We have the Absolute then," I proclaimed. "Separating itself into male and female principles and by the subsequent unity of the two, it gives birth to itself; the dragon. What then?"

Valsaris and Zurath glanced at each other and then at me. Zurath spoke first.

"Well, we have the birth of the cosmos, the realms, the worlds, the consciousnesses."

"And each is made in the same way, as the dragon procreates in himself, creating each consciousness as the younger dragon," said Valsaris.

"Correct. All of creation takes place, step by step. The dragon, upon his manifestation, exhales fire, creating mist in the waters of life. The dragon, though, holds seven flames, each with its own attributes, giving matter and consciousness their individual potencies."

I gave them a few moments for their brains to readjust as the light of knowledge made its way around it.

"These flames spring forth into space, colouring it with their light, individually, collectively and always interrelating. The first contains all the others. It is in a great sense the dragon itself; the Law, the will that thrusts the law into motion. From that first flame, two more come forth. The second is the flame of Wisdom, whose application is Love; the third is the flame of Creative Activity. And from that creative activity, spring forth the remaining four, that of Harmony, Knowledge and Devotion; all to be solidified by the seventh, the flame of Order.

Contemplate these forces. For the entire cosmos consists of them."

I met Cereena in our small garden. She watched over our daughters while my wife and I carried out our duties. Volitia cheered for her sisters, telling them to keep moving as they crawled on the ground next to the pond.

"Can you take them inside?" I asked.

Her mouth withheld her words, before vocalising her thoughts. "The little ones just woke up. It will be good for them to..."

"Now, please."

She took a step back, examining my face.

"Yes, of course, Aletheos," she finally exhaled and went for the kids.

Volitia already complained, but she rushed inside as Cereena picked up the twins.

"Please, let Idhatora know I will be back here."

"I will. Is she at the temple still?"

I nodded and took off my crown. I placed it in the water and moved the pyramid to head below.

T he sunlight no longer reached me in the cave of forefathers. Only the faint light of the symbols on the walls gave me some sense of direction. The light of each one intensified as I brought my hand closer, going through them one more time.

I gasped at a touch on my shoulder.

"Idhatora! You scared me."

I turned back to the symbol.

"My love," she pleaded, "what are you doing? You have been going over the symbols for days. Come up, you missed the girls again."

I said nothing as I narrowed my eyes at a symbol.

"Aletheos, you are exhausted," said Innok from the bottom step, whose presence only now did I notice.

I moved my hand a few fingers away from the symbols, tracing the shape of each one.

"What are you looking for down here?" asked Innok.

"A sign," I said.

"My love," said Idhi with a sweet tone, "you engraved them yourself. If the answer isn't here, you must know why."

I turned to her, waiting for more explanations.

"It was eons ago," she said. "Maybe this entity didn't exist back then. And if it did, maybe you didn't know about it. Which would mean that there is nothing in here to help us. Or..."

"Are entities born?" Innok interrupted.

"Of course, they are born; sometime during the process of creation and cycle of existence, their consciousness springs forth as well. But this one is strong. I can't assume he wasn't around back then."

"Back when?" said Innok.

"If the beast was indeed around," continued Idhatora, "and you knew about it, maybe you thought that his nature was somewhat of a given, that you didn't need to include him in the knowledge passed down to the new era. And in any account, that knowledge still exists within you, accessible somewhere in the records of your lifetimes."

All my energy pulsated in my forehead. "What are you saying?"

"What if the answer is so natural, so obvious, that we dismiss it before we even bring it to awareness?" she said.

She came close, touched the symbols as well.

"You told me," she said as she made her way around the cave, "that his appearance is similar to how the scriptures of tradition describe the father of gods."

"That can't be. The father of gods described in the old scrolls is a symbol, used to denote divine attributes, the inner faculties and principles of the cosmos. This is an entity, a beast powerful enough to rule over the lower realms. Malevolent and dark."

"So, the exact opposite?" said Innok.

"Exactly," said Idhatora. "What if Altazadeh created him like Chaa did Udenas and you the crocodile?"

I sighed. That couldn't be right.

"The beast must be a creature of old. And he is too strong to be created by one man alone. And from what I saw, it's the beast that lends it power to Altazadeh, not the other way around."

She paced around for a little while.

"What if the distinguishment of the two..." she said. "What if people cannot distinguish the symbol from the entity? So much so that through their prayer to the father of gods, they give their power to this beast instead?"

The crown of my head was getting heavier. I turned within, let the light come in and fill my head. The image of the beast projected out into the room in front of me. The beast was small, almost as small as a man. But for the first time, I saw him with wings attached to his back. Wounded, weary, dying, he dragged his wings on the ground. His pain burned in my stomach. He wished to die. Almost; he didn't really want to die. He preferred being in anguish. He deserved it. He crawled through the desert towards a river. Two man-like creatures were fighting next to the water. Darkness burned vividly in them. The beast fed on it. He got stronger; strong enough to distract himself from his pain.

They pray through their darkness. It is the beast who answers.

"What if that's true?" I asked my friends, who remained unaware of my vision. "What if the beast is indeed fed by the darkness of people who mistake him for the father of gods?"

As he grew stronger, so did the darkness in the two men. The darkness rose through one of the men, and as it reached his head, the beast got closer, stood by him, and stretched his wings before thrusting them on the fiend, who dissolved into droplets of darkness that fell and corrupted the ground.

"If that's true," Innok said, "the beast is fed with the collective unconscious power of almost everyone in the kingdom!"

The images vanished. The cave was dark again, with only the dim blue light of the symbols casting shadows around us.

"We need to scrape away the image from people's minds," I said.

"What? How?" protested Idhatora.

"Take down his image from all temples in the kingdom! And strip the symbol of its title as father of gods!"

"My love, no," said Idhatora. "People hold that image sacred. Conflict will create more conflict, more darkness. It's what your father did..."

"I know Idhi. But this may be our only way in. Removing his image from public access may help people realign themselves away from him. People must know the order of things. If the beast gets weaker, I may be able to reach Altazadeh! And save us all."

"What if we are wrong?" she cried. "We will only fuel them!"

This will work. It has to! Otherwise... I turned to Innok. "Send our soldiers! By first daylight!"

Idhatora shook her head. Innok stared back at me. I remained unmoved.

"And issue another decree," I said. "No more searching in silence. Make it known that Altazadeh is wanted for crimes against the kingdom! Anyone who shelters or aids him will be trialled as an accomplice!"

CYCLE

I pulled my crown from the pond with refreshing droplets sliding through my hair. It was past the time I should have visited Muttiya. I wouldn't. She would just try to talk me out of desecrating the temples.

Hanjya's room was empty; she had been staying with friends who also worked the land. In the front yard, the kids played with Cereena; Idhatora already spoke at the temple. And Valsaris was probably with Zurath at the library.

I went through the stables, fondled my horse's head, and silently mounted away. Guards walked the green streets next to the gently flowing streams, bowing their heads as I rode by. Innok was nowhere to be seen, probably instructing the messengers on visiting the wardens of our cities and carrying out my command.

I rode away from the harbour, towards the mountains. The small crystal pyramids on top of the obelisks glimmered with the sunlight, setting the horizons around the city. I passed through them and out onto the steep slopes. The path widened in front of a cave, sealed with a rock that depicted a disk with seven rays emanating from it, my future resting place. I halted for a moment. *May darkness be dead before I finally lay inside.*

The path narrowed again all the way up. I dismounted, watching my city below the cliff, humming with life. People filled the temple. Others worked in the fields. Ships sailed up and down the river. And if I focused hard enough, the dome of sigils guarding the city was almost visible to the physical eyes.

"Finally sneaked out of your hiding place?" asked a man from behind me.

I smiled. *My decree drew him out.* I turned to face him.

"I am hiding, Altazadeh?" I opened my arms under the light of the sun. "You are the one lurking in the shadows."

"You have been searching for me," he said.

I nodded. We both moved, walking across each other in a circle.

"Why?" he asked.

"I wanted to talk to you. Let you know of your grave mistakes."

He laughed. "Inform me of things?" he mocked me. "All that you are unaware of have you running in circles around your shadow, Aletheos."

"You give yourself to a false god, Altazadeh."

We stopped moving, seeing into each other's eyes. He switched direction. I switched as well.

"Anthelios is not a god," he said.

My eyes widened. *Anthelios!* I kept walking, withholding any reactions. *Did the name slip his tongue?*

"So, you do know," I said. "Do your followers know?"

"They believe what they want to believe. They see what they want to see."

"And you just use their delusions."

"They plead; no, they beg of me to use them."

"You used to be a healer, Altazadeh. What happened to you?"

His eyes twitched. Moved rapidly for a moment. He either did not expect me to know or he didn't remember himself. He kept walking.

"What happened," I repeated, "that twisted your morality so much? So much so that you purposefully mislead people?"

A glimpse of light sparked above his head, but disappeared as fast.

"To what end, Altazadeh?"

"I want everything!"

"So you've said. But darkness separates, dissolves. Whatever you are trying to gain, you will dissolve before it even reaches your hands."

"And what do you want?" he asked.

"I want the truth. The only stable thing in the cosmos. The one that unites and keeps us together."

He burst out with laughter.

"You can't, still, be so naïve!" he said.

"I am not naïve, Altazadeh."

"Then what are you? A champion? A leader? You are naïve, searching for the truth in a world of consciousness. There are as many truths as there are consciousnesses. And each one separates us even more, holding us apart from each other. The very thing you are looking for will be your fall. And that of all that you are trying to solidify."

"A noble cause," I said.

"A stupid cause; a futile one."

I halted. Looked directly into his eyes. He did the same.

"What are your plans?" I asked. "What scheme are you playing out?"

"The fall."

"And then what?"

"Then I rise as god."

I shook my head. "Become the beast yourself," I said.

He smiled.

"You will never be a beast, Altazadeh. You are a snake, slithering amidst the feet of pilgrims on their path. Yes, you may bite them. Yes, they may stumble because of it. But there is no good outcome for you. Not a meaningful one."

He opened his arms. Dark flames burned around him. "Everything," he exclaimed and turned into a dark fire to fly away.

I smiled. He hadn't noticed. He bashed on the sphere of light I had slowly raised around us. He hit the floor, turning back into his human form. I brought Innok's sword to his throat.

"I may fail, Altazadeh. But I am not naïve. I will throw myself into your dark flames before allowing you any hold on one more of my people."

My stomach flared. An image flashed before my eyes, a memory from eons past, something I had said as a keeper of flame to the dark magician. 'You cannot maintain the darkness separated from the light without it consuming you!'

Altazadeh turned into the black flame again. And all I could perceive of myself was a white flame. We swirled and struck each other within the sphere of light. I fumed and expanded until I encircled him whole and threw him to the ground. I stood above his kneeling body. I raised my blade. It came down with a swing that shook the mountain and threw me away. I didn't get him. Anthelios came out of nothingness and crashed my walls of light. Altazadeh disappeared.

I panted. But I could not lose them! I turned within and up through my pillar of light. As my consciousness grew around the beast, I kept gathering light around him. I became the all, darkness, space, with the white dragons of fire spiralling within me. In peace. In serenity. Silence. I could see him no longer. He vanished somewhere in my nothingness.

I came back, breathing myself into the flesh, atop the coarse sandy mountain. They got away, again. I sighed. But at least I had a name.

I rode back through the obelisks and under the trees that sheltered me from the afternoon sun. A couple walked in the shade, speaking tenderly, leaning on each other. I hopped off my horse and walked by them towards my house, searching in my mind for more clues Altazadeh might have given away.

"Aletheos, is that you?" asked Innok.

He moved a few steps away from his friend and stayed quiet. I smiled at him and nodded at the other man.

"I will meet you later," said Innok to his friend, who kept on.

"Are you just coming back?" he asked. "Idhatora said you left in the morning."

"You didn't have to send him away," I said.

He blushed.

"He seems like a decent guy," I said.

"Sahran... he is a good man."

"You don't have to worry about me, Innok. You should take care of your happiness." I turned away. "You may deserve it more than any of us."

"Is something wrong?" he asked.

I tilted my head at his question.

"Yeah, sorry," he said.

He looked up at my crown, down and up again.

"Your crown changed again," he said.

I brought it close to my face, observed it closely. I caught my breath. The sapphire, my father's third gem, had fused itself on the gold, shaping a triangle with the ruby and diamond. I turned to Innok.

"Bring the horse home!" I said and let go of the reins to run through the narrow passages.

OF GATES

The torchlight glimmered through the windows against the indigo sky. A guard opened the door for me. Inside, Cereena lined some small pieces of gold on the table.

"Idhatora?" I asked with an urgent smile.

"In the garden," she said in a calm tone.

Our kids were already asleep. I went through our bedroom and out to the small haven. Idhi sat on the ground with her back against a tree. She waved her hands in the air, moving orbs of water around her. She glanced at me and looked away, letting the spheres splash on the ground.

"My love," I said and sat next to her. "Look!" I showed her the crown.

She touched the third gem. She said nothing.

"Are we pregnant?" I asked.

She stormed up.

"What's wrong?" I asked.

"Your daughters have been trying to stay awake, waiting for you. Volitia cried herself to sleep."

I am so sorry.

"I had to give her that pendant of yours she likes so much," she said. "She broke it!"

"Chaa's pendant?"

"Yes. Cereena gathers the pieces while I am here, by myself, trying to figure out what to do."

"Figure what out?" I asked.

"Really, Aletheos? You let me take care of everything! The temple, the people, the kids!"

I sighed. *How nice it must be; a normal life, a good life.* How I longed for it.

"You disappear for most parts of the day!" she continued.

"My love," I approached her, opening my arms.

She pulled away.

"You said we would be safe here. Instead, this city is beginning to feel like a cage. We didn't keep him out! We just locked ourselves in."

"I am doing my best," I exclaimed.

"It's not enough. I don't care anymore. About his war, about the hidden mysteries, about your duty to the order. I want to live my life with you and our daughters. But you are always away, hidden in that mind of yours. And now..."

She touched her belly. I forced a smile below my tears. She sighed and brought my hand to her belly.

"Listen," she said.

I let the force in my hand connect with the baby. One. Two. Three. Three separate heartbeats sparkled with light. My shoulders relaxed; my chest calmed with their rhythm. Idhatora pulled away.

"My love," I repeated. "This is a good thing. This is a moment of joy."

"I am tired, Aletheos," she said and looked at me with wet eyes.

"I know," I said. "I am getting closer. Things will get better." I slowly pulled her into my embrace. She relaxed in my hands. "I will do better," I said, inhaling the jasmine scent of her hair.

Idhatora lay exhausted in our bed. Her face looked so calm now. As if all of her worries had disappeared into a dream. How I wished to join her in our life. How I wished I could. I promised to do better. *Can I?*

I got out of bed, careful of my movements. In the common area, Cereena picked up her things.

"You are still here?" I asked. "It's late."

"I was just about to leave. I left all the pieces I could find on the table."

I sat, inspecting Chaa's shattered pendant.

"Cereena," I said, "thank you for being here for us, for my wife and children. You don't have to..."

She nodded with a half-smile and headed for the door. I rearranged the pieces on the table to resemble the pendant's original form. As I laid it in position, a miniscule parchment dropped from the golden cone. 'My grandson. Power,' it said in the ancient language. I jumped off my seat as she opened the door.

"Cereena!"

She gasped at my outburst.

"Are these all the pieces?"

"I think so, yes."

"Is everything all right?" asked Innok from outside.

"What are you doing here?" I asked.

"I brought the horse and waited to walk Cereena home."

"Innok, come in!"

My fingers shook as I tried to show him the parchment. "Did you know about this?"

"What is..."

"Chaa's pendant. The word. It was inside!"

His eyes sparkled. "You can open the library?"

"Who had the other words?" I asked myself out loud.

He didn't answer.

"Chohanatma," I said. "And probably Father."

"And did they..."

I shook my head. I let the pieces drop back on the table.

I lay next to my sleeping wife. I kept my eyes beyond the open window, focusing on nothing of this plane. Only the song of cicadas reached my consciousness every now and again. I tried to retrace my interactions with Chohanatma and my father, searching for the words within their words. But only their deaths kept flashing to awareness.

'Be wise, my grandson,' were Chohanatma's last words.

Chaa's parchment moved on my bedside table with the small breeze. 'Power.'

"Power," I whispered to myself, and closed my eyes. I gave up. Then, I opened them wide. Of course. Power. Wisdom. 'Be wise,' Chohanatma said! I searched in my brain again. The events prior to Father's demise. He was in the throne chamber, pointing outside while struggling to breathe. 'Library,' he had said. 'Love,' he repeated.

I sat up. *How stupid of me!* The attributes of the threefold flame in the heart. *Power, wisdom, love!*

I turned to Idhatora. I had the words! I jumped off the bed, went around to her. I touched her shoulder. She didn't move. *She is tired, alone.* Her hand tenderly rested on her belly. I sighed. *Three more babies.* 'I don't care anymore...' she had said. 'I want to live my life with you and our daughters. But you are always away..."

I retrieved my hand. All the excitement slipped away from my chest. I leaned and kissed her as softly as I could. The cicadas were loud with their song outside, underneath the glimmering stars. I returned to my bed and brought the sheet up to my nose. My eyes were still open, looking beyond the thin curtains into the night.

NEOPHYTES

A *nthelios.* I threw the scroll aside and grabbed another from the case. *The dark flame is part of the light.* That's what my former personality had said. *Anthelios.* I searched amidst the symbols on the parchment. *Anthelios.* Nothing. I moved for the next scroll, the last one in this part of the library. The higher aspects of Altazadeh insisted on appearing in my mind, separated from his lower ones. *What if I help him reunite with his light?*

"So, you think you know the words, but you won't go," said Innok.

"I can't leave now, Innok."

Anthelios. I moved my hand on the scroll, guiding my gaze. Nothing.

"Why?" Innok insisted.

I moved around the small amphitheatre to another case and grabbed the first scroll within my reach.

"Aletheos?" he followed me.

"Innok! I can't leave! The journey alone would take about a sun cycle. Idhatora is a few moon cycles away from giving birth. And the people... The temples... The city..." *Anthelios.*

"What if you tried creating another body? Like Chaa, who kept visiting her island."

"I don't know how to do that!" *I tried. I failed.*

"What if you reach the library through your..." He brought his finger to his head, searching for the words. "...mind or however you do the thing?"

I took another scroll. "I tried. The doors don't respond; probably for the best. Paradchi is not trustworthy. To whom would I open it? And why?"

"What if..."

"Innok! Stop! I am trying my best. I can't go. If you know a better way to keep the city safe and the kingdom in order, do let me know!"

He shook his head and looked away. "I don't mean to impose," he exhaled.

"I am doing the best I can, Innok. And it's not nearly enough, it seems. So, stop."

He raised his arm to my shoulder. "I can't imagine how you experience all of this. And I am sorry if I don't understand. I am trying to help. Always."

I nodded. *I know.*

Zurath brought his students inside. Their chatter stopped when they saw me.

"My king," he exclaimed cheerfully.

"Hello, my friend," I answered and turned to the people behind him. Fifteen, maybe twenty; men and women. "Welcome, everyone. Your presence fills me with hope."

They made their way down the amphitheatre for their discussion to commence. I pulled Zurath aside.

"Have you found anything?" I asked.

He shook his head. "Valsaris kept looking through the night. I sent him home when I came in this morning."

"Okay. Thank you. Keep looking," I said and went for the exit. "And Zurath..."

He turned to me.

"This is magnificent," I said and pointed at his students with my eyes.

"**H**ow are you and... Sahran was it?" I asked Innok as we walked down the streets of cobble.

"We are fine," Innok responded. "We..."

"Pad!" little Volitia yelled, running towards me.

I kneeled for her to fall in my open arms. Cereena was a few steps behind, holding hands with Fiave on one side and Noees on the other, supporting them as they stepped on the uneven path.

"We are going to see ma," Volitia explained.

"Right on time," I said, and raised her in my arms.

Hanjya leaned on the pillar to the entrance, listening but not joining the others. Beyond her, hundreds had gathered in the temple. We could barely see Idhatora on the podium. I helped Volitia stand on my shoulders while holding her arms to pass through the crowd.

"...So be kind, to yourselves and others," Idhatora said to the people. "There is no other way that can, so practically, so beautifully, connect us to spirit within us."

"Is it midday already?" she asked when she saw us below.

"It is," I said.

She came down to meet us. The twins escaped Cereena's hands to reach their mother while Volitia leaned forward, crying 'ma.' Idhatora fondled our daughters while touching her belly as well. Soon, our girls got bored and let her go. She came to me with a kiss, and we proceeded to the inner part of the temple, alone.

The white stone of the walls looked like solid light under the midday sun. We went to opposite sides of the pond, projecting light on the marble sphere, and bathed the city in mist.

THREADS

T he old capital seemed unchanged, other than the new houses that replaced the ruins of the earthquake. People went about their daily businesses; merchants, fishermen, craftsmen, children running around. Together, they orchestrated the familiar noise of Eos, the city I used to call home.

"I haven't been out in a while," Muttiya said, pinching her dress in place while stepping down a small pathway.

People bowed as she passed by them, some with a smile, others with a greeting.

"I miss this place," I said. *Or rather, what it used to be before any of this began, back when I strolled the streets with my mother.*

"Are you coming any time soon?"

"I don't think I can leave Esperos."

"Any developments?" she asked.

I shook my head. "Not after I met them up the mountain. Both Altazadeh and his beast are in hiding. Maybe they were weakened by the light."

"No. Not so soon," she said. "Not if the beast is fed by the darkness of the people. It's too much, it's in everyone. No person is immune to it, even your father. It was guilt for him."

"That's what we, or rather, Idhatora, has been trying to teach people; to embrace their darkness with love and acceptance, work through their issues instead of feeding them with fear and more conflict."

"How about the little ones?" she asked, changing the subject. "Are they happy?"

"They are growing fast. Cereena and Valsaris help out a lot. You should come meet them. Get some rest from all of this."

She looked into my eyes, frowning.

"Hetta and Cyrus can come take your place as warden of the capital," I proposed.

She stopped in front of the temple of old tradition. The pillars and statues had patches scraped away from them, as per my decree. Muttiya pointed at them.

"Was this necessary?" she asked.

I sighed.

"Is it helping at least?"

"I don't know," I responded, shaking my head. "I can only hope."

She nodded at some priests that arrived at their temple. They replied with a rigid look as they made their way up.

"This absence of a response," she said, "their silence on the matter, is a sign of danger, Aletheos."

Passing by us, people stepped on the path through the desert that led to my temple.

"I am so glad to see people gathering under the light," I said, trying to focus on what good I could find.

"No one did anything, neither the people nor the priests!" she insisted. "There is a reason we haven't had retaliations yet. They are brewing something. You know that, right?"

I did. If we only knew what. I said nothing more on our way. We reached the pillars and walked around the winged lion statue with a human head. At the podium, my old student, Auffia, prepared to address the few people that joined her. She smiled as she became aware of my presence in the higher realm; I had trained her well.

"We gather again at this time of day," she exclaimed, "as the sun is closest to us."

I turned at Muttiya with wide eyes. "Is it midday already?"

She narrowed her eyes at my urgency.

"I have to go. I am grateful for all that you do. Stay safe!"

Before she had the time to respond, I let my surroundings fade away as I returned to my body in my small garden. I was late again.

I ran through the streets and down to the temple. I had promised her we would act together, at least during the mist ritual. Maybe she was still talking to the people.

The temple was packed with murmurs. They all got quiet as they saw me, clearing a way for me to proceed. Idhi was not on the podium. I paced onwards, further inside to the second section. She was not around there either. I found her in the third part of the temple, lying on the ground next to the pond with Cereena on top of her.

"Something's wrong!" Idhi screamed in pain.

I turned at the crowd. "Get Valsaris and Zurath!" I yelled and threw myself to the side of my wife. "Now!"

T he cries finally dissipated. Our three babies had joined us in the physical world, now asleep next to Idhatora. Our elder daughters, also lay asleep in another bed of the infirmary; they would not leave their mother.

I watched the tiny faces, weary from all they endured coming into this world. Above them, like their older sisters, they, too, had little flames. Mynia's flame was white, steadily swirling around within itself. Gnolia's burned green, solid, and sharp, almost in the shape of a pyramid, while Delia's red kept growing and dissipating like a heartbeat.

Zurath whispered from the door. With soft movements, I joined him outside.

"True embodiments of the flames," he said.

"Thank you, my dear friend," I said and patted his shoulder.

He stayed still, looking at me.

"What's wrong, Zurath?"

"It's Idhatora," he said.

MESSENGERS

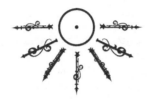

A re Cereena and Valsaris managing with all the children? I hope Volitia is behaving. She was upset. What If they get away and jump on Idhatora? They just want their mother. Are the curtains drawn? Mosquitos could go in.

Loud whispers forced me to focus. My fingers were numb; I had been rubbing the stone engravings of the podium. Around me in the temple, hundreds of people waited for me to resume the teaching and perform the mist ceremony. *What was I saying? I need to go home.*

I coughed, maybe get a few moments to remember. Behind the crowd, four guards carried an ornate chair on their shoulders. It was my wife who sat on it, beautiful as ever, wearing a linen dress with turquoise beats woven below a chest plate of gold. Topaz earrings and golden armlets caught the sun.

"Make way," I told the people who cheered when they saw her.

I stepped down the twelve steps of the podium as the guards gently placed the chair on the ground. She struggled, pushing herself up.

"Are you okay? You should rest. You don't have to be here."

She just looked me in the eyes, decisive. I gave her my hand. She accepted my assistance.

"We do this together, remember?" she said and leaned on me.

"Together," I repeated and gave her a kiss.

I held her close and took half a step towards the inner temple. We moved together, slowly, half a step at a time. I helped her to her usual position while she caught her breath.

"Do you want to sit down?" I asked.

I looked at the guards next to her chair.

"No, my love." She touched my chest and held my gaze. "I am fine."

I nodded and moved to the other side of the pond. We let the light come through us and onto the sphere that sent it out into a mist.

Only when the mist faded, lowering towards the ground, did she finally nod for the chair. The guards brought the seat.

"Let's go home," I said, holding her hands and helping her down.

"Sit with me," she said. "Let's stay for a while. The mist is healing."

She leaned back as I sat on the ground by her side, resting my cheek on her warm arm.

T he guards carried Idhatora in her seat high above us. The temple was almost empty. Horns sounded from the harbour, just as we got out in the street. The unrest in my chest turned into a smile, and my shoulders dropped.

"She is here," I said and looked up at my beloved. "You should go home, get some rest."

She shook her head and told the guards to move her to the docks. *Stubborn woman.* I smiled at her, gracious even in her pain. *Fierce woman.*

Guards had assembled in lines according to Innok's commands. My council was present as well. Horns sounded again as Muttiya left her ship to join us. People came from their houses to feed their curiosity.

I opened my arms as I approached. I hadn't seen her in the flesh for a couple of sun cycles. Dry or appropriate as she may have wanted to appear, she did embrace me back.

"Thank you for coming, Muttiya!"

She nodded. She walked away before uttering any words. She went to Idhi, lowered on the ground by the guards, who stepped back at Muttiya's presence.

"How are you, my dear?" she asked my wife.

"In pain," she finally admitted. "But I am handling it."

"Don't worry too much. I had similar injuries when I gave birth to Hetta. You will be fine. But you should be resting," Muttiya said and proceeded up the slope of the unknown, to her, city.

P ast the front garden, Cereena opened the door of our house and rushed to welcome her aunt. Valsaris joined as well.

"My dear sister!" he exclaimed.

"Hello, Valsaris," she said, and indeed hugged him. "You are changed. I am glad to see you like this!"

Our three elder daughters came out to welcome their mother. They were all stunned to see Muttiya and her servants among us.

"It's okay, little Volitia," Muttiya said and lowered herself. "You may not remember me. But I do. And who are you, little girls?"

She smiled towards Fiave and Noees. We exchanged glances with Idhi, both amused with Muttiya's playfulness we had never experienced before.

"This is grandmother Muttiya," I told the girls.

I leaned back in my chair. The afternoon air below the trees moved with the laughter of my daughters and friends. Maidens came out in the front garden, bringing more fruits and wine around our table.

"Your room is ready, my Queen Mother," her maiden said.

"I hope you find it to your liking. It captures a cool breeze," Idhi said.

"Don't worry about it," she replied without moving her eyes away from the girls.

Innok banged the door of the garden, coming in from the street.

"I am sorry to interrupt," he said, panting. He bowed to Muttiya before speaking. "There is another ship, sailing in from the north. They just turned behind the island."

I brought my awareness beyond my body and out towards the river.

"Not a supplies vessel?" asked Idhatora.

"We expect no more ships today!" Innok replied.

I raised my arm. I turned to the maidens.

"Prepare another room," I said with a smile. "More family is here."

Severance

Torches lit the dark harbour as Cyrus's ship finally reached the city. He and Hetta looked down from the deck in each other's embrace.

"Welcome, my dear ones," I exclaimed as they stepped foot to shore.

Cyrus hugged me tight. Hetta walked a little slower behind him. I gasped, excited, as she approached.

"Aletheos!" she said with a smile. "Let me introduce you to our son, Rarou!" She moved the sheet to uncover the baby's sleepy face.

"Congratulations Hetta! And Cyrus! May he be wise and strong!"

"Thank you, my brother," Cyrus said.

His features slowly dropped into a frown.

"You should have sent correspondence of your coming," I said. "We would have prepared a feast and a house for you!"

He pressed his lips against each other and looked behind at his servants, unloading chests from his ship.

"I couldn't send a message. We need to talk," he said.

The previously cheerful people in our front garden now sat in contemplation around the table. Muttiya held her new grandson, with Hetta by her side. Cyrus's servants brought in the last chests. Innok opened them all. Hundreds of stone tablets, scrolls, and leather parchments were neatly placed inside.

"All of these..." Idhatora said.

"How did you find out?" I asked, standing with my fists on the table.

"Our correspondences went unanswered for months. I sent a few diplomats to the neighbouring states. They all blamed us for the same. They had been reaching out with no response. They even accused you of capturing their messengers."

My forehead trembled with anger.

"I sent a few men on the corresponding routes," Cyrus continued, "while soldiers spied from a distance. The messengers were ambushed. We captured the attackers and uncovered their operation. They had been killing the messengers and destroying the messages. They even had people back in our kingdom who hid any messages that did reach our cities before going out to you. These," he pointed at the chests, "are all we found in underground crypts."

"Do you think it's Altazadeh?" asked Innok.

"He changed his focus," I said. "That disgusting snake of a man! Instead of isolating me from our people, he is isolating the kingdom from our alliances."

"To what end?" asked Idhatora.

"He would have us all buried in the sand," Muttiya said in calm voice over her sleeping grandson, "bring the kingdom to ruins."

"Meneir is looking for his sister," said Innok, reading a scroll.

I turned at Muttiya. "Is she alive?"

It was Idhatora who answered. "She is."

I looked at her in silence.

"I have been visiting her," she said. "She was a friend."

"Savghana is the least of our worries," Cyrus proclaimed. "We have found our-selves amidst a war." He dragged a chest close and pulled the parchments out, one by one. "Most of our affiliated states have been at war with Hytai for many moon cycles. Many of them have already fallen."

I opened one of the letters that mounted the table.

"They have all been asking for our help," Cyrus explained.

No, no, no!

"How did you not know about this?" Muttiya asked me.

My stomach burned.

I remained alone in the garden with the light of a sole torch still burning. I kept going over the letters.

'... great ruler of land and sky, commander of water and fire, why have you for-saken us at our grave need? We have been relentlessly attacked. Gorean has already fallen.'

Ruler of land and sky. Ha!

They all said the same; exalting me in the hope of receiving help. Dozens of letters from each state; first reporting their situation and thereafter marking the position of the enemies, who got closer with every letter. Until the trail of correspondence stopped and that of another state began.

'...your greatness... magnificence... Hytai is close to the city. If your silence is the answer to my father's actions, please... he found his demise as he very much deserved. Your father himself forgave our state and wished for our good relations. My sister, a nurse, must have surely shown the true nature of our people. Please carry out your father's sentiment as we have remained loyal..."

Innok drew a chair and joined me.

"You are back," I said.

"You are not alone, Aletheos."

He unravelled another scroll.

"Don't bother," I said. "They all say the same. Hytai has marched through their cities. Most of the states surrounding our kingdom are now his. He is building an empire."

"Hytai? He was supposed to be an ally!"

"He was."

"What should we..."

"We must help. For their sake. And ours."

I let Meneir's parchment drop on the table. Innok brought it to his eyes.

"Meneir," I said.

"Has he fallen?" Innok asked.

"Not yet. This is one of the most recent accounts."

"Aletheos." He looked up with unblinking eyes. "Khantara is a few days from the sea. If it falls and Hytai decides to come against us... The first part of the kingdom he will attack will be where our presence is weakest."

"The Five-Pointed Star," I said and looked away.

I paced around. My lungs expanded with fury. I reached for the table and flipped it to the ground. The scrolls and parchments and tablets, all bashed in the sand.

SPILLED WINE

I nnok came to the front garden.

"I looked for you in the assembly room," he said with a cheer.

"I needed the fresh air of the leaves," I said.

I could not bring myself to stay within the thick walls of the administration building. All I could do was wait. So, I came back here following the morning reports.

"Correspondence is secured!" Innok said and showed me the letters. "Only the Towers haven't made contact yet. But it's natural from so far south."

"Good. What do they say?"

"Harapi marched from the south and Cyrus from the north, as we discussed. Several cities are already freed. Hytai is dead."

"Have they reached him already?"

"He was dead before all of this even began; at the hands of his sons. It's them who led the rebellion."

I only shook my head and stared into his eyes, waiting for more.

"Cyrus contacted his father on the island. They are prepared. But Cyrus's troops have already secured the passage to the sea."

With a deep breath of relief, the morning sun could finally warm my stiff body. From the house, joined us Idhatora in slow steps. I pushed myself up, ready to help her.

"I am fine, my love," she said.

"How are you, Idhatora?" Innok asked, drawing a chair for her.

"Thank you, Innok. The pain has dissipated. I just need to get strong again."

"All is according to plan," I told her.

"Good," she responded. "What's next?"

All three of us remained silent, in contemplation. The vibrant greens of the garden, together with the songs of the birds and the cicadas, faded again, out of awareness, as grey clouds of uncertainty took their place.

Idhatora spoke first. "They will still see us as the ones who abandoned them to Hytai's sons' deadly ambitions."

"But," protested Innok, "we didn't!"

"She is right, Innok. Nobody will care why we didn't help. They will care of how late we were to join them."

"We should do what your father did at his coronation; and yours," exclaimed Muttiya from the door. "The reports of your administration are astounding," she continued as she joined us around the table.

"Are you just returning from the council meeting?" asked Idhatora.

"Yes. I went through the annual reports, and your chiefs were eager to exhibit their achievements."

"What do you propose?" I asked.

"You have nothing to apologise for, Aletheos. You are the king. Invite them here, throw them a festival and give them gifts and support to rebuild. You can explain the dark conspiracy that condemned their cities and re-declare your supremacy. The supplies in storage should be more than enough to cover both the festival and the needs of the city until the next harvest."

"It's risky, Muttiya," I said. "All those strangers in our city... Who knows what Altazadeh has corrupted them with?"

"The power of our kingdom relies heavily on our relations with neighbouring states," she replied. "We can't lose that."

"If we give in to fear," Idhatora said, "if we lose our affiliations, it seems to me that he has already won."

They were right. But they didn't know him; not as I did.

"And we can keep our eyes open for his clouds around the people," Idhatora continued.

"Do you really think we can keep guard in the higher realms against everyone?" I asked.

"I do," she said.

"We don't really have a lot of choices," said Muttiya. "Not if order is to be maintained."

"Let's hope you are right," I said. "For all of our sake."

HARVEST

O ur little triplets crawled around in the small garden while their elder sisters
galloped with toys around them, with Volitia orchestrating the game. The
flames in the invisible planes above their heads burned bright. All of them.

I sat on the ground next to the pond. Idhatora rested in my arms, leaning back
on my chest. The rustling leaves above us made the sunshine sparkle on the ground
while our daughters, innocent and bright, enjoyed their day in the sun.

"Do we have to go?" Idhi asked in low voice. "I can't stop watching them."

"They are life itself, aren't they?" I said, giving her cheek a warm kiss. "We don't
have to, not until midday. I asked Zurath to take Valsaris and their students and
appear in the temple. We don't have many days before hordes of people arrive for
the so-called festival."

"Will they perform the mist ritual as well?"

"They can't yet," I said. "But I can go alone."

"No, no. I like it. I told you, it's therapeutic."

I leaned my head back on the tree and closed my eyes with my children's voices
and my arms around my wife.

"Aletheos?" Cereena's voice. The warm calmness in my chest vanished, seeing her
eyes. "You are needed."

Idhatora jumped up. "I will go to the temple for the mist ceremony. Go."

I nodded. A guard waited outside my house with my horse readied.

"What's going on?" I asked him.

"It's Zurath! He's gone mad!" he said.

I kept my breath with a sinking heart. I mounted immediately. "What happened?" I asked.

The guard didn't answer, only shook his head with terror in his eyes, leading me
towards the obelisk at the south boundaries of the city, next to the river. On the
banks, a small group chattered around a strange mass.

I hopped off the horse and walked amongst them, pushed people out of my way. They all silenced themselves upon seeing me. Streams of blood ran down the muddy ground towards the river.

"Who is it?" I cried at no one in particular as I ran to the body. *Zurath?*

"It was the crocodiles," answered one from the crowd.

The flesh of the abdomen was torn apart. A cracked bone stuck out of the leg. Mud and blood all over. I tenderly moved the hair away from the face. And tears blurred my eyes.

"No," I cried, stroking her cheeks, "my dear Hanjya!"

I leaned, hugging her face, wanting to stay with her, protect her from pain, knowing very well that she wasn't feeling it anymore.

"I saw it," a man said. "Zurath sent the crocodile away before the beast took her in the water."

I shook my head with tears falling down on Hanjya's empty vessel. *Where is he? What happened?*

"Aletheos!"

It was Innok from a little further, by the obelisk. Around him shouted more people and guards. I pushed myself up, legs shaking, and rushed to them. Guards yelled at Zurath, others at another.

"My friend," I said swiping my tears, "what are you..."

Zurath held a spear, raised through the etheric boundaries of the city at a man's neck on the other side.

"Terran," I said, empty of breaths.

Terran crossed his arms around his chest, pushing them hard, as if to keep his daughter close, safe from disappearing at the teeth of the reptile.

"My little girl," he cried, "my beautiful little girl."

"Let him through," I said. "It's her father!"

Zurath never moved his eyes, nor the spear from Terran. I put myself between them and pulled his face to me.

"Zurath," I said, and pushed away the blade from Terran's throat. "What lunacy has gone over you? It's her father! Let him..."

"My king," he mumbled, "he brought him here!"

I turned to the old, heartbroken father and back to Zurath. "What..."

The muscles in my back twitched. A familiar stench stuffed my nose. I closed my eyes for a moment.

"Oh, Terran," I said.

Stripes of dark smoke moved around him. A few steps behind him, stood Altazadeh; invisible to Innok and the guards. A disgusting smile filled his thin, bald face with satisfaction.

Terran burst in screams. "It's your fault! You took her from me!"

He pushed to come through the invisible barrier. The guards now turned on him. Zurath raised his spear again.

"You took her away!" he cried. "We should have never helped you! We should have left you die in the desert!"

He threw himself on a guard, bashing him to the ground.

"No, no," I yelled to the guards, signalling them to calm down as they pointed their swords at him. "Zurath, it's his pain talking. Don't!"

Zurath's spear spilled a single drop of blood from Terran's throat. A stripe of smoke followed the droplet down the blade and all the way to Zurath's hands.

"It's Altazadeh," shouted Zurath.

"No," I grabbed his face. "Look at me! Zurath, please! He is not Altazadeh. He is using Terran's pain."

"He killed Lohar. He killed our friends and patients!"

"It's not him! Zurath!"

Terran screamed through his tears from behind me. And then he stopped. Zurath's eyes widened; his hands shivered. Terran froze, nailed in place by Zurath's spear. And he fell amidst our feet.

Altazadeh's smile grew wider as his eyes stayed on mine from beyond the obelisk. His form burst into dark clouds that rushed through dead Terran and into Zurath, who gasped for air. His body stretched, turning red. His eyes rolled back in his head, and neck bent to the back, bringing him down. Darkness flooded out of him and burst towards the city.

I jumped on my horse and pressed my legs. The temple glimmered with white mist. Anthelios's blank eyes opened, covering the sky above us.

LAYPEOPLE

I went up the steps to emerge from the cave of forefathers. The sun blinded me for a few moments. I raised my arms to the crystal pyramid. *No.* I decided against it. I left the cave unsealed and met my children, playing in the garden. Hetta had finally allowed her son, Rarou, to play on the ground as well.

"Cyrus should be back today," I told her.

"You are leaving?" she asked.

"Cereena and the maidens will provide everything you need," I said.

She grabbed my arm. She said nothing.

"We will be fine," I said. "Your son is safe here."

I didn't know that. But I hoped that the mist did help against the infiltration. She slowly released her grip. In my house, Innok sat with Valsaris.

"Any development with Zurath?" I asked Valsaris.

"No. Still locked in; his mind is somewhere I can't reach."

After all these days, still nothing. "Stay here," I told him. "Hetta needs you. And the children. If anything goes wrong, and only then, take them all down to the cave in my garden."

He frowned, unaware as he was of the cave. He nodded nevertheless, and joined the others in the small garden. I exchanged glances with Innok, took a deep breath, and proceeded. He opened the door for me, out to the front yard, where dozens of guards stood with their backs against the walls surrounding the garden. None said a word. Before reaching the other end of the yard, I turned to them, looked at each one for a few moments.

"We should go," said Innok.

I raised my hand, commanding him into silence while I took my time examining the guards. *No perverted darkness. Only their personal one.* I bowed my head at them and joined Innok.

Silence was locked behind in my house. Two rows of guards raised their spears as we passed through them and into the city. In the streets, busy with preparations, people carried sacks of nuts, and wheat for cooking, and jugs of wine. Students of the higher sciences prepared the great temple with the initiates. And Starani men stood at every corner.

"Is the bridge from the administration complex sealed?" I asked.

"Anyone who tries to go through the bridge to your house will be met with blades," Innok responded.

I nodded as we walked through the courtyard of the administration building and into the throne room.

"We are insulting them!" said Muttiya, receiving me.

Gnomnas and other councillors stood around the room.

"This was a mistake. We are not letting the hordes that arrived from all over the world in the city," I responded, as calm as I could.

"So, you are leaving our allies outside in the desert?" she yelled, echoing in the chamber.

"The tents and supplies we present them with are more than what is left of their cities," I responded. "Only the chief commanders will enter Esperos!"

"Aletheos!"

I walked to her. "I should have never listened to you. His darkness is inside. And we still don't know its effects; nor his plan!"

My advisors stayed silent at my outburst. Idhatora spoke from her throne. "Don't you think," she asked in a sweet tone, "the mist might have protected the people?"

Her shoulders dropped to the front, making her seem smaller. She should have never agreed with Muttiya or pushed for her suggestion.

"Maybe in the moment," I said. "But we don't know whose inner issues he may have nested in."

"We will stand guard at the realms beyond!" she said. "We will make sure..."

"Idhi," I interrupted her, "they are coming from war! Even the kindest man amongst them is now fuming with darkness. Who knows what Altazadeh's seeds may flare up within them. You really think we have the mental capacity today, or any day for that matter, to search amongst thousands of people and accurately distinguish their darkness from Altazadeh's? Or protect them from it, as we planned, inside the city? It probably already lurks amongst us! After the infiltration, we haven't even had the capacity or time to do that for our own people yet!"

She only sighed and lowered her gaze. Muttiya opened her mouth, but Idhatora spoke before Queen Mother could vocalise her objections. "Zurath?"

"He is still in the infirmary," I said, "his consciousness still locked somewhere within."

Guards opened the door for Cyrus to join us; triumphant from war. I smiled at his safe return. Harapi followed a few steps later.

"Welcome, old friend," I said.

"Good to see you, my king." Harapi bowed. "I remain at your command."

"Is she here?" I asked him.

"In our ship. But I bear some news. We received reports from the capital. Your temple has been desecrated, much like we did to the old ones."

Now they retaliate? "Is Auffia safe?" I asked.

"No one was hurt. Scenes and statues were scraped, though."

As long as Auffia was safe, we would deal with the rebels later. I turned around to the members of the council.

"Is everything prepared?"

Everyone nodded affirmatively.

I dhatora and I crossed the river towards the narrow island that hid the city from the western desert. We climbed the steps carved on its hill and reached the obelisk at the top. The land on the other side of the river was separated in patches of colour, tents that filled the horizon with the emblems of each visiting nation. Chariots arrived among equestrians and people on foot. Behind and around them all, stood the tents of the Starani men.

Officials from each state lined up on the western banks. Idhatora and I raised our arms to the obelisk next to us. The crystal pyramid on top reflected our light down on the river before white mist erupted on all sides.

The desert wind carried the voices of those scared by it. They all ceased when the mist enfolded them in its warm light. We waited for the light to dissipate, looking down at the foreign rulers and diplomats.

"Our kingdom welcomes you all!" I said. "We receive and accept you within our protective light. May our bonds grow stronger from now onwards. No aspiring usurpers may hope to intimidate us ever again! Together we stand!"

The officials kneeled and so did the men behind them. Drums broke the courtesies. It was time for a feast.

B eyond the throne room, the courtyard was lit with hundreds of torches. The scenes of nature and beauty flickered alive from the walls around us. The great yard was split in groups of each nation; rulers, representatives, diplomats. The rest enjoyed the feast across the river.

My beloved wife sat next to me. So did Muttiya and Gnomnas, while Innok and Harapi stood to the sides, in command of the guards that lined the walls.

Gnomnas took notes of a ruler's particular requests. When he finished, the man returned to his friends and several guards took away the gifts he presented us with; wheat, fruits, wine, cedar oil, scented reeds, ostrich eggs, and peacock feathers.

Another foreigner stepped forth; a bald woman with skin as dark as Muttiya's. She was dressed with leopard skin and decorated with hanging turquoises and red corals.

"Medja of the free southern tribes!" she said of herself.

"It is an honour, your great king," she continued in broken language. "Our cities stand strong. We only ask of you to nurse our men across the river. They are sick and exhausted travelling here after the war. And we bring shields and bows. Together, we stand strong!"

People at the back were getting upset, moving unrestful. A few moments later, the reason became apparent. Medja's companions had brought a leashed leopard.

"And we bring a guardian of the night," she said.

A guard went around the leopard to safely get a hold of the leash, while Innok and Harapi stepped forward, ready to draw their blades. The guard was particularly shaky. The feline must have sensed it, roaring back at him; a roar that shook the yard and made the guard stumble and fall, losing his grip on the leash.

Muttiya gripped her chair while Idhi and I stood up. Medja ran to take control of the now free leopard, but Idhatora nodded at her to stay back. My wife took a deep breath and slowly descended the throne stage. Her arm hung to the side with an open palm. I turned within, ready to intervene, as the big cat approached.

With a wagging tail, she rubbed her back on Idhatora's hand and circled around her before sitting by her side. In swift movements, Idhi removed the leash and threw it to the ground, resting her hand on the cat's neck and gazing back at the yard.

Medja bowed to Idhatora's display of power, as did the rest of Medja's people, and, after a few moments of silence, my wife returned to her throne with her cat, while Muttiya was trying to maintain her posture on the seat.

Meneir now stood in front of us. "Meneir of Khantara!"

"I know who you are, Meneir," I replied.

"My king," he said, please excuse me. I wish no disrespect to this court. But in order to stand strong together, I must be forward."

"Speak, Meneir. I wish nothing but the truth from you."

"My king, this court has left our cities exposed and vulnerable to Hytai's sons. What alliances are we discussing here if we cannot trust and rely on each other?"

I sighed, exchanging glances with Muttiya. "As I have explained before, dear Meneir, your calls for help had not securely reached us. This falls beyond our control and..."

"We come here bringing our most valuable gifts then, staying in the desert outside your lavish city, and we remain at your mercy and the capacities of your officials to deliver our messages, our cries for help."

"You will not interrupt me again," I said with a calm tone.

His eyes widened. He glanced at my guards.

I spoke again. "Your messengers' safety is not a responsibility that burdens my officials. And you speak of trust, Meneir..." I smiled at the irony. "I have graced you and your nation with an undeserving amount of trust. May I remind you that your father's actions almost drowned us all, villages whose chiefs stand here today, and me personally, and that your failure to control your men after his death has killed many of my people."

He moved his mouth but spoke not, searching for words.

"As of my mercy, Meneir... You will find my mercy in your sister's life."

He gasped. "Savghana!"

"Your dear sister, Savghana, has murdered my father, your king, by her own confession," I said, "by means of oils and herbs; those you, yourself, gifted us with the previous time you wanted to ensure our affiliation."

The yard filled with whispers.

I continued. "Consider the bare existence of your city and nation, Meneir, as the most grandiose demonstration of my mercy. One that will not be equally offered if you dare defy me again."

Idhatora's feline friend echoed my sentiment with a raging roar at the courtyard. Meneir swallowed whatever thoughts he had prepared to confront me with.

"You may leave," I said. "My only gift to your nation is your wretched sister. Take her and leave my kingdom at once."

He looked around. Harapi brought Savghana in chains; thin, dirty, weak. I turned to the crowd while Meneir took Savghana in his arms.

"Enough with unpleasantness," I exclaimed. "A feast awaits across the river!"

People dispersed. Only one from each nation remained, to make sure our guards received their gifts and noted the provider of each one. My council discussed with Gnomnas what we promised to each nation while slowly making their way outside. Behind them, Meneir, still helped his sister slowly walk towards the exit. Even against my anger, my heart ached at the sight. *A sad sight in any case.*

"She did that to herself," said Idhi next to me, with wet eyes. "Thank you for freeing her. May she find peace."

"Maybe she will," I answered with clenched stomach and kissed her forehead nevertheless, still uncertain whether Savghana deserved peace after what she did. Or her freedom.

"You did well to expose Khantara's actions in front of the others," said Muttiya, with eyes locked on her husband's murderer. "And by warning them of defiance, any notions they might have had about an alliance without us are now ruined."

"Are you okay?" I asked, ending any further discussion on the political affairs.

She exhaled through flaring nostrils. "I will be," she said and walked away.

"I will go check on the girls," Idhi said, wiping her tears away and petting her leopard.

"Just take care to introduce them first." I nodded at the feline. "I'd much rather come home than deal with more courtesies."

"I know, my love. Try to enjoy. I will come find you."

Harapi waited for me below the throne stage.

"Are you coming?" I asked Innok.

He made sure Harapi was present before answering. "Sahran was not feeling well, and I sent him home. I will go check on him and join you across the river."

I nodded, and made my way to the harbour.

I escaped the loud noises of drunkenness and sailed back to the city, back to my wife who never joined me. I jumped off to shore and tied the boat. Below, in the water, splashed movement. *Crocodiles*. Hanjya's last image appeared in the night, soon followed by her father's deleterious pain. With a loud sigh, I shook the gruesome sight out of my mind, and moved on.

The city was quiet. The pathways seemed darker than usual, probably in contrast with the western banks that burned with multiple fires around the camp. Along my way, I only got glimpses of the moon through the leaves.

A guard opened the door for me. My front garden was still surrounded by men who acknowledged my presence by moving their spears in an upright position.

"Have you rested since morning?" I asked no one in particular.

One of them took a step forward from the left wall.

"Yes, my king. We had others assume our position before our evening duty."

"Good," I said as he stepped back, even though I hadn't check the replacements' inner planes. "Thank you."

Inside, Valsaris and Cereena sat silent around the table, both resting on their hands, almost asleep with eyes open. Cyrus had returned, so Hetta should already be asleep in his hands with baby Rarou.

"You should have joined us after Idhatora returned," I told them.

Volitia screamed from another room before they could answer. I ran through my bedroom and out to the small garden. My first born was riding the leopard, yelling and laughing. Fiave was close to her mother while the triplets crawled around the feline and Noees chased the dotted tail.

I laughed with relief. "Are you sure that's safe?" I asked Idhi.

Her laughter of joy left no space for doubt. I took Fiave in my arms and stood by my wife's side, watching wild Volitia and curious Noees ran with the leopard among their sisters.

THE OLD PLAGUE

The birds chirped in the shade of trees outside. The kids had not yet marched in the room, and Idhatora lay asleep next to me. Her eyelids covered her eyes so softly that any outbreath of mine could wake her up.

A bang of the front door broke serenity. Reality was back. The thoughts of Anthelios and Altazadeh lurked back to mind. I had to resume my search for them in the higher planes. At least they had remained quiet during the festival. Also, the council's members probably waited for me with reports on the festival expenditures. Some foreigners were still across the river. And Zurath's students would be at the library soon.

All I wanted to do was stay watching my beloved sleeping, calm and carefree. I hopped off the bed to address the voices at the door.

"Is everything all right, my love?" she asked before I left the room.

I returned to kiss her good morning. "Don't worry my love, it's probably Cereena. Stay, rest, I will see you later at the temple."

Muttiya paced around the common area, mumbling by herself.

"Do you have to keep that beast in the front garden?" she complained.

I smiled with relief. "Tet is a part of the household now. The girls love her."

She coughed as she shook her head in disapproval.

"Is Innok outside?" I asked.

"No," she said, clearing her throat.

My brow furrowed. He should be; as every day.

"Are you joining the council meeting?" I asked.

"Already taken care of. Everything is in order."

One less thing to worry about. "Any news of the rebels?"

"Harapi should be at the capital by tomorrow. He will take care of it."

"Good. Thank you. I will be at the library until midday."

The guards no longer stood within the front yard. Only Tet dwelled here now. She laid on the ground, wagging her tail at the sight of me without moving otherwise. Two guards stood out in the street.

"Has Innok passed by?" I asked them.

"No, my king, not today."

I took a step towards the library behind the administration building; then turned around. I paced towards Innok's mansion. Guards protected their commander's door.

"Is Innok okay?"

"My king," one said, "he seemed fine this morning. But he called for a nurse."

I pushed inside and rushed through his garden and up some steps. The door was open to a dark interior. Amidst sharp pieces of a ceramic bowl, a chair lay on the ground.

"Innok!" I yelled and waited in silence for a few sharp breaths.

Nothing. I ran up more steps to a sunlit veranda leading to his bedroom and some noises. Behind the door, he held Sahran, who coughed and vomited.

"Aletheos, quick!" he said.

Blood stained the ground. Sahran, sweaty with red eyes, struggled to expand his lungs in between spitting blood.

"How long?" I said as I touched Sahran's burning forehead.

"Last night," Innok said. "It was very mild! But today..." He looked at the door. "Where is that nurse?" he yelled.

"We have to get him to the infirmary," I said, "right now!"

I pushed the door to the infirmary with Innok carrying Sahran behind me. The chamber was full of people, coughing and vomiting. Some laid on beds, others pushed their arms against the wall as they puked. Nurses were trying to treat them. Some mixed herbs with milk while others held patients upright, and others brought linens to clean up the mess.

I pushed some scrolls aside for Innok to place Sahran on the table; no vacant beds.

"They keep coming since last night," said Pathia, who came to help Sahran.

Medja leaned by the door. She had removed the leopard skin from around her shoulders, sweating bear-chested with her hand to her mouth.

"I sent the healthy home. I stayed back with our sick," she said and turned to the site to vomit.

Light sparkled in front of the window across the room. I walked towards it, among the ill. Zurath lay still on his bed, as he had been for days. The sparks were coming from him. He gasped and opened his eyes, shouting. "It's him! The plague!"

In a heartbeat, I breathed out violet light that filled the room and made time stand still. I brought my awareness to the subtle planes. Dark patches slowly floated among the ill, like big burning leaves. Behind me, mere fingers away from my face, Altazadeh's black flame had frozen in place with his hand stretching out to me. Several stripes of dark smoke stretched above the floor around the room.

"You would really bring the kingdom to ashes, wouldn't you?" I asked.

Among the slowly flaming darkness, his grim smile was taking shape. I focused on the threefold flame in my heart; wisdom, love, power. The flames burst out of my chest, creating an orb of light in between my hands. And I brought it to his face, pushing it deep into his forehead.

His dark flames swallowed the light that flashed like lightning in the dark clouds. The orb sent a single ray down to his heart. The stripes of smoke above the ground shone from within them as well. I followed them outside, avoiding the patches of darkness that floated around in the halls, the yard and out in the street.

Guards stood like statues, people frozen mid-step. Several branches of dark force stretched throughout the city, around the temple and towards the houses. My heart pounded in my chest. *It's everywhere.* I followed those that connected to Altazadeh's consciousness, still shining with light, down to the river at the source of all darkness.

Altazadeh stood still. I moved on. Not by choice; as if magnetised. I reached him. His lips were slowly moving. But trying to form a sound would take him an eternity, it seemed. His eyes moved the same. But he knew. He was in there. He was aware. I brought one hand to his forehead, the other to his chest. I took a deep breath, and exhaled my light through my hands and into him.

As I tried to reach his innermost planes, I turned to my pillar of light above my head, called for that white electric fire that could dismantle his connection with the beast, like it did to Maya. The fire appeared from the highest of planes, swirling down towards me.

Altazadeh's eyes moved fast as he struggled against my light, already inside of him. My stomach burned. I focused on the fire above. *Please! I am losing him!* The fire's descent was slowing down as my urgency and the pain in my stomach clouded my mind.

Altazadeh blinked, and shattered my grip. Time resumed. His dark flames swarmed out of the infirmary, reuniting with him with a strike that threw him on the ground. He coughed and coughed.

"What did you do to me?" he asked, swiping drops of blood from his lips.

"I am trying to help you, Altazadeh! Your highest aspects cannot reach you. You are blinded. You are hiding away from yourself."

He swung his arm, bringing dark clouds towards me as he missed his steps, coughing. I raised my arm, dispersing his darkness.

"You need to see Altazadeh! Take a good look at your actions. Anthelios is using you! He cares not for you! He wants the kingdom; to abuse peoples' pain! The powers he promised you are better attainable through your own spirit!"

"You moron," he yelled. "He only wants you! The kingdom is mine!"

I narrowed my eyes. His brain sparked with light. The pillar of light that would connect him with his true self was upon him. But behind him, Anthelios's eyes opened in the sky. He materialised in an instance; a monumental giant of darkness with blank eyes and black feathers floating around him.

He swung his sceptre, crushing through Altazadeh's pillar, and falling down on me. The jackal's head at the top of his sceptre struck my open hand that burst with light, and disappeared in an explosion of force that shaped a pit of sand around me.

From behind me, a spear pierced the cloud of dust and flew over me. Altazadeh grabbed the spear with his mind before it reached him, and threw it deep into the ground.

"Father!" Innok shouted.

"Stay back!" I yelled at Innok as Altazadeh pulled the spear from the ground.

He spat on the blade and raised it high, stretching back his arm. The urgency vibrated within me. The white fire had finally reached me. I opened my arms to the sides and raised electric fire from the ground upwards.

Altazadeh catapulted the spear before the fire turned into a wall of light in front of my city. The spear flew high, arching as it headed for Innok. With a jump, Innok threw himself on the ground, and the blade punctured the tree to his side.

From behind him, a cloud of white mist flooded the city, swiftly coming for us. *Idhi!* I turned to Altazadeh, connected with the wall of fire, and let it fall down on him as the mist enfolded us. Anthelios covered him before the wall reached them, and, together, disappeared in a swirling tornado of dark clouds.

I ran through the mist, down to the river, the white flame flashing in my hands. *If I had only reached him in time...* I breathed heavily, looking at his footprints in the sand; my missed opportunity.

"Aletheos," shouted Idhatora, coming down from the temple.

"He is gone," I said to myself, panting. *The others!* I hurried up the slope to Innok. "Let's go! Treat Sahran and the others!"

Innok grabbed my arm before I could proceed. He shook his head with tears in his eyes, desperately looking into mine. *No.*

I pulled him into my embrace, held him tight as he freed his cries from his chest. Idhatora halted a step away. I shook my head over Innok's shoulder. And her eye filled with tears. She took a deep breath and put her arms around us both.

FOUNDATIONS

I nnok said nothing the entire morning. He looked straight ahead with the procession. Sahran's vessel was raised one last time, together with that of Zurath and dozens of others that succumbed to Altazadeh's plague. Amulets, prayers, blade. Citizens of our sanctuary laid to rest; teachers, healers, soldiers, friends.

"Each where he belongs," I said; the final farewell.

With the sound of my words, Innok left for the city. I escorted my wife to the temple for the mist ceremony. Outside, guards scraped the wall from signs of fire.

"They are blaming us," said Idhatora.

I pressed my lips and nodded. Not many gathered inside today. We proceeded to the inner temple and pushed the mist outwards, through the entire city.

Our way back home was met with shouts.

"You left our loved ones die!" one said.

Guards pushed the protesters back.

"You killed them!" said a woman among the yelling.

I pressed my eyes shut for only a moment, holding my wife's hand as we headed to our daughters. Before we entered the yard of our house, I kissed her goodbye.

"I will go to Innok," I said.

She nodded as the guards reassumed their position in front of the door. Dozens of them stood strong, with spears in hand and swords around their waist. Still, my feet were heavy on the ground. I didn't want to leave her.

After a deep breath, I did, I had to. Innok wasn't at his house. I found him at the administration building discussing with his troops' commanders and Cyrus.

"We go again tomorrow," Innok said and dismissed them.

My steps brushed against the stone floor as I approached them in the dark room, lit only by the afternoon sun through the narrow windows. The commanders bowed as they passed by me. But Cyrus halted.

"We should be going home soon," he said.

"It's good that you are here," I responded.

"For us as well," he said. "Hetta is happy to be with her mother. But we should return at Dessha. I may be of more use at the North boundaries. Besides, Rarou is being tortured by your girls," he joked.

I exhaled with laughter that broke the veil of sadness. "As you wish, my brother." I patted his shoulder before we separated ways.

"Nothing yet," Innok said, looking down on the maps.

"I don't think we will find him in the desert," I responded.

"He must be somewhere! He does have a body, doesn't he?"

"With whose face?" I asked. "I don't assume it difficult for him to appear with a different face to our soldiers' eyes."

"Then what do we do? Wait for his next attack?"

"I think I got to him this time. But you are right. We can't just wait, especially now."

"Why especially now?" he asked.

Is it joy? Is it insensitive to tell him in his pain? He expected an explanation.

"Idhatora is pregnant again."

He managed a smile through his grief.

"That's beautiful," he said, finally looking up from the maps. "Get some sense of life in all of this!"

"I am happy you see it like that."

"How else?" he asked.

Why would I expect anything less spirited from sweet Innok?

"Is it a girl?" asked Valsaris from the door, his face only appearing as he came closer to the table.

"From all I can see at this point, yes."

"So, the seventh?" he asked.

"Are you done with the initiates?" I asked.

"We were just talking about the flames!" he said. "Do you think she will carry a flame as well? If she brings the light of the seventh in our midst, it could solidify our efforts, bring order."

"You've seen them on the girls..." I said.

"You trained us well! And I spend most of my time with them. Of course, I saw them!"

"Yes, Valsaris, I assume she will bear the seventh flame."

"Maybe that will save us," he said and turned to Innok. "I am sorry for your loss, my boy."

Innok nodded. "We all have lost."

"We have," I said.

"Don't despair. If the seventh is upon us, we still have hope," Valsaris said, and left with a smile.

I waited for him to go away enough.

"What was he talking about? Is it true?" asked Innok.

"I don't know. My children embody special forces within them, but are not means to any end. None of us is. I will not place the responsibility of our survival on my unborn daughter."

"I won't assume to understand your esoteric terms. But one thing I do understand. We draw our own paths. And from them, we harvest our responsibilities. The burden of our survival is upon us."

"My beloved friend... To that end, I have already told Idhatora, but I need you to know as well. I will never give up on our people. But I need my family to be safe. If anything ever happens to me, if I don't manage to triumph over Altazadeh, there is a path through the mountains. At its end, a ship is anchored in a narrow stream that branches out to the river. I will need you to take them there."

"Your family is my path, Aletheos. I will do anything to protect them."

Oh, Innok. Determined even through your grief. Knowing that my wife and daughters would be looked after relaxed my stomach.

"Have you met Sahran?" he asked. "I mean... beyond."

"I have," I answered. "He is on his own path. People with kindness in their hearts have no trouble finding it, even if we lose it for a while."

"Will Altazadeh assume responsibilities for his actions?" he asked.

"It won't be his choice. But we still need to stop him."

LABYRINTH

T he higher aspects of Altazadeh showed the way. A single thread of light pierced
through his dark clouds. I floated to it.

"I saw the pillar appear above your body," I said, "but Anthelios broke the connection."

"The connection cannot be broken," Altazadeh's light responded. "Only denied by the personality. Your intervention sparked within him; created this opening."

Should I pass through? He could sense me. I had to try.

I touched the ray of light that connected his lower with the higher aspects. I merged my consciousness with it, leaving as much of myself behind as I could, to go unnoticed through his denser planes.

Slowly, I floated down to the realm of men's fire; only, his fire was black. Faint spheres of force appeared as thoughts. I could, maybe, gather his plan from them. The one closest to me, vibrated in greys. It dissolved as my awareness contacted it. So did the next one and the next. *Futile.*

I moved down to his world of mud. Darkness roamed abundant. A black snake, as thick as tens of times my height, slithered in the brown and red storms, with venom gathering at its teeth. From the clouds, emerged insects, rapidly flying above us.

The thread of light leading downwards was even thinner here. Behind a brown cloud, a violet lotus glimmered with light. I opened my hands and willed it to approach. I sensed my father; an image of him as a young man appeared in my mind. My heart beat faster at the vision, pushing tears to my eyes. He looked at Altazadeh with kindness, offering his open hands to him. The image disappeared. The lotus turned to ashes and withered through my hands, taken by the dark storms.

In the distance, a young Altazadeh dragged his feet in the storms. His form was not solid. Parts of him turned into liquids before reassuming their position on him only to redissolve. He brought his palms to his face, inspecting them closely. He was holding a bird, a sparrow with a crooked neck; dead. He cried, bringing the bird close to his chest.

"Who am I?" he asked, slowing facing up towards me.

"You are Altazadeh," I said, "the healer, the disciple, the friend."

He stared at his hands. "No, no, no," he yelled as the bird melted away. He struggled to contain the liquid, but his hands turned to ash, only for a moment, before their form was gathered again. "Who am I?" he repeated.

I breathed out my light towards him. He breathed it in with closed eyes and opened them wide as if from deep sleep. His form was more solid now.

"I am Altazadeh!" he yelled to me. "They locked me out!" He marched with heavy steps, raising his fist at me. "They defied me! Me! They took my future from me!" His mouth and lips twisted with every word.

"Do you remember what you did?" I spoke.

He stopped. He brought his hands to his head. And hit it hard. Again and again. I focused on the light I had given him; inhaled it back from him. He stopped punching his head. His form was back to liquid. He brought his hands to the front, and fixated on them, as stripes of smoke slid through them in the shape of a bird.

My chest ached at his affliction. I looked around at the snake and insects wandering around with no reason nor purpose. *If I could get down to his body, maybe I could help with his memories.*

I focused on getting lower, down to the physicality of his existence. The darkness was fading, his surroundings in the flesh were taking form. With the sound of shattering glass, the clouds reappeared. The snake moved in circles around me. Its enormous scales were closing in, ready to crash me. *No! So close!* I floated upwards and out of his lower planes.

"He became conscious of your presence," his light said. "He no longer wanted you to pierce his pain."

"Wanted me?"

He nodded. "You can never intervene if one's corresponding levels don't allow you access."

"What now?"

"Let's see whether his conscious mind will deal with what you triggered. If so, he may allow for more help."

I nodded. I retrieved my consciousness back to my body and opened my eyes to the glowing symbols in our forefather's cave. The garden above was alive with my daughters' laughter and loud voices.

Muttiya waited amongst them. She coughed, clearing her throat. "Any news?"

"I don't know how twisted he was before," I said, "but Paradchi taking his memories doomed him."

"Who, pad?" asked Volitia.

I smiled and took her in my arms. "Nobody, my love," I said, as cheerful as I could be.

"Grandma won't let us play with Tet!"

"Is that so?" I laughed and looked at Muttiya.

"The beast is at the front," she said.

"Let's go," I told Volitia.

My younger girls followed with shouts and laughter and my nephew Rarou soon behind.

MELTING CANDLES

I folded the scrolls on the inner structures of men. Helping people deal with their darkness was our only way to protect them from the clouds that now roamed the streets.

"Go to the temples," I told our students. "Help the aspirants. Knowing how our issues affect each centre of force can help us recognise and heal them. Share the knowledge with people." *Before it's too late.*

"We will need more guards," Phir said.

"We have more incidents every day," Pathia added.

"Their anger blinds them towards violence," Noina explained.

"Their grief, pain, and anger is like fertile soil for him," I said. "Talk to Innok. Take all the protection you need. We should keep the fire lit, even for the few."

"It is our duty," Gaos replied as they made their way outside.

Idhatora had been silent the whole day. She rubbed her small belly with one hand and tidied scrolls with the other. I kissed her cheek as I stretched to place a parchment on the appropriate shelf. Innok entered the library as Idhatora focused on me.

"So, you know the words to open the library?" she asked. "And you never thought to discuss this?"

I left the scrolls on the table. Innok widened his eyes. "Was it a secret?" he asked.

"My love," I said with a smile. "What is there to discuss?"

"You need to go, Aletheos," she replied.

I sighed. "When would I go, Idhatora?"

"We can take care of everything!" she said. "Muttiya will help me."

"How about Altazadeh? And Anthelios? How about our daughters? I would be away for several moon cycles."

She brought her hands to her belly.

"I have been trying to live our lives," I continued. "As you wanted us to. As I wanted us to."

"Yes, Aletheos. I get that. And I love you for it. It's not fair. Neither for you nor our family. But this is something you must do for everyone else."

I looked away.

"It seems all I do is for everyone else," I mumbled through my teeth.

"I know," she said. "And I am sorry. But your path is yours alone. Maybe after I give birth? If things are going well?"

Her eyes were confident. *Maybe.*

"My friends," said Innok and showed us a parchment in his hands.

We moved to the throne chamber. Muttiya, Valsaris, Cyrus, and Gnomnas joined us.

"It's Harapi," I said to the silent room. "He reports sickness around our cities. And instances of dark magic practiced on the ill."

"It's back," Valsaris said.

"What's the answer to this?" asked Cyrus.

I turned to Muttiya. She was there with Father when her parents fell to the sickness, when they had to deal with it before.

"Prohibition and exile," she commanded.

"Father tried this before," I said.

"We need to stop this," she insisted, "before it overtakes the kingdom and takes thousands at its pass."

"Can't you help them?" asked Valsaris. "Like you did to me, push the darkness out?"

"You were conscious, Valsaris, and willing. You should have seen what happened to Maya! It was an entirely different process."

"Father," said Idhi, "have you seen the clouds out there? The people's pain is strong. We can't even be sure whether Altazadeh hides in them anymore."

"Do it anyway!" he said.

"Valsaris!" I exclaimed. "You would have me forcefully tie down every single person in this city, and then the kingdom, and scorch them with electric fire?"

"Aletheos," spoke Muttiya again. "Even if you should, that's impossible. Prohibition and exile. You tried the other option. You have made the sacred science accessible, opened temples, given people the choice to reorient themselves toward the light," she said.

"It's not working," added Valsaris.

"It is working!" Idhatora declared. "But people need time. A new paradigm does not establish itself in a day."

"We do need time," Muttiya said. Her raised voice made her cough. "But this is an immediate threat," she finally resumed. "I have no other way of addressing it, but with immediate measures!"

"No," I said. "Let's make it abundantly clear to all. Valsaris, send all students but the seven initiates to our cities. Guard them well. And let them make it known to all that it's the dark practices that make them sick. And guide each person through it. The people do need more time to come to us. So, let us be more immediate and take the light to them; give them hope before they look for it in the faces of dark magicians. Nurses will consult only with our students."

"It's too late for that, Aletheos," Muttiya protested, coughing in her hands. "People are weak. You are surrendering our fate and that of the kingdom into the hands of sheep. Altazadeh will devour them! We need..." She couldn't speak over her cough. When it stopped, her eyes widened, looking at her hands. From her lips dripped drops of blood.

Idhatora rushed to Muttiya. Before she reached her, the Queen Mother leaned against the wall, vomiting blood.

LOCUSTS

"**I**t was never his intention," said Altazadeh's higher self. "He is losing control. The spark of light you ignited in him created doubts and awakened the pain he had sealed away from his consciousness."

"This was not his intention?"

"No. Sickness was to take your city alone. After your fall, he would raise himself in the eyes of people as the bringer of light."

"You can reach him now." I smiled in relief. "Can you tell me anything more?"

"His confusion hides him, yet again. He struggles against seeing the reality of his actions. Even the slightest of suspicion brings him immense pain. And he will do anything to distance himself from it."

I shook my head. "Anthelios?"

"The beast feeds Altazadeh's illusions."

I sighed and returned to my body and my front garden. My arm was numb from leaning on the wall.

"How is she?" Cyrus asked as he joined me.

"Did you make arrangements?" I asked.

"I sent all instructions to my council. We won't leave you at such a time. Nor would Hetta leave her mother."

Hetta sat by her mother's side while Tet laid with her, resting her head on Muttiya's chest. Valsaris stood with his back to the wall; his arms crossed above blood-soaked linen.

"How are you?" asked Cyrus.

She didn't speak, only waved her hand. Cyrus touched the big cat on the bed, trying to gently nudge her away.

"No," Muttiya said with a hoarse voice, "let her be."

"Mother," said Hetta, "you will be more comfortable."

"I said no," Muttiya responded, placing her hand on Tet's back.

"Grandma!" Volitia barged in.

Idhatora joined us with the girls, who jumped around the room. Muttiya's mouth stiffened as the kids climbed on the bed. Idhatora tried to bring them back down.

"Let them," Muttiya said, reaching out to enfold within her embrace as many of the girls as she could.

"What's wrong, Grandma?" asked Fiave.

"Nothing, little one. Everything will be fine," Muttiya said.

Volitia balanced herself standing up on the bed. She grabbed Muttiya's head with both hands. "You are sad!" the kid declared.

Muttiya wore a smile below her wet eyes. "It's because I will miss you so much," she said.

Hetta looked away at the sound of her mother's words, hiding her face from the kids. Her son, Rarou, looked up at her from the floor, with a grip on her dress. Above Muttiya's head, now flashed sparks of light. None seemed to acknowledge them; only Valsaris shared a glance with me.

"This is ruined," said Volitia, serious. She touched Muttiya's chest. "Don't cry! You will get a better one."

Muttiya closed her eyes as tears slid down her cheeks. And smiled. "Let me kiss you all," she said, and leaned on each one.

Hetta, already in tears, raised Rarou to get a kiss as well.

"Everyone out," Muttiya commanded. "Give me a few moments with Aletheos."

Valsaris hugged her first. "Through everything, you have been there for me!" he said. "I hope you will forgive me."

She touched his temple. "We have been fighting since we were kids," she said. "But we have always been there for each other. I am glad to have spent time with you in peace."

He kissed her forehead and left the room. Hetta fell in her arms. Muttiya kissed her as well.

"I love you," said the mother. "You may be the one good thing I have achieved."

Hetta forced a smile through her tears.

"Go now," said Muttiya. "I will see you later."

Muttiya shared a moment of silence with Cyrus, nodding at him with a smile. She did the same with Idhatora, who led everyone outside and closed the door behind her.

"You are saying goodbye," I said.

She gave no response.

"We can still help you. If you let us."

"It's too late, my son," she said. "I know my issues. My guilt and anger will not heal now. There is no time. But I want nothing unsaid."

"Muttiya..."

"I am proud of you," she said. "You have all the power to destroy. But you choose to be kind and loving and stand by your principles. None of us has achieved that in our lifetimes. And you have done it by yourself. None of us was there for you as you needed us. Not your father, not your mother, nor Chaa. They taught you things. But none was there for you. And neither was I; especially not I. What you have achieved, what you have become, you did that yourself. And it is magnificent. Don't be scared to embrace it in their absence. You don't need anyone to hold that mirror for you. You are the fire. That fire that your father always mumbled about; the sun. Go out there and shine for all to see."

"I want to help," I said through my tears.

"I have Tet," she said, petting the leopard.

I smiled and sat by her side; held her warm hand. "You are never alone," I said.

She leaned back in her bed. We stayed silent. Days could have passed in that touch.

"I am not," she said. "Your father is here."

She smiled as her last breath loosened her grip on my hand.

SCHISMS

The colourful sceneries painted on the walls of the burial chamber flickered with my torch. After almost two moon cycles preparing the body, Queen Mother would be the first to lie in this room for eternity. I smiled at the thought of old Muttiya, dry and rigid, laying in my own tomb. I would have never imagined it a few sun cycles ago, but she had become family after all family was gone.

I moved the torch around to take another look at the beautiful rivers and flowers and animals on the walls. The room was ready for the following morning. Outside, two guards waited under the stars, making sure no one messed with her final resting place; a risk that arose with the general upheaval that now plagued the city. I nodded, thankful for their service, and took the twisted way down the mountain.

Below the fading symbols that projected in the sky from the cave of forefathers, the city was mostly asleep. Only our guards' torches shone around a storage facility that had been vandalised the previous night.

I stepped through the mountains while focusing high in the realms above to reach Altazadeh's aspect of light. I merely took a glance at it. It shook its head. After all this time, slowly planting seeds of light in his lower planes, he still refused to let them grow.

"Too much pain," his higher self said.

I focused on my path as I passed by the obelisks, wondering what good they served now that the darkness was already inside. Below the trees, the pathways were dark. No moon tonight. Only the flame of the torch lit my steps. Three people ran towards me through the shadows.

"Who goes there?" I asked, holding the torch high.

One of them rushed to me, swiftly placing his face close to the light.

"Innok! What's wrong?"

"It's Idhatora!" he said.

I followed him, Pathia, and another nurse back to my home. I ran by Tet and pushed the door open. Cyrus and Hetta stood among the children while Idhatora screamed from our bedroom. I bashed inside, with Cereena holding her hand and Valsaris trying to adjust her position. The two nurses came inside as well, while Innok gave us some privacy.

I kneeled next to my wife as she squatted on two blocks of amethyst engraved with a circle and seven rays shining out of it.

"I am here, my love! Our daughter is coming!" *The seventh. A gift of life; after all we've lost.*

She screamed, pushing. "She is early," she yelled through tears and sweat.

"We are here, my love; everything will be all right!"

She faced upwards with a scream and a tight grip on my hand. Pathia pushed linen in between the bricks and Valsaris sank his hands in water infused with frankincense oil. Idhatora cried with another scream.

"She is coming," Idhatora repeated through sharp breaths.

Valsaris kneeled and caught my daughter at my wife's next cry.

"Bring her to me," Idhatora said, anxious.

"It's okay, my love, you did it," I said and kissed her forehead.

We helped her up to the bed. I turned to Valsaris, waiting for him to bring our daughter. He stayed still, looking down at the little human.

"Valsaris?" I asked.

"Father!" Idhatora yelled. "Bring her to me!"

He finally looked up. "She... She is... not..."

We both stayed silent, staring into his eyes. Valsaris slowly made his way to us. And placed the baby in Idhatora's arms; peacefully.

"No, no," Idhatora cried, leaning over her and hugging her tight.

I focused within; turned to the little one's subtle planes, looking for a heartbeat, some light in the chamber of the heart or a centre of consciousness in the head. Nothing. Empty halls for winds to howl through. Above her head, a flame had solidified like glass; dark, void of life.

I opened my eyes back in the flesh. Idhatora looked into my eyes, pleading in silence. I uttered no word. I was cold. My chest was empty, freezing.

She shook her head and leaned back, crying. I lay next to her, held her in my embrace together with the seventh that never managed to take a breath.

"My king, should we take..." Pathia murmured.

"Get out," I said, without turning away from my beloved. "All of you. Get out."

The door soon creaked closed. I was alone. Trying with all my heart, with all my dissipating light, to console my wife, who never let go of our daughter.

T he room was cold. Candles had long gone out. Idhatora was finally asleep in my hands, still holding the little one. I was dry. Empty. Only one thought now banged around in my head.

The seventh is gone. What now?

I got up, careful of my beloveds and softly opened the door. Innok looked up from his seat with red eyes. The people who loved us were all there, waiting, awake with swollen eyes. So close they were... So distant I felt...

"Cyrus." I coughed. "You are staying. You shall be king."

SETTING STONES IN THE SAND

I placed the scrolls back in their places. The seven initiates that remained in Esperos had left the library to assume their position in the seven temples. I had no more knowledge to share. The development of their capacities was up to them now; and it would come through service to humanity. On the table, next to melted candles, rested my crown.

"Do you need anything else?" Valsaris asked.

"My dear Valsaris. You have done enough," I said.

He gave me an empty glance.

"If you still carry guilt from your past," I continued, "please shed it away. Your sister died with it. Unnecessarily. You have fixed your mistakes."

He shook his head.

"Valsaris, I ask only one thing of you."

He stood straight, waiting.

"Please! Take care of Rarou. And teach him all that you know and all that you have learned here."

He furrowed his brow.

"Don't ask. Just assure me you will."

"Yes," he said, looking down, and then at me, "of course!"

"You may go," I interrupted him before vocalising any thoughts.

Innok entered as Valsaris left, exchanging a concerned glance between them. turned back to the cases, full of the wisdom of old.

"It was nothing serious after all," Innok said with low voice. "A neighbour quarrel. Something about a goat."

I sighed, still with the scrolls. *My people... Fighting over a goat...*

"You are seriously going through with this?" Innok asked.

I glanced at him and then away.

"Aletheos!" He demanded my attention.

I stayed silent for a few more moments, going over all the thoughts I couldn't expect him to understand. I sighed at having to justify myself.

"It's for the best," I finally exhaled.

"Really? That's all you are giving me?"

"I don't know what you want, Innok. My daughter..." My throat refused to say the words. "I don't know what explanation you want to hear."

"I get that! Seriously. I cannot even imagine..."

"No."

"How is this helping anyone?"

"Cyrus is a good man, and military trained. And Hetta is kind and smart, takes after her mother. And royalty by blood. They will be good rulers. And they have a son. They fit easily into tradition. People will be happy with them."

"Is this helping you? Or Idhatora? That's what I am asking. If it's your pain talking or your hope."

"Only in pain, one can hope," I said. I smiled and brought my hand to his cheek. "I am not giving up, if that's your worry. But I can't be everything for everyone; not all the time. I choose to be a husband and a father. When I go, Anthelios will probably come after me and leave the people alone. Altazadeh said it's me the beast wants. And I will keep working on Altazadeh from afar. From the realms of light. While my family is safe."

"Leave? You are leaving?"

"We will talk about this tomorrow, after Cyrus's coronation. I want to go home, to Idhatora."

He said nothing as I walked away.

C ereena sat with Hetta and Rarou. They welcomed me in silence as I headed to my bedroom. Behind the closed door, Idhatora lay in bed with our daughters around her. Tet growled from next to the bed. I smiled at the big purring cat and went around her, slowly lying behind Idhatora with my arms around her and a warm kiss on her cheek.

A knock broke the quietness. Innok whispered from the door.

"People damaged the temples," he said.

I sighed and leaned back, next to my beloved.

"Take care of it," I whispered, relieved that Idhatora was still asleep.

VIOLET LOTUSES

I joined my wife and kids out in our small garden. The girls were in the pond, splashing water on each other among the violet lotuses. Idhatora sat on the ground, leaning on a tree.

"Hetta and Valsaris left with Rarou for the capital," I said.

"Cyrus?" she asked in a low voice.

"He will stay a few more days, go over a few more things."

"Any more upheaval?"

"Some. Outside the infirmary," I said as I sat by her side. I held her hand. "You don't have to worry about it. We are taking care of it. And we will soon be away from all of this."

Her blank face seemed void of hope.

"You will love Areteia," I said, forcing a smile below my dry eyes. "There are trees and streams of water everywhere. And flowers, and a whole jungle around it, full of colourful birds and monkeys. And elephants!"

"The girls will love the elephants," she said and brought my hand to her lips. She sighed. "Can we help from that far?" she asked. "Anthelios? Altazadeh?"

"All that we have done is from up high anyway," I said.

"Is this the right thing we are doing? Cyrus's coronation as co-king went smoothly, but we are leaving him a kingdom in disorder."

"That's why we are leaving, my love. Our path deviated from tradition too harshly. If we go away, things may evolve more naturally."

"What about there? The library?"

"I will open it up below the sanctuary and leave it up to Paradchi and whatever council he formed for the continuation of the order. The sigils of the library will keep Anthelios out." *And the library may tell us more about Anthelios.* I dismissed the thought. "We can live in peace in Areteia. Maybe help at the infirmary if we want, or find something else. And the girls will play free."

"Sounds nice," she said in the same flat voice.

"It is. You will see," I said with a kiss on her cheek, forcefully cheerful.

THE LIFE OF FIRE

Riots had damaged the administration building, now covered with my banners. My sigil, the dot in the cycle amongst two wings, embroidered in gold threat, shone with the sun. My vision for the future, for our development, hung from columns and walls only to hide the cracks in the stones.

I walked through the cobble pathways, taking in the greens that gave a sense of livelihood, the streams that burbled on the side of the streets and the colourful flowers of the bougainvilleas; some fresh on the trees around the houses and others blown away with the wind or floating in the water.

My sanctuary. A naïve plan, as Altazadeh had pointed out, built with the best of intentions; a place to stand as a beacon for all who aspire to find the truth, safe from darkness, safe from wars. But pain followed us here. *Not for long.*

I passed by the temples. The one for the builder was empty. No farmers or land workers gathered here anymore. So was the temple of the artist, the soldier, the healer. Master Gnomnas alone sat in the fifth, the temple of the scribe. He got up upon seeing me.

"My king! Are we resuming the mist ceremonies? People have gone astray since you and the queen stopped performing them."

I smiled at him, a tired smile. "Will you join me for a walk?" I asked of him.

We slowly made our way towards the sixth. The seven initiates were gathered in the temple. I didn't enter. My heart warmed with glimpses of light, seeing them in silent contemplation. *There is still hope.*

"No, my friend," I said to Gnomnas and resumed our walk. "We will not carry on with the ceremonies. People will have to face their own at some point. It saddens me to see any one of them suffer. But they now know the way. They have to walk their path. It's humans that must look for spirit, not the other way around."

He nodded. He knew. "How is the queen?"

I shook my head. "Don't worry, my friend." I stopped and touched his shoulder. "We will be fine."

"You are leaving, aren't you?"

I gave him a smile. "I have to. For the sake of all of us. But Cyrus..."

"Thank you, my king," he said and bowed his head. "For everything. You have truly shown the way. May we all walk it."

His sentiment brought tears to my eyes. *Maybe it wasn't all in vain.*

"Go on, my friend," I said. "I will see you tomorrow before we leave."

I reached the great temple. I passed by the black cubes, now empty of offerings to our neighbours, and proceeded to the third section with the marble sphere in the pond. *Maybe one more time, then.*

I took one deep breath, bringing mother and Chaa to mind. I took the sunlight in, let it fill me whole, before projecting it on the sphere to come out with a mist. I pushed as much as I could for the mist to go beyond the temple and out through the pathways of the city. Its warmth was soothing to my skin and heart.

I thought of our next step, the route we would follow, the places we would see on our way to Areteia where Father, Chaa, and Chohanatma came together to bring the light into the world. Surely it had been stained by dark days. But we would form new memories there, with my daughters diving into the waterfall and Idhatora smiling, watching them grow.

The image of my wife changed. Her body and face shone bright as she took the form of her previous lifetime. I took the form of mine, the personality of that flamekeeper. We came close. Touched our hands.

"Almost," she said.

I nodded. "Almost."

"Until next time, my love," she said.

"Until next time."

I held her hands in mine until the image dispersed. It was now replaced with the memories of crystal city's fall. The clouds of darkness that expanded through the city corrupting everything in their path. The steps that dissolved beneath the feet of people, throwing them to their deaths. The fall of the temples. The dark magician defying the order of the cosmos. And all those we left behind to save the flames; all those I left behind to die.

My stomach burned from deep within. The pain was accompanied with anger and shame and guilt that gripped on my heart. I was tired. My own darkness was catching up. The mist around me, almost down to the ground, was now cold, denser than ever. Its light was muddier as streams of darkness from the streets reached this inner part of the temple, corrupting it.

I got up, ready to withdraw in the company of my wife and daughters. Beyond the temple, the streets were loud. People rushed up the slope from the river. A woman screamed; her last scream before an arrow landed on her back. With a pounding heart, I ran against the crowd, searching for the intruder. A man laid on the street. Gnomnas! I threw myself next to him. An arrow was already deep in his chest.

"I have you, Gnomnas!"

I looked around. More arrows landed around us. Among the chaos, a guard stood still. I called for him.

"My king," said an elder man from behind me as he leaned over Gnomnas to help.

The guard finally reached us. He drew a dagger and stabbed the man's back. One, two, three times. The man fell to the side as the guard locked his eyes on me with the bloody blade in hand. Before he took his next step, an arrow punctured his skull, bashing him down on the ground. Another grabbed my hand, pushing me up. Cyrus!

"Run, run!" he said.

I left Gnomnas's lifeless body and pushed onwards through the city. A man swung a sickle through a woman's throat. Others fought with swords and spears. A group of aggressors emerged from a house, catching and killing anyone they could lay their hands on. Men, women, children, all screamed as the intruders hunted them down. Arrows killed anyone.

No guards kept my house safe.

"Where is Innok?" Cyrus asked.

I pulled him inside and closed the door behind us.

"Where did they come from?" he asked.

"This is our people, Cyrus! The intruders were hidden by our people. It's neighbours butchering each other out there."

Tet's eyes looked at us from the other side of the yard; blurry, muddy. Her mouth was open with sharp teeth showing, ready to attack. But she moved not. A spear was coming out of her neck.

Inside my house, Cereena lay in a paddle of blood. Cyrus placed his hand on her neck while I bashed on my bedroom door. Empty. Across the room, the thin transparent curtains moved with the wind. I passed through them, tearing them apart.

Our garden was empty. No sight of my wife and daughters. The crystal pyramid was bright with refractions of light, sealing the cave. My mother's big white pot still stood above the silent pond of violet lotuses.

I took a deep breath, silencing my thoughts of fear. Rocks from the wall were thrown to the side. I exhaled, deeply. The shouts of pain from outside faded. My heart beat calm. Only the rustle of leaves reached my ears. *Until next time.*

Cyrus barged out into the garden with his sword in hand.

"Cereena?" I asked, already knowing the answer.

He shook his head. I sighed and slowly walked to the pond, reaching for my crown. My shoulders dropped as I placed the wet metal on my head, gathering my mind in accepting our ordeal.

We walked outside to people screaming in pain. A guard leaned over an elderly man, bloody on the ground. The elder shared his last words, fatherly urging the guard to leave. With tears in his eyes, the young man finally stepped back, accepting his father's end. But an arrow brought him down as well.

"We can't fight this," Cyrus yelled.

"The mountains," I said.

We ran beyond the trees of the city, through the sand, and towards the steep pathways. Before we reached the obelisks, the edge of the cliffs above us darkened with archers. I halted with the lashing wind. Cyrus grabbed my hand, pulling me onwards. I grounded myself in the sand and stopped him.

"My brother," I said with a calm voice, "you need to go. You are needed for the future to unfold."

"No!" He pulled again.

I escaped his grip as the archers pulled the strings on their bows. I raised my arms, breathed whatever light I still had in me, out into a dome. The burning sensations of my stomach had reached my heart, aching as I held the light above us.

"Go," I yelled.

He came towards me. The arrows flew high into the sky, under the blank eyes of Anthelios.

"Now!"

He took a step back. Stopped. Looked into my eyes. I nodded goodbye to my dear friend. He had no other choice. The arrows hit the dome of my force. Some bounced away while others dissolved into dust. A few landed in between us.

Cyrus finally backed up through the sand and hid behind the obelisks, waiting for the second wave of arrows. I breathed in. And out, sending the force of the dome bursting on the archers. The edge of the cliffs trembled, forcing them back. I nodded at Cyrus. He moved on through the mountains.

I turned back. The sun was setting through the streets of Esperos. Ashes floated down on us. The library was ablaze. The infirmary as well. The streams of water along the streets ran red as people lay on the ground, some with arrows in them, others from the blades of their friends. Dark clouds now flooded the streets, invisible to the physical eyes yet reflected in death which now roamed free.

Killers alone walked our streets. They all saw me. None came close as I walked into the burning administration building. I pushed the door to the throne chamber. The candles lit with flames as I passed through the columns, presenting one last time the natural scenes of serenity on the walls. I stepped up the twelve steps and sat on my throne.

A solitary dark feather floated down in the middle of the room. I smiled as Anthelios materialised.

"How did you ever think you could escape me?" he spoke without opening his mouth.

"We are connected, aren't we?"

"You witnessed my story, and you have yet to understand," he said with a loud, heavy voice.

"You are no god," I said. "You are a wretched entity, Anthelios."

"People were desperate for a god that reflected themselves. And they found me."

"How are we connected?"

He groaned. And laughed.

"You were there when I was born," he said.

I narrowed my eyes and turned within, conscious of the light above my head stretching through all realms. *I was there.* His words were at peace with my heart. *But how?* I went through the scattered memories, the dark magician holding his sceptre, pushing his corruption on me while the crystal city fell to darkness. I had pushed his force back at my only chance to escape. A beautiful black bird flew by me to survive.

I sighed and opened my eyes to Anthelios, growing bigger with dark clouds in the room. I exhaled with a single laugh.

"I see you now," I said.

"Yes. But I see you too."

"I am not giving myself to you, Anthelios."

"You will die," he answered. "It will take dozens of sun cycles for you to reembody. And even then, you will not remember this. You will start anew. Again. While I will be growing stronger. The people are thirsty to give themselves to me. I have already won."

"I will see you next time, old friend."

He banged the base of his sceptre on the ground, angry at my calmness.

"So be it," he said, disappearing with a burst of darkness.

Altazadeh walked through the beast's clouds. He stood at the gate while other marched in from behind him to surround me. Some had been our guards, other our neighbours. And others wore that cursed golden mask with the shades of green and brown of age.

"You have condemned yourself, Altazadeh," I said. "You will burn in your own light."

"You have condemned your people," said Altazadeh, pointing at those around the room. "You have condemned them in sickness and misery, spending their live to fulfil your desires of living as a god."

I smiled and looked around. People, my people, stared at me; disappointed desperate, angry.

"I am very sorry," I echoed in the room. "I tried to offer you a choice. Show you the way. But those that came before me knew better. You must learn through your own suffering. And you will."

A guard struck my temple with the handle of his sword. My head trembled with sharp pain as blood dripped down my cheek.

"Don't you dare threaten us!" the guard declared.

I pushed myself up from the chair. The masked magicians fed the black clouds that filled the room. Altazadeh blew out dark smoke that reached my nose and branched out within me in a rotten smell that heavied my blurry mind.

I struggled to take the reins of my mind. My stomach burned as if hot red metal had pierced through it, my heart still aching as if ripping apart with every beat. Altazadeh's darkness found shelter in my own, now with a tight grip on my consciousness. I projected no light in the room to disperse the magicians' tricks. I couldn't. Above me, a sense of hope shone in the pillar of light that remained intact. The clouds had not subdued it. I let my consciousness float through it, expand as high as I could reach, still aware of my body.

Altazadeh twitched his eyes, alerted by something behind him. He swiftly turned and grabbed the hand and throat of Cyrus, throwing him to the front. Cyrus looked at me from the corner of his eyes. *No, my dear brother. There is no escaping today.* I sighed. *But you are not alone.* I gathered all sense of peace I could find within me and looked at my friend, who had already taken his last breath. Cyrus's sword dropped as the people in the room pushed their blades and spears through his body.

Hot drops ran down my cheeks with him thumping on the floor. Altazadeh coughed over the dead man. He bent his body, holding his stomach. He stretched his neck, and spat blood on Cyrus's empty vessel. His red eyes focused on me, confused.

"I told you, Altazadeh, your light is catching up."

My higher aspects met with his in the realms above, overlooking the dark storm over Altazadeh's muddy realms. A ray of light shone upwards through his clouds.

The flames from the library and infirmary finally reached the throne chamber, burning the wooden doors to my sides and painting the walls black. The rebels and dark priests pulled back, away from the fires behind me.

"Keep your ground, your fools!" spat Altazadeh.

Flames blasted towards them as the doors collapsed. The guard who hit me was overtaken by fire. He ran disoriented towards the others. Altazadeh extended an invisible grip on him, keeping him away as the flames melted his skin and his screams turned into smoke. At the gruesome sight, still ablaze, the others ran behind Altazadeh, pushing each other to save themselves through the gates.

Only one walked calmly behind them all, his mask shining close to Altazadeh. He raised his sword. Altazadeh turned, grabbing with his mind the throat of the attacker. The poor man kneeled, struggling to breathe behind his mask. His robes fluttered behind him, exposing a missing right arm, as his sword hit the ground.

"Altazadeh!" I yelled. "That's your son!"

The ray of light in the realms above, burst through his clouds. I dropped my consciousness in his muddy aspects, with the enormous snake slithering in circles. I opened my arms and breathed out white flames that swirled in his darkness and pushed away the snake. In the flesh, Altazadeh froze still.

The snake spiralled around me, high in the muddy clouds. Black feathers emerged from the storm around me and, like blades, burned me with excruciating pain as they rained down on me. The dark clouds pushed to drown the light from above.

Altazadeh, still stunned, struggled to move. He clenched his jaw and tightened his fingers in the air. Innok, choking, reached for his sword and pushed it deep into Altazadeh's stomach. His father screamed, tightening his palm into a fist. Innok stopped struggling. His neck twisted with a crack that brought him to the ground. The golden mask fell, uncovering his innocent face as it hit the floor.

The roaming snake came down on me, opening his mouth and swallowing me into the darkest of planes.

Silence.

Black space.

Altazadeh slowly took form across from me, panting, looking at his open hands with tears in his eyes. Whatever realisations he may have accepted were now fading. He shook his head, off with the tears, and stood straight. Dry, calm, he observed me with a satisfied grin.

My boiling stomach now burst out. I bled with freezing black liquid. I pushed my hand on the wound. Nothing stopped it from pouring out. And as it did, the cold sensations spread within me as well, passed to my chest, restricting my breathing, and coming out with black liquid floating out of my mouth. I closed my eyes in dark space with the voices of all those dead because of me; back in the crystal kingdom and now in the city of stone. The freezing liquid filled my head, drowning all thoughts, and gathered around the one last core of light at the centre of my forehead.

All of me held on to that core of light, now smashed with black waves. My whole being was ripping apart. *I cannot.* I let go; I left it all.

I was no longer me. I broke myself in two. Again. The darkness fell. What remained rose as an orb of light, floating beyond the darkness untouched, beyond the realms of mud, and up into the realms of fire.

My darkness, my guilt and pain, all drowned, weighed down as a mass of darkness through all realms and into my body. The crown's metal now shrieked around my head, the golden, delicate dragon shaking. Before my darkness was about to open my eyes, the dragon, with a swift movement, thrust through my forehead, breaking my skull. Across from me, Altazadeh, still paralysed, bled out over his son's sword, falling to his own demise.

All ceased to be in a last cold outbreath.

OF DARKNESS AND LIGHT

All links to my body were dismantling as the threefold flame retrieved from the sacred chamber of the heart. The pillar of light no longer incorporated the physical vessel, for it was destroyed. Around me, the winds of silence howled in the burning throne chamber. My consciousness remained in the world of sand. No judges appeared to decide on my path.

I went outside, floated over the city. People ran wild, destroying all in their path. My temples fell to ruins. The library with all the scrolls of wisdom was now ashes. My house, ravaged; my mother's pot thrown from its pedestal, crashing the lotus flowers in its fall and breaking the pond. Water and mud escaped through the cracks, down into the cave of forefathers, eroding the ceiling that came down, together with the shards of the crystal pyramid. The sanctuary had fallen at the hands of its people.

I wended higher in the sky, having the whole kingdom stretch below me along the great river of life. Storms of darkness ran rampant in my nation. Around it, an ocean of darkness waited to drown us all, kept away by walls of light.

Several pillars of light appeared above the cities. Hundreds. Thousands. Some of them extended over dead bodies. Others, above barbaric rebels; guards, farmers, dark priests. They all shone bright.

Their light spoke as one. "Save us."

Currents of white electric fire waved, spiralling above me. The higher aspects of each person gathered together in solidarity with myself.

"One more stance," I said.

I called the fires to me. They did the same, collectively piercing through the higher realms with our pillars of light. The currents of fire responded, as if we drew close the whole spiritual plane, forming a flaming whirlwind that came down and took roots in my heart. A heartbeat gave the signal. The flames ran through me, turning into dragons of electric fire spiralling within me. I could barely bear them. T centre of consciousness focused in a golden sphere in the head. I took a deep breath. And exhaled with all my might.

The dragons of fire burst out of me in a sea of fire over the kingdom. And I held all that flaming plane in my hand. And I let it drop. The light poured down on the people in a rain of fire that touched everyone, revitalising to the innocent and burning to the victims of darkness, severing the dark channels the connected them to Anthelios and any access to his powers.

No priest would bring about phenomena out of darkness. The sacred sciences would no longer be abused and dragged through the mud. Such power would now be attainable only through the personal efforts of each individual, through the reorientation of the mind and the physical application of wisdom.

"Thank you," everyone shone from their hearts.

No more self-proclaimed gods would abuse the darkness in people. The gods were dead. The false prophets now powerless. Truth must be rediscovered.

The pillars of the living faded away from the sky. Those of the dead remained. I called upon the fires one more time, drawing them towards each person to help them ascend further on their path. One by one, they moved forward to the passing of judgment and the infirmaries of high.

I remained alone. I looked at the walls that kept the darkness from swallowing the kingdom. My heart ached again. How could I do this again?

"My son." The voice filled me with warmth. Father approached from behind me. "It's all right, my son. So was your duty. And such is the people's path."

I turned back at the world one more time, at the people, conscious of all and each one simultaneously. My initiates had escaped, hiding in the fields of reeds.

"May you have the strength to walk the path," I said with no hope of response.

Father stretched his arm, waiting for mine. With one last breath of hesitation, I touched his hand. And the invisible walls around the kingdom broke, as I withdrew my presence from the world of sand. Darkness fell upon the nation, eradicating our history, our efforts, and hiding the light even deeper within each incarnated consciousness.

Father guided me higher into the light. Smiles waited for me. Chaa, Chohanatma, Muttiya, Cyrus, Cereena. Innok hugged me tight with both arms. They all rejoiced with me as one, and I finally felt lighter in their embrace; amongst my people. Behind them stood one more spirit with a violet flame in her chest. No form, no features, only a bright, familiar essence.

"Hello, Father," she said.

"Oh, how I yearned to meet you," I said and hugged my stillborn daughter. "And so did your mother!"

She took my hand and led me on further into the light, until all that remained was bright white space. I stood alone again.

"I am here," I declared. "I stand alone. In truth."

Space vibrated with an unspoken voice that rang only in my mind, simultaneously male and female.

"To whom shall I announce you?" the voice said.

"To it, whose progeny is fire and water," I responded. "To the parentless parent who gives birth to the dragon in the image of its own."

In front of me appeared the dragon with the body of a lion, the tail of an ox, and white wings stretching from its back.

"What is your condition?" the being asked.

"I have repelled falsehood. I have stood for truth. I have done falsehood. Truth brought death. The fate of people burdens my chest."

The fourfold entity raised itself, turning into a man with white wings. The man approached with a smile. He was a reflection of me. He leaned towards me, touched my heart, and kissed my forehead.

"So be it."

AN END

EPILOGUE
MOONRISE

WATERS

T he boat moved with the splashing waves far beyond the great river. The stars above guided the way. Idhatora struggled to paddle through the waters with our daughters cuddling close to each other.

The boat followed the shattered path of the moon. A woman stood alone, bright with the moonlight, waiting at the shore. Her black and silver hair blew with the wind around her wrinkled eyes.

She raised her arm as the boat thumped on the sand.

"I have been waiting for you," said my mother.

ABOUT THE AUTHOR

anagiotis is a multidisciplinary artist with a passion for exploring the intricacies of the human experience and the cosmos.

As a fantasy author, his writing is inspired by his studies in philosophy and mysticism, adding depth and meaning to his epic stories.

Visit **www.panagiotisdimitriou.com** to find out more.

@PanagiotisDimitriouAuthor

@PanagiotisDimitriouAuthor

And sign up to Panagiotis's **Mailing List** to get all updates and new stories!

Made in the USA
Monee, IL
21 January 2024

52165989R00261